Double or Nothing

KIM SHERWOOD is a novelist and a lecturer in creative writing at the University of Edinburgh. Her award-winning debut novel, *Testament*, was released in 2018, and in 2019, Kim was short-listed for the *Sunday Times* Young Writer of the Year Award. *A Wild & True Relation*, following a woman who joins a smugglers' crew in eighteenth-century Devon, is coming soon. *Double or Nothing* is the first in a trilogy of Double O novels expanding the James Bond universe.

🐦 kimtsherwood
kimsherwoodauthor.com

WILLIAM MORROW

An Imprint of HarperCollins*Publishers*

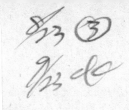

Double or Nothing

A DOUBLE O NOVEL

Kim Sherwood

FIRST EDITION

Designed by Kyle O'Brien

Library of Congress Cataloging-in-Publication Data

Names: Sherwood, Kim, 1989– author.
Title: Double or nothing : a double o novel / Kim Sherwood.
Description: First edition. | New York, NY : William Morrow, [2023] | Series: Double 0 ; vol 1 |
Identifiers: LCCN 2022007090 (print) | LCCN 2022007091 (ebook) | ISBN 9780063236516 (hardcover) | ISBN 9780063236523 (trade paperback) | ISBN 9780063236554 | ISBN 9780063236530 (ebook)
Subjects: LCSH: Bond, James (Fictitious character)—Fiction. | LCGFT: Spy fiction. | Novels.
Classification: LCC PR6119.H49 D68 2023 (print) | LCC PR6119.H49 (ebook) | DDC 823/.92—dc23/eng/20220523
LC record available at https://lccn.loc.gov/2022007090
LC ebook record available at https://lccn.loc.gov/2022007091

ISBN 978-0-06-323651-6

23 24 25 26 27 LBC 5 4 3 2 1

For Nick. Nobody does it better.

ONE

An Appointment with the Devil

The White Helmet said, "To save one soul is to save all of humanity."

Sid Bashir didn't take the shot. He lowered his camera. His finger lifted from the shutter release.

The White Helmet gave him a friendly knock on the arm. "You must know this, brother. The White Helmets are committed to these words from the Quran: Whoever saves a life saves all of humanity."

Bashir bowed his head. "My mother used to tell me that."

"May Allah bless her. She taught you well. I used to carry arms. But it is better to give my life to my people than take lives."

"May Allah bless your family also." Bashir gripped the bench seat as the truck swerved to avoid a crater. His chest was tight with smoke, which had poured down his throat like concrete eager to fill a void as he followed the Syrian search-and-rescue volunteers into the fire, digging through rubble for survivors in the long minutes' wake of a cluster bomb, the Red Crescent warehouse groaning, keening, until it swayed, walls crumpling, and crashed in a cloud of render. Bashir pulled the sleeve of his battered Barbour back from his Casio watch. There was a gash on his forearm. He wiped blood from his watch face. Every vanishing second reduced her chances. Five minutes until the drop.

The man beside him removed the white helmet with his name written in indelible pen, shook dust and debris free from his hair, and replaced the helmet. He played along as Bashir took his portrait, but the gaze fixed on Bashir was probing. "I have known other photojournalists, sir. Even other men from Reuters. I have seen them pull victims into their cars and drive them to hospitals under live fire. Shield children from shells. Give their flak jackets away." The White Helmet sniffed. "But I've never seen a photojournalist do any of that without taking a photograph first. You ran into the fire, and you didn't take a single shot. Not until we'd cleared the dead for burial. You might be a noble man. But you are not a war photographer. And you hold your camera like a gun."

Bashir looked down. Three fingers on the grip, thumb on the barrel, finger at the trigger. His heart was haring. "It's my first war." He tried a smile. "I haven't developed a defense against my humanity yet."

The man studied Bashir. The thick sweat of the other volunteers in the cabin, the squeak of their fireproof overalls, the screams of pain from the medical truck behind, the wind chasing down the mountainside to push at the wheelbase, the sudden rumble overhead, the muscles in each man's thighs tensing, carrying them to their feet before anyone exchanged a word, until one raised a hand and called, "It's only a civilian aircraft"—it all filled the breach of silence. The White Helmet shrugged. "I do not think so, sir. I think you are more concerned for your own little war than ours. But I thank you for your help. You may have saved your soul, today. I believe this is where you wished to be dropped . . . for your next photo assignment."

Bashir could not summon a reply, and had no chance to do so, the truck rolling to a stop.

The White Helmet clapped his palms together, a slick stickiness, as if wiping his hands free of Bashir. But still he added, "Remember, brother: To save one soul is to save all of humanity."

Bashir had to stoop as he rose. His mother had raised him to keep that sentiment tucked into his heart, though he had long since subscribed to another philosophy. Sid Bashir had been given a number and license to kill. He was 009, and to him the faith that saving one soul could save something of the world's humanity was harder to maintain in the face of the calculations his job demanded. He would more readily sacrifice one life for the good of the many. It might be cold, but then logic didn't have a heart with corners to spare.

Tonight, though—tonight Bashir would try to save just one life, one soul, and if it did not matter a great deal to the world, it mattered a great deal to him.

The doors opened. Bashir gave his thanks and jumped onto a single road snaking the foot of the mountains, the beaten earth and blistered tarmac etched by a faint moon.

The trucks rattled on, headlights fading, and with them the sound of the engine, until the only thing that moved on the hulking slope of the mountain was one small black spot, the figure of Bashir inching ever upward, his outline stretched, flung, and swallowed in the pinstripe shadows of pine trees. As the minutes ticked down, high above a second black spot seemed to ripple from the lily pad shadow of drifting clouds, descending the mountain. This second black spot zigzagged, and its own shadow was distorted by the unmistakable silhouette of a gun. The gun, and the shadow, belonged to Corporal Ilyasov, who was serving his first mission for Rattenfänger PMC.

Rattenfänger PMC offered a year's average salary in whatever denomination you worshipped for just one month's service and a trip to the Front, wherever the Front happened to be, however official or unofficial—Yemen, a concert hall or temple, the Central African Republic, a subway in a world capital. PMC stood for Private Military

Company, or Pretty Much Crap, because to call Rattenfänger a private military company was like calling the mafia a social club. Registered in ever-changing shell companies, Rattenfänger were terrorists for profit, marauders who turned fluid situations into war zones and peaceful streets into settings for the nightly news. Their soldiers and bases were international. Their fingerprints were suspected on embassy bombings, kidnapping, grand larceny, underreported civil wars, and data breaches. But those fingerprints could never be traced, and neither could their backers.

None of that mattered to Corporal Ilyasov, apart from the 1,240,000 rubles a month. He had a wife and three children, and that mattered a lot. Before Rattenfänger, Ilyasov might have hoped to earn that in a year, if he held his pockets wide open. This was his first posting. Pulling off his mask so he could spit out the taste of that evening's third-rate vodka, Ilyasov continued down the mountain, treading carefully, just as they'd taught him in Molkino, though there was little risk of attack so far into Assad's territory, and so far up this godforsaken rock where nothing worth a damn grew. That was why they'd chosen the eastern slopes for the makeshift black site, the mountain showing its back to the Mediterranean and the few towns that straggled down toward Tripoli.

The ground beneath his boots was hard but the trees clung to their fir coats. Ilyasov peered up to locate the moon, but she was sulking, just like him. He didn't see the point in patrolling so far out from the base—suspected Colonel Mora of punishing him for winning at cards. The other boys were watching the show, and he was listening to the wind.

Ilyasov was calculating how much longer the woman they were holding would last when a shape in the trees moved too quickly to be a swaying branch, and then a glitter in the black told him a knife was spinning toward him. That information registered too late. The knife found his jugular and Ilyasov pitched sideways.

The last thing he was conscious of was a boot tipping him onto his back, and then a needle-thin light on his face. In its trembling beam, Ilyasov made out eyes like antique gold and a nose that bumped over a break. He had only another thirty seconds to live, and would not report this to anyone.

Ilyasov's body would be returned to his wife by a courteous silver-haired gentleman, who would leave five million rubles of "insurance money" on the kitchen table, along with a medal for blood and bravery. When his wife called up newspapers and her local councilman to demand answers, she would be shown her error by foreign men in cheap dark suits.

Bashir pulled the flat throwing knife free and cleaned the blade on the dead man's arm, at the bicep, where he expected a Syrian flag. He turned the flashlight onto the man's sleeve. Nothing. He looked back at the face.

Bashir tapped his earpiece. "How do you feel about surprises, boss?"

A chirp, then Moneypenny's voice: "Depends who jumps out of the cake, 009."

"I know you were hoping for worn-out soldiers of the Syrian Armed Forces. But how about a well-armed, well-trained, if very dead, soldier with no flag?"

"Rattenfänger?"

"Quiet extraction is looking like wishful thinking."

"Stand by, 009."

Bashir scanned the trees, hunting for a sign of a second patrolman. He remembered Bill Tanner briefing him and the other new recruits about Rattenfänger. Bill had been perched on the desk at the front of the seminar room, and rolled his sleeves up as if settling into a bedtime story: a folktale for the ages. "Rattenfänger are out to make money, whether that's by holding a city to ransom, or lending their services to the highest bidder. Every member has a stake in the profits. Like a diabolical Waitrose." Bill laughed at his own joke, then hunched closer for the grisly part. "For those who flunked German, Rattenfänger means The Ratcatcher, the original name of the Pied Piper. They earned their name bombing a school track-and-field day after a Russian oligarch refused to pay Der Rattenfänger for their services kidnapping the son of this oligarch's rival. They killed their own client's son, and his whole class too, and were paid for their efforts by the original target. The US leveled both businessmen with sanctions. The rival shrugs and says: *I am a businessman. That is all. If they want to see the devil, let them see him.* But that's overstating his position. He's only a disciple. Rattenfänger are the real devil."

009 waited for the devil now. M had denied permission to carry a handgun into Syria, in case he was searched as a photojournalist. Bashir was glad of the throwing knife now, which he'd concealed in the hinges of his camera case, knowing customs would consent to a hand search in order to avoid X-rays damaging the kit. Rattenfänger had shot 008 in the head last month and left him in the scrub in the Central African Republic. And Donovan had been good. Still, Bashir bent down, prized the RPK-74M from the dead mercenary's hands, and slung it over his shoulder. Then he took the man's radio, lowered the volume, and pocketed it.

"Home front to 009. Stand down. I say again, stand down."

Bashir felt his body temperature drop. "That's a bad copy, say again?"

"Listen, 009. Rattenfänger must be leasing the base. Q says Rattenfänger's SOP is to station at least thirty agents inside the compound, most likely alongside the Syrian Armed Forces. The chance of mission success is less than zero. We don't even know she's alive. It's been nineteen days. You know the odds."

Bashir chewed his lip. He wondered if Moneypenny was conscious of slipping from the language of a strategist, the language she used when hoping to appeal to Bashir's better angels, to the language of a gambler—into *his* language. So: What would Bond say? *Life is nothing but a heap of six-to-four against, Penny. That doesn't mean I leave the table.* But that didn't help him. What would 009 say?

"She's more valuable than I am. This isn't a zero-sum game. My death is worth the chance of her life."

White noise. Then: "As romantic as that is, 009, the bank wins this time. Stand down. It's too dangerous."

Bashir clenched his jaw. What now? Leave her to die, if she wasn't dead already. Leave her to the devil, and only in order to save his own skin. Exfil to Istanbul, back to London, and then the Tube to the Regent's Park office, the silent journey in the lift, the walk along the corridor, avoiding the commiserating or disappointed eyes of the others, refusing Moneypenny's understanding, and finally facing M's sympathetic eyes across the table, his "better luck next time," when, of course, there couldn't be one, because Bashir would have failed to save her, just as he had failed James Bond.

Bashir straightened up. "Someone once told me it's always too dangerous. That's the fun."

"Sid—"

A soft sound, and then that stern voice came on: "009?" It was M.

"Sir."

"Try and bring it off. And watch out."

Bashir smiled. "Sir." He heard Moneypenny raising an objection, and then tapped his earpiece, silencing the debate on how short his odds were. It was then he heard a boot catching in the undergrowth.

He turned, drew the knife, threw.

A thud.

Bashir inspected the dying patrolman. A second pawn.

He slid his knife out of the man's thorax and eased the RPK-74M into a comfortable grip. He searched the soldier, found more magazines, which he pocketed. The camera hung from his left shoulder, and Bashir raised it now, switching to infrared. The forest was clear of moving bodies. A walled-off compound with a single watchtower crouched at the peak of the mountain, another fifteen minutes' sharp hike. Bashir brought the sniper waiting there into focus, and then moved off, considering where they might set up the kitchen. In private military operations like this one, locals put on the food, usually in poorly constructed huts with little regard for regulations. That would be his strategy.

TWO

Bête Noire

The compound occupied a half-moon of cleared forest at the peak of the hill: inside the walls, a grid of tents surrounded a stone barracks. At the rear of the compound, a soldier guarding the service entrance stood whistling the same few bars of a song. He seemed to be having trouble finding the bridge. It wouldn't bother him for long. He slumped forward.

009 caught the man's Makarov PM before it could clatter across the ground. The favorite pistol of Soviet policemen, before Bashir's time. Eight rounds in the chamber. Hauling the body into the shadows, Bashir stripped the man of his jacket and pulled it on. He skirted around to the kitchen, a tent with wires straggling from it like the tangled limbs of a dead octopus. Bashir ducked through the door, and found the cook reading on a cot—a skinny man who, Bashir imagined, lived on leftovers. The man started up. With one hand, Bashir covered the cook's mouth. With the other, he held the pistol to his head.

"One chance," Bashir whispered, and then switched to Levantine Arabic. "The back door is open. Disappear, quietly. Or burn to death."

The hand Bashir had clamped over the man's mouth grew clammy with sweat. The cook nodded. Bashir let go. The cook glanced around, as if the fire had already started and he was considering what to save.

Then he looked back into Bashir's eyes, where he seemed to recognize something. He swallowed, picked up his book, and ducked through the back.

Bashir made a study of the kitchen. He wanted as big an explosion as possible. If he was right, it would draw most of the Syrian troops from their posts, and at least half Rattenfänger, who would have the urge to take command of a crisis. Bashir supposed four or five Rattenfänger had been ordered to remain with the prisoner at all times, and would not stir despite the kitchen finally doing what everyone on base would have joked about at one time or another, given the state of this generator: gone up in flames. Their fear would be the fire spreading to other tents, hovering in the wind, roosting in trees. It would be the forest that killed them, a slow collapse of blazing timber.

Well, there was no point being subtle about it. Bashir kicked over the petrol generator. The back end clunked to the ground. Liquid oozed onto the dirt floor. He popped the back of the camera, prized out the battery, and chucked it in the microwave. He set the thing to one minute, maximum heat. This represented only a marginal departure from his usual culinary skills anyway.

Bashir grabbed a small knife that smelled of onions from the sink, and retreated out the back. After forty-two seconds a bolt of hot air and flame shot from the tent. Twelve seconds later, the whole kitchen went up, slapping the night white with shock. The air twanged, and then there was the sound of boots running and soldiers shouting.

Bashir raced toward the stone barracks, keeping his head down, buffeted by the panic of running Syrian soldiers, who saw his jacket and did not question him. Inside was the usual filth of men in close quarters. Bashir hurried past the Officers' Mess, where a game of cards had been left abandoned. He was about to take the next turn when he heard orders barked in choppy English. Bashir drew up against the wall, and held his breath as at least five Rattenfänger passed by without looking around the corner.

As the fifth man passed, Bashir grabbed him by the collar and jerked him back. The man twisted in his grip. Bashir slammed his elbow down on the man's wrist. He dropped his gun in shock.

Bashir jammed his gun into the man's gut. "Take me to her."

A moment's hesitation, then a quick nod.

Bashir followed the soldier deeper into the compound, tracking left turns and right. The hallway lights were doused, replaced by the flickering aqua of a backup generator. He noticed prison tattoos crawling up the man's neck.

"In there," the soldier whispered. "The bitch is in there."

Bashir peered around the next corner. At the end of the short passage was a locked steel door.

"Do you have the key?"

"No."

"And you had so much potential."

Bashir struck the man with the butt of the pistol. He stepped over his unconscious body and around the corner, considering the locked door. And him without a wall charge to his name.

Bashir was slinging the RPK-74M around when he heard the door rattle. He pulled back to the corner.

Three soldiers came out, locking the door behind them, and formed up in front of it: the Rattenfänger men ordered to stay with the prisoner.

He could take them with a burst from the machine gun, but that would draw the others back—if they heard it over the hunger of the fire.

Regardless of whether the troops outside heard it, the Rattenfänger undoubtedly behind the door with a gun to her head would. A steel door could muffle only so much. And the man would follow his orders without question, just as Bashir would.

Quiet it is.

Let's call it a sample of convenience. Can two knives kill three guards?

Bashir moved into the open, registering three masked soldiers coiled with excitement, fingers on triggers. Before any of them could make a sound, Bashir threw his own knife and the kitchen knife, picking off the left and right men. The man on the right staggered and fell, eliminated. The kitchen knife was poorly weighted and found the cheek of the man on the left. He was about to howl, just as the man in the middle raised his rifle. Bashir rolled forward, hooked one foot behind the man's ankle, and then smashed the man's knee. He went down flat. The rifle clattered away. Bashir pulled the knife out of the cheek of the man on the left and slashed his throat just as the man in the middle clambered to his feet. Bashir elbowed back. The soldier hit the wall, drawing his pistol for a point-blank shot. Bashir slammed him into the wall, nothing clever in it, just body against body. Bashir's ribs shuddered, close to breaking. He held on.

"You think you beat Rattenfänger?" the man spat. "Pied Piper is unbeatable."

Bashir clamped his hand over the soldier's mouth, as he had the cook's, only this time he did not let go. The soldier thrashed and pounded. Bashir held on.

As the man sagged, Bashir panted: "I don't believe in fairy tales."

"I see you don't like to give your enemy the chance to surrender, Mr. Bashir."

Bashir hunched, absurdly readying himself for a bullet to the back of the head. None came. The next thought: they know my name. Bashir turned, his back to the steel door now. At the end of the short passage stood a man whose presence seemed to make the nearby crash of fire seem irrelevant, foolish even. He was a giant, with at least fifteen years on Bashir. He had buzzed graying hair. He wore the uniform with no flag of Rattenfänger. His arms were unusually long, his empty hands hanging by his sides unusually big, seeming to wait for something. The stripes on his shoulder said he was a colonel. The king, and probably the only man who knew who was funding Rattenfänger, who was calling the shots. In the flickering light, Bashir could see the man was smiling indulgently.

The colonel gestured to the bodies. "Not very sporting. I thought you Englishmen had rules."

"I skipped civics," said Bashir, and hurled the kitchen knife.

The colonel plucked it from the air. He laughed, and then weighed the blade in his great palm. "Next time, I suggest stealing a bigger knife."

Bashir was about to pull the Makarov PM and fire when he remembered the gun to her head, just behind the door.

"No need to give less than your best," said the colonel. "It doesn't matter who hears. She's already dead."

Bashir rocked a little, then planted his feet. "She's a high-value target. You'd keep her alive as long as possible."

The colonel shrugged. "She broke." He said it lightly, as if they were discussing a faulty bicycle. "We extracted what we wanted, and disposed of the remains."

Bashir listened, tried to locate noises from behind the door. There were none.

"And now all that's left," said the colonel, "is to break you." He tossed the knife away, and came on with his arms still hanging loosely.

Instinct told Bashir to shoot. There was no sound from behind the door. She was dead. He was too late, and she was dead. But he did not draw. His mission was to bring her home. So what if this man said she was dead? A certain event with a probability rate of one hundred percent still might not occur.

Bashir crouched forward in the starting position of Krav Maga. He threw a right. The colonel swayed back, quicker than Bashir imagined, despite his bulk. Then the colonel's hand shot out, his fingers stiff, and jabbed Bashir in the brachial plexus.

Bashir almost threw up. His right hand went numb. It would not form a fist. Shock sliced through him.

The colonel stabbed Bashir's tibialis anterior muscle with his boot. Bashir folded to his knees. He swung with his left.

The colonel caught the punch, and dug his thumb between Bashir's fingers. Bashir's hand was suddenly boneless. He was attacking Bashir's nerve points. The colonel knocked behind Bashir's ear with one knuckle, finding the pit between jaw and neck. Bashir choked. He couldn't move. He was paralyzed.

The colonel sniffed. He seized Bashir by the lapel and hauled. Bashir swung from his fist. His eyes were streaming.

"This does not reflect well," said the colonel. "Not well at all. I was led to believe you were something special. 009: the next bright thing from Her Majesty's Secret Service. Strategic, smart, ruthless. First-class degree with honors in philosophy and mathematics from King's. Fights with tenacity. High threshold for pain. A promising young man with an exciting future as a professional murderer. Only weakness that *big brain* of his, persuading him to take measures a mere mortal might shudder at. But this overthinking looks very much like not thinking at all. You are letting yourself down, boy. You couldn't even die for her. You're too late. You failed her. And now you're failing me. Come on, son. Play up, play up and play the game—isn't that what M would say?"

Bashir flailed about inside, but his limbs would not respond. He'd been rendered impotent with just a few jabs. Fear and revulsion gripped him.

Remember your training. Remember Bond's words. At the heart of every agent is a hurricane room: in the tropics, the room a house keeps empty at its center so that when a storm begins to shake the ⸻ an retreat to this citadel without fear of flying chairs ⸻ smashed crockery. The hurricane room inside you ⸻ o clean it shines. You retreat there when a situation ⸻ ntrol and no other action can be taken—retreat ⸻ the storm to rage into exhaustion, for the moment you can step out and ask the heavens: Is that all you've got? The moment you can say: Give me your worst, I'll take it. So, retreat to your hurricane room, and wait for your nerves to come back. They'll come back to you, and then you'll stick your thumb into this man's eye. Until then, lock the door, Sid. For God's sake, lock the door.

"What would dear Moneypenny think, if she could see you now? Her shiny new toy, to replace all the toys she's lost, but you're broken out of the box. Bête noire of the world's terrorists and criminals?" He laughed. "You're just a scared little boy, hoping Mother will come along and save him—and knowing she never will."

The hurricane door burst open. The storm was coming in.

Bashir kicked out, aiming for the colonel's groin. The colonel caught his ankle, and hurled him against the wall. Bashir hit the floor.

He was trying to shift his arms when the colonel stamped on Bashir's solar plexus, with all the pressure he'd give a cockroach.

Bashir almost blacked out.

When the colonel knelt down on his chest, the weight was an ocean. Bashir tried to buck and thrash, but he could not move the monster an inch—he could not move.

Hands like giant pink crabs closed around his throat.

He could not scream.

The walls of Bashir's hurricane room caved in. She was dead. He had failed her. He could not move, could not breathe, could not scream. He was a child, screaming from night terrors after his mum's funeral. There was a malevolent ghost squatting on his chest. For all he'd prayed, it was not his mum's spirit that returned to comfort him, but something vicious and hateful, and his mum did not cross over to save him.

This is how he would die. A child again. A failure. Alone.

As the light faded, Bashir noticed a tattoo spread over the colonel's chest and neck. A death's-head hawk moth. His mother had designed her garden to attract butterflies and taught Bashir their names.

Must report the tattoo to M, Bashir thought, and then laughed at himself. The moth's wings fluttered as the cords in the colonel's neck bulged, and then began to flap as the colonel started to pant, not from any exertion—he batted away Bashir's protests—but from pleasure. The moth came closer. It wanted to smother him. The monster seemed to want to drink his last gasp. The fingers squeezed. Bashir could not breathe. He could not breathe.

A single gunshot.

The moth panicked, wings hot against his face, and then reared away.

Bashir gasped, swallowing the bitter smell of gunpowder.

The colonel lay on his side next to Bashir. Blood pooled under him, warming Bashir's fingers back to life.

Air rushed into him. His stomach folded inside out. His nerves blazed. He sat up.

003 stepped through the smoke.

Bashir rested his head against the wall. Breathed out. Tried to laugh. "I'm here to rescue you."

Harwood smiled back at him. "I can see that."

She put out her hand. Bashir's skin crawled as he moved his arm, took her hand, and got shakily to his feet. He looked over her shoulder. The steel door was open, revealing a room with no windows, a chair with restraints hanging from the back, a table with a box of used syringes, and a man lying on the floor, bleeding from the temple.

"I like what you've done with the place," he said.

Her eyes glittered in the half-light. "I thought you might."

"You got any plans this evening?"

"What did you have in mind?"

"How about breakfast in Istanbul?"

003

J ohanna Harwood had stayed with James Bond in the Golden Horn suite of the Pera Palace Hotel twice, once on their first joint mission, and then for a weekend away. Built in 1892 by a French-Turkish architect to neoclassical proportions for passengers of the Orient Express, the hotel was within firing range of crowded Istiklal Avenue, as well as a roulette of consulates, from British to Russian. The guest list had once included Mata Hari and Ernest Hemingway. On that second visit, the concierge gave Bond the keys to the Agatha Christie suite, where Harwood tested whether the typewriter still worked, now preserved behind a velvet rope. It did. Things like that happened with Bond. He was fun. He made her laugh. Bond lived up to his belief that an agent should take refuge in great luxury to efface the memory of danger and the shadow of death. She knew that if he were here now, that's what he'd be doing: four in the morning by the Belle Époque mantel clock on the marble sideboard, and Bond would be pouring them both a glass of Dom Pérignon.

"What shall we drink to?" said Bashir.

Harwood looked down at the glass of water now in her hand. She couldn't remember taking it. In fact, she couldn't remember sitting down on the bed, with its polished mahogany headboard, and the antique Turkish silk rug employed as a wall hanging. She was no longer wearing the jumpsuit they'd forced her into. Instead, she wore a red peshtemal dressing gown.

Yes—that was it. She had stripped from the thing with Bashir's help, her own hands trembling. Then she had spent fifteen minutes at the bathroom sink with the first aid kit and a glass of whisky. She studied her bare feet. The bruises had soured yellow.

The last few hours—stealing a UAZ, the breakneck drive down the Homs Gap, Bashir at the wheel, Rattenfänger close at their heels, Harwood spraying the forest with machine gun fire, reaching the Druze militia, who smuggled them into Tripoli, and then the sigh of relief as they made it to the boat Bashir had arranged—it felt just as much a dream as the last nineteen days were a nightmare.

Bashir seemed to know this, for he didn't sit down beside her, but in the corner armchair.

Harwood said, "Let's just drink."

"I'm too scared of that look in your eyes to argue."

"Coward." She noticed the suitcase in the corner. "That's mine."

"That's good news," he said. "Otherwise I broke into the wrong flat."

"You *broke* into my flat?" she said, sitting up a little straighter.

"Well, if you're going to insist a man returns his key when he breaks off the engagement, what else do you expect? Besides, living in that brutalist eyesore attracts all the wrong elements."

"The Barbican is a groundbreaking mixed-use site of housing and art for the people."

"I should've brought your Little Red Book too, I see. I thought you might want your own things, after . . ."

Harwood swallowed, then laughed shakily. "A little overconfident of mission success there, 009?"

A shadow seemed to touch his face. "Not much point being anything else."

"That's what they teach us," she said, studying him in the glow of the bedside lamp. The black curls swept into a haphazard quiff, which fell into his face more often than not; thick eyebrows; eyes that deepened to near-black in the gloom; cheekbones that threw shadows down his face; nose like a blade and lips so full he always seemed to be pouting. He was perhaps the most beautiful man she'd ever met. All sharp angles, he kept himself from feeling ungainly by stooping a little over the person he was talking to, and shoving his hands in the pockets of his trousers, giving him the habit of gesturing with his elbows—something he did now, hunched in the armchair, the muscles of his right arm twitching indignantly. His well-tuned body, framed by the close-fitting black cashmere—which made the bloodstains harder to see—was quietly wringing out his panic and pain. She knew she'd have to tell him her story for the initial report soon, and bear the look in his eyes. "I suppose this is the part where I say, Oh, Sid, I knew you'd come for me."

"Did you?"

She put her empty glass down on the bedside table. "They caught me in Damascus. I thought I'd picked up Bond's trail. But it was a trap. I should have taken more precautions, after . . . after everything."

He colored, took her glass, filled it from the bathroom tap. When he returned, she did not look up at him.

"I know what comes next," she said.

Bashir sat down, reclining so that his face was in shadow. "I don't."

"You need to know if I broke," she said. "What I told them. How many assets I jeopardized. If I could have been turned. My loyalty, scale of one to ten. Anything under six, you take the Glock 17 you removed from the safe when we walked in here, shoot me in the head, and save M the paperwork. My only question is why Moneypenny sent my ex-fiancé to do the job. Does she think you're that cold?" She opened her hands. "Maybe you are."

He shifted in the dark. "I know you didn't give them anything."

"Your faith in me is touching."

"Those are fresh injection marks on your arm. I'd guess a cocktail to relax you, and disorientate you. Possibly make you hallucinate. And those are new burn marks on your shoulder. New, and angry. You didn't tell them anything, because you didn't break. And they were pissed off about it."

Harwood stood up. She opened the curtains of the French windows, and looked down onto one of the most famous views in the world. On the right, the still waters of the Golden Horn streamed in pink and green neon, the lights from floating fish restaurants, and on the left the unsheltered Bosporus surged, black and gold, a winking semaphore that told the story of sleepless shipping. The Pera Palace was at the tail end of a tourist district; diplomats and delegates used most of the surrounding hotels, and the night was soft. Soon, the cough of engines and the call to prayer would herald the working day, and the two continents threaded together by water would carry on about their business. Someone once told her Istanbul is a small town that just happens to be very big. It reminded her of Paris, of home.

Harwood closed her eyes, steering away from that thought, and toward the last time she was here, to breakfast with James on this balcony—remembering the deep yellow yogurt in the blue china bowl, the blushing figs, the jet-black Turkish coffee, that burnt taste of freshly ground beans; sitting in James's lap, taking his cup from his hand, and untying her peshtemal gown; the smile on his face when he saw she wore nothing beneath it—remembering all this so vividly it made this moment seem like nothing but a dress rehearsal.

Except it wasn't make-believe, and it wasn't Bond, because she still hadn't found him, and he was probably dead by now. It was Bashir, the man she'd finally left Bond for, the man she loved, the man who now could not love her back because he'd been on a joint mission with Bond when 007 went missing, and could no longer hold her gaze. But still, perhaps the person who knew her best, and the best person she knew.

She said, "I was close. I almost broke."

"We're always close."

Harwood turned to face him. "So that's my debrief? You don't want to give me a physical?"

Bashir cleared his throat. "Are you suffering from any life-threatening injuries?"

"No."

"Anything else you want me to know?" he said.

Harwood let go of the curtain's velvet cord. She didn't remember gripping it. "No."

"Then, no, I'm not going to give you a physical." Bashir stood up, and stepped into the light. He was smiling suddenly. "Unless you want me to."

"I'd rather you order room service."

"I'll never recover," he said, loping across the room to the phone. "What have you missed?"

Harwood's shoulders dropped. The urge to laugh came over her. She considered him, the hunch of his broad shoulders, refusing to put down some weight. The pull of his sweater as he glanced at his watch, revealing two inches of his stomach, straining muscle and a line of dark hair disappearing down. The urge to laugh was replaced by the urge to kiss him.

She crossed the carpet to stand beside him, drawing his chin down with her finger and thumb, and pressing her lips to his. He remained stiff for a moment, and then he pulled her to him, kissing her with an intensity that matched their first time.

Then the voice of the concierge desk interrupted them.

"Your order, ma'am?" said Bashir, his voice the way she remembered in these moments, heavy with want.

"I don't care."

Bashir chuckled, bent to kiss her again, tangling a hand in her hair—and then told the desk they'd have the biggest breakfast on the menu, twice. "It'll be half an hour," he said.

"Half an hour?"

"That's what the man said."

"Enough time to wash my hair."

Bashir nodded. "That's a serious job. You'll need a safe pair of hands."

Harwood felt the mood slip from her, but she wanted to stay in it, wanted to stay in this warmth, away from reality. "Are you a safe pair of hands?" she asked, looking into those eyes, which weren't black anymore, but gold. She knew it didn't quite make sense: was she asking whether she'd be safe with him, or whether he was safe with her? But he didn't seem to mind, for he simply drew a gentle hand over her shaking arms. His arms were shaking too.

"Yes," he said.

003 woke with the call to prayer floating in through the window, which had been cracked open an inch, admitting the mixed scent of the Bosporus rushing coldly on; the market nearby, selling spices, sugar, nuts, paprika, baklava; and beneath all that the mulch of rotting vegetables and broken drains.

Sitting up, she winced as the bedsheet brushed her burns, and looked around, expecting to find Bashir on his knees.

"Over here."

He was standing naked in the doorway to the bathroom, holding her jewelry pouch. "I know you can't be separated long." His chest was a spider's web of bruises.

She said, "If you've ordered coffee too then I'll know you love me."

He grinned. "On the way up. I've got your Charlotte Perriand ball bearing necklace, and those earrings we found in the flea market in Nice."

Harwood stroked a thumb over the needle marks on her arm. "I feel more human already."

"And this." He tipped something from the bag into his palm, a lapis lazuli ring. "You kept it."

"I'm thinking of starting a collection. Engagement rings in transit."

"Oh yeah? How many men have proposed to you lately?"

"That depends. What do you think you're doing right now?"

He ducked his head, then sat down on the edge of the bed, making the mattress bounce with the jerks of his foot. "Listen, Johanna. I know I owe you an apology."

"Never accept a man's vowels."

"I'm good for it."

She bit down on the lurch of feeling. "We're all sorry, Sid. Was there something in particular you were thinking of?"

"In particular?"

"Yes."

He closed his fist around the ring, bent down, and kissed her, a kiss that tugged at her like an undercurrent. "I never stopped loving you, Johanna."

"Say that again for the people in back."

The sun swung on its axis, puncturing the curtains and scattering jewel drops across the floor, casting him in stained glass. He pulled back. "You don't believe me?"

"Should I?"

He swallowed. "I thought I'd never see you again. I thought you were dead. Everything that happened—I don't want to lose you again."

"You didn't lose me, Sid. Just like you didn't lose James."

Harwood linked fingers with his, tracing the bump of his knuckles. He bowed over her, and she felt a tear fall into her hair.

She said, "I did know."

"Know what?"

Harwood drew a quick breath. "I knew you'd come for me. That's
why I didn't break. I knew you'd come."

FOUR

Blank Sun

The security officer who presided over the lifts of the Regent's Park office was a navy veteran called Bob Simmons who rested the stump of his left arm against the panels only he could operate. He could read the building like few others. When a Double O stepped on at the basement, he would sniff the gun smoke on them, and either congratulate or commiserate on their score that day in the shooting gallery. He was always right. When the doors sighed open on the eighth floor, the offices of the Double O Section, Simmons could tell from the pace of activity in the corridor—whose drab Ministry of Works green had long outlasted the ministry—whether a crucial flash meant good news, or loss had thrown its shroud over the screens. When 008 had been killed in the field last month, the floor was muted. No one on Moneypenny's staff let doors swing open, or bang shut. It was as if they had all agreed to a minute's silence that would not end.

Simmons had only recently grown accustomed to thinking of the office on ninth as Moneypenny's domain. Sir Emery Ware was mostly based these days at SIS HQ on the Thames—M described the building as a bureaucrat's Aztec temple stranded in Vauxhall Pleasure Gardens—and he always hummed in the lift whenever he was called back to his Double O's. Simmons knew that was how M still saw the Double O Section, himself the only Double O to survive the racket, granting him legendary status and the crown, first as Section Chief and then M when his mentor Sir Miles Messervy retired. He'd over-lapped with 007 and Moneypenny in their first years in the Section, introducing Bond to all brands of fun trouble, all the while telling Moneypenny he was giving her the gift of experience as she fished them out of it. Sir Emery appointed Moneypenny as Section Chief when he moved to Vauxhall to become Chief of MI6. But he'd never let go. These vainglorious but effective weapons were his children.

Today, Simmons felt the good news in the straining cords of the lift as staff came in and out, carrying word from floor to floor, though the message would have crossed every station already. This was news to share personally, a moment to savor. Regent's Park had been liv-ing under a cloud for more years than Simmons cared to count. The original 009 was shot on a job. 0011, Harry Mace, disappeared on assignment in Singapore. Elizabeth Dumont and Anna Savarin, 002 and 0010, were killed in Dubai and Basra. 005, Ventnor, had fallen to his death while on a mission with 000, Harthrop-Vane, or Triple O as he was dubbed. 000's wrist and fingers remained bruised for weeks, a souvenir of his efforts to pull Ventnor to safety. Add to that the day Bashir limped in without 007 at his side. He did not meet the security officer's eyes. Bob understood Bashir and Harwood split up after that. But today, finally, some good news. 009 had brought 003 back home.

Simmons rode down to the garage, and stood to attention with-out quite realizing it as the doors whispered open. He looked past the Aston Martin, which remained under dustsheets, to Harwood's Alpine A110S in matte thunder gray, expecting to hear its 1.8-liter, 4-cylinder, 16-valve turbocharged engine easing to an echo. But the car was just as quiet as the DB3. Instead, there was the hiss of Ms. Moneypenny's Jaguar E-Type, whose quiet electric engine Simmons thought of as almost indecently spy-like.

Moneypenny pushed the door to with her elbow, waving at Simmons over the bonnet of the car. Simmons saluted.

"Ninth, please, Bob."

"Ma'am." He touched his fingertips to the panel, and a set of symbols only he understood glowed briefly, then disappeared at a tap. She stepped on beside him. Simmons tried to detect any sense of satisfaction from her, but her cool stare was as direct and quizzical as usual, with no spark to give the game away. She wore oxblood brogues, gray slacks, a green silk shirt with the gold-and-turquoise insect brooch that Simmons thought she wore when she wanted to get away from here to warmer climes, and an amber trench coat with the collar up, catching her curls, which glistened wet. The splotchy newspaper under her arm showed a photograph of Sir Bertram Paradise posing outside his satellite megafactory in Wales. Simmons caught the clench of her jaw. "Rain again?"

"Thirteen consecutive days," said Moneypenny. "I should have placed a bet."

"You want to bet on something," said Simmons, "bet on the sun."

A small smile. "I don't think bookies would take a bet on whether the sun will rise."

"Not rise, ma'am. Whether it will blink."

She glanced up. "Excuse me?"

"The sun is blank. No sunspots for over one hundred days. That's a record."

"Does that mean anything?"

"Now is a good time to take risks," he said, "but don't be surprised if those closest to you, either at home or in the workplace, deliver a surprise. At least, that's what my daughter posted on Instagram this morning."

Moneypenny freed her hair from her collar. "I'll look into that for her."

"Obliged, ma'am."

"Don't expect 009 or 003 today." She looked at him sidelong. "I know the building's humming, but Bashir is due to debrief at Vauxhall, and Harwood is bound for Shrublands."

"She got seven days without the option?"

"Something like that." The lift slid to a stop. "Thanks, Bob."

She turned left and walked past Communications, where sunspots and the movement of the Heaviside layer used to hold great significance. She made a note to ask the listeners if they ever got any intelligence on the sun these days, and pushed through the green baize door. Her assistant, Phoebe Taylor—a petite young woman with a purple fringe, a smile brighter than the sun, whatever the sun's movements, and an IQ brilliant enough for Op Management—rose from her seat.

"Morning, ma'am. 009 and 003 have touched down."

"Thank you." She looked past Phoebe to the window, the glistening treetops of the English Gardens. "Any word on when he'll be arriving?"

"Not yet."

Moneypenny touched her brooch. "Let me know." She slipped off her coat, turning to find Phoebe waiting; smiling, she let her take the wet thing. Moneypenny opened the door to her office, hearing the hum of the red light go on overhead—signaling she was not to be disturbed—and closed it behind her, resting for a moment against the soundproof padding.

So, Mikhail Petrov, the subject of Bond's final mission, was dead.

Moneypenny crossed to the window, forcing the sashes to relent and let it up by the inch allowed by security. She wanted the smell of rain, wanted to wash the whole place out. Raindrops bounced on the sill and ran to the ground.

She sat behind the glass desk, and tapped her screen. Her fingerprint swelled for a moment across the sensitive surface as if rippling across a pond, and then the crime scene photographs flashed up along with the report. The body in the bathtub. The wet tiles. The complimentary toothbrush glass broken.

Mikhail Petrov was dead, and Anna Petrov was missing.

Her first instinct: tell Phoebe to alert James. She and Bond had grown up in the Service, she as an agent runner in the field, he as the agent she was running. They had performed funeral rites and miracles over old wars and new wars, twenty years fighting nouns concrete and abstract, from drugs to terror; they had been rising stars, first sternly doted on by Sir Miles, then pinned together by Sir Emery to the top of the firmament. James would always be her first instinct.

Moneypenny pinched her fingers over her forehead, minimizing the images of Mikhail's murder in her mind. She imagined the swing of her door—for James never knocked—and there he'd be. The black comma of his fringe, always a little out of place; the gray-blue eyes that looked back at her with a hint of ironic inquiry; the longish nose; the straight and firm jaw; the slightly cruel mouth, smiling now as he said: "Miss me, Penny?"

She would start, hand to her heart. "Day and night, James, day and night."

He'd sit down on the corner of her desk. "I hate to think of you losing sleep over me."

"Especially when it's so much more fun losing sleep with you," she'd say, picking up her letter opener and tapping him on the shoulder. "Or so I'm reliably informed."

A gasp. "Who's been playing kiss-and-tell?"

"Who hasn't?"

"You know you've spoiled all other women for me . . ."

Moneypenny wasn't sure whether that was an actual conversation they'd once shared, when the idea that James Bond might one day fail to appear at her door seemed impossible, despite his insistence that he would die before the statutory retirement age of forty-five. An age he'd recently passed, refusing a promotion and a desk, in a grudging compromise between field work and training. Why worry about the end, he'd say. Every mission carries a high probability of death. If it didn't, Penny, you'd give it to somebody else. And the moments when it seems touch-and-go, he'd tell her—they just remind a man that being quick with a gun and easy with a smile doesn't mean he's invincible. He might be tarnished with years of treachery and ruthlessness and fear, but what waits in the dark isn't afraid of him. Why should it be afraid of his cold arrogance and the flat bulge of a Walther PPK beneath his left armpit? There's nothing to do about it. The whole of life is cutting through the pack with death. If a man makes it home to flirt with an old friend, that comes courtesy of his stars. Better thank them.

And then his stars had failed him. The sun went blank.

FIVE

Institutional Memory

What would James say about Mikhail Petrov's death? Money-penny remembered the briefing over at Vauxhall with M and Bill Tanner. 009 was in attendance too, the simple mission a chance to kick the boy wonder's training wheels.

If Bond could have been said to have modeled himself after one man, it was M. Not in style, M was far too relaxed for Bond—scuffed red Converse, crisp jeans, striped T-shirt, and linen blazer—but in charm. Under Sir Miles's gruff oversight, Sir Emery had been an incorrigible older brother to Bond. When Sir Miles retired, Sir Emery took up the role of father at the point where Bond most needed one. A voice like honey over gravel that sometimes had to slip an octave higher in order to escape his closing throat. When M looked you in the eyes and smiled, you blushed and smiled back before you knew what you were doing. M had been a Double O himself, kicking up trouble in every quarter of the Cold War. There was something debonair and devil-may-care about M, a quality lauded then lamented by the four wives in the rearview mirror. He had the body of a dancer or a fencer, though his arms were skinny and knotted now. Bald, a short white beard, white-gray eyebrows—which he just had to lift ever so slightly to make you feel he understood the weight of your pain, the whole world's pain. This display of compassion was something he gifted to cabinet secretaries and his driver, but it was out of place that day.

Bill Tanner, M's roving Chief of Staff, was perched on the windowsill, hands shoved in his pockets, foot tapping.

Bond unbuttoned his jacket and sat down. "Didn't expect to see you here, Bill."

"I'm protesting the cafeteria lunch."

Moneypenny took the seat next to Bond. She read the coding upside down on the two files on M's desk, then studied M's face.

Adjusting his cuffs, Bond looked across the desk at the spy chief who after all these years, Moneypenny knew, held a great deal of his love, and all his loyalty and obedience. 009 remained standing behind them at the center of the rug, hands clasped behind his back—Moneypenny observed his unusually erect posture in the reflection of the framed portrait that hung over M's head. If M was Bond's mentor, and Bond was Bashir's, the man behind the glass—Sir Miles Messervy—had been M's, and his battleship eyes peered down on the generations now.

"New call sheet," said M. "Mikhail Petrov's grown bored of the walk-on husband bit. Thinks he deserves a better billing."

Moneypenny heard 009's shoe scuff the rug as the latest Double O brought all his attention to bear on Bond's current case. She wondered if Sid Bashir truly represented the new and improved model, or only the next best thing to 007. She also wondered, with a grim smile, how Johanna Harwood would answer that question.

Tanner leaned forward. "Mikhail, Russia's foremost climate scientist, wants you to wine, dine, and fuck him. If you're not too busy doing the same to his wife."

Moneypenny spoke before Bond could. "When did this come in?"

M slid one of the files to her. "Confirmed in the last hour. Mikhail wants to come over to our side. Quaint, isn't it? But only if Bond will meet him and Anna in Barcelona and do the niceties in two weeks' time." He considered Bond. "We sent you to woo the wife in question so you could use her access to his files. We never imagined it would endear you to her husband."

"Mikhail Petrov wanted to be a poet," said Bond.

M sighed theatrically. "Didn't we all?"

Bond gave a one-shouldered shrug. "When Mikhail told me that he knew about the nature of my relationship with Anna, he wasn't angry. Had the idea it made us closer. Affection for the same woman, I suppose. Poetic."

Bond was silent as Moneypenny, M, and Tanner discussed how best to use Mikhail's kamikaze love for poetry, Anna's kamikaze love for Bond, and Bond's kamikaze love of—what, duty?—until it was decided that Bond would meet the Petrovs in Barcelona. Bashir would shadow him, observe how to bring in a defector.

As the angles were debated, Bond's gaze drifted to the portrait of Sir Miles Messervy, where 009 was reflected in the glass. Moneypenny could only imagine what Bond was thinking at the prospect of taking Bashir with him so 009 could study Bond's charm with another man's wife, when Harwood had so recently chosen Bashir and accepted his ring. Moneypenny glanced over her shoulder. Bashir's hands were loose now, and he was fiddling with his ring finger.

But when M gave a friendly rap on the table, Bond's expression gave nothing away. M said: "Let Bashir learn from the best, hmm?"

A small smile. "That's what I did, sir."

M pushed back from his desk. "You'll get me all aflutter, 007."

Bond winked to Moneypenny. "I meant her, sir."

Moneypenny remembered this with a stone dropping through her stomach. Because now James was missing, presumed dead after seventeen months, Mikhail had been found poisoned in a hotel room in Sydney, and Anna had disappeared.

She tapped the intercom. "Any sign of him, Phoebe?"

"The lift's just gone down, ma'am."

Moneypenny twisted her brooch. James had stopped her as they summoned the lift that afternoon, told her he knew what Tanner had said to Harwood: *James is a good-looking chap, but don't fall for him. I don't think he's got much heart.* That might be true. His heart might have been buried in Scotland at his parents' empty graves, or Royale-les-Eaux, or on the road north of Rosenheim, under the careless gaze of the white peaks. Perhaps he wasn't willing to hazard what remained. Or perhaps he'd never had much of a heart to begin with. Perhaps that's how he ended up in this job.

Bond had been brought to his knees by love and luck only twice before, and knew if there were to be a third, Harwood could be the author of it. Either way, whatever was left of his capacity for love he had shared with 003, no matter how drifting the relationship—not that Bond would ever use such a word—and no matter what status their connection was given by those watching for vulnerabilities in Regent's Park: active, inactive, as they pursued weekends away and embraces on his doorstep or hers, then retreated, then came back together for another mission, another night. Until Harwood chose Bashir. There were few people in the world Bond cared about, and would do anything for. She was on a very short list.

Moneypenny thought of Harwood on her way to Shrublands now. A formidable agent, adaptable to the point of camouflage. Olive skin, brown hair so dark it was almost black, which curled at her shoulders. Eyebrows just as dark, a thick sweep. High cheekbones, a jawline that commanded respect, and a soft nose. Bronze eyes that could wither a man at forty paces, or light up with mischief. She'd gone undercover as everything from Albanian to Afghan to Ukrainian. Tall and slim, with a young face, she'd also cut off her hair and passed for a boy in Saudi Arabia. Bond liked to say they were both products of European unions, him Swiss-Scottish, her French–Northern Irish. Both were products of colonialism too, in different ways: Harwood's mother Algerian-French, and Bond the poster boy for a waned empire.

He'd realized on their first mission he could fall and stay fallen, when 003 performed a tracheostomy on a boy under live fire in a public square with a Biro for a tube. It's not difficult to get a Double O number if you're prepared to kill people in cold blood in the course of a job. You were told to take care of a bent Japanese cipher agent in New York or a Norwegian double agent in Stockholm, so you did. Your victims might have been decent people, but they were caught up in the gale of the world. But one wanted it to count. And Harwood made it count.

There by the lift, on that last day, Bond asked Moneypenny if she thought he had a cold heart.

"No," she said. "That's the problem."

Before she could add another word, M had called James back, and she never told him what she meant. That his heart, or his sentiment, or whatever you wanted to call it—the wounds that never healed, the emptiness—that this broken heart of his would get him killed unless he gripped tight to that list of people he cared about. Because Moneypenny knew, and perhaps only she knew it, that James Bond, CMG, conqueror of SMERSH, and defender of the realm, was running out of reasons to live.

And she very much wanted him to come home.

But she never got the chance to tell him any of that.

The door opened.

Moneypenny stood up, ludicrous hope at her throat.

004 said, "You expecting somebody else?"

SIX

004

H ow was Jamaica?" asked Moneypenny. "Nice leave?"
"Twenty-nine degrees in the shade," said Joseph Dryden,
"and my auntie wouldn't stop feeding me curried goat."

Moneypenny waved to the window. "Sorry to be back?"

"It's peace I can't figure."

Moneypenny was caught by that, but continued: "In that case"—
sliding a tablet across the desk—"take a look at this."

004 had come up through Special Forces with a heavyweight's
build, six feet four and fourteen stone of muscle, shoulders straining
against the pink shirt he wore unbuttoned at the throat with a loose
purple tie, and midnight-blue trousers. His sleeves were rolled to his
elbows. Dryden always had the air of a man relaxing at the end of a
long day, despite ticking nearly every box of what experts called Operator's Syndrome, one symptom of which was hypervigilance—the
legacy of being a killer since he was sixteen years old. But, as 004
said, it was peace he couldn't figure, peace that had spun him out.
Here, ready to jump into danger once more, his looseness came with
the reassuring solidity of authority—a soldier who knew he could
command any situation and didn't need to prove it. When Moneypenny first sat beside him, she'd been struck by the rumble of laughter

from so deep in his chest, the languid survey of the room, and his ramrod back. She believed that if she simply took a seat beside him on the Tube, she'd wonder: Who is this man?

Joseph Dryden's name first crossed Moneypenny's desk after an IED in Afghanistan fractured the base of his skull and lacerated the vestibular nerve beneath his right ear, cutting the wire and leaving him sensorineural deaf on one side. The shock wave that followed resulted in a mild traumatic brain injury and damaged the language center in the brain, meaning his left ear received speech as a wall of sound which took huge effort to discern and comprehend. Dryden was medically downgraded. Then he faced a medical board. Then he was exited from the military. That was when Moneypenny made him an offer. Dryden's close-cropped hair gave no indication of the microphone embedded in his ear canal, or the brain-computer interface threading sound directly to his language processing center, bypassing both the cut nerve and the damaged tissue. The work of Q.

Moneypenny considered 004 the most experienced of her new generation of Double O's. 009, Aazar Siddig Bashir, had been a student when his place at the quarterfinal of the European universities chess championships in St. Petersburg brought him to her attention. M made the approach, asking him to carry out a small job for his country. That was how it began, if one wasn't already in service. He was young, and there was still something naïve about him; perhaps his faith that the ends justify the means. He had yet to meet the means that would haunt him. Triple O, Harthrop-Vane, was an Eton man like Bond. Though where Bond was expelled at twelve, Harthrop-Vane became Captain of School, and went on to meet all the right people at Cambridge. Bond had said to Moneypenny, "A Cambridge spy? Don't you know not to tempt fate?" She told him they couldn't all be Kim Philby.

Dryden closed the file and slid the tablet toward her. "What do you buy the man who has everything?"

"You tell me."

"You don't," he said. "Only thing he hasn't got is risk. You put him in debt."

"So, you think Bertram Paradise is a man for whom the world is not . . ." She trailed off.

A half-smile. "Something like that. Tech billionaire who claims his geo-engineering project can save us from the climate crisis, now Q discovers his chief science officer and head of security are missing and he's regularly dropping money in shady accounts around the world? I'm not surprised the Treasury is worried. It's either blackmail, or gambling. Suspicions of foul play in the missing persons?"

"Q says yes. This technology of Sir Bertram's, Cloud Nine"—Moneypenny gestured at the tablet—"represents a significant disruption to the status quo. Since the sixties, every decade has been hotter than the one before. If we stopped emissions tomorrow, which we won't, the current emissions in the atmosphere would still drive up temperatures in the next decades. Modeling shows that if we continue business as usual, we could see a five-degree increase by the end of the century. Melting Arctic. Rising seas. Extreme storms, flooding, droughts, fires, deadly heat waves. Add to that rapid urbanization, poor land and resource management. We're looking at pollution. Food and water insecurity. Decreased water, air, and food quality, combined with disease vectors and waterborne pathogens. We are already seeing increased migration, with communities temporarily displaced into neighboring territories by climate emergencies. After twenty forty, this will become permanent. Whole regions of the world will be unlivable."

"Best-case scenario?"

Moneypenny raised an eyebrow. "I've always loved your optimism, 004. Best-case scenario, a shift toward a global commons, in which we survive by the survival of others—sustainable, inclusive development that respects environmental boundaries, and is oriented toward low material growth and lower resource and energy intensity, driving down inequality across and within countries."

"And the worst?"

"It's an old story," said Moneypenny, "but it won't sell theater tickets."

"Rich get richer," said Dryden. "Poor get poorer."

"We stand on the brink." Moneypenny raised both hands. "Two worlds that are divided by income, degradation of social cohesion, conflict, and unrest." She closed her left fist. "One, a highly educated, internationally connected society that benefits from capital-intensive sectors and targeted environmental policies. This world exploits the other"—she closed her right fist—"poorly educated laborers working in highly intensive low-tech sectors, while bearing the burden of environmental collapse." She dropped her hands. "For some people, the brink was miles back. They exist in a closed bubble of superyachts and private jets. Or they just sold an organ to feed their family. All of this represents one of the most urgent threats to global security that we've ever faced."

Dryden nodded. "Enter Sir Bertram."

"Exactly. As time runs out, one camp is placing its faith in competitive markets driving rapid technological progress and development of capital as the road to a sustainable future. Calls for geo-engineering—large-scale interventions in the earth's natural systems—from states and nonstate actors are growing more aggressive. Sir Bertram is answering the call."

Dryden frowned. "I heard his family money comes from mining."

"Yes—a long line of imperial 'speculators' with interests in mining, from diamonds to today's rare earth metals." Moneypenny gestured at the damp newspaper. "Paradise says his forefathers grew rich taking from the earth on the backs of those they deemed less human. Cloud Nine is his atonement. He promises to use his fortune to heal the earth."

"Can he deliver?"

"Until now, geo-engineering research has been academic, existing almost entirely in computer models. Sir Bertram is the first to attract large-scale funding and more or less international backing to undertake live tests." ·

"In the army, *more or less* support leaves you stranded without backup behind enemy lines."

Rain swept in sudden static against the window. "If the Cloud Nine tests go wrong—if *anything* goes wrong—we are looking at blowback and increased risk of global unrest. More than that, the side effects of geo-engineering are completely unknown. If there are victims, there will be blame. Where there's blame, there's grievance. It's the government's job to mitigate the climate crisis. It's our job to mitigate conflict. And that's putting it nicely. Maybe Sir Bertram is just as saintly as he seems. Maybe he isn't. It's your mission to find out."

"What do you need me to do?"

A loaded gun. Just tell me where to aim. "You know the sun's gone blank?"

"I don't think I can do anything about that."

Moneypenny sat back. "Your old friend Luke Luck is on Sir Bertram Paradise's security force. He's been promoted since the head of security's disappearance—a man named Robert Bull."

Dryden held his breath, then seemed to go loose through his body, a mental shrug. "Guess I shouldn't be surprised you know about Lucky Luke."

"We can do the surprise portion of the conversation, if you'd like. Or we can just get right down to it."

He crossed his legs at the ankles. "Luke was more than my friend."

"I know. You served together. Won the Army Boxing Inter-Unit Championship together. And loved each other."

"You make it sound easy."

"I need it to be easy now."

"Gain his trust again?"

"Yes. Robert Bull's sudden disappearance does not augur well, especially combined with Dr. Zofia Nowak's. She's credited with designing Sir Bertram's computer and cloud-seeding device, though only in whispers. Now she's gone. Our fear is that Sir Bertram's whole setup is under attack. Another actor, state or otherwise, have got him in their pincers enough to bleed him for a fortune. It could be that he's trying to pay for Dr. Nowak's release. It could be something else entirely. Whatever it is, he's not asking for help. I need you to convince Mr. Luck to recommend you for the security team, without him realizing what you're really doing. He thinks you went into private security too, yes?"

"He blames me for not getting him a job when he discharged out."

"Well, now the tables have turned. Let's hope he's in a forgiving mood. I want you at the heart of Paradise's operation. Discover his vulnerabilities. Where is Dr. Nowak? What happened to Robert Bull? And is Cloud Nine vulnerable? If these large deposits are not the result of blackmail, what are they, and what does that mean for Paradise's claims to be able to save the world? The clock is ticking. Extinction is not a theoretical possibility. It is a lived reality, right now. I'm not waiting for the sun to blink. No last-minute miracles. Humankind has a short window to act, and it's closing. I want to keep breathing. How about you?"

"Yes, ma'am."

"Then you can do it?"

Dryden stood up and smoothed his tie. He grinned. "With pleasure, ma'am."

"Good." Moneypenny turned back to her screen. "Go some rounds with Triple O and then check in with Q before you leave, make sure everything's in working order."

"I didn't know Q leaned that way."

Moneypenny glanced up quickly, then smiled. "Who could resist you, Joe?"

SEVEN

The Sweet Science of Bruising

Joseph Dryden was boxing his shadow, and his shadow was hitting back.

Conrad Harthrop-Vane was not a man to shy away from targeting Dryden's skull. Human preservation told 004 to shield his vulnerabilities, to raise his guard in order to stop the blows aimed at his implant. But preservation had no place in the ring. Boxing is more about getting hurt than hurting. The body cannot shrink from it, or fear it. That's why Dryden boxed. In the ring and out of it, his body belonged to boxing: his teenage years had been a climb from welter to heavy, from middle to cruiser, to reach the point where his body alone said, *Hit me and I'll kill you—so don't hit me.* He'd been told by his father that a good big man will always beat a good little man. He couldn't afford to be the good little man. Boxing invited a person to dance to their limit, to lean out against the ropes and ask: Can I take another blow? Well, can you?

000 asked him this with a hook that came straight from childhood. Every boxer had a style, and Harthrop-Vane's was that of the

bully who waited for you after school: he wanted to inflict damage, he wanted to make it public, and he wanted to make it last. Afterward, he'd laugh and pretend it was a joke, pretend he didn't enjoy it, that he wasn't here for the hurting, and that getting hurt was the price of admission. In Dryden's view, this style lacked heart, but right now it was also taking his lunch money. He couldn't call Harthrop-Vane a coward, for he didn't exhibit that trait of human behavior that would be so fatal in the ring—a survival instinct. He had the boxer's gift of denying his own self-preservation.

It was also the gift of a Double O, and Dryden had to admit that Harthrop-Vane had that and many other effective gifts: endurance, education, style, armed and unarmed combat specialties, especially with a sniper rifle. And he had to admit that the reason he only half-laughed at Harthrop-Vane's jokes was that Harthrop-Vane had been born with all those gifts, fed to him on a silver spoon. Now Harthrop-Vane failed to defend against a blow to the ribs, his whole body shuddering at the end of Dryden's fist, but still he was laughing. He was the bully who knew he'd never get into any trouble, because his big beautiful blue eyes took care of that. Dryden delivered a right that sent Harthrop-Vane stumbling back. Now close in. A left. Don't stop. Don't show mercy. Knock him out of the ring, out of body, out of time. Kill him with a smile on your face.

Harthrop-Vane hit the mat. "Truce!"

Dryden hesitated over him, fist raised. Harthrop-Vane was so blond his hair shone white under the strip lighting of the gym. His eyelashes were the same: pale fringes over eyes the color of an iced pond, which glimmered up at Dryden now with an innocence that seemed to ask, *Who, me? What did I do?* His cherubic lips smirked.

Dryden shook his head.

He pulled his glove off with his teeth, and offered Harthrop-Vane his hand.

Harthrop-Vane accepted Dryden's offer, then tugged. Dryden

lost his balance, pitching forward. Harthrop-Vane rolled him onto his back, pinning Dryden down, hammering him with punches.

Knocked out of time.

"I knew you white boys couldn't box," said Dryden. He head-butted Harthrop-Vane with all the force he had. Blood gushed over him.

Dryden rolled away as Harthrop-Vane got to one knee, cupping his nose and laughing. He said, "All right, all right. Only following orders."

Dryden moved to the ropes. His chest was slick with Harthrop-Vane's blood. "Whose orders?"

"M's," said Harthrop-Vane. "Told me to get in your face today. Test you."

"How'd that work out for you?"

Harthrop-Vane sneered. "Five rounds to you. And I'll thank you not to suggest going the distance."

Dryden wiped his face, then chucked the stained towel at Harthrop-Vane. "Guess that's why we call you Double O Nothing."

Harthrop-Vane flinched, caught the towel, then smirked. "Hearing OK?"

"Depends how long this conversation lasts."

Harthrop-Vane waggled the towel. Blood fanned in the air. "I surrender." He dabbed his nose. "Of course, this isn't a real test."

Dryden leaned into the ropes. "How'd you figure?"

"An SF operator like you can be dropped behind enemy lines alone with just a stick of gum and a pocket knife and he'll work the problem."

Dryden grunted, "So?"

"This isn't the field," said Harthrop-Vane, "and you're not alone. You never will be, not with Q in your head. You're not self-sufficient anymore. Must sting. Being vulnerable."

"What do you know about vulnerability?"

A slow smile. "Oh, only that I don't enjoy it." Harthrop-Vane pulled his gloves off.

Dryden ran his thumb over his throbbing jaw. "You ever think about what you'd do if you faced something in the field beyond your limits? When extra muscle won't cut it, and you're just outpunched."

"No need to indulge in thought experiments," said Harthrop-Vane, ducking his head, but Dryden caught a grimace of something close to self-deprecation, or self-hatred. "I met it, and I failed. 005 plunged into the crevasse and I only realized my hand was empty when I heard his body hit the ice. Ventnor was a good man." Harthrop-Vane flicked his thumb against his index finger. "As I said, I don't like vulnerability. You tell yourself, never again old boy, say your prayers and make amends, honor his memory by doing whatever it takes to protect the next man beside you. But you know it's nothing but a lullaby. We do not traffic in death, Joe. It traffics in us."

Dryden ran his tongue over his teeth. He had the urge to ask Harthrop-Vane, Don't you think I got what it takes anymore? But he didn't want the answer. Harthrop-Vane's privilege came with an unsavory gift—telling the truth, because he didn't need tact to get by. So Dryden pulled off the other glove, popped his knuckles, and bounced forward.

"Come on then, Double O Nothing. Let's give death a run for his money."

Harthrop-Vane raised his bare fists, his feet tracing a pendulum in the chalk. "Well look at you. I'll have to tell M there's no chinks in this hardware."

Dryden threw a punch, buzzed contact, threw another, landed: the satisfaction of bone on bone.

Harthrop-Vane stumbled, laughing. He spat blood, holding up one hand for time. "Rumor is you'll be under the covers on this one with your old beau. If Sir Bertie is in trouble, I wonder what your man knows. Suppose you'll have some fun finding out."

Dryden hunched.

"Nothing quite like fucking someone over for queen and country."

Dryden's guard flickered. The blow was perfect, smashing his right temple. The vacuum in his skull was crushing, but not as bad as the tinnitus that followed it, the roar of an ocean filling the hold of a ship. Dryden staggered, hit the floor. Harthrop-Vane was standing over him. His mouth was moving, but the sense was cutting in and out, arriving in tatters, out of sequence and out of time. It felt like trying to understand a language he'd last studied at school. Dryden clutched his head.

Conrad Harthrop-Vane sighed, patted him on the shoulder. "Don't worry, 004. Q to the rescue."

Dryden caught Harthrop-Vane's wrist, wrenched until the man was off-balance, and then swiped his legs out from under him. He raised a fist ready to murder. Harthrop-Vane spread his hands, shouting something—peace. It was peace.

Dryden eased back onto one knee.

It's peace I can't figure.

EIGHT

Q

Families queuing for the boating pond, art students sketching the modernist Elephant House, the faithful chatting outside the mosque—none of them knew what lay beneath Regent's Park, as they crisscrossed its sodden lawns and found shelter beneath its trees. The Double O building looked like any other Regency terrace converted into tired offices and clung to with a creaking lease. But beneath it, a whole world followed the paths of defunct canals and tunnels, coring like a peeled apple to the central control room—to Q.

004 sagged in the corner of the lift. Bob Simmons had greeted him by asking who 004 thought would emerge victorious in the upcoming prizefight between Chao and King in Macau, before recognizing something was wrong. It wasn't the blood. He was used to Dryden shrugging that off. It was the way Dryden controlled his breathing, attention fixed to the floor. Controlling fear. Simmons pressed basement level twelve and watched the floors count down, working his jaw. Then he rested his arm on Dryden's back.

Dryden glanced up quickly. He swallowed, then smiled.

Simmons nodded. The doors slid open. It was usually here that Dryden rolled his sleeves down. Simmons would remind him that he wouldn't feel the cold outside of the chamber. And Dryden would say: "What my brain knows and my body feels are two very different things." Now, Simmons threw Dryden a salute, and left him to the things his brain and body knew.

Level twelve was the final strip of the peeled apple. Dryden followed the padded white corridor round past the lab, the noise swelling like the screeching of cicadas on a Mediterranean night. He tapped his watch in vain, knowing the implant was not responding. The lab had no walls, just windows. A knot of technicians hovered over the crystal growth chamber. At the end of the corridor, glass doors opened into a crescent-shaped office, a tangle of workbenches and fabrication machines clasped between a transparent floor and transparent walls, seeming to lean into the core. Dryden's heart always tripped as he stepped into what felt like nothing.

Below: a white sphere, with what looked to him like a golden chandelier suspended at its center; or a hazel eye, the gleaming gold-plated copper pipes like nerves descending to a great cylinder. The quantum computer was gripped in place by magnetic hinges. Inside the vacuum chamber it was absolute zero, minus 273 degrees Celsius. All that stood between him and a plunge to the death, if absolute zero didn't kill him first, was world-class engineering and a few inches of solid matter.

Dryden cleared his throat. To him, it made no sound.

The two engineers tasked with Q's design and maintenance shared a desk pressed up against the glass wall, as close to the chamber as possible.

"Could you get our attention in a less manly way?" said Aisha Asante, not looking up. "The vibrations of your chest could distract Q from nailing this arms deal transaction."

Dryden raised an eyebrow. He could only hear ringing as loud as a siren.

Aisha glanced around and leaped to her feet, becoming tangled in the spin of her chair. She pushed the thing aside and closed the gap between them. She cupped his cheek with a warm hand, tilted his head, as if she could see inside him.

Ibrahim Suleiman was slower to realize what was happening, asking questions Dryden couldn't fathom, before Aisha hushed him, steering Dryden toward a medical bench.

Dryden read her lips: *Fuck Triple O.* He laughed and the rumble suddenly pierced him, as if he were laughing into a megaphone.

Aisha didn't seem to care about getting blood on her hot-pink blazer, which she wore over a black top with black jeans and a matching braided headband. She clicked her fingers, mouthing: *Shirt off.* Dryden helped her pull the undershirt over his head.

Ibrahim seemed to hunker inside the oversize fisherman's sweater, which Dryden knew would be the result of charity shop rummaging. Last time he visited, Ibrahim denounced his luxury brands and fast fashion. Dryden didn't want to attempt speech, afraid his words would slide out of position, and he wouldn't know if he was making sense or not. So he signed to Ibrahim: "How's Q today?"

Ibrahim perked up. He'd been learning BSL since working with Dryden. "We've told you," he signed, "it's a machine. It doesn't emote."

Dryden rested against the bank of consoles with a sigh. He clicked his neck while Ibrahim attached all the wires he needed—Dryden had made it a point to only half-understand what went on in here. He was still uncomfortable with being Q's first hyphen subject. Where the other Double O's had Q implants in their watches or phones, Q and he were bound to each other beneath the skin. He focused on Aisha and Ibrahim's chatter. At first, he could only interpret their warmth. Then words returned to him, relaxed him inch by inch as they isolated the problem and fixed it remotely using the link with Q, circumnavigating the deaf right ear, and bringing the left ear back online, bypassing the damaged brain tissue. Dryden closed his eyes. He felt as protective of the two prodigies as they did of him. If he was a test subject, so were they under Q's unblinking virgin eye. And all of them knew the sensation of quantum superposition long before this chamber, coexisting in more than one state.

Aisha was a state school Londoner like him, and like his, her grandfather had also served in Britain's colonial forces in World War II before immigrating to Britain, Aisha's parents from Ghana, his own from Jamaica. Very much unlike him—Dryden reflected as the screens started translating the murmurs of his body—Aisha was a Cambridge-educated genius with multiple degrees in quantum physics.

Dryden put his faith in their genius now, humming softly, listening for it in the receding din.

Ibrahim's parents had both worked as locally employed civilians, or LECs, for British forces in Iraq—they'd served as interpreters for three years. They had been resettled in the UK as refugees after local militias started targeting LECs for assassination. Ibrahim's mother was refused a job as a cleaner because she didn't have "UK cleaner experience." When Ibrahim told his parents he was going to join the army in order to become an engineer, they reminded him of the one bedroom he'd shared as a teenager with them and his three younger siblings in Sheffield as a thank-you for their contributions to Britain. But Ibrahim signed up anyway, from there going on to study bio-engineering.

For all of them, Ambalavaner Sivanandan's aphorism—*we are here, because you were there*—included either direct or generational experience of serving Britain's interests, while growing up in a country that more often than not refused to accept them as British, and dedicating their minds or bodies or both to its cause despite that. It was an exhausting kind of contortion, one that blinked at him baldly now in the form of numbers on the screen, reminding him what he'd lost and gained courtesy of Her Majesty's Government.

"Are you still with us, 004?"

Dryden focused. They were staring at him with concern. He

winked. "Triple O ain't that hard." He rubbed his ear. "Q back in sync with me, then?"

"It doesn't emote, and it doesn't lose time," said Ibrahim. "And I don't design faulty equipment."

"I thought Q doesn't bother with time."

"Score one to He-Man," said Aisha.

Dryden stood up. He wore tracksuit bottoms, his chest and feet bare. He moved, a swift footwork drill.

"Just like new," said Aisha. "You're welcome to use the staff showers through there, unless you enjoy the cut-up and bloody look."

Dryden said, "Ask my assistant to send down some new clothes, would you?"

"Sure," said Aisha, "that's a thing I'll definitely do before you get out of the shower."

Dryden drank lungfuls of steam, the water sliding over him, turning red around his feet. He watched his and Harthrop-Vane's blood thread the plug. The cascade was the drop of multiple grenade pins—no, it was only water. It was only blood.

"What do you think of Bertram Paradise?" said Dryden, knotting his tie. "You think his quantum computer is better than Q?"

"He claims it's the best in the world," said Aisha, passing him black coffee.

"You don't believe him?"

"The data's good."

"Then what's the problem?"

"Him. I look at him sitting in front of parliamentary committees and donating money to good causes and giving YouTube tours of his autonomous survey yacht—he's too good a showman."

"You can't be a tech genius and a showman?"

"She's just jealous," said Ibrahim.

"I am very happy to hit you," said Aisha, raising a magazine above Ibrahim's head as he threaded a minute camera into Dryden's ear for a full systems check now that normal functioning had resumed.

"Please don't," said Ibrahim.

"It's not jealousy, and it's not that I consider his Q *necessarily* inferior to ours. I just don't think he developed it. I look into his eyes and see nothing. No spark. My money is on Dr. Zofia Nowak."

"The missing science officer."

"I'd consider her *my* rival, *if* I was a jealous person. But as I'm not, I merely appreciate the beauty of her brain."

Dryden smiled. "You ever feel like a Numskull, living in here with Q?"

"Should I be offended?" said Aisha.

"You know He-Man but you don't know the Numskulls? *The Beano.* They lived inside someone's skull. Ran about maintaining his brain."

"She knows He-Man because it's a meme," said Ibrahim. "And no, we don't feel like Numskulls, because we didn't come of age before the Internet was invented."

"Can't beat *The Beano.*"

Aisha's touch on his forearm was gentle. "Maybe you feel like we're living inside your skull too?"

"Aren't you?"

"Trust me, 004. The only person inside your mind is you." She watched Ibrahim thread the camera out. "But wouldn't it be less lonely, the other way?"

"You're not lonely," said Ibrahim. "You're never alone."

"And how did you come to this astonishing insight, Numskull?" said Aisha.

Ibrahim nodded at Q. "None of us are."

Dryden considered the machine. The device implanted beneath Dryden's skin was able to read his brain waves, understand whose voice he wanted to focus on, and select and amplify that voice until its owner was whispering secrets into his ear. The microphone in his ear canal streamed everything he said and heard to Q for processing. The manual controls were secreted inside his Garmin MARQ Commander watch, which, with a few tweaks, meant Dryden could receive Aisha's voice inside his skull without anyone else hearing her.

Where a regular computer had to process information in a linear sequence, ones and zeroes, a quantum computer could contemplate the one and the zero simultaneously, allowing it to process data so quickly it could solve equations that would otherwise take the lifetime of a universe. One day, Q might solve the climate crisis, space travel, even time travel. For now, Q was fighting terror. Where cryptocurrencies and stronger encryption had allowed terrorists to become smarter, Q was filtering unfathomable data sets to identify and follow threats. Q had not yet met a personal privacy it couldn't invade, including Dryden's.

Not that it could solve everything. Q had been running facial recognition through every closed-circuit surveillance system it could access since 007 went missing, and come up with nothing. It was as if James Bond had lost his face, his identity scraped off without leaving so much as a death mask. Or, he had stopped existing. For if the smartest mind in the world couldn't find him, then surely Bond was just another dead agent in an unmarked grave. To Dryden, the point was academic—he'd never worked with Bond, knew him only as attractive, sometimes arrogant and surly about it, sometimes charming. But if Q wasn't up to the job—that directly concerned him.

A sharp rap on the doorframe made him turn. Mrs. Keator wore her usual black—this time, high-waisted black woolen slacks and a black turtleneck beneath a long white painter's smock that consumed her shrinking frame, the rolled-up sleeves just revealing hands wrinkled as crushed magnolia petals, swollen knuckles gleaming between globules of gold and precious stones. "Ma'am."

She peered at him. "Returned from my lunch to alarms hollering. But you look like you're operating on full efficiency."

"Yes, ma'am."

"I understand Moneypenny has put you onto Sir Bertie." Mrs. Keator was the co-founder of Q Branch with Major Boothroyd. She was rumored to have begun her Service life decoding Spektors. When the Major died, she arrived to work dressed in black, which she never threw off. Eyes and mind like a hawk, she still gripped Q Branch in arthritic talons, and would until the living computer—as she was sometimes known—stopped processing.

"Yes, ma'am."

"Define air gapped, 004." This delivered with nothing to entertain the notion he might not have an answer.

Dryden shot Aisha something close to a smirk. "A computer that's not on any network. Invulnerable to hacking. The way Q picked up that cabinet minister being paid for his vote with sexual favors last month, it was periods when his phone was stationary at a certain sauna, right? But if your phone or your computer or whatever's not on a network, it can't be monitored."

"I like an agent who does his homework. The future of security is the past. Sir Bertie likes to think he has the most sophisticated technology in the world, but his personal devices are air gapped. Absolute radio silence. Same for everyone in his inner circle."

"And the outer circle?"

She peered at him over her heavy tortoiseshell glasses. "You might actually be worth the money we've poured into you. Dr. Zofia Nowak, the opposite number to our Dr. Asante and Dr. Suleiman, has disappeared as perhaps only she would know how to do. Q has been trawling her social media for anything useful, and come upon something with such sublime coincidence I don't know whether it's good or very bad luck. Zofia Nowak recently contacted Ruqsana Choudhury, a human rights lawyer and childhood friend of 009. Bashir will make contact with Ruqsana soon, an innocent hello. We're prompting Facebook to feed Choudhury memories of more innocent times, soften her up. She'll ask 009 for help. Then Bashir can use Choudhury to locate Dr. Nowak. If she is the brains behind Sir Bertram, we want to make sure those brains fall into *our* hands, no one else's."

Dryden drummed his fingers against his stomach. "If Paradise knows we have the capability to get up to brainwashing on the weekends—because he has the same capability, presumably—and he's air gapped his devices, how did we pick up his irregular payments?"

"With all the difficulty of detecting flaws in the dodgy dossier. He wants someone to know he's been behaving badly."

"A cry for help?"

Mrs. Keator laughed, the crackle of a broken exhaust pipe. "Or a fuck you."

Dryden smiled. "To us?"

"Young man, I don't think we register on this demigod's radar."

Aisha tossed her hair over her shoulder. "Time to correct that. You're good to go, 004. Give the demigod a kiss from us."

Medical History

T hank you for talking with me today," said Dr. Kowalczyk.

"I'm glad to be here," said 003.

Surprise flickered over Dr. Kowalczyk's face. She was young to be the psychiatrist on duty at Shrublands. A small woman with bulging eyes, which Johanna Harwood put down to overactive glands, magnified by a pair of rimless glasses. The effect was like sitting under a microscope. The office was dressed up the same as any therapy room: a small table with an innocent box of tissues, a vase of wilting flowers, a cheerful clock, a sofa, and an armchair for the doctor. Stale, warm air. She'd been encouraged to kick off her shoes at the door, as if this were the living room of a friend. All designed to relax. To make you believe Dr. Kowalczyk was here to help, rather than evaluate. There was no two-way mirror. Harwood guessed a camera was embedded in the clock.

Dr. Kowalczyk said, "Previous Double O's have made it clear to me that they're only here under orders."

"We're a touchy bunch. I promise not to make your life difficult."

Those hungry eyes narrowed. "Perhaps you can tell me how you're feeling, 003, in yourself?"

"Tired."

"You look like you might be in pain."

"Yes," said Harwood. "My shoulder. And my left arm."

"Are you comfortable there? Would you like another cushion?"

"Sure. Thanks."

Dr. Kowalczyk pulled a cushion out from behind her armchair. Harwood did nothing to hide her grimace as she reached out.

"What words might you use to describe how you're feeling emotionally?"

"Tired." Harwood laughed. "That's not really a feeling word, is it? I guess I'm . . . relieved. Happy."

"Happy about what?"

"Happy I'm alive."

"Yes, I can imagine that. Anything else?"

"Frustrated."

"Frustrated at what?"

"Myself. For getting captured. And that I killed the man who did this to me, instead of capturing him for interrogation."

"Might frustration be an understatement?"

Harwood crossed her legs. She flicked an invisible bit of fluff from her trousers. "Yes, you're probably right. I'm angry. Angry I was caught, angry I was treated like an object of amusement by cowards and sadists, angry I killed the bastard, angry I have to be angry that I killed the bastard."

Dr. Kowalczyk took off her glasses, cleaned them, and slid them back up her nose. "You said you weren't going to make my life difficult."

Harwood opened her hands. "Save us both some time."

"Do you have another place to be?"

"I have a week of massage and saunas until I'm fighting fit. I should nearly die more often. But you—it's six o'clock in the evening, and you're drinking a large cup of coffee."

"What does that tell you?"

"It tells me it's been a long day, with a long night ahead. It tells me you might be as tired as I am. I just want to go to bed. So, I'm not going to hold things up. I'm all yours."

"Good observational skills," said Dr. Kowalczyk.

"That's what they pay me for," said Harwood.

"You have a background of medical training, is that right?"

"I was studying to be a surgeon before I joined the Service, yes."

"That was your dream?"

"It was my intention."

Dr. Kowalczyk made a show of opening the file balanced on her knee, though Harwood would lay down good money she had it memorized. "It says here students in medical schools are ranked on skill and knowledge. You came top of your year on that metric. Then they rank students on interpersonal skills. Bedside manner. Getting a patient to trust you, or divulge sensitive information. Defusing difficult situations. Usually the student who achieves the number one spot on skill and knowledge drops to the bottom of the pile when it comes to interpersonal skills. They've been so busy studying, they've forgotten how to talk to people. But not you. You achieved the number one spot in interpersonal skills as well."

Harwood felt herself blushing, though she knew she wasn't embarrassed. "So?"

"So they pay me for my observational skills too."

Harwood pulled the cushion out from behind her and fiddled with its seams.

"And what I'm observing," continued Dr. Kowalczyk, "is that while other Double O's conceal their discomfort and disdain for this process—their *fear*—with bluster, you are concealing it with openness. You know what I want to hear and see. You know how to defuse this situation. You started with transparency. Now you're trying vulnerability."

Harwood's fingers stilled on the cushion. She tossed it onto the floor.

"Want to stop bullshitting me, 003?" said Dr. Kowalczyk.

"I hope they pay you the big money," said Harwood, looking at the clock. "Shoot."

"Interesting choice of word. Let's start there. The bastard, as you call him, could have been a high-value capture." She turned a page in the file. "Identifying feature: a moth tattoo on his neck and chest. Known as Mora, developed from the Kikimora, a folk character: a spirit, usually female, that enters a house at night through the keyhole, and sits on her victim's chest until he suffocates to death. We have traces of Mora leading Rattenfänger in Lebanon, Libya, Albania, the US, Russia, and Indonesia—his activities blur the already hazy lines between multinational terrorism, multinational organized crime, legitimate business, and narcotics money laundering. What we know for certain is that he's considered a nightmare by those experienced in giving nightmares. So why did you kill the bastard, instead of capturing him for interrogation?"

"I was pumped full of chemicals. He was kneeling on top of 009. I took the shot I had. It wasn't supposed to be a kill shot."

"Which is it?"

"Excuse me?"

"Did you make a kill shot because you were pumped full of chemicals, or because you valued Aazar Siddig Bashir's life over capturing the target?"

Harwood's jaw pulsed. "I took the shot I had."

Dr. Kowalczyk said, "Why didn't you take your cyanide pill after you were captured?"

"I like my life."

"Do you?"

Harwood opened her mouth to snap a reply, then stopped. "What makes you think I don't?"

"Look at you. Is it worth it?"

"I discovered a chemical weapons stash in Syria and reported it to Moneypenny, potentially saving thousands of people. Yes. It's worth it."

"So that's your motivation? Saving lives?"

"Of course it is."

"You have a license to kill."

Harwood sat forward. "You're not that naïve."

Dr. Kowalczyk blinked. "What about the Hippocratic oath? You swore as a doctor to do no harm."

"I took another oath."

"Your word is worth so little?"

Harwood tilted her head. "You're trying to rattle me. You're testing for PTSD."

"Do you think you have PTSD?"

"I don't have any of the symptoms."

"Is that a no?"

"That's a no."

"It says here you were given a lie detector test to find out if you were telling the truth—that you didn't divulge any information to your interrogators."

"Yes," said Harwood.

"And you were telling the truth."

"Yes," said Harwood.

"Do you resent the implication that you might lie?"

"It's standard procedure."

"Lying, or checking whether you lied?"

No answer.

"How did you stop yourself divulging any information?"

"We're given training."

"You didn't persuade them to go easy on you, somehow?"

"How exactly would I have done that?"

Dr. Kowalczyk said, "Tell me about your childhood."

Harwood wriggled her toes. "When testing for PTSD, we ask

rapid questions on different topics, and observe how the patient responds. You don't want to hear about my childhood. You want to test how I stand up under stress. They know they can trust my loyalty. Now they need to know if I can be trusted to return to the field."

"And you don't want to talk about your childhood."

"God, who does?" She'd been sitting here for twenty-five minutes. "It's all in that file, anyway."

Dr. Kowalczyk said nothing.

Thirty-five minutes to go. "Fine. I grew up in Paris. My mother worked for Médecins Sans Frontières. I followed in her footsteps. I got into medical school in London. Then I joined the Service."

"Do you call that the redacted version?"

"I call it the hurry-up-and-go version."

"What about your father?"

"Is this the part where I flinch?"

Dr. Kowalczyk said nothing.

Harwood looked at the floor. Then, slowly, she smiled, and shrugged. "My mum and dad met in Paris. He'd moved from Belfast. He was older. A failed photographer fantasizing about a second life, falling in love with a pretty Parisian girl. He got his wish. My mum—I don't know if she was in love. But she was pregnant, so they got married. We lived with my grandmother. Money was tight. When my mum got a job as an administrator with MSF, it was a good opportunity. She was promoted quickly. They saw her abilities."

"She traveled for her work."

"Yes."

"Leaving you with your father."

"She didn't leave me. She traveled for work."

Those eyes opened and closed in empty semaphore. "Your father didn't have a job?"

"He looked after me."

"With the help of your grandmother."

Harwood fingered her necklace. "He couldn't hold a job."

"He was a paranoid schizophrenic," said Dr. Kowalczyk.

"We didn't know that. Not at first. When he was diagnosed, he took the medication. He managed it. Most of the time. It was hard for him."

"What effect did it have on you?"

"I learned adaptability," said Harwood. "That's what you want to hear, right? I learned how to defuse situations."

"Is that how you feel?"

"I guess if I told you I'd never really thought about it, you wouldn't believe me?"

Dr. Kowalczyk raised her eyebrows. "Let's say I'd be highly surprised."

Harwood smiled again. "He'd see things, sometimes. He'd think people were following us. When I was young, I believed him. As I got a little older, I realized it was in his head, but it was best to go along with it. We'd spend days riding on the Métro, evading pursuit. Sometimes I had to talk him down from attacking people he thought were after me. He wanted to protect me."

"How much did your grandmother and mother know about this?"

"You think they were endangering me?"

"Do you?"

"I think they were doing the best they could under difficult circumstances."

"And your mother? She didn't change jobs so she could be at home more?"

"You don't change the course of your life for an accident."

Dr. Kowalczyk slowly pushed up her glasses. She linked her hands.

"You're just going to leave that lying out in the open?" said Harwood, gesturing to the space between them.

"Tell me about Frankfurt."

Harwood ran her tongue over her teeth. A minute passed. "My dad said we had to get away from Paris. We were in danger. He made me get on the train to Frankfurt. He said he had to meet his handler in the post office outside Frankfurt Süd Bahnhof. He believed he was a spy. Funny how things turn out. When we got there—he said we should wait for his handler. We slept outside. A man tried to take me in the night. I always thought he was homeless. I'm not sure why. Anyway. My dad stopped him. He broke his hand on the man's face."

"How old were you?"

"Nine."

"What happened to your father after that?"

"Hospitalization. Then he disappeared."

"Did your mother try to find him?"

"We all did. My grandmother was too old to look after me."

"So your mother took you with her, around the world. You were home educated. Except you didn't have a home. You moved to London to study. And you found your father."

"He was living in the Barbican. He was very ill. He'd starved himself."

"You were with him when he died."

Harwood scrunched her toes into the pastel-blue fibers of the carpet. "That's right. Was that all?"

"You managed to free yourself when 009 arrived. Convenient timing. You didn't want to free yourself before?"

"I tell you, the cuisine there is just to die for. Why bother with a little thing like freedom?"

"Do you bother with freedom?"

"What does that mean?"

"You've signed your free will and body away in service to your country."

"In service of an idea."

"Tell me about that."

"I want to stop bad things happening to good people."

Dr. Kowalczyk said, "You're not that naïve."

Harwood lowered her lashes. "Nothing more dangerous than an idealist, right? I must be setting off alarm bells right now."

"Your father is Northern Irish, your grandmother was an Algerian radical. Don't you think you set off alarm bells the minute you appeared as a candidate for the Service?"

"She fought for independence."

"You wouldn't call her a radical?"

"Only if you call the notion a country has a right to freedom and justice radical."

"Freedom again. Tell me how you got free."

Harwood ran through it: hearing the explosion; how she forced her heartbeat to slow down, making them think they'd overdosed her so they wouldn't kill her once they realized they were compromised; withstanding their efforts to "rouse" her; simulating coming round once most of the guards left; talking the remaining guard, a Syrian soldier low down on the command structure, into believing the SAS were staging a rescue—he'd better escape now, and take her as a hostage for his own safety—then disabling him once he'd cut the restraints.

"Did you kill him?"

"He was just doing his job. Not very *well*, but still . . ."

"Have you ever failed to persuade someone to do something you wanted?"

Harwood squinted. "I suppose it would gratify you to hear I couldn't talk my father out of dying?"

"Tell me about joining the Service."

Harwood ran her hand through her hair. "I was doing a trauma fellowship in a hospital in Beirut."

"Unusual choice."

"Not really. I'd lived there for a while with my mum. I had a patient—I can't tell you his name. He came in for burn treatment. It was a resource-poor environment. We were left alone and got talking. He trusted me. Next time I saw him, it was chemical burns. That's when Moneypenny made the approach. She told me he was a bomb maker. MI6 needed to know certain things. He would talk to me. I was in a position of trust."

"And you abused that trust."

Harwood straightened up. "I got the information they needed. I saved lives."

"Then what?"

"He took me from the hospital one night. He forced me to go with him to a house where a friend of his was hurt. There was a young woman being held captive there. A girl, really. I talked my patient into letting her go. But his friend wouldn't go along with it. He started waving his weapon about. He said he'd sell me and the captive."

"What did you do about it?"

"I had my medical kit. I used my scalpel. I killed the friend. My patient was going to shoot me. I didn't let him. I saved the young woman. After that, Moneypenny asked if I'd like to serve my country."

Dr. Kowalczyk said, "You don't change the course of your life for an accident."

Harwood glanced at the clock. "Like I said, the big money. That's our hour. Have I passed? Or do you think Rattenfänger's game of pin the tail on the donkey has left me a shaking wreck?"

"That depends. You said you discovered a chemical weapons stash in Syria. Is that all you were looking for?"

The minute hand quivered. "No."

"You went off mission, afterward, to follow a lead in the search for a missing agent. That's when you were captured."

Time spilled over. "Yes."

"Under whose authority?"

"Call it a question of loyalty."

"You realize you jeopardized two more assets—yourself and 009—in search of this missing agent?"

"Yes."

"And that this missing agent is likely dead, or turned, by now?"

"He wouldn't turn."

"Because he's loyal to you?"

Harwood laughed. "No. Because he's loyal to an idea."

"Would you call your love for James Bond a danger in the field?"

"I don't accept the premise of the question."

"That love constitutes a danger, or that you love him? An agent, by all accounts, of significant weaknesses—women, drink—and mental health that was, at best, exceptionally unreliable."

Harwood breathed out slowly. No answer.

Dr. Kowalczyk wet her lips. "One more question."

A sneer. "Shoot."

"Ms. Moneypenny asked if you'd like to serve. You said yes. Why?"

"I decided I didn't want to mop up the damage the world wreaks. I wanted to prevent it. And I do, every time I accept a job. Good enough?"

Dr. Kowalczyk closed her file. "Do you ever see your mother?"

"You've had your last question."

TEN

Human Nature

King's Cross had changed almost beyond recognition since
Dryden was young. Striding through Granary Square, the fountain rising to greet him and the whole world out to lunch or shopping
for Christmas, Dryden thought its new beautiful skin was rather like
his own: modified, prettified. But inside, was it the same old King's
Cross, the thunderous and stinking crossword puzzle of main roads,
back alleys, and railway tracks suturing Camden and Bloomsbury? He
crossed the old tramlines to the thread of the canal, which remained
an artery to another life, when he spent whole schooldays, dawn until dusk, walking with his crew along the water, from Shoreditch to
Wembley and back again—looking, as his ma said, for trouble.

He was looking for trouble now, knocking on Luke's boots, asking for help. When a judge told Dryden that he had a choice between
army and prison—recognizing, perhaps, that he was a patsy, a teenage
lookout stranded on a park bench, meant to keep his mouth shut for a
five-year stretch and be looked after when he got out; or maybe only
recognizing useful fodder—Dryden chose army and expected exactly
what he'd expected his entire life: absolutely nothing. But instead he
found something in himself that was unbeatable. Confidence in his
own body. And Lucky Luke. Dryden remembered the feeling that

Luke had somehow been waiting for him, holding open a door to Dryden, welcoming him home.

Dryden stopped on the edge of the grass bordering Gasholders. He and Luke belonged to different houses now. The three great cast-iron gas rings shimmered in the winter light, showing off their new skin too, triple-glazed glass and perforated steel screens. The 145 luxury apartments inside the empty stomachs of these Victorian monuments to power were finished only recently. Bertram Paradise had been the first to move in. Dryden mounted the steps to the central atrium, which tunneled through the Venn diagram of the three rings. The humidity of a rainy season enveloped him. Tree ferns stretched their arms in the vast shaft of light.

Dryden slipped his hands into the wool and cashmere pocket of his peacoat and nodded to the concierge. "Sir Bertram is expecting me. Joseph Dryden."

The woman tapped at a computer. "Oh, yes. Straight to the top."

Straight to the top. Not bad, Luke. Dryden entered the glass lift and watched London drop away beneath him. He turned to peer down into the spiral of the building. Nine floors and counting. You could easily kill a man just by shoving him off the walkway. Or kill yourself. He wondered briefly what Bertie Paradise had got himself into. And whether Lucky Luke was in it too.

The doors slid open on the man in question. Dryden stood still, his vision warped for a moment by Luke—the short white Cockney bastard, as he was affectionately known once upon a time, blond hair, blue eyes, impish good looks; he could get away with breaking into some fucker's flat and taking a nap on their sofa during a burglary, his life before the army; get away with rugby-tackling an insurgent in an S-vest and holding on to the man's trigger finger while the rest of the team ran about like headless chickens; get away with . . . anything. He got away with you, didn't he, Joseph Dryden?

"Hey, Joe, whaddya know?"

Dryden cleared his throat. "Thanks for seeing me, man."

"Miss a chance to show off this palace?"

"Straight to the top, huh, Luke?"

"Nowhere to go but down. You gonna get off the lift at some point?"

Dryden snorted. "Always ruining my cool."

"Yeah, you need it, mate, that's the truth. Well, come the fuck in."

Dryden stepped onto a tiled floor. The lift let on to a sweeping foyer, which dropped down into a curving room stretching sixty feet to the floor-to-ceiling windows. The parquet was checkered with rugs in bright geometric shapes, and the furniture was mid-century modern, with a look of little use. The bookshelves were mainly empty. No TV. No sound system. In fact, no technology at all. A series of what Dryden took to be ancient Greek vases were arranged on plinths along the window, bordering a model of a ship on a baize table. Unlike the vases, the model was encased in glass.

"You said on the phone you're looking for work," said Luke. "What happened to your fancy job?"

Dryden shrugged. "Client was arrested. Firm felt I should've done something to keep him out of cuffs."

"Did you try?"

"Man was arrested for sex with a minor. No, I didn't try to save his arse."

Luke bounced on his heels, then nodded. "I think Sir Bertram could use your help."

"I hope so. You know me. Can't be still. You tell him about my hearing?"

"Figured that was yours to tell, or not." Luke looked him up and down. "I don't see a hearing aid."

Luke had been the one to drag Dryden from the mounted vehicle. He'd learned sign language during Dryden's recovery. Dryden said, "My old employers fixed me with this new therapy."

Luke sniffed. "Always the best for Joe. Happy for you."

Dryden pointed at Luke, then signed: "You look happy."

Luke made an inverted OK sign: "Arsehole."

Dryden grinned. He signed: "Let's meet your mad titan."

He waited for a flicker of confirmation, as he had after raising sexual assault. But there was no sign that Luke thought Paradise should be struck from the honors list.

Luke led Dryden into the apartment, switching to speech: "By the way, something I never had occasion to ask you, all our years together."

Dryden steeled himself. "What's that?"

"You scared of tigers?"

Dryden stopped in the middle of the floor. In front of a column of sandstone with a hole-in-the-wall fireplace was a golden cage, and inside the cage was a sleeping Siberian tiger. It opened one blue eye now, and inspected Dryden.

Luke laughed. "All the times I've done that, *of course* you're gonna be the fool that don't blink. One day, Joe Dryden, I'll make you jump outta your skin."

"Don't put ideas in its head," said Dryden. "You know it's illegal to own exotic animals in the UK, right?"

"It's not like that. Sir Bertram rescued it. He's just waiting to house it somewhere. I call it Tony."

"What does Paradise call it?"

A voice from the next room: "Nothing. Humans have no right to name nature."

Dryden turned. Sir Bertram Paradise stood in the doorway to the bedroom, wearing a white shirt, white linen trousers, and uwabaki slip-on shoes. He was a florid man, somewhere between overweight and muscled, with red cheeks that spoke either of too much sun, or of too much drink. He wore a signet ring on his pinkie, and a Rolex Submariner on his wrist.

"You don't believe in taxonomy, Sir Bertram?" said Dryden.

"It was the nineteenth-century obsession with empiricism and cataloguing that gave rise to our belief we could stuff and mount any bird or tortoise unfortunate enough to pass our ship—if we didn't eat it first." Paradise crossed the blood-red carpet. His voice was nasal, Kensington meets the Upper West Side. "The West drew up new maps and dug for treasure. We thought we could collect the world. A map is a set of human intentions. Now we map the stars, as if we can simply fly away from this exhausted planet. We must do away with taxonomy. We do not have the naming of nature. It has the naming of us. Soon it will attach a pretty label: *extinct*."

"I'm surprised, sir," said Dryden. "Cloud Nine can save us. But you don't seem to think much of science."

Paradise almost pouted. "Yes, I can save the world. But it won't be a stroke of science. The science to halt the climate crisis has been in place for decades. Those with power have denied it. Do they want to listen to my warnings that if they keep drilling here, or deforesting there, they'll tip the global balance? That it's already tipped? If I save the world, it will be because governments listened to their savior. How very rare that is. They'll probably assassinate me first."

Dryden looked in Paradise's watery blue eyes for a spark of genius, or a spark of madness. He wasn't quite sure which he was seeing. But he did see silver moons under the man's eyes, and that his lip was chewed.

"Not on my watch," he said.

Paradise raised an eyebrow. "Gung-ho, I like that. My lucky charm here tells me you were a senior man at Steel North Security."

"Yes, sir."

"And you were awarded a George Cross and Conspicuous Gallantry Cross during your time in Special Forces?"

"Yes, sir."

"What did you do, squat on a live grenade?"

Dryden glanced at Luke, wondering whether that kind of talk ruffled his feathers. It didn't seem to. "I killed a lot of people," said Dryden. "And then jumped on a live grenade."

Paradise laughed. "You'll forgive any cynicism you detect, Joe—may I call you Joe? I learned to abhor war, seeing the legacy of imperial conflicts as a boy raised in my father's shadow. But I have never abhorred soldiers. I appreciate your valor." He swept one hand over the other. "I could use some of it now. Luke tells me you're the best he's ever seen in action. You boxed together?"

"Among other things," said Luke, with a shit-eater grin.

Paradise looked at Dryden as if together they were disapproving parents. "What a rascal. Has Luke shared any of my concerns?"

"Just that you need another man on your security team."

"That's right. I'm promoting Luke to head it up, but he'll need someone reliable underneath him."

Dryden avoided Luke's gleam. "Anything worrying you in particular, Sir Bertram?"

Paradise gazed at the white tiger. "I suppose the end of the world is worrying enough."

Dryden narrowed his eyes. He decided to take a chance. "You don't believe in naming nature, but you're happy to keep a live animal in a gilded cage?"

Drifting silence.

Then: "We're all in cages, Mr. Dryden. If I open the door here, that tiger would kill you. If I open it in an animal sanctuary, as I intend, the tiger will kill no one." He faced Dryden. "Which would you prefer?"

"You open it here it'll kill you too."

Luke eased from foot to foot.

Paradise laughed. "Yes. That's the trouble with only having the power of God, not being God himself. God gets to watch. I'm down here in the muck with the rest of you." He heaved a sigh. "Still. It has its pleasures, and I'd like to keep enjoying them. Come and see the fleet you're joining."

Paradise slipped a hand onto Dryden's elbow and urged him to the model of a superyacht—Dryden understood from Moneypenny's briefing—that looked like it was alive with spines.

"*Cloud Nine by Paradise*, my marketing team have called it. Sounds like a perfume, but what do I know?" A humble chuckle. "I have spent the last year establishing ground sensors in remote wildernesses around the globe. Soon I will launch my low-orbital satellite array. My sensors and satellites communicate with each other to map the climate crisis minutely. All of the information is fed into Celestial—more loathsome branding, I'm afraid—the best quantum computer known to man, which itself controls both the sensors and satellites. A closed circuit. I use the information that circuit yields to predict the future, if you will, and so direct *Ark*." He gestured to the yacht. "I came up with that name."

Dryden decided to poke again. "I read somewhere that super-yachts produce over seven thousand tonnes of carbon dioxide a year, fifteen hundred times more than a family car."

"My hybrid diesel-electric propulsion system makes this the cleanest superyacht on the ocean. It is a little flashy perhaps, but sometimes one needs a little flash to get the world's attention. Future yachts will be smaller, autonomous vessels, with no pilot required."

"Where's Celestial? On the yacht?" asked Dryden, knowing perfectly well a quantum computer couldn't exist on a yacht, but also knowing the location of Celestial was undisclosed.

Paradise only smiled benignly, returning his hand to Dryden's arm to urge him to study the spines on the yacht. "These release my cloud-seeding particles, spraying an ultrafine mist of sea salt bonded with silver iodide particles, through which I can encourage cloud formation, defending against the sun, and cooling the sea ice. I can stop the ice melting. Spraying around ten cubic meters per second would undo all of the damage wrought by the climate crisis. Through cloud seeding, I can tame extreme weather events. I can change the formation of the marine layer. Put it this way, Joe. I can move clouds. I can make it rain. I can control cyclones." His milky eyes—so much like the tiger's—settled on Dryden. His voice was ethereal as he said, "I've hijacked the heavens."

Dryden worked his tongue against the inside of his upper lip. "That's a lot of power for one man. A burden, some might say."

Paradise's jaw tightened. "The strongest poison ever known came from Caesar's laurel crown."

Dryden said softly, "Who placed it on his head?"

The ghostly look on Paradise's face vanished in a vivid grin. "No man appoints Caesar. He crowns himself. And no man can dethrone him." He clapped. The tiger sat up with a growl that curled in Dryden's stomach. "We're about to embark on a press tour of my good works, culminating in the launch of the satellite array and then front-row seats at the championship fight in Macau. It *must* go well—goodwill is the most important currency in geo-engineering. Would you like to help save the world, Joe?"

Dryden took the smooth palm being offered to him. "I'd be honored, sir."

"Good man," said Paradise, repeating in a coo, "good man."

Dryden glanced at Luke. He saw him release a long, quiet breath.

ELEVEN

The Sky Is Falling

O04 had never understood the point of gambling: either so little money was hazarded, it was no more than children playing at war; or so much was hazarded, it was a fool's game. But tonight, watching Sir Bertie and his pals fritter away their wealth, Joseph Dryden tasted real danger at the back of his throat, and liked it. He looked around the French roulette floor of the Casino de Monte-Carlo, the second stop on the tour, for the source. Yesterday, Paradise's hydrogen-powered vehicle had placed third in the Rallye Monte-Carlo. Tonight, the taste of danger didn't come from the six bodyguards under him and Luke keeping to the background. They were men like 004, or at least like his legend: men who'd fought national wars and private wars and washed up here to fight corporate wars because they hadn't died and couldn't quit. The leader of the pack was a merc called Poulain. But Poulain didn't bother Dryden.

Nor did Sir Bertie's friends and entourage.

The friends: shipping magnates, Internet giants, tech developers in lifelong batteries and self-drive AI automation, all with glowing zero carbon promises. They were among the world's wealthiest ten percent, whose lifestyles produced half of global carbon emissions. Dryden's implant fed their conversation to Q, and their bios and known associates burred inside his skull in Aisha's voice, which she kept hushed not for fear of others hearing, but because she didn't want to shout at Dryden: who here had recently received 1.3 billion in funds from Saudi Arabia to build their first large-scale auto engineering plant; who got their start aged twenty-seven sending ships into the Iran–Iraq wars to pick up oil; who was currently negotiating a non-prosecution deal for tax evasion with the US Department of Justice. In other words, they were whatever the collective noun was for a bunch of rich arseholes.

Sir Bertie's steadier entourage were a more curious collection. PR types and any number of loosely termed advisers. Yuri, whose principal job seemed to be to lose to Bertie at cards. Ahmed, a fatherly provider who took care of the diary, eager to arrange luxuries on which he'd grown fat, lavish entertainer yet vacant behind the eyes, as if permanently claiming deniability. St. John—pronounced in a slur as *Sinjin*—a cryptocurrency enthusiast and wealth manager always patting his pockets for his phone, but there were no phones allowed around Bertie.

But it was Lucky Luke at the center, Lucky Luke who managed the swinging doors, limited and gifted access, read his master's moods as a son reads an alcoholic, and managed them that way too, tempering, cajoling, amusing. For the closer Joseph Dryden got to Sir Bertram, the more he felt that sort of vulnerability shaking beneath the surface, though so far the man seemed only vaguely interested in the pleasures Yuri and Ahmed and St. John produced. Yes, it was Paradise himself who gave Dryden the taste of danger. But did he pose it, or was he a victim of it? What had happened to Dr. Zofia Nowak, his science officer, and to Robert Bull, the man tasked with maintaining security—whose shoes Luke now filled?

Dryden leaned on the brass rail surrounding the table. The Salle Blanche gleamed. The chandeliers dripping from the gilt ceiling vaults scattered gold over the yellow fleur-de-lis floor. Landscape paintings that some prince probably lost on a roulette turn punctuated the discreet faces of clocks. Dryden had never seen clocks in a casino before. He imagined the admission of time had something to do with Le Train Bleu, a restaurant modeled on a dining car marooned outside the Salle Europe. Before the hive of hotels, back in the first days of the casino, gamblers would anxiously check the time, ready to run to the station for the last train. Now the last train had been recast as a restaurant and would never leave. Arranged above the clocks Dryden counted eight windows from which God's eyes once watched proceedings, replaced by CCTV cameras. Those were the cameras you were supposed to see. Dryden counted a dozen more hidden in the ceiling.

Dryden turned his attention to Sir Bertram himself, who sat at the head of the table, with Lucky Luke at his shoulder. Yes, his wealth was a moral obscenity and his eccentricities a nightmare from a security perspective—an insomniac who insisted on breakfast at dinner and dinner at breakfast, a gambler so confident with chance he would bet on minutiae, winning a thunderous side bet at the Rallye Monte-Carlo yesterday by guessing how many inches of snow would fall over the Alps. But there was something in the set of his shoulders, as he watched the spin now, and the grim line of his mouth, that suggested he knew all of these affectations were expected of him, were mere drama, and his mind was fixed beyond where the ball fell now, beyond the casino, the Riviera, the race, to a grander goal. Dryden wondered if it was Paradise's focus that sent the thrill of danger up his spine, or Paradise's exposure. The snow couldn't fall to his wishes every day.

Luke whispered something in Paradise's ear. Paradise clapped him on the wrist, where Luke wore a Richard Mille RM 11-05 watch, the blues and oranges popping against his navy jacket, the cogs turning beneath a new material that combined the lightness of titanium with the hardness of diamond. Luke said it was a birthday present from Paradise. For the same price, Paradise could have bought the winning car straight from the rally. Lucky Luke.

The wheel ticked to zero. Paradise had bet on *chances simples*, and now faced losing whatever sum the tower of chips represented. The safe option would be to divide his bet. The danger play was to wait for the next spin, when his bet would be freed if it won. Dryden was certain Paradise knew exactly what the odds were on that.

Paradise circled his finger in the air: spin again.

The croupier bowed his head. The wheel sounded to Dryden like the *clack-clack-clack* of a carabiner the moment you jumped over a cliff edge.

The CEO to Paradise's left—a flabby man in shipping Dryden recognized from the cover of *Time* magazine—snorted: "I could bet you the sky's going to fall down and you'd take it."

Paradise murmured, "The sky is falling down."

"Don't give me one of your hug-a-tree lectures." A guffaw. "*The sky is falling.*"

Paradise's circling finger pointed straight up to the painted heavens. "It's raining."

"Raining? Pull the other one, Bertie, it makes a funny sound. No windows. No phone in your pocket, never is. And we've been sitting here so long my balls are itching like the devil."

Paradise nodded to the slowing wheel. He'd lost. "Double or nothing?"

"Double or nothing that it's raining?"

Paradise shrugged. Behind him, Luke appeared caught between pride and fear.

The flabby CEO laughed. "I'll take that bet."

The croupier raised an eyebrow, and then bowed deeper to Paradise.

"Mr. Luck," said Paradise, "go check the weather, would you?"

Dryden watched Luke walk away, seeing how two or three women turned to take a look too. Well, he was worth watching.

Yuri said, "You are too, too absurd, Sir Bertie."

"You keep looking at your watch," said St. John. "Don't tell me you checked the weather twenty-four hours ago, or whenever it was we stumbled in here. That would be just like you."

The CEO grunted. "I bet you used to look up football scores as a boy and rehearse conversation pieces."

With friends like these . . .

Paradise stacked his chips. "Ours is essentially a tragic age, so we refuse to take it tragically," he said. He was no longer smiling tolerantly. His voice took on a new confidence, an orator at his pulpit. Spines stiffened. Faces fell. "The cataclysm has happened, we are among the ruins, we start to build up new little habitats, to have new little hopes. It is rather hard work: there is now no smooth road into the future: but we go round, or scramble over the obstacles. We've got to live, no matter how many skies have fallen . . ."

It was then Luke appeared at the brass rail at Dryden's shoulder. Dryden felt electricity crackle across the base of his spine as he almost reached for his weapon, and stopped himself. Lucky Luke had always been able to sneak up on him. He smelled of damp earth. His shoulders were wet.

Luke ran a hand through his wet hair. "I can report it's inclement as fuck, sir."

Bursts of laughter like live fire. The CEO sheepishly stacked his chips and nudged them into Paradise's orbit. He moaned: "But how could you have known?"

"Luck," said Paradise.

TWELVE

The Last Train

Le Train Bleu was fitted out like a train carriage from the Belle Époque. Teardrop lamps coated the wood paneling and deep-red leather in a simulacrum of dawn. Following Lucky Luke to a table in the corner, Dryden watched Paradise sway a little as he walked down the narrow passage of the restaurant, as if he were really leaving a station. Yuri kept him upright with a quick hand at his arm, and a tight grip. Ahmed and St. John were already ordering, shouting at a waiter who was attending to another party. Paradise told them to behave. The reporters who had followed Sir Bertram at the rally had retreated now, set to rejoin the party en route to Central Asia, where Sir Bertram would perform miracles in the desert.

Luke picked up the menu. "I've got in the habit of dinner for breakfast. But the chef will make you anything you want."

After the waiter got through laughing at Ahmed's jokes about leaves on the line delaying service, Luke ordered the steak and an old-fashioned.

The waiter bowed. "And for sir?"

Dryden said, "Coffee, black."

"Very good, sir."

Luke spread his legs and drummed on his stomach. "You gotta learn to live a little."

"You'll have to teach me."

"Again," said Luke, smile fixed. "I already taught you once, remember?"

Dryden wanted to hunch over but instead relaxed in his chair. "We had our fun. Not on this scale, though. What did Robert Bull get fired for? Didn't know his D. H. Lawrence from his Thomas Hardy?"

"What you going on about now?"

Dryden nodded to Paradise. "That monologue. It was from *Lady Chatterley's Lover.*"

Luke shrugged sullenly. "Never had much patience for reading. Who said Bull was fired?"

"Who would quit Paradise?"

"Bull left a mess I have to clean up, that's all."

Dryden raised an eyebrow by a fraction. "What kind of mess?"

"Sexual harassment in the workplace kind of mess. It's all cool. I'm sorting it."

Dryden stroked his coffee cup. "Who was Bull harassing?"

"Dr. Zofia Nowak. She's on compassionate leave now. I've got it covered."

"I'm sure you do." Another look at Paradise, who was sipping miso soup. Yuri wolfed down a veal. A man is judged by the company he keeps, Dryden's father said. But then, as Dryden had read in a gushing profile of Paradise, *there are always unexplained corners in the life and history of a billionaire.* Dryden said to Luke now, "You've kept Bull's harassment of Dr. Nowak out of the papers. Where is Bull now? You sure he won't mouth off?"

"I can handle my responsibilities just fine. I'm not your 2ic anymore."

"No," said Dryden, linking his hands on the linen. "You're his."

Luke sniffed. "I'm not his morning delight, if that's what you're thinking."

Dryden said nothing.

"And he's not the father I've always been searching for, or some bullshit like that."

Dryden tapped Luke's watch. "He's not?"

Luke adjusted the strap, finger brushing Dryden's. His voice dropped. "He never had any kids. That's all. Likes to spoil me. Says I'm worth it."

"I don't need Sir Bertram to tell me that. You shouldn't either."

Luke twitched in his tux. "Easy for you to say, mate. Believe me, you don't feel like God's gift when you're sleeping on the street with a sign written on some soggy cardboard, telling strangers you're an army vet with no home and no hope. You don't feel like nothing special when you see the people walking by don't *believe* you were a soldier, don't *believe* you miss the patrol base in Helmand because at least there you didn't sleep for a good reason, don't *believe* . . ."

The waiter set the plate before Luke, who looked at it, sighed noisily, and pierced the steak with his fork. "Sir Bertram noticed me. Saved me."

"I didn't know you were on the streets," said Dryden.

"You gotta be around to know something."

Dryden was quiet as Luke ate. He raised a hand. When the waiter appeared, he ordered a whisky—Octomore Orpheus, neat. Dryden watched his retreat, then asked Luke, "Paradise always have such luck at the tables?"

"Has since he met me," said Luke. "Says I'm golden. Shame I never brought that luck to myself, huh?"

"You brought it to the unit. To me."

Luke shrugged. "Now I'm Sir Bertram's good luck charm."

"Then he can't lose. Plain sailing from here on out."

"What you getting at, man?"

Dryden sat back as the waiter lifted the glass from the silver tray, and the smell of hiking peaty mountains with Luke at his six as day turned to night and licked the rocks dry came to him. "You don't look like life's coming up cherries."

Luke hesitated. "Maybe there is a storm ahead. I've been weathering 'em on my own lately."

"I'm here now."

Luke didn't meet his eyes.

"What'll happen to Cloud Nine without Dr. Nowak?"

"She's just on leave."

"She's coming back soon, then? From . . ." Dryden left the sentence dangling, but Luke did not provide a location. Dryden stretched his legs beneath the table, brushing Luke's calf. He lightened his voice, saying, "You're lucky that CEO's off his head. It's not raining."

"How'd you figure that?"

"You went out front and stood in the fountain for two minutes."

A beat, then Luke's raspy laughter made the other diners turn and look, including Paradise, who gave Dryden a benefactor's smile.

"Man, I missed you," said Luke.

Dryden loosened his purple tie. "What happens now?"

"What are you fishing for?"

Dryden cupped his chin in his hand. "You," he said.

Luke laid his knife and fork to rest. "And what would you do with me, if you caught me?"

"Make up"—Dryden knocked back his drink—"for lost time. Last train out, Luke. What do you say?"

"I say you're mixing your metaphors."

"Fuck metaphors."

"That's what you wanna fuck?"

Before Dryden could answer, Sir Bertram rose noisily, activating the hangers-on and security like a director calling for a scene change. Dryden lingered, rolling his sleeves down, shaking the waiter's hand

and leaving a tip, so he brought up the rear as they left the restaurant—too far back for anyone to bother about the new guy. Focusing on Sir Bertram and Luke as they walked out onto the Place du Casino, Dryden slid through the still-surreal moment of entering a conversation out of ordinary earshot. He remembered how Luke used to boast, "No shot my man can't make."

But the memory was cast aside as he heard Luke whisper in Paradise's ear, with a furtive glance to the palm trees crisp against a fresh sky: "That was a risky bet, sir."

Sir Bertram patted him on the back. "Can't lose with you around, my boy."

Luke cleared his throat. "I thought we weren't going to do that kind of thing anymore. Not while we've got a vulnerable point."

Sir Bertram hesitated in his step. "I'm not worried. You shouldn't be either. You're going to protect Cloud Nine, aren't you? Protect me?"

Luke drew himself up. "I wouldn't let you down, sir."

Dryden didn't like the way Paradise took the time to smile into Luke's eyes, and he didn't like the relief on Luke's face. Didn't like it because he'd shared that fixity countless times with Luke, pulling each other out of the fire. It was the pride Luke took in being Dryden's oppo. They'd been bound together, once, in common cause. Now Dryden was bound to Q, to Moneypenny, to MI6. And Lucky Luke was bound to a man who seemed to know just what tune to play to make him dance. Whether Paradise's intent was malevolent or not, Dryden didn't know—but, breathing in the sea air, he admitted to himself that it stirred envy in his gut.

THIRTEEN

Contest of Kings

The Soviet chess grandmaster Mikhail Botvinnik was once asked if he ever played blitz chess, the sped-up version of the game, in which each player has an average of ten seconds to make their move. Blitz chess is considered the fast food of the chess world by champions of the classic game. Botvinnik answered: "Yes, I have played a blitz game once. It was on a train, in 1929."

009 liked to imagine that game: who persuaded Botvinnik to play, where was he going, did he win? He might have been on his way to play for the Leningrad student chess team against Moscow, a game he won in 1929, bringing himself to the attention of the deputy chairman of the Proletstud, who arranged for Botvinnik to transfer to the Polytechnic Electromechanical Department, beginning his leading career in computer sciences. Botvinnik was the first son of Soviet chess. He was closely watched by Stalin. When ministers suggested Botvinnik's Russian opponents throw games so that he could be sure of keeping his world title, Botvinnik said he would rather knock over his own king.

Sid Bashir identified with Botvinnik—not because he matched his skill, though he was pleased to achieve 241 for standard play, and 229 for rapid, in the latest English Chess Federation ratings—but because Botvinnik also played to satisfy greater masters, for whom the game of chess belonged to the Great Game. Bashir was glad to have nights like this, at the Battersea Chess Club.

The Contest of Kings—a rapid tournament—was taken seriously by the mostly gray-haired men who bent over the tables, cradling their heads in their hands as they peered down at the boards, but it wasn't a matter of life and death. It was a welcome distraction, a chance to care about something that belonged to Sid Bashir, junior civil servant on the fast track, who was now in the semifinal, and the favorite to be crowned king before Christmas.

Not the Sid Bashir who proposed to Johanna again because he was under orders to reignite their relationship, grow closer to her—and spy on her movements.

Still, when Bashir glanced over his opponent's shoulder and saw M in the corner of the hall reading the messy noticeboard, he felt his heart pick up. He moved his queen without looking back.

"Checkmate."

His opponent, Simon, groaned. "Good game, Sid."

"You too."

"No need to rub it in," said Simon. He looked around. "Who's that? This is sport, not a social."

"My future father-in-law," said Bashir. He shook Simon's hand. "Thanks for the game, mate." He stood up. "And—it isn't a sport."

Simon huffed. "Chess might be included in the Olympics, actually."

Bashir grinned. "All right, Simon. But I enjoy it as it is."

"Of course you do. You keep winning."

Bashir bounded over to M. "Evening, sir. I didn't think you'd come."

"Missed most of it, I see," said M. He nodded at the board. "Says here you're top of the London league, Sid."

"For now. Stand you to a pint, sir?"

"Don't be ridiculous."

Bashir laughed, and led M upstairs to the bar, an overlit room in pretend blond woods. Hits from the early two thousands hissed through cheap speakers. He felt a moment's insecurity and then shrugged it off. He couldn't think of anything worse than an evening at the Hurlingham with the owners of football clubs and oil fields. M ordered a double whisky, and a Guinness for Bashir. They settled in a corner, both with their backs to the wall, surveying the room. The tables were painted with chessboards, and Bashir fiddled with the Tupperware box of scuffed pieces left out for anyone interested.

"Set it up, then," said M.

"You play, sir?"

"You may have to remind me of a few points."

Bashir closed his fists around a black and a white pawn, swapped them a few times behind his back, and then offered his hands.

"White," said M, and then tapped his left hand.

It was the white. "How did you know?" asked Bashir.

"You tell me."

Bashir shook his head. "You go first then, sir. Good luck."

"Are you being impertinent, young man?"

"No more than usual. Etiquette is taken very seriously. Ivan Cheparinov refused to shake Nigel Short's hand once and the game was forfeited."

"Quite right," said M. "Good luck, then."

Bashir grinned, and said solemnly, "Thank you, sir." He finished setting the board, and hunched over the game. After the opening moves he said, "I spoke to Johanna this morning. She's feeling a lot better. Passed all the tests, too. She got one hundred percent in her marksmanship."

"Bravo," said M. It was strange seeing him out in the world. Bashir noticed a new frailty, which seemed foreign to M, something he'd decided not to entertain. He crossed one leg over the other, pressing forward on his elbows, reminding Bashir of a wire coat hanger twisted out of shape. Then he moved his pawn, taking Bashir's knight off the board.

Bashir sat back. "Are you hustling me, sir?"

M grunted.

Bashir tapped his chin. "If Johanna's passed all the tests, maybe it isn't necessary for me to watch her, sir."

M looked up. His eyes were searchlights. "Pray to God it isn't necessary, son."

Bashir's hand hovered over the board. Then he retreated. "She wouldn't betray us, sir. Not Johanna."

"We have a leak, and we're bleeding, Sid. Rattenfänger knew where to find Donovan. They lured Bond out."

Bond had disappeared in high summer seventeen months ago. Mikhail Petrov was delivering a paper on shrinking sea ice to an academic conference at the Fira de Barcelona, built for the 1929 International Exposition on a wooded hill in the southwest of the city, from which the guns of Castell de Montjuïc guarded the sea. Bond would make contact on the last day of the conference.

Station S had set them up in a sad apartment squeezed between two-star hotels on the outer circumference of Montjuïc. On previous surveillance missions, Bond and Bashir had passed the time playing chess or cards, making use of the one bottle of Haig Dimple that always seemed to be stashed in an otherwise empty safe house. They'd talk of Bond's past missions or Bashir's training. When Harwood and Bond first crossed the professional line, Harwood was only another new Double O to Bashir. It didn't mean much to him. As the relationship faltered and Bashir got to know Harwood, then tangled up his lines with her too, Bond and Bashir didn't address their shared feelings. Perhaps like Petrov—Bashir had wondered during the briefing with M and Moneypenny—Bond was also something of a poet, and believed that love of the same woman connected the two men. Perhaps he didn't care. At last, Harwood broke it off fully with Bond, and

Bashir proposed. The Barcelona safe house was silent. No games. No reminiscence. Bond tersely told Bashir to brush up on his tailing, so Bashir followed Bond, who followed the Petrovs.

A long weekend spent looking for signs of betrayal, any hint that Mikhail's defection was a trap. Montjuïc hill was a pleasure ground of the past, and Bashir trailed Bond on Mikhail's shadow between conference halls. Anna kept to Montjuïc but did not attend the conference. Bashir kept his distance as Bond did the same, tracking her while she took in the local sights without really looking at any of them. Poble Espanyol, a mock village of different regional architectural styles; the Olympic Ring; the Mies van der Rohe pavilion, where Anna's lone shadow slanted across the four linear slabs of marble, and Bond's shadow hovered ever closer.

If they'd been speaking, Bashir would have asked Bond if that was longing or pity in his eyes, as he read whatever dreams or nightmares he chose in Anna's pale, pensive face. And if it was more, why did Bond give a damn who Harwood chose?

At the Teatre Grec, Anna watched the performance blankly with an empty seat beside her, Mikhail failing his promises, and she left before the end to drift around the Magic Fountain, whose water played to the melancholic second movement of Beethoven's *Emperor Concerto*—Bond told Bashir the name over a game of two-handed canasta later that evening, the silence finally broken. Bond had moved to stand behind Anna as the lights of the Magic Fountain changed from blue to red. She rested her head, minutely, against his shoulder. Bond whispered something by her ear.

Later that night, with Bond and Bashir retreated to the safe house and the infrared showing the Petrovs asleep, Bashir fell into nearly every trap Bond laid at canasta, handing over the deck. They talked about chance and responsibility. Bond said he liked gambling because luck was a servant and not a master—there was only oneself to praise or blame. In the field, one was so often set into motion by a train of coincidence, a tiny acorn of chance that grew into an oak so tall its branches darkened the sky, and a Double O must cut down its growth. When Bashir asked what the seed of chance was here, Bond only shrugged and said it didn't matter—"I have only myself to blame."

Bashir took the risk: "Do you blame yourself, that Johanna picked me?"

Bond's smile was somewhere between grim and ironic. "Don't you know better than that, Sid? A man makes his own luck. A woman makes her own choices."

Bond's phone murmured, a soft flash lighting the darkened room. Bond checked it, seemed to hesitate, and then stood up. He said he had a lead to follow and Bashir should stay on the infrared.

"You don't need any help?" asked Bashir.

Bond tightened his tie. There was a gleam in his eyes. "I think I can handle it. Just remember what I said."

When Bond didn't make the next radio check, Bashir held tight, studying the Petrovs' room—no movement. When he failed the one after that, Bashir called it in to Moneypenny. She told him to rein Bond back in, as if that were possible. Q guided Bashir in Bond's footsteps across the empty Teatre Grec as spectacular heat spilled over the city, the dawn a pot of yellow paint kicked over. At the hotel, the Petrovs were picking at a limp continental breakfast without meeting one another's gaze. Bashir pulled on the maroon jacket of a waiter and took their coffee order, angling the pad so Anna could read the location of the meet in ninety minutes. She did so coolly, reminding him she wanted oat milk—she'd not got it at yesterday's breakfast. An old hand at pretense. Bashir exited to follow Bond's ghostly beacon down the funicular railway, his scalp pricking.

Moneypenny asked him, her voice in his earpiece: "Did 007 say anything to you? Anything out of the ordinary?"

"He told me to remember what he'd said."

"And?"

The funicular stuttered to a stop. Which part of what Bond had said was Bashir to remember? His heart began to race. He felt, ludicrously, like a child lost at the supermarket. Q pulled him through tourists emerging from the Metro, sweaty and confused; the dance of street sweepers and pigeons; the ice-cream swirl of rooftops; to Parc Güell, where Bashir ran the curve of the hill, palm trees shaking angrily above him, Gaudí's pillars twisting like dancers all turning their faces from him. He tripped on a loose stone, almost twisting his ankle, feeling even more ridiculous.

Then he found it. A bench overlooking the city. A cigarette stubbed into the sand. Next to it, a spot of red, as innocent as a spot of rain. That was it. Q had lost James Bond. Security cameras and phones and social media—they'd all lost him. Moneypenny told Bashir not to worry, Bond had probably slipped the leash for a play at freedom somewhere. He did that sometimes. A last hurrah. Bashir briefly wondered who that last hurrah was with, and then moved to the rendezvous, a station café. Anna sat at the high bar, her feet dangling over a gutter filled with tickets and other detritus. Mikhail was pacing the tiles.

"Where is James?" asked Anna.

Bashir urged them together, creating a tight triangle by the counter. "007 sent me."

Mikhail shook his head vigorously. "*Nyet*. I told him. James or no one."

"007 will see you in London."

Mikhail grabbed Anna by the arm. "We are leaving."

"You can't, we've already made contact, it's not safe—"

It was no use. Mikhail hurried Anna out onto the concourse. She tossed a look of apology back to Bashir.

Mission failure. A routine op busted. Bashir returned home with no Petrovs and no James Bond. Moneypenny said he'd turn up. Q Branch swore it. They were all wrong.

Q concluded it must have been Rattenfänger. They'd been responsible for the death or disability of all of Bond's contemporaries in the field, and finally they'd collected Bond. But, capturing a white pawn and tossing it in the Tupperware, Bashir still whispered to M now, "We don't know that was Rattenfänger."

"I do not think the leak is 003," said M, cracking his knuckles with a heavy sigh. "I do not want it to be her. But I can't afford not to ask the question. You understand that. All I am asking is that you keep your eyes open for any incongruities."

Bashir shook the Tupperware. The casualties rattled gently. "Yes, sir. Do you really think—you think her relationship with me, and with Bond, was to gain leverage over us?"

M spoke softly. "Rattenfänger are a terrorist group for profit, led by the lately departed Mora, now presumably by his second-in-command. It only makes sense for Rattenfänger to embed an agent in MI6 as an early warning system. If I were sending an agent to infiltrate Rattenfänger, I would order her to compromise as many of their team as she could, by any means at her disposal. The three of you lost parents: you, Harwood, and Bond. You share a sensibility, perhaps, a natural affinity. She *resonates* with you both, to the exact pitch you require, though you and Bond are very different instruments, if you'll forgive my putting it that way. He a blunt instrument, some would say, you a fine one. One hates to overextend metaphor, but one mustn't discard the possibility that Harwood is a scalpel. With you, she is the scientist, a meeting of rational minds. With Bond, she is the hedonist who has seen the world and wants more of what only he can offer. I have every faith in Ms. Moneypenny and the whole Double O operation to root out false cover stories. But Johanna Harwood—she might well prove too good to be true. A good thing usually is."

"You don't think she's in love?"

"With you?" said M. He looked impatient. "Or him?"

Bashir pulled ruefully at the lock of hair curling over his forehead. "I don't know."

"You've done well, Sid. You've reestablished your connection, just as we discussed. 003 was wearing your engagement ring around her neck, I saw. Stay close to her, and tell me if you suspect anything, that's all. I realize it's indelicate. But this is an indelicate game." He countered, and took another of Bashir's pawns.

"I know. Sir."

M sat back. "I know you do. You can see the next twenty moves. You already know how you're going to beat me. You are the best strategist I've got, Sid. So tell me. Can you swear to me that Harwood's all she seems, and no more, with the possibility of a leak in British Intelligence giving information to Rattenfänger, and whosoever might be behind Rattenfänger?" He gently probed the pawns in the Tupperware. "At least Ms. Moneypenny was able to recover 002's body from Dubai, and 0010's from Basra; 005 is in a mountain pass somewhere. The former 009 took eleven hours to bleed to death, alone. 0011 has been missing for over two years. One prays he's dead. Then Donovan, discovered with enough insect life in him to inspire several significant studies on degradation in desert ecologies. I hope you don't think me cold. It's my job to count the bodies. It is also my job to make that count stop."

"You didn't count Bond."

M pushed the box away with his index finger. "An old man's hope." There was a catch in his throat, which he cleared, a sudden crack. "Tell me then, Sid, with a count like that, can we take the risk that Harwood was simply a victim of bad luck when she was captured? And even if she was, can we take the risk that she didn't turn in captivity?"

Bashir's throat was suddenly dry. He was pinned by M's eyes. "I want to say yes."

"What we want rarely comes into this game. Believe me. I'd planned to retire and see Bond replace me. Now here I am, waiting like an old fool for my prodigal son to return so I can pass on some ridiculous baton, while mandarins dig me a grave and ministers snip at my heels and obit writers count my ex-wives."

"Sir—why not tell Moneypenny what I'm doing? She must share your concerns."

"I trust Ms. Moneypenny with my home address. But in this game, son, it's the person you trust most who has the most power to hurt you. I have to suspect her as much as anyone else. Now"—M fixed him with a look—"you can do what's needed?"

Bashir nodded.

M smiled. "And that's why I'm trusting you."

"She won't forgive me," said Bashir, quietly.

M crossed his arms. "Are you going to win this Contest of Kings?"

"I think so."

M raised an eyebrow.

"Yes, sir. I am."

M nodded. "If she's true to us, she won't ever know. You love her, don't you, Sid? Want to marry her?"

"We only broke it off because—because I let my partner follow a lead with no backup, and I couldn't handle that I'd lost him. But a man makes his own luck."

"Then I'm not asking you to do anything you wouldn't have done otherwise. You'll only report to me, if you observe any—infidelity, shall we say. But I'm sure it won't come to that, hmm? First Double O marriage." M bent over the board. "Just stay the course, my boy. Keep this between us. I need your focus. Your mind. And then—I'll walk her down the aisle myself. Now, tell me how many moves I have before there's no chance of victory."

Bashir shrugged. He said, "You've already lost."

FOURTEEN

Barbican (I)

Bashir arrived with the moon and mist, knowing the latter would swallow the view from the twenty-eighth floor of Cromwell Tower on the Barbican Estate, the best in London. The porter knew Bashir on sight, and waved him through the redbrick and glazed terra-cotta foyer to the panel of buzzers, stacked in the arrangement of the tower itself. The slip of card over Flat 285 read C. J. H. in boxy letters, hovering ten floors from the top. Johanna had never replaced her father's handwriting, her father's name, with her own. Even he had wanted to conceal himself, Charlie John Harwood truncated to three letters. Johanna would say a spy could never wear too many masks. Bashir believed she was unwilling to exorcise her father's ghost. Johanna's voice came over the speaker: "Hurry, would you? My sparkling beauty is wasted without an audience." He laughed. The architects had designed the Barbican Estate for "young professionals, likely to have a taste for Mediterranean holidays, French food, and Scandinavian design." And a license to kill. Johanna Harwood ticked all of these boxes.

It was a long ride in the lift. Bashir wondered if they would greet each other as lovers or friends now she had returned from Shrublands. Their night in Istanbul existed in the shadow of her captivity, the limbo in which an agent is alive and dead at once. The limbo James Bond flickered in now. She was out of that shadow and perhaps out of the secret inner life of Bashir's heart, too. He hoped otherwise, aware of the quickening in his body, how much he wanted her and loved her even when she was nowhere around. A desire blind to the possibility she was a double agent. A love blind to caring.

The doors opened into a triangular hall, from which three flats spun off, each on its own axis. Harwood was standing in her doorway wearing her satin dressing gown, and questions of betrayal dropped out of Bashir's mind, as did tomorrow's mission to make contact with his childhood friend Ruqsana Choudhury in order to locate Dr. Nowak, Sir Bertram's missing science officer; and the cold fact that Bashir would be lying to two of the most important people in his life, though one might already be lying to him. Johanna raised a faintly ironic eyebrow, as if she had followed his thoughts. Bashir grinned and brushed his hair from his face. She moved, one hand on her hip, leaving space for him to enter the flat. Lovers it was. His heart rose as if he was still climbing the height of the building and the lift had given that sudden lurch. He never wanted to meet the day again when Johanna Harwood didn't greet him as her lover. Bashir pulled her warmth to him, kissed her as they stepped inside, softly tangling his hand in her hair. He kicked the door shut with the heel of his boot.

The flat was a long line, and down the corridor he could see a bottle of champagne waiting to be opened by the sofa, and the doors leading to the balcony, which wrapped around the flat like an oyster clasping a pearl. A pair of glasses waited on the concrete table in a dust of snow. Beyond, the splintered crown of the Shard disappeared into pale cloud. He stopped paying attention to the view as Johanna freed him from his damp coat.

They never made it to the champagne. Bashir and Harwood stripped on opposite sides of the bed, Harwood winning the race and laughing, their bodies replicated in the windows, rippling with the lights of St. Paul's slicking the haze. They threw the bed linen to the floor as a silvery lace descended over Shakespeare Tower opposite, dousing the lights, until all that was left was the drift of final birdsong and first sirens and soft words. Outside was inside and inside was out. They were floating in the sky. Floating in each other.

Bashir woke alone. He listened to shortwave radio in search of sleep, something Johanna indulged with only the comment that late-night trucker rock and roll was the best. It was cycling through what sounded like whale song now. Johanna's side of the bed was still warm.

"Johanna?"

Nothing. He sat up, taking in her messy console table—a tangle of necklaces and bracelets and perfumes and scarves—to the open door of the en suite. The box lights did not glow. The flowing white tiles were dry and blank, the pipes silent.

The bed was low to the ground, and the clamber to his feet always made him feel even more ungainly. He pulled on his boxers, then on second thought stepped into his chinos and jammed his gun—which he'd left on the bedside table—into his waistband.

Bashir edged down the hall into the kitchen. The ancient Creda fridge hummed. The side was a long steel sheet. He popped the discs covering the hobs—none were hot, so Johanna hadn't recently boiled the stove top kettle that took ten minutes to whistle forlornly. He didn't quite admit to himself why he was uncovering the plug in the sink, where they scraped the remains of the chocolate torte they'd shared as a postmidnight snack. The sink sucked food waste into the mysterious pipes of the Barbican.

Johanna had once joked: "A good way to dispose of evidence."

He checked it now, but the last crumbs of cake were still there— cake only partially attended to along with half-drunk champagne, curled together on the sofa afterward watching the end of *Charade* because it happened to be on: Cary Grant as an undercover agent, Audrey Hepburn as a wide-eyed widow, tearing around Paris after a set of stamps worth a small fortune, Bashir telling Johanna how he'd first watched this with his mother and his friend Ruqsana when his mother was ill.

Now Johanna's joke about evidence hung over him. Evidence of what? A lack of fealty? When M was in a reminiscing mood, he'd hark back to nineteenth- and even eighteenth-century spies as if he'd been there with them, recalling that in the American War of Independence, British and American intelligence gatherers refused to remove their uniforms when behind enemy lines, because it would be deceitful, conniving—ungentlemanly. If pushed, they might remove their bright coat, but would keep their boots. So many early spies were caught and hanged because their boots gave them away. A spy might be a hero, the fate of a nation might depend on them, a spy might be a brave man or a bold woman, a person of great daring and courage, but they could never be a man or woman of honor. Spies lied and thieved. So what did fealty mean to such a spy? Everything. Because they were throwing away their honor for their country. A spy who wasn't loyal, then, was really nothing but a liar and a thief.

Bashir moved into the dining room, where a door would have been concealed invisibly in the wall were it not for a panel of glass behind which the original hand-cut Letraset read:

Emergency
escape door
Break glass
Press handle

Bashir thought of this as a fragmentary poem, the words emergency/escape/break/press bashing and jostling together. The glass was intact. No one had escaped that way.

The darkroom safety light, a relic of her father's photography, was on the coffee table. Johanna had been trying to fix it of late. Bashir imagined its red light sinking, the number of times it might have answered the slow semaphore on the nightly horizon with its own semaphore, not a light by which to clean a gun, but a light to welcome or to warn. A signal of betrayal. What if every night when she told him she hadn't been able to sleep, she'd sent up this flare and slipped away from him, ready to meet Rattenfänger? James Bond had gone missing seventeen months ago. 008 had been killed just last month. Could it be that Johanna only offered a timeline of death? What would she betray for?

Bashir shrugged into his T-shirt, denim shirt, and Barbour. He was lacing his chukka boots in the hall when a shadow from the balcony splashed its edges. Bashir pressed himself against the wall, peering into the bedroom. A shape on the balcony left mist roiling in its wake.

A maxim of Bond's: "It's not in a Double O's makeup for our own safety to give us concern."

Bashir strode across the living room, hauled at the heavy door, and edged around the corner of the balcony. Icy mist opened and closed around him, revealing the twenty-eight-floor drop. Vertigo threatened but he ran into the blank gray, drawing his gun. Nothing lunged at him from the gray, nobody tried to hurl him over the edge. He reached the fire escape at the end of the balcony.

Johanna had said once, "There are four escape routes from the top of the tower in case of fire. Or in case of anything else."

He found the cool steel handle of the escape door, counted to an odd number—his ritual, a perhaps vain belief that it was less predictable—and pulled, entering the stairwell gun-first. Empty. The skylight at the very top dripped light into the vast chamber. Bashir peered up, then down. The stairwell was arranged in a triangle, the stairs jacking this way and that downward, the same shape repeating and repeating on itself like an M. C. Escher painting.

A scuff of a shoe from below. Bashir pulled back. Had someone on the lower level seen him? And who was it sneaking around Johanna's balcony—Johanna herself? He counted to another odd number and ducked his head over the side. A bullet whistled past him and pinged off the concrete. Bashir's first thought was that Johanna would be annoyed the Barbican had been damaged on her watch. The second was that it might be Johanna shooting at him. But Bashir dismissed this as quickly as he'd moved on from the sink and their passing jokes of burying the bodies. The third thought was that whoever it was, they were trying to shoot him, and that pissed him off.

Bashir threw himself down the next side of the triangle, sprang out, and fired. An answering bark of a gun as Bashir drew himself back. Another miss. He hugged the wall and ran down to the next level as fast as he could. Just twenty-seven more to go. Bashir saw the figure before they shot this time, a blur in the gloom, a blur with dark hair. He fired again, but knew his aim was off, and somewhere deep inside, knew why. But still, as he took the stairs three at a time, he knew there was another possible reality, in which Johanna was in trouble, Johanna was being chased, Johanna needed him. Then a bullet zipped past his ear from above. Bashir looked up and saw a figure descending on him from the top floor.

An enemy above, an enemy below, and little old me in the middle.

FIFTEEN

Barbican (II)

Bashir fired up at the shooter above, put his hand on the banister, and jumped to the far side of the triangle, the open stairwell yawning beneath him for an infinite second. He landed with a clatter, smashing his knee on the concrete. But it did afford him a look to three levels below, where the other would-be assassin peered up at him. An Asian man around six foot, square shoulders, the black clothes of any mercenary—including Rattenfänger.

"How about identifying yourself now," Bashir called, "save me turning out your pockets?"

A bullet was the reply. Another exploded from above, this time smacking the wall and rebounding, grazing Bashir's arm in a singeing line. Bashir swore, loosed off two rounds, and launched himself down the stairs again, as death pincered him and the stairway twisted and something in him wanted to laugh, wanted to ask: It doesn't end like this, does it, when I don't even know who I'm chasing and what I'm dying for?

"Sometimes you don't know," Bond would say, with a cold smile. "You do it anyway. You do it to be a man of honor in a world of spies. Sometimes you don't know."

Bashir took aim at the man below, fired, and a pained howl filled the stairway. He muttered to himself in satisfaction and hurried down the stairs, wanting to put distance between himself and the man above so he could search the body. But he was putting the funeral cart ahead of the horse, as Johanna would say, because the merc was getting to his feet with a groan, and the pursuer was catching up.

Hoping to cut them off from below, Bashir darted through the next fire door, scrambled across the carpet to the fire escape on the opposite axis of the tower, raced down seven flights, and cut back across to the previous shaft. But the stairway was empty. The faint trace of gunpowder was the only evidence that the figures weren't marshals from his nightmares. No trail of blood. So his shot hadn't proved fatal, and the enemy were regrouping somewhere.

Bashir fought for breath. He checked his arm. If Johanna was in trouble, why would she leave the flat without alerting him? If Johanna was meeting someone, where would she go? If Johanna needed help but couldn't—for whatever reason—turn to Bashir, whom would she turn to? He remembered Mrs. Kafatos in Defoe House, a compatriot of Johanna's father whom Johanna spent Sundays with, when her Sundays were hers. It was not lost on Johanna that Daniel Defoe had been a spy too. Bashir backed into the hallway, punching the button for the lift. His ragged panting filled the wait. He stepped inside. The polished steel showed him a face contorted with doubt. He turned his back on it.

He rode the lift down to the basement, jogging past Harwood's Alpine—the engine was cold—between the slender columns that held up Cromwell Tower, ascending through a ventilation shaft that curved like a head of lipstick in concrete gray. He used Johanna's keys to cross the Podium level, his steps swallowed by the Rubik's Cube of flyover walkways and hidden stairs to Defoe House, a long building overlooking the artificial lake, which was electric jade no matter the weather. The blocks alternated paint from a Barbican Approved Palette. The last time Bashir had joined Johanna at Defoe House, Mrs.

Kafatos informed him the banisters and doors were Mariner Blue. Now they were Flame Orange-Red, and the two flashed in his mind like a siren.

The flats in Defoe House each had a window that opened onto the common stairwell, and the residents blocked this intrusion into their privacy in different ways: bookshelves and tapestries. Reaching Mrs. Kafatos's floor, Bashir paused in the murky glimmer of the vaulted skylight. Mrs. Kafatos blocked her window with postcards. The messages faced into the stairway, telling half the story of her life. There was one particular postcard that Bashir always tried not to read because it was so personal. Written in stubborn block hand, perhaps from an old paramour, it contained something of an apology—*You saved my life, and I never thanked you. I regret that I have, in fact, always taken you for granted* . . . Bashir privately dubbed the old lady Mrs.-Kafatos-Taken-for-Granted, but she wasn't neglected by Johanna, who would answer the phone to her at all hours. But Mrs. Kafatos's hall, glimpsed in the gutters left by her postcards, was dark, and no murmurs came from inside. No Johanna.

As Bashir turned away, it occurred to him that the postcard of regret was missing from its spot. Someone had peeled it away, and replaced it with a postcard he'd never seen before. An Austrian stamp. The same block letters. Four words clamored for his attention: *I come bearing gifts.* Could this be the oldest of tradecrafts, a signal to Rattenfänger to meet and accept whatever gifts Johanna had to offer?

Bashir's senses pushed into something above alert, the kind of panic he'd enter as a kid when his mother was ill, when numbers seemed the only way to wrestle monstrous proportions into manageable sums. He counted the number of bicycles crowding the base of the stairs as he pulled at the heavy steel and noted the remaining flecks of Mariner Blue in the rim of the door. He jogged to the lakeside terrace, which was lit by lamps, its bright surface dappled with fine, cold rain. The gate to the residents-only gardens was open. He heard the soft fall of steps ahead.

Bashir stood still. Held his breath. Looked up at the triangular towers guarding the corners of the lake, each swiveled one turn so they seemed to shrug him off. He stalked down the stretch of the lake, checking each "igloo," sunken spheres which the water did not fill, so one could stand in the lake totally dry—when it wasn't raining. A single trumpet note pierced Bashir. Someone practicing in the music school in the early hours, hoping to be selected for the city orchestra.

Then the mist opened and closed on the opposite side of the lake, and Bashir saw a figure entering the hothouse.

He ran around the lake, beneath the waterfall—the crash of it surrounding him and spitting him out onto the other side—to the conservatory. A voice. Bashir pivoted, both hands on his gun. He looked up through the fronds of giant tree ferns pressed to the sweating glass. Shadows on the roof.

Bashir tried the rusted handle of the conservatory door. Locked. And him, once again, without a wall charge on him. But silence was the name of the game. Bashir pulled back his cuff. He slid the inch-long pick from his Casio watch and knelt, rain trickling down his neck. He was shaking. When had he last shaken during a routine task?

The door shuddered slightly, and swung open. The humidity of a jungle licked him. He edged around the stack of plant pots and sacks of fertilizer. Ivy and straggling vines lolled over his shoulder. The magenta burst of berries drew his eyes. Bashir inched around the terrapin pool, remembering Johanna telling him that the terrapins had been re-homed from Hampstead Heath after they'd bitten a duck in the Ladies' Pond.

"They're calling them *terrorpins*, get it?" she'd said.

"No," he'd replied. "Please explain it to me slowly."

Bashir crept to the stairs. The door at the top was locked too.

Bashir's hand was steady this time. He cracked the door by an inch, holding his breath, but it did not whine. It was used regularly, he remembered now, Johanna telling him the conservatory roof housed a bee hive. "The keeper gave me the best honey you've ever tasted in your life."

Sid: "Gave you?"

Johanna: "Be sweet to the world, Sid, and the world will be sweet to you."

Sid: "That's a philosophy to die by."

Johanna: "Maybe I'm just sweeter than you. Want to find out?"

The drone of the hive fought with the voices, but Bashir could have sworn one was laughing. The speakers did not match the outlines of the enemy in the stairway.

Then the wind picked up and the door squeaked in his grip.

The two figures stopped talking. They turned toward the source of the noise. Bashir ducked down, just catching the smaller figure move gracefully to the edge of the roof and jump off. That left the bigger figure, who pulled something from his coat—a balaclava—and lost his face. Then something slender, that winked teasingly. A baton. And in his other hand, a Taser.

Bashir drew his gun. Cocked it.

Stand up, double tap to head and chest, call it in.

The drone grew louder. Bashir pushed through the door. The enemy seemed to amble around, no hurry, and then shoved at the nearby box. The droning became a roar. Bees crashed over Bashir. He lunged through the storm, thick bodies battering him, unsure if he'd been stung or not, until he made solid contact and hugged the man around the waist, hurling himself forward—and through the sheet glass roof of the conservatory.

Had he been stung everywhere, or was it the glass, or the cacti in the concrete rafters, into which both men had just fallen? Bashir shook himself, grappled with the limbs around him, and rolled, falling through branches and smacking into the rocky border of the pond. His side screamed. Bashir grabbed a rock and thrust upward, meeting bone.

A curse, then the sound of crashing and tearing.

Bashir sat up. Wiped his eyes. The enemy had forced a path through the undergrowth. Bashir got first to one knee, then both feet. He swayed, waiting for the pain to let itself be known. No stings. A few cuts. Maybe a busted rib. A lucky toll. Be sweet to the world, Sid, and it will be sweet to you.

And no gun. Bashir patted the earth for it, sinking into a bog. Gone. Bloody terrorpins. She'd laugh at that, if he told her.

Bashir limped after the enemy, out of the jungle, onto the champagne terrace, picking up a bottle of Moët as he went—an effective weapon, according to his trainer and mentor, a man who'd spent more nights in honeymoon suites than a onetime widower ought to, a man who'd even spent nights in honeymoon suites with Johanna, when Bashir never had; a man who Bashir hadn't kept safe, a man whose ghost was still between them so that now Bashir was standing out in the start of snow, just trying to breathe, just trying not to want to kill, because a license shouldn't mean a desire—when the dark took form and attacked him. Bashir brought the bottle around in his best crossbat shot—Dad would be proud—except it struck bone and the weight took Bashir with it and he fell into the lake, and hit the floor.

Johanna: "The lake's not even a meter deep in places. It follows the line of the Tube between Barbican and Moorgate. Any deeper and commuters would be swimming to work."

Sid: "Then it can't really be called a lake, can it? Glorified pond, at best."

Johanna: "I guess I won't be inviting you skinny-dipping."

Bashir spat, reared, flailed around for his ghost. But the enemy was lying facedown. Unmoving. You can drown your opponent in less than two inches of water. He grabbed the man by the neck and hauled—the man's elbow snapped up and smacked Sid in the chest. Sid doubled over, tasting vomit in the back of his mouth. He wiped his eyes. The ghost was gone.

Sid splashed to the side of the igloo, gripped the bricks, and hauled himself into its protection. He lay spread-eagled on the shallow stair, empty-handed, empty.

"You match the machines."

Bashir stood in the doorway to the Barbican Launderette and tried to find something to say. Johanna was sitting on the low wooden bench that ran along the wall of baby-blue washing machines. The machine behind her shoulders was turning slowly. She called it a Swedish massage for a quid. A battered copy of *Ashenden* lay in her lap.

"I couldn't sleep," she said. "Decided to get some laundry done. And you decided to go swimming, I see."

"I got caught in the rain," he said.

"And it dyed your fingernails blue?"

Bashir raised his hands. "That's how they keep the lake blue?"

"When something's too good to be true, Sid, it usually is."

His mouth was dry. "What did you just say?"

Harwood tilted her head. "You could've invited me nighttime skinny-dipping. I might have been amenable."

"I couldn't find you. I thought something was wrong. And then I . . ."

"Had a bust-up with my surveillance? I have to say, primordial ooze is a good look on you."

"Your surveillance?"

"Keep up, Sid. I thought you were a genius." Harwood pushed a hand through her curls. "I passed all the tests at Shrublands. Doesn't mean they gave me a halo. Moneypenny has to do her due diligence."

Bashir wanted to say: *Your surveillance has itchy trigger fingers, and likes to shoot at their own.* He wanted to say: *When M told me to watch you, I said you'd never betray us—don't make my calculations wrong.* But instead he forced a jolly smile onto his face and said, "I'm afraid I just gave her due diligence a black eye. I thought—I thought maybe you were in trouble . . ."

"My knight in sopping clothes." Harwood put her book down. "We could do something about that."

Bashir gestured at the machines. "That was the idea." He was grinning now, a real grin, despite himself. It was all a dream after all. Johanna wouldn't betray him. Johanna wouldn't betray Bond. "Maybe you could help me out?"

Harwood leaned back. "Maybe you could tempt me."

Bashir dropped his coat to the floor. Peeled off his shirt. She said nothing about the hot red graze of the bullet, just tugged at his T-shirt. More cuts, more bruises. What's a few more between friends? You lie to me, I'll lie to you. Maybe we'll get good at it.

Harwood hooked her finger around his belt buckle and pulled him closer.

SIXTEEN

The Island of Rebirth

Three fishing vessels, red with rust, studded the desert.

Joseph Dryden sat with his shoulder pressed against the oval eye of the Gulfstream G650ER. The USSR had pulled the plug on the Aral Sea, draining so much water to their new cotton fields they left behind a bone-dry basin of salt, a blank canvas stretched taut from Uzbekistan to Kazakhstan. A dam to the north and rising temperatures did the rest. Nothing would float here. Nothing would grow here. Fishing villages straggled along the vanished shore, beached in the long shadows of oil pumps, newly minted, cracking the white crust in search of black gold.

Lapping the fishing vessels, snow drifted toward the island of Vozrozhdeniya, now baked into the mainland. Soviet military scientists had chosen this site because it was isolated. When they abandoned the island, they buried canisters of anthrax and smallpox and bleached their footsteps behind them. Still, today, a whole herd of cattle might die in an hour, an ill wind drifting overhead. The next stop on Sir Bertram's press tour.

The wheels of the Gulfstream reached for the poisoned earth. Dryden zipped his parka halfway up his chest, leaving a free draw to his shoulder holster.

"Are we ready to make history?" said Hester Garnier, Sir Bertram's publicist. She laid her hand on his sleeve.

Paradise looked up from his papers with surprise, then peered over the edge to the window. Dryden thought he could see the man's pupils widen, as if ready to swallow the whole landscape.

A brisk smile. "Always."

The airstrip was a scar of salt and snow. The second plane, carrying journalists, banked behind them. Wind slapped Dryden across the face. They were greeted by a committee from the villages, hard-faced men with stares that said they'd believe in miracles when fish swam in the desert. Little girls in traditional dress began a welcoming dance. Paradise's videographer scrambled for his equipment. Paradise strode forward to grasp the hand of the eldest man present as if they were long-lost brothers. The elder presented Paradise with a convoy of cars peeled of paint. They were to drive into the shimmering expanse.

The field of ground sensors looked like truncated pillboxes tossed here from a forgotten war. Standing sentinel beside Luke, Dryden only half-listened to Paradise's speech officially opening the latest crop. These stations had already found homes in the Scottish Highlands and the Alabama plains. Now, Paradise was bringing industry and rejuvenation to this corner of the former Soviet empire, retraining fishermen in tech maintenance, keeping the ground sensors gazing up at his network of satellites above, communicating air temperature, seismic shifts, cosmic ray levels, wind changes, and precipitation.

"Moses parted the sea," Paradise said to a shivering convoy of journalists. "With this technology, I'm going to do him one better. I'm going to turn the desert into water."

The applause of the villagers was carried on the wind. Hester Garnier pushed the videographer's elbow so he got a shot of a kid cheering.

"Sir Bertram!" A journalist with the air of a raw and hungry recruit. Dryden remembered her face from his security pack: Elena Ilić, studied at the University of Belgrade, recently joined Al Jazeera after three years at Radio Belgrade. "What do you think about the new oil fields here?" she asked.

"It's deplorable. This land is a trauma victim. Instead of calling a doctor, the powers that be are cracking open the bones to suck the marrow."

Dryden could see Hester's eyebrows rise over her sunglasses. He brought his gloved hands together and signaled to Luke: "Colorful imagery."

Luke did not respond.

Elena pushed her hair from her face: "What do you think about the Sea of Okhotsk?"

Luke jerked. Dryden thought he was about to signal something, but he only tugged at his watch.

"It's the heart of the Pacific," Elena continued. "We rely on its ice to pump oxygen and iron to the ocean. But the ice is thinning to dangerous levels. You advocate closing the oil fields here, yet you've done nothing to advocate curbing the fishing industries in Japan or Siberia. Could the Sea of Okhotsk one day be as barren as this desert?"

"Salmon fishing is a fundamental cultural tradition in the Japanese island of Hokkaido," said Sir Bertram, glancing at Hester. "Even more urgently, Siberia has little economy. We must not let the most vulnerable suffer, in order to stanch the damage wrought by the world's most privileged."

"Couldn't that be said of the oil fields here? They bring work. But they're part-owned by one of your rivals, whereas you've invested significantly in international shipping."

Sir Bertram sneered. "You think miracles come cheap?"

Hester Garnier pulled her sunglasses off and waved them like a flag. "Next up ladies and gentlemen, we'll be taking a tour of the island of Vozrozhdeniya, which translates to the Island of Rebirth. Sir Bertram has committed to an ecological cleanup of this secret biowarfare base, which was abandoned by the USSR to condemn the land for generations to come. As you'll have seen in your briefing package, you'll need full hazmat suits."

The convoy speared the desert, Paradise and Luke riding up front with a threesome who'd been described to the press as brave volunteers, but were actually salvagers, who only agreed to take the mad Westerners to Vozrozhdeniya on the promise they could take any valuable metal, and make use of Paradise's hygiene showers. Dryden was in the next vehicle, riding shotgun.

The man at the wheel shouted: "Shut window!"

Dryden cranked the window as a brown wave billowed across the desert, swallowing the car. Salt rasped Dryden's throat. He wanted to heave.

The driver floored it, spinning free from the cloud and into the maze of oil rigs. Shepherds on donkeys scattered before them. The driver spat in the footwell. "Toxic levels of sodium chloride, pesticides—they get into everything, food, water, everything. Your Mr. Paradise talks about the apocalypse like it's the future. We are living it now."

The biocontamination suits were made of a silver foil that glittered hard as diamonds beneath the high sun. Dryden checked his breathing apparatus, then Luke's, the muscle memory of checking each other's parachutes dunking him like a riptide: back in the army with Lucky Luke at his side about to jump into trouble because they had orders and that was it. Now he was walking into trouble because some billionaire wanted to one-up Moses.

Seeming to read his mind, Luke caught his eye and drew a smile from him. "Didn't you ever want to be an astronaut when you were a kid?" His voice crackled through glass and tubes.

"Sure—why?"

"Just pretend you're visiting an alien planet. It's all cool, mate."

Dryden checked the zip on Luke's suit. "Did you want to be an astronaut?"

"Nah. I wanted to be a soldier."

"And you were."

Luke turned away, light blanking his face. "I was."

It was a strange party to tour the end of the world—the journalists cradling their cameras and phones like lifelines, Yuri and Ahmed and St. John jostling each other like kids playing bumper cars, Dryden and Luke guarding their flock. The town of Kantubek, built to house the scientists and their families, whistled emptily. The salvagers moved between the peeling schools and homes with familiarity and purpose, clattering over debris: timber, bricks, the copper wiring and light fixtures already stripped. In the playground, a mural of a duck and a little boy had paled, leaving a faint ghost. The bleached skeleton of a red fire truck. A cratered football field. A garage, where two T-54 tanks and two armored personnel carriers waited like dogs tied up outside a shop. They would have been used in tests: could germs penetrate their shells? Dryden had ridden in vehicles just like them during his three tours of Afghanistan. He turned away, searching for the relief of birdsong or the chomp of insects. The sea where the scientists swam after work had long since disappeared. Nothing.

The labs lay two miles to the south. Animal pens, punctured and crumbling, told them they were getting close. Dryden picked his way around the eastern corner, maneuvering a landslide of cages. Fifteen miles north and fifty years ago, on a plateau, donkeys and horses had once been tied to telephone poles. Between two and three hundred monkeys had been arranged on the plateau in cages next to devices that measured the concentration of germs in the air. Scientists monitored the animals' deaths over a matter of weeks, and performed the autopsy. A germproof suit lay resigned in the corner of the lab, its glass mask intact, the air hose flopping from the back. Dryden wanted to draw his gun, but there was nothing to shoot.

He raised his arm to cover his eyes. The structures ahead were nothing but rusted girders, but the floors shone as if encrusted with white gold. The sun spun off the glass, and he realized that whoever had been in charge of decommissioning the complex had simply trashed it. The glitter wasn't gold: it was petri dishes and beakers forming a snake's skin, each scale glistening and clinking as the group crept through the labs. Dryden alone walked closer to a wall of vast glass tanks, in which liquid remained.

Dryden did almost draw his gun when an arm landed around his shoulders. It was Yuri.

"I am surprised you Yankees do not do a better job of cleaning this up."

"I'm not American."

Yuri shook him. "You are not? Funny." He grinned into Dryden's eyes. "You people all look alike to me."

Dryden sighed. A beeping told him the oxygen was depleting. If the air filters were failing, that was the first sign corrosive chemicals had slipped into their suits. He shrugged Yuri off and double-timed through the journalists filming at the edge of the enormous pit at the center of the complex, finding Paradise and Luke. The anthrax grave, canisters interred here and forgotten.

Paradise was explaining the effect of inhaling anthrax. "A spore will attach to your lymph nodes. There, it will hatch and multiply, entering the bloodstream. It will eat your tissue from the inside. You will bleed internally for months. But that wasn't enough for these men of military science. Anthrax is nature's poison. They perfected it. A strain resistant to antibiotics. A strain that can rupture red blood cells and rot human tissue. A strain just five micrometers long, narrower than a strand of human hair. You'll never know you inhaled it. And it sits beneath us, a toxic stain on a world we insist on destroying."

Dryden tapped Luke's shoulder. "Exfil."

Luke muttered: "I know."

Dryden wanted to ask, Then what's the problem? But then he saw that, behind his mask, Paradise was smiling. He was having fun.

"Eight out of ten people who inhale anthrax die. There are nineteen of us here, against the wishes of Moscow's comms department. I wonder which four of us would survive. What about you?" said Paradise, turning his gaze on Elena Ilić. "Young reporter, career to build, prepared to take big risks. Do you want to go viral?"

Elena Ilić swung her phone toward Paradise. "Would you repeat what you just said, sir?"

Paradise suddenly lunged, as if intending to push Elena into the shallow pit. Then he pulled up short and laughed.

Dryden relaxed his grip on his gun. The cackles from Paradise's entourage reminded him of hyenas. The titters from the press were queasy. Luke wasn't laughing. He was studying the edge of the pit.

Dryden raised his voice. "Time to go."

Paradise chuckled. "Forgive my gallows humor. One develops it when one attends to the dying. As I do over the earth. From this site, I pledge the rebirth of the natural environment. We will all be reborn."

SEVENTEEN

Cosmonaut Hotel

Paradise had bought the stars. Constructed in 1955 to serve the Cosmodrome, Baikonur had retained its purpose long after most other Soviet satellite cities had faded. It was known as Star City. The past was glorious: *Sputnik I*; Yuri Gagarin; Valentina Tereshkova. The future was uncertain. When the USSR collapsed, Russia and the US leased the city from Kazakhstan, but both countries had now grown tired of spending millions on renting the last gateway to heaven and were building their own sites. Star City was dying on the Kazakh steppes. Men huddled on the railway platform selling smoked fish, hoping a train would stop and someone hungry enough would climb out in the blizzard. The only thing left to do was wait for summer. On the riverbank, the ice-cream parlor with its yellow-and-pink parabola bleached by heat and frost waited for when people would sit by the Syr Darya and drink deeply of the sun, talking over the groan of the Ferris wheel, now too old and too dangerous to use.

Sir Bertram said—with a modest chuckle—that a new monument should be built for him. He had bought the Cosmodrome to launch his satellites, and so, unofficially, Star City. But if Sir Bertram was the people's savior, the people had not yet got the memo. That, or they were weary of men who called themselves saviors and asked for monuments.

The staff of the Cosmonaut Hotel didn't care about offering good service when they first opened their doors, and the construction was shoddy, but the building looked good, its concrete grid more striking than anything else around here for one hundred miles and one hundred years; they didn't care because they were Kazakhs and they were being paid to open doors for Russian officials who gave them subsistence wages and a meal a day while standing on their necks. Now the wage was worse, the meal was gone, the dictator had a different name, and the concrete grid wept with water stains. When the Paradise party checked in that evening, the ancient receptionist's face said, If I didn't give a fuck about Stalin, then I *definitely* don't give a fuck about you.

Lucky Luke met this with a stare Joseph Dryden had seen stun superior officers and arms dealers alike, but the receptionist merely jammed an open hand under Luke's nose.

"Passports."

The photocopier was as loud as a passing train. Dryden surveyed the empty lobby. Wood paneling cracked and flaking at the edges. The doors to the restaurant were closed; they had round windows set at the center, like a child's drawing of the windows in a rocket, and through them Dryden glimpsed a ballroom with all the chairs stacked upside down on the tables. Cosmonauts and astronauts quarantined here, planting a sapling in Cosmonaut Grove, the last ritual before they strapped themselves into a tin can and made their prayers. Luke asked if they could have their passports back now and the receptionist said with great lamentations that the photocopier was defunct and he'd need to keep them a little longer, his English borrowed from nineteenth-century classics in bootleg translation. Dryden drifted closer to the round windows and spotted a bar back there too, with

Moskovskaya Osobaya vodka, Ararat brandy, and Jack Daniel's. All the bottles were empty. It was a dry high noon at the O.K. Corral.

"You can give me those passports back any day now, mate. You might be three hundred years old, but some of us are dying standing here on this shit-awful carpet."

Dryden flanked Luke at reception, putting a calming hand on the small of his back. "You don't have any other guests tonight?"

"Only your illustrious company, sir."

"Suppose the chef's at his daughter's wedding and can't possibly come in?"

A begrudging smile twitched the man's mustache. "Sir is clairvoyant."

Dryden dug out his wallet. "How much to fix your photocopier and open the kitchen?"

The money was gone from Dryden's fingers before he finished the sentence.

"The machine has made a most fortunate recovery, sir, and your staff may use the kitchen with our compliments and lasting pride."

Dryden said to Luke, "Reckon you can still improvise a distillery? We're dry back there"—with a nod over his shoulder.

Luke turned around, looking to the ballroom. Dryden slid the passports into the inner pocket of his jacket. Something about Yuri had caught his attention today—not so much the racism as the gleam in Yuri's eyes, as if the two of them shared a secret. He wanted Q to run Yuri's ID.

The receptionist scattered keys across the desk and inched closer. "If both sirs would enjoy real local drink I can give you directions to a bar, very close, where you will have a dancer each. Beautiful girls. For an inconsiderable fee."

"I bet."

Dryden ushered the security detail on. Poulain glared at him—

the member of security who most threw his weight around, and seemed least eager to take Dryden's commands, perhaps wishing for the number two spot. But he followed as Luke hoisted Paradise's bag to the penthouse suite.

The Paradise entourage kicked into gear: Ahmed promising to show them all what a man with appreciation for food could create even in the most meager of circumstances, St. John paying the porter to bring them real alcohol and wake up the disco.

When a maid knocked on the door with the drinks, Yuri grabbed her by the skirts and insisted she dance with him, tugging her into the center of the suite. Hester, the publicist, tried to intervene. Yuri seized Hester by the hips with one hand, his other still gripping the maid's skirt.

"You can both party with me!"

Dryden lowered his hand onto Yuri's shoulder. "I'll party with you, Yuri." He squeezed.

Yuri released the maid, who stumbled. Luke caught her and ushered her out of the room.

Dryden kept squeezing.

Yuri pushed Hester away. He spat at Dryden. "I am not Lucky Luke. You are not my type. Put on a skirt, then maybe I close my eyes."

Paradise relaxed in his chair, linking his hands in his lap and watching from beneath lowered eyelids. St. John was baying. Ahmed told Yuri to stop being a bore and accompany him to the kitchen. Luke stood stranded on the carpet between them.

"I don't think you closing your eyes would make you any more attractive," said Dryden.

"I'll close your eyes forever."

Paradise sighed. "You're *drunk*, Yuri. We're here to generate goodwill, not make a show of ourselves."

"Only a little drunk, boss."

Dryden smiled. "You wanna step back, Yuri, before something gets broken?"

Yuri moved closer. "What is going to be broken?"

Dryden pulled Yuri the rest of the way and planted a kiss on his forehead. "Only your heart, darling."

Then he let go. Yuri staggered and fell on his arse. Paradise clapped. Luke flushed.

Dryden wiped one palm over the other and slipped from the suite, taking the stairs down a level to his own room. A doorman gave him a disinterested look but did not move aside. Dryden produced another tip and the man performed such an obsequious bow Dryden had the urge to give a royal wave. He strolled down the hall, noting the little desk with a little lamp by the lift doors where once upon a time a little old lady would have hunched over a pad noting down who came to this floor and who left and at what time. One hundred percent employment, much of it in Dryden's stock-in-trade: watching. Now the desk was empty, and the lamp had no bulb. He checked, tapping it and enjoying the echo that pulsed inside his skull.

Room 106. The door had warped in its frame and Dryden gave it the kick he'd been famous for in Afghanistan—Joe Dryden, Door-Kicker, never mind the frightened family on the other side—and the veneer thing bounced open. The stink of a museum basement kicked back, bad water leaking into bad walls. The carpet belonged to a lost empire. The single bed had been wrapped tightly in peach-colored sheets by a babushka who'd washed the linen so many times it was translucent, and Dryden had to give a violent tug before the corners would relent. He swept his hand underneath the mattress. Nothing. He patted the floor-to-ceiling curtains. Dust puffed into his face. The windows were two panes of glass with an inch of air between them, in which flies had collected for the last half-century. They seemed to be the only bugs present. Dryden pressed a button on the side of his watch, and the screen strobed as it searched for waves that would inter-fere with his hearing aid, which would mean someone else was having help listening too. Nothing. Q Branch would ask him, Why bother checking manually first? They didn't understand that Dryden wasn't looking to be a perfect machine. Only a good version of himself.

The bathroom was a three-piece in avocado green, the water slug-gish and brown, like tea dribbling from a pot clogged with leaves, and the soap gave no lather, only stuck to his hands. Dryden looked at himself in the mirror and loosened his tie. No steps closer, but several lies deeper. He pulled his jacket and shirt off and splashed himself at the sink. It didn't help.

He was pulling the passports from his jacket pocket when a wolf whistle made him fold the coat over and drop it onto the toilet lid.

Lucky Luke was reclining on the bed, his bulk making it look like something intended for a dollhouse. The grin was in place, but something was missing from his eyes.

"Feel like being my dancer for the night?" he said. "For an incon-siderable fee."

Dryden leaned in the doorway, crossing his arms over his bare chest. "There's a party upstairs, ain't there?"

"Sir Bertram has got the posh boys for that. Come on. Let's go sample the moonshine and embroider our war stories."

Dryden knew he ought to tell Luke no—he'd seen this hardness in Luke's eyes before, and it always meant he was spoiling for a fight. But there was a tether running from Lucky Luke to Dryden's heart and it tugged now, saying, You were only in love once in your life, and it was with me.

"All right," said Dryden. "Buy me a drink and I'll dance for you."

The bar was a windowless hole where hard fun and hard sorrow were exchangeable. The locals brewed their own liquor, colored it, and stoppered it in branded bottles. Dryden and Luke were sharing a bottle of Smirnoff by any other name at a table so small their knees were jammed together and their hands locked over the scarred surface. Dryden was aware of the hum of the light fittings above, the cloying smoke, and the conversation boxed up so tight it threatened to overwhelm his hearing implant, when all he wanted was to give Luke his focus. But whether it was the drink or the noise, Q didn't want him to give Luke everything he had.

What Q would want him to keep an eye on was the factory worker with no factory but fists like meat hooks, clinging onto the bar alongside another barrel-chested gentleman chewing over the sour taste in his mouth. Dryden wasn't sure why the two men had locked onto him and Luke when they entered. For sure, he was the only black man around, and as Luke's bowed head inched ever closer to his, it was readily becoming apparent they were the only openly gay men around too. Well, he was used to both, and the sneering stares didn't overly concern him. What concerned him was whether Sir Bertram had paid a couple of locals to stay on their six—and whether it was Luke he mistrusted, or Dryden himself. There was the taste of danger again, and Dryden calmly acknowledged to himself that he liked it. That's why he was here, and why Luke was here, and perhaps even why Paradise himself was here.

He murmured by Luke's ear, "Your boy likes his deadly chemicals, huh?"

A snort. "Sir Bertram gets a little Napoleon sometimes, but that's how you get the *really big* portraits. He who dares."

Dryden shrugged. "Those kinds of portraits, you got the general or the king wearing their robes, the globe in one hand, a book in the other, a map and a sword on the wall. Conquering hero."

"So?"

"So who's Paradise conquering today?"

Luke took another shot, banged his glass on the table. "Haven't you heard, he's saving the world?"

The two men at the bar were discussing something, and one of them had his hand near his coat pocket.

Dryden threw a shot back too. "Or else, those portraits, the great man's got his loyal servant behind him in exotic silks, usually some black kid who's been forced into slavery and now told to pose all grateful. No one knows his name. No one knows his deeds."

"That's 'cause nobody *wants* to know," said Luke.

"I do."

Under the table, Luke's boot tapped on Dryden's. "You gonna stop talking in code, some point?"

Dryden took a breath. His instincts told him: use the emptiness you saw on Luke's face at Kantubek. Emptiness that looked a lot like dread. Luke had spent his childhood years parceled out between his aunt, grandmother, and great-grandmother, as his mother disappeared from rehab clinics onto the streets. His father would reappear periodically with presents that had fallen off the back of a truck and take his son by force if he had to, but he'd soon forget why this had been so important, abandoning Luke in rooms over alien pubs or at petrol stations, where Luke would place a reverse call at a telephone box with trembling fingers, praying his aunt wasn't on nightshift. But still, Luke always hoped his father would return. He first used with his mother at age eleven, getting by after that on his charm and his beauty and his fists. But his luck was a sand timer with a hole in the bottom, and he would have died on the streets before reaching eighteen had he not one day slept rough in the doors of an army recruiter. The poster told him he could be more, and even if it proved bullshit, it had to be better than this. Luke got clean when he signed up, before the opioids flowing through Afghanistan gripped him and grayed his striking looks with a sapping dread. Until he met Dryden. A therapist once told Dryden that he and Luke reignited one another's capacity for compassion.

Dryden said, "Your deeds. I want to know your deeds, if you want to share 'em. I know when you're in the grips of something."

Luke spun the empty glass. It trembled on its base. The vibration threaded through Dryden's bones.

"Sir Bertram wants me to do something, something I've not . . ."

Dryden brushed his thumb over Luke's hand. "I've got your back."

Luke looked up, and Dryden was struck by how red his eyes were.

"Do you? I served for nearly twenty years. Fifteen combat deployments. Hundreds of individual direct-action missions. I lost track of my kills—those are in the hundreds too. I haven't lost track of the number of friends I saw die. I didn't quit the army. My body quit me after one too many injuries and kept on quitting, and all the army could give me was a course on how to write a CV. I can't go to bed without triple-checking the locks and even then I can't sleep for migraines. My joints are fused. I couldn't even handle executing a shopping list for my half-sister. A car backfires and I fling her kid to the floor because I think it's live ammo. Terrified him. But I miss the action like I miss getting high. I'd go back in a heartbeat. I can tell you how many weapons there are in this bar, who doesn't fit, where the best exit is—but I don't need to tell you. You know already. I'm good like this. I'm *me* like this. I can't stop operating. Without it, I couldn't concentrate on shit, couldn't remember appointments, couldn't plan where I'd get food, just kept asking myself—Am I next?"

"Next what?"

"The next one to hang himself. I never expected to survive. Here I am. Me, not any of our brothers. What was the point of it all?"

Dryden said softly, "What does Paradise say?"

Luke thumbed his nose. "I called you. After my half-sister kicked me out. Some stranger answered your phone. Said you'd moved on. I called Steel North. They said you'd be in touch. You never were."

"I didn't get the message"—Dryden's voice was stone rubbing on stone. It was true. He imagined Moneypenny shaking her head at her assistant: kill it. No former attachments. No attachments at all. But now he was being asked to convince Luke it was safe to believe in him again. "I'm here now, Luke. We were each other's home once. We can be that again."

"I heard once Special Forces look for a certain mindset—lads who can operate by themselves, entirely self-sufficient. That's why so many of us come from chaos, from care systems, from fucked-up families. We join to get away. Never had to wonder who would feed or clothe us or put a roof over our heads. Then it all disappears. Sir Bertram gave me a new home. Not you. He's a good man."

"Then what is it he wants you to do?"

"It's no big deal. Just a bet. It's harmless. I can control the situation."

"Who's the mark?"

Before Luke could speak, the pair at the bar made up their minds and flung a slur Dryden would prefer not to translate or deal with right now. But Luke's head snapped up, and a glimmer appeared, which Dryden knew presaged nothing good. "Leave it, man."

"You got my back or not?"

Dryden sighed, and stood up as Luke rose and asked the unfortunate souls if they had a problem.

The decibels of the bar were suddenly swallowed. The usual toe-to-toe, eye-to-eye, get it out and measure. The usual curt words. The usual drift to the coat as the man with the sour taste in his mouth prepared to pull a knife. The usual clench of muscles as the factory worker folded his meaty fingers around a bottle on the bar.

Dryden said, "Remember your fists are classed as lethal weapons."

The man on the left demanded to know what Dryden meant.

"I wasn't talking to you," said Dryden, and then ducked under the swing of the bottle, blocked the follow-through with his forearm, and landed a punch to the gut that would reconstitute the man's insides. Next to him, Luke snared the other man's knife hand, just as they'd done a thousand times, but instead of moving to disarm and disable, he delivered a headbutt that broke the man's nose. Now things would get serious. Dryden glanced around the bar, read the expressions of men with a whole lot to be angry about, facing two Westerners with big wallets. And the passports of the Paradise party in Dryden's breast pocket.

"Just like Tangier?" said Luke.

"You lost half your teeth in Tangier," said Dryden.

"All right, maybe not *just* like Tangier."

That time in Tangier meant, in Luke's language, a stunning act of violence to rival God's own fury—Luke being biblical at times. But these two weren't worth it. So close the situation down while the crowd is still on the right side of the fence.

The man with the bottle was rearing up. Dryden used the man's momentum, clanging his fist against the top of his skull, shunting him to the floor. On the way down Dryden delivered a knee to the throat, leaving him gasping and retching. As the man slid past him, Dryden's hand darted inside the man's coat, palming his phone and tucking it inside his sleeve. A roar from the man with the shattered nose, which Dryden knew would chime all of Luke's bells, a resonant call of bloodthirst. Dryden put one arm across Luke, a safety bar on a fairground ride, and swung with the other, a left-cross right hook that landed in the messy center of the man's face and lifted him from his feet. He didn't get up again.

Dryden planted both of his feet and looked around the room. A stretched second, and then the drinkers dodged his gaze, and went back to their business. Dryden bunched Luke's shirt in his hand and pulled.

Snow howled around them. Dryden urged Luke down ghostly streets until they stumbled into a square, where the sculpture of a cosmonaut glittered as if dusted by stars. The concrete buildings were dark, and where before Dryden had seen only decay, now he saw something inviting in a city that had for so long kept secrets. Luke was ranting—you should've let me have 'em—until Dryden tugged him closer, slipping his arms around Luke's waist, pressing his face to Luke's neck, searching out warmth, searching out home. Then he heard that rumble from the depths of Luke's chest, that purr, which sent electricity shivering down his spine.

"Hell's frozen over," said Luke.

"I didn't notice."

They were kissing, and then they were hurrying through the snow like a couple of kids hearing school's closed for the day. It was your room or mine, it was walking at a six-inch distance down the corridor, it was Luke pressing him to the wall as soon as the lift doors closed. Luke was different. Luke was hungry. Luke was desperate. Dryden was the Door-Kicker again, he was in Afghanistan, he was in Luke's tent discovering the truth of who he was and who Luke was and the world felt limitless.

Dryden took off his coat and threw it onto a chair so Luke wouldn't feel the outline of the passports. He double-tapped his watch, so the sound would stop transmitting to Q. They didn't use the bed. Luke said the peach sheets were a nightmare too far. They used the floor, and afterward, lying together on the carpet, Luke yanked at the curtains, opening them by just enough inches to reveal a plateau of space above them. Dryden tipped his head back, drinking in the dust of comets. He reached for Luke's hand, but Luke said he was cold to the touch.

Dryden sat up on his elbow. Watched the shadows play over Luke's closed eyes. "What did you mean earlier, about hell freezing over?"

Luke reached for his boxers. "I said to myself—when you got your fancy new life, when you stopped answering my calls—the day I forgive him will be the day hell freezes over."

Dryden swallowed. He skirted a hand up Luke's back, feeling the dents of his spine, the old scar tissue. "I told you I'm sorry."

"Did you?"

The transmitter was off. Dryden could tell Luke the truth now—I'm a Double O, I was ordered to cut off all ties to my past, I did it for our country, I did it so getting my brain scrambled wasn't the end of me as a warrior, I did it so that all the lives we've taken and the damage we've wrought was worth it. He could say—I'm here because there's a missing scientist and a missing security chief and your boss is dropping a vast treasure on the dark web and we've got to know why. He could say—You used to walk with pride and now you don't. You saved me once. Let me save you this time.

But instead he said, "You're gonna have a bruise from that head-butt. What will you tell Sir Bertram?"

A one-shouldered shrug. "He likes to see me fight. Just like you, once upon a time. Guess you don't now, holding me back." He twisted and looked down at Dryden. "Got too dangerous for you, did I?"

The honest answer would be yes, in so many ways. But Dryden said nothing.

Luke dressed, stepping over Dryden's coat—which had slid to the floor—on the way to the door. As he slammed his elbow into the warped wood, Dryden said, "I missed you"—but Luke didn't hear him.

Dryden closed the curtains. He picked up his coat, sat on the edge of the bed, and turned his transmitter back on. He pulled the stolen phone from his pocket and photographed each passport, capturing the vital statistics, the stamps, the warp and weft. Patterns of a life.

EIGHTEEN

"Dead or Otherwise"

Q's got something," said Ibrahim, pushing into Mrs. Keator's office without knocking. Immediately, the swelter of computers whose fans had resigned and the sweat of the spider plants and monstera choking the street-level window engulfed him. Mrs. Keator was grinding coffee using a gadget made deep into the last century. The steel handle looked chalky with age. He spoke up: "We fed the details from the passports 004 sent us into Q. They're legit except one, which is a near-perfect fake. Q cross-referenced the passport with old case files and it tripped an alarm. The file is marked ultra-hush."

"Now there's a bit of ancient history." That was Bill Tanner's voice, the Chief of Staff under M, promoted one rung behind him their whole careers. Ibrahim closed the door after him, finding Tanner slumped low in a chair with foam bulging from the seat, which he picked at now. He wore a sardonic grin on his overworked face, like a rosette pinned to the mane of a long-exhausted horse. "Crash dive and ultra-hush . . . remember those days, Dolores?"

"Whose ancient history?" said Ibrahim.

Mrs. Keator's hands were shaking as she tipped the grounds into a cafetière, and the kettle wobbled when she lifted it, water sloshing across the tray. "The dead."

Tanner crossed his legs. "He's not dead."

She fixed her eyes on Tanner. "Know that for a fact, do you?"

"Bond's whole mission statement is miracles. Besides, he owes me fifty quid. Lost at golf. Wouldn't skimp on a debt, James, would he?"

Ibrahim climbed over the sliding piles of books and lifted the tray onto the glass coffee table, which had suffered a deep crack and never been repaired. He reminded himself to do something about it. Mrs. Keator patted him on the forearm—he could feel the tremor of her body through his sleeve. She wore black velvet Vivienne Westwood—vintage, before his time, style, beyond his interests, but Aisha told him it meant she was just as much a class-act rebel as ever. How she survived in so many layers in this heat trap was also a mystery to him. He wiped his brow.

"Miracles are for little boys," said Mrs. Keator waspishly. "Make yourself useful and plunge the coffee." She pointed a swollen finger in Ibrahim's direction. "You, speak."

Tanner sighed and got busy with the coffee.

"Yuri Litvinnof, joined the target as a consultant over a year ago."

"Target?" said Tanner, without glancing up. "Thought we were protecting Sir Bertram."

Mrs. Keator waved impatiently.

"It's the signature on the passport," said Ibrahim. "Q compared the handwriting with everything we have on file and came up with a match. A business card given to one of our agents by a Michael Dobra, back in the late nineties. We only have the card because it was turned in by Operative 765. The rest of the file is pretty blank. But the business card includes a printed signature, a needless flourish typical of the subject. Yuri's signature is different, obviously, but Q says the penmanship is the same. Set an alarm ringing."

"Metaphorically or literally?" asked Tanner, wincing as he scalded his fingers. The spout was cracked.

"Well, both," said Ibrahim, frowning at Tanner.

"Lead on, my swain," said Mrs. Keator.

The screen at Aisha's station showed a photograph of Michael aka Yuri in his twenties. A pale face so gaunt it seemed to have been stretched by his long fingers from chin to forehead. Slicked-back black hair. Red-rimmed eyes with an appetite. Aisha hooked her foot around a nearby chair and pulled it over for Tanner. He'd been the one to interview her, and she enjoyed his sardonic ennui, reminding her of physics professors at Cambridge who viewed the everyday through a screen of lighthearted detachment verging on disappointment.

Tanner sat down, swapping a quick smile. "Looks like he's got quite the record."

"Yuri's—or Michael's—father was an Albanian mobster. Yuri started life as an enforcer. He was set to inherit the kingdom but when his father was assassinated, Yuri was rejected by the lieutenants. They didn't like his temperament."

"Who spooks the Albanian mob?"

Aisha raised an eyebrow. "I looked up his criminal record. No convictions, obviously. But it says here that the police found a restaurateur in Yuri's area who was late paying protection money cooked alive in his own fryer. Not long after that Yuri's pregnant girlfriend was discovered drowned in a fish tank."

"Theatrical," said Tanner.

Mrs. Keator snorted.

Aisha continued: "Drinking, drugs, gambling, torture. Yuri's not a guy you want heading up your operation if you want that operation to remain stable."

"And we've encountered him before?" said Tanner.

"It would seem so," said Aisha. "Number 765, Station F, based in Paris. She started as a grade two assistant in field operations, and was promoted after a joint op with 007—says here she saved his life. She quit for the private sector nineteen years ago. She's in crisis management now. Real name Mary Ann Russell."

"Waste of resources," said Mrs. Keator.

"Quitting for the private sector?" said Aisha.

"Saving James's life," snapped Mrs. Keator. "Look what he went and did with it. Disappeared or died without leaving any valuable intelligence behind. What was the nature of the contact?"

Aisha scrolled down. "Russell met the subject in a Paris casino after the joint op with Bond. She reported the contact, but there was no follow-up. There's not much detail on the nature of the encounter, either. Yuri's just tagged here as not an active threat."

Mrs. Keator peered closer. "Tagged by whom?"

Aisha tapped her nails on the desk. "No case officer mentioned. Hold on—it says here that Russell recently saw the subject again and flagged it."

"Maybe not such a waste of resources," said Mrs. Keator.

"Russell met Sir Bertram when she was working for a friend of his, a shipping magnate whose oil spill upset his shareholders, among other things. Russell spearheaded the cleanup operation."

Tanner sighed expansively. "She probably goes by Mary Ann now."

"You'll go by Mary if you don't learn to mind your tone in my workshop," said Mrs. Keator. "Go on."

"There's not much else—Russell contacted us a year ago to flag that she'd seen Yuri with Sir Bertram."

"Aisha, Ibrahim—explanation for why there was no follow-up from us?"

Both of them glanced sidelong at the transparent wall separating them from Q.

Ibrahim said, "None forthcoming."

"Unless there was a follow-up," said Aisha, "and it was eyes-only."

Mrs. Keator jabbed Tanner. "You tell us lowly technicians, then, hmm? What have your eyes seen?"

Tanner clapped his hands on his thighs and stood up. "Not Mary

Ann Russell, sadly. I bet James fell in love before she did so much as flash her smile. I'll hunt down what came of her report and get back to you lowly technicians, how about that? Happy?"

"Not for years now," said Mrs. Keator, scowling at Aisha's screen, "but I can't blame that on you, Bill."

"Imagine my relief." He pulled a face at Aisha, then glanced at her second screen, which showed Ruqsana Choudhury's file. "When is 009 making contact with his childhood friend the crusader?"

"Tonight. Q's been feeding her memories of childhood on Facebook, and it looks like call-to-action algorithms really work. I'm almost alarmed by my own power. Choudhury has asked 009 for help. There's only one problem. She's currently occupying a police building."

"It wouldn't be government work if it didn't involve some red tape. Good work. And let me know if Q hears any other voices from the past, hmm?" He was sliding the chair under the bench when he paused, drumming the back. Then he added: "Dead or otherwise."

Mrs. Keator watched him leave. Then she walked back to her office, breathing in the damp soil, relieved to return to its heat. She had no warmth left inside her bones. She picked up the ancient Bakelite telephone and dialed Moneypenny.

NINETEEN

Old Friends

It was a beautiful morning for a drive. Moneypenny had recently asked Q Branch to convert her 1967 Jaguar E-Type Series 1 4.2 in British racing green to electric, and she let the lithium-ion engine free now, the 402 horsepower and 442 pound-feet of torque delivering the same jolt to the body she felt in a fighter jet haring from the runway, but there was no roar, no rattle, no rumble in the bones. She was flying silently above the valley, which dropped away steeply to her right, a basin of mist. Beyond, railway and telephone lines crosshatched bronzed fields.

Moneypenny slowed as the road snaked into the hills where villas of Bath stone and glass hid from sight. It surprised her that Mary Ann Russell had settled down in a converted barn to the north of Bath, a city that always struck Moneypenny as a contradiction, grand yet somehow wistful, a monument to Roman and Georgian pleasures that never quite recaptured its purpose. Cresting the road, she briefly shielded her eyes. Crescents drawn in loops of gold and green delicately clasped the valley, sun spinning from lattices of vast and symmetrical windows. She wondered if Mary Ann Russell would share the city's wistfulness. It was very rare indeed to retire from the Service. She took the next dip into a wood, finding the almost hidden entrance to the drive. Moneypenny pulled up to the crunch of gravel and turned off the engine.

Mary Ann Russell was waiting on the doorstep. One whole side of the barn had been walled with glass, and Moneypenny could see a barefoot man with curly hair and a dark complexion making breakfast at granite countertops. He was kept company by a girl on the edge of being a woman, who was rolling up a yoga mat.

Mary Ann Russell raised her hand. "Welcome to retirement," she said.

"I could get used to this," said Moneypenny. "But I thought you were working with your husband—crisis management."

Mary Ann pulled a face. "I've had enough crises. I lend Assim the grace of my wisdom, let's put it that way."

Mary Ann was over six feet tall, with the grace and poise of an athlete. Her blond hair hung heavily to her waist, just as it always had. She wore a black beret and a beaten-up Driza-Bone. She obviously wasn't planning to invite Moneypenny inside. There was a scuffle at the door, and Mary Ann opened it to release a German shepherd that bounced to Moneypenny, ready to land its paws on her chest before Mary Ann whistled shortly. The dog promptly sat. Moneypenny stroked its ears.

"Thanks for seeing me on such short notice."

"Always nice to catch up with old colleagues." Mary Ann glanced over her shoulder, catching the sidelong attention of the inhabitants of the kitchen. "Come on, the dog likes a mad dash around the pond."

The pond was a natural swimming pool in the back garden whose surface drifted with brown reeds. The water ran over the side in a constant trickle, keeping a bank of bulrushes damp. The garden was set out in layers, a walkway threading up the steep hill. Moneypenny followed Mary Ann, who deadheaded as she went. The dog crashed between them. In the far distance, Moneypenny could make out a glimmer of Clifton Suspension Bridge slung between clouds.

"How old is your daughter now?" asked Moneypenny.

Mary Ann smiled over her shoulder. "You know the answer to that. I left the Service when she was born."

"Second-year student at Edinburgh. Home for the Christmas break?"

"That's right. Clare doesn't know what I do—I mean, what I used to do. And I'd like to keep it that way." Mary Ann faced her on the path. "Don't take this the wrong way, Penny, but I haven't missed you."

"If that's true, why did you report your contact with Michael Dobra to us last year?"

Mary Ann held her breath. Then she bent to stroke the dog, who bowled on up the path. "Come on." She led Moneypenny to a bench at the top of the garden. She sat down, sighed. "I suppose I never found an off switch on duty. I can see you didn't either."

Moneypenny crossed one leg over the other. "I never looked for it."

"Try it sometime," said Mary Ann, gaze flitting over the roof of the barn. "It's not a bad feeling. Though there are points . . ."

"Yes?"

"We were doing some work with a rather odious toad in the oil industry, a contact of Assim's. I wasn't thrilled but the environmental cleanup was important, and it was a big client. There are times I miss the clarity. I mean, we did things that were morally gray, of course we did. But there was still that sense of clarity—the clarity of duty, I suppose, even if all it amounted to was a game of cops and robbers. That last time I worked with James . . ." She buttoned her coat. "How is James? He missed our yearly date."

Moneypenny kept her face cool. "You know James. If he's not standing you up he's letting you down."

Mary Ann laughed. "That's right. Anyway, Assim and I were invited to a party where we met Bertram Paradise—I suppose he's on your radar?"

Moneypenny said nothing.

Mary Ann nudged her knee with her own. "Same old Moneypenny. That's when I saw Michael Dobra. He sent a chill down my spine."

"There's not much in your report on that first encounter."

Mary Ann frowned. "There isn't? I gave chapter and verse to Bill Tanner at the time. James included it in his report on the operation too—it was Operation View to a Kill. I can't remember why you weren't running James then."

"I was sorting out a mess in Vienna. James was supposed to be heading home to have his wrist smacked by Sir Miles Messervy but he stopped in Paris and got seconded to your op."

Mary Ann nodded. "That's right—it was the first time we worked together. I remember James saying he'd been hoping to find out if there was any stuffing left in that hoary old fairy tale of a good time in Paris." She looked down at the palm of her hand with a compressed smile. "After the op, James and I did the Paris in springtime routine, which included a night at the poker tables at Club Elysées. James cleaned out a young gangster, who invited us for drinks afterward. Well, it wasn't pink champagne and violins, but as I said, there's no off switch on duty, so we went. The gangster's name was Michael, and he had a proposition for James. He ignored me, mostly. He wanted to tell James about a new venture, a venture that could use a killer like 007. I remember the smugness in his eyes as he said that, the desire to shock, I mean. Of course James was absolutely notorious for blowing cover, so he didn't blink. Michael got over his disappointment and made an offer. A new international outfit of thugs and terrorists. As much booze and Benzedrine and springtime in Paris as you like. In return, you only have to betray your country. Join Rattenfänger."

The dog barked. It was snuffling at the border of the garden. Another dog nearby joined in the baying. Moneypenny pulled her coat closer. "What did Bond say?"

Mary Ann raised an eyebrow. "What do you mean, what did he say?"

"He didn't go along with it?"

"He took Michael's card. Then we reported it all to Tanner. You said the report was incomplete?"

The sliding doors at the back of the barn opened. Assim whistled for the dog to come inside.

Moneypenny said, "What did you make of Michael keeping Paradise company?"

"Nothing good. If you were Rattenfänger, wouldn't you want to hold the power to end droughts or stop coastal erosion in the palm of your hand, to sell to the highest bidder? If you want a longer rainy season, or to boost your fisheries, Sir Bertram can provide that. If you want to put out wildfires, he can do that for you. Or he can let them burn. That's a valuable asset to a group like Rattenfänger."

"Weaponizing the climate crisis."

"It's already been weaponized. I mean, it's only now when more privileged communities are feeling the impact of floods and fires that we're caring to do anything about it. Better not get me started, Penny. The thought of leaving my daughter to this . . ."

Moneypenny watched Clare join Assim at the door and give a sharp whistle. "Did you get a sense that Sir Bertram was uncomfortable around Michael? Or Yuri, as he calls himself now."

Mary Ann waited for her husband and daughter to retreat inside with the dog. "There was something between them—I felt that Michael was somehow guarding Sir Bertram, though his head of security was there too. A man called Robert Bull, I believe—a nasty look to him, too. I told Bill Tanner all this."

Moneypenny fiddled with her watch, designed by Nanna Ditzel for Georg Jensen in silver with a satin finish. If Sir Bertram was feeling pressure from Rattenfänger, and his own security was falling apart, what might he do? Perhaps find a solution in the deep background of his second-in-command. How difficult would it be for a man with his own quantum computer to find Joseph Dryden in Luke's past?

Moneypenny imagined it as a mirror. She had ordered 004 to exploit his relationship with Luke and infiltrate Paradise's circle. Perhaps Paradise had ordered Luke to find an extra security man, knowing he'd call up his old friend, perhaps even knowing—depending on how good his computer really was—that Steel North was a front, and Dryden was a Double O. Sir Bertram recruits his own Double O, and Moneypenny does the legwork for him, spurring Dryden to make the contact.

Had Sir Bertram let 004 get close in the hopes he would dispatch Yuri? He seemed arrogant enough to believe he could supersede MI6. And, if so, how much did Luke Luck know about Dryden's real identity? It seemed from the reports coming through Q that Luke had no idea.

Perhaps this really was Paradise's version of a cry for help. Moneypenny flicked soil from her woolen trousers. He might have just picked up the phone to Her Majesty's Government. She sighed. She really could have used the deep background on Yuri when she was putting the op together. But it would seem Bill wasn't in a sharing mood.

"Moneypenny?"

"Hmm?" Moneypenny looked up.

Mary Ann was studying her. "Is everything OK?"

Moneypenny gently touched her knee to Mary Ann's. "You've been a friend, Mary Ann. Thanks."

"Let me know if I can do anything else." Her voice was steady, and there was steel in her eyes. Nothing wistful about this professional.

"No off switch on duty?"

Mary Ann's lips turned down in something of an inverted smile. "Not on me."

Moneypenny drove away with Mary Ann hugging her daughter in the rearview mirror. She called Q Branch, and told Aisha to give 004 new orders. Isolate Yuri, discover the nature of Rattenfänger's involvement with Sir Bertram—and exercise his license to kill.

TWENTY

Government Action

It was three weeks since Europe's highest-security police station had been occupied by the Better World Coalition. CCTV cameras clinging to the concrete shell of Paddington Green streamed traffic on the Edgware Road to screens inside reception, now monitored by feminists, anarchists, socialists, and advocates for climate justice. In the windows of the tower, spray paint spelled out sixteen letters: NO JUS-TICE NO PEACE. But the real action was belowground: a reflection of the tower above, as if cast in a dirty pond. For almost fifty years, these subterranean cells held IRA terrorists, suicide bombers, and detainees returned from Guantánamo Bay. Then the police transformed Paddington Green from a prison into an urban warfare training center, before abandoning it. Now, protesters had turned it into a venue for workshops, skill shares, film screenings, music, and lectures. Ruqsana Choudhury, 009's childhood friend, was giving a talk this evening about new government legislation intended to curb climate activism. As one reviewer of Paddington Green posted on Google: "a great living space and anti-capitalist party center."

003 wasn't getting party vibes. She was getting maybe-you'd-make-a-good-hostage vibes.

"You're a civil servant? What sort of civil servant?"

The question came from a teenager who, were proceedings being observed by a drone pilot over the Middle East, would be described as a military-age male. He was standing behind a desk wearing a hoodie and a mask. On the desk itself, hundreds of keys glittered in the flickering generator light.

"The underpaid kind," said Harwood.

"You got more than a zero hour contract," said the boy, "you're more paid than me and mine, lady."

Harwood looked at Bashir. "Can't argue with that logic."

"Look, we were invited here," said Bashir, "by Ruqsana Choudhury."

"You tight with Ruqsana?" The boy smirked, looking Bashir up and down. "Sure you are."

Harwood put a placating hand on Bashir's sleeve. "Maybe Ruqsana doesn't go in for men in made-to-measure shirts anymore, but don't hold that against my friend. He's got an inferiority complex to work on. Every little helps." The boy snorted. Bashir glared. Harwood continued: "Ruqsana told us she needed our help. You're here because you want action from the government? This is what it looks like."

The boy clicked his tongue. "Action with you I could enjoy."

Harwood leaned a hip against the counter. "Satisfaction guaranteed."

Another snort. "You ain't government issue. Hold on." His face lit up blue as he bent over his phone and sent and received a message. "You're cool to go down. Watch out for the mess. Police don't know how to clean up for shit." Another look at Bashir. "And you. Watch out for target practice."

A pause. "I don't need any practice."

"These police—you're the target. Stairs are that way."

Harwood maintained silence, reading the posters pasted in the stairwell until they were beneath the city: 200 MILLION PEOPLE CLIMATE DISPLACED BY 2050; RICHEST 10% RESPONSIBLE FOR

50% LIFESTYLE CARBON EMISSIONS; EARTH AT ITS HOTTEST IN 125,000 YEARS. Shotgun shells and grenade pins rang beneath her feet. From below, the rumbles of shouts and bass. Glancing at Bashir, she saw his frown was only growing. She felt herself running out of air, as if the staircase were closing in.

"It's called charm," she said eventually.

"Calling me inferior certainly is charming."

"It was charming to the target. Besides, if you play the tapes back, you'll find I didn't call you any such thing. I said you have an inferiority complex."

"Well I'd hate to be simple about it. I know how easily you bore."

Harwood winced. "Rook takes queen, Mr. Bashir. I'll never recover. You tell me, then, why you're suddenly buying shirts from Turnbull & Asser, if not because James took you there to size you up when you first joined."

Bashir sniffed. "Ruqsana thinks I'm a civil servant who tore through the fast track. I've got to look the part."

"Dress to kill, you might say."

A baleful look. "You might. Look, Ruqsana's gone off the deep end. First she represents protesters for free. Fine. Now she's on watch lists herself. She's not the girl I knew. Our mission is to find Dr. Zofia Nowak and secure whatever it is she knows about Sir Bertram and his technology. So I'll go to Turnbull & Asser if I have to."

"For queen and country, then?"

"Something like that."

Harwood laughed. "You know, one of these days you'll have to pick a side."

"Funny, coming from you."

Harwood ignored that, stepping over a crack in the stairway, imagining it lasting as many miles as the breach between her and Bashir. "You make a big show of being on the outside, no queen and country for you, just the life of the mind. But your friend makes a stand and ends up on watch lists you and I *know* are drawn up to justify over-surveillance, and you think she's gone off the deep end."

"It's about reason," said Bashir. "This kind of protest—any kind of protest—what's it going to achieve? The game is rigged."

"What would you suggest? Blowing up the game? That only works for people with a cozy penthouse from which to watch it burn. People like Bertram Paradise, come to think of it."

"You don't like the messiah?"

"What incentive does a billionaire have to change the system that made him rich?"

"He wants to live, just like the rest of us."

Harwood looped her arm in his briefly. "Not everyone has your logic, darling." Then she uncoupled and shoved at the fire door at the bottom of the stairs, minding the splinters of shattered safety glass, a radiating fracture she attributed to a shotgun blast. Practice makes perfect. She was met by air trapped in a bottle for decades, and with it human desperation, human fear, now thrumming with grime music. The hallway was free from bullets left over by police training for tower block assaults; she found a broom leaned in the corner over a neat triangle of brass. But still stapled to the wall was a life-size poster of a South Asian man in a business suit holding a gun, with a bull's-eye over his heart. Bashir drew to a stop.

"So that's what he meant," said Harwood. "We are the practice."

Bashir wrinkled his nose. "We're not target practice for the establishment, Johanna."

"No?"

"You and me? No." He pushed ahead. "We *are* the establishment."

They passed a kitchen with a sign on the counter that read INFO-SHOP next to a stack of pamphlets, and another written in felt-tip offering a menu of tray bakes for dinner. A group of women around Harwood's age were looking at a map and discussing defenses against a police raid. A door stood open to a staff room, where a meeting about inviting the media in was growing heated. The next corridor was a row of blue metal doors. The cells.

Harwood's stomach clamped. She felt suddenly weightless: lifted from the floor, ready to be carried down the hall thrashing, chased by laughter. But the laughter wasn't that of Rattenfänger guards hoping for some entertainment. It was a knot of people stacking chairs, swapping papers. At the center, Ruqsana Choudhury was offering out her card with one hand while awkwardly bouncing a baby on her hip. From the way Bashir's eyebrows shot up, a baby was news. From the way his eyebrows stayed up, Ruqsana was more than a friend. Harwood considered the lawyer's look of absolute focus, and the fun in her smile, and could see why.

"Sid!"

Bashir's shoulders dropped, and he bounded over to her. "Ruqsana, don't tell me that baby is a political prop."

"Hearts and minds, Sid, what do you think. Meet Hope."

Harwood hung back as Sid bent at the knees in order to come face-to-face with the baby, waggling his fingers for her, and laughed when she laughed.

"Thanks for coming," said Ruqsana, and then hesitated, seeing Harwood. "I thought you were coming alone."

"I'm his protection detail," said Harwood, finding an open face to wear. "Here to stop him tripping over his elbows."

"You're a lawyer too?"

Harwood picked up the presumption and nodded. "From one to another, when this place is taken back by the Met you're going to be in serious trouble."

"She's right, Ruqsana," said Sid. "Come out with me now, we'll get a drink and you can tell me how I can help. You don't want Hope to get hurt."

"I was breastfed at Greenham Common," said Ruqsana, "so save the spiel." She looked over their shoulders—Harwood followed her gaze, seeing a column of young men carrying boxes with masks, ready, she presumed, for tear gas—and then Ruqsana nodded her head to cell number twelve. "Come in here. Close the door behind you."

"It won't lock, will it?" said Harwood.

The cell had a bench, and that was it. No window in the door, no window in the brick, no window in the ceiling. Tatters of brown paper shivered against the walls. When suicide bombers were brought here, it was vital to retain any evidence of explosive on their clothes. The brown paper would stop them rubbing it off. Harwood sat down, holding her hands in her lap, running one thumb over her wrist, which was free of restraints, and healed of needle marks. She tugged at her watch. Bashir closed the door, and blocked it.

"Your message said this had something to do with the next UN climate change conference."

"In a manner of speaking. It's Dr. Zofia Nowak. Bertram Paradise's science chief in Berlin."

Bashir sighed. "If you've dragged me here to talk to my minister about a whistleblower, you should know that's his least favorite word."

"Strange, I thought his least favorite word was child support," said Ruqsana, poking Bashir in the ribs.

"That's two words." He glanced down at Hope. "Don't tell me . . ."

"Please, you think I'd call that pig's hell spawn Hope?"

"I take it you've met the good minister?" asked Harwood.

"He glad-handed my behind at a benefit for refugees."

"And you and your behind weren't charmed? I'm shocked."

A scoff. "So was he."

"I imagine you and Zofia Nowak set the world to rights when you met," said Harwood, crossing her legs.

Ruqsana nodded. "COP24 in Katowice. We've been close since. Zofia knew about this planned action. She was considering coming along, giving a talk on technology and climate, but she knew it would jeopardize her job. Then three weeks ago, I got an email from her telling me that Sir Bertie might call me and make some offer of support. A complete about-face."

"I highly doubt a friend of the government like Sir Bertram is going to offer support to glorified squatters," said Bashir. "No offense."

"A great deal taken." Another poke in the ribs. "I said the same thing—minus your robotic cynicism—in my reply." She turned to Harwood. "I got an auto reply telling me Zofia was on leave. She hadn't mentioned any leave to me. At first I thought she must be coming to Paddington Green, but I've called every contact I have for her. She's disappeared off the face of the earth."

Harwood met Ruqsana's eyes. "And you started having dreams. Worst-case scenarios."

Bashir eased from foot to foot.

Ruqsana swallowed. "Zofia told me something once."

Harwood, softly: "She told you she was afraid of someone."

A nod.

"Who?"

Then the building shook.

TWENTY-ONE

A Suit

P olice!"

The shout split the building, followed by another percussive round. Hope's cries bounced around the cell.

Harwood rose with her heart rate.

"I have to get out there," said Ruqsana.

Bashir barred her way. "Wait." He looked at Harwood. "We could tell the Met who we are. They'll let us go with Ruqsana."

The lights went out.

"I'm not abandoning the people who need me because you have club membership," said Ruqsana.

The conversation was interrupted as a scream cut the air: "*They're coming down!*"

Harwood said, "Where's the fuse box?"

"Fuse box?"

"Ten floors, ten doors. I saw the mechanisms. I can lock them electronically from down here."

"But the police have cut the electricity," said Ruqsana.

"Doors work on a different circuit, in case this happens."

"How do you know that?"

Harwood glanced at Bashir.

Bashir took Ruqsana's arm. "I'm not the kind of civil servant you think I am."

"Then what kind are you?"

Harwood said, "The fuse box, have you seen it?"

Ruqsana was studying Bashir with narrowed eyes. "The Info-shop."

"OK." She turned to Bashir. "You know what I'm thinking?"

"I'll get her ready."

Harwood gave him a smile, not because he needed it, but because she wanted to smile at him, wanted to tell him—I love moving in time with you. But instead she turned to Ruqsana and gripped her arm.

"Who is Zofia afraid of?"

"There isn't time—"

Harwood squeezed. "I lost a friend. I would do anything to bring him back. You've got the power to act."

Hope wailed.

Ruqsana whispered: "A man named Robert Bull. Paradise's head of security."

"What did she tell you?" said Bashir.

"Zofia thought he'd bugged her phone—I don't know—I can't talk to you until I know these protesters are safe."

Harwood laid her hand flat against Ruqsana's arm. "Then let's get to work."

Harwood slipped out of the door. Boots in the stairwell, the pinball bounce of canisters, the shuffle of shields coming together like plated armor. Activists streamed around her. Each faction had come here with a different agenda—to get arrested, to occupy the building as long as possible, to bring media attention to their cause, to escape while they could. It was chaos, some hauling furniture to barricade the doors, others shouting for a vote on whether or not to surrender, others saying they'd only surrender if they set the building alight first.

Harwood reached the door where a group of university students and anarchists were stacking up filing cabinets. She helped topple the last cabinet and then grabbed the arm of a young man dressed in black with a jean jacket quilted in protest badges.

"Hold the door," she said. "I just need two minutes."

"I've not seen you down here. Who are you?"

"The fuse box. I can buy us some time."

The filing cabinets jumped at their feet as the police rammed the doors. He nodded.

Chants swelled as more and more people flooded into the hall, some contradictory, some overlapping, all growing noisier:

"No justice, no peace!"

"We are peaceful, what about you?"

"Who shut shit down? We shut shit down!"

"Show me what democracy looks like—this is what democracy looks like!"

Harwood vaulted over reception and dragged a chair so she could reach the fuse box. Then she picked up a paperweight, climbed on the chair, and brought the weight down on the lock to the fuse box. It pinged free. The world's most secure police station came down to a lock bought on the cheap bulk from China. But the fuse box itself was complicated enough for a light show in Leicester Square. Harwood glanced down at the CCTV monitor screen, which must also run on a different system, because it was showing her police at every level on the stairwell.

"The people, united, will never be defeated!" The voices joined as one. "The people, united, will never be defeated . . ."

The door boomed and groaned beneath the battering ram, but held.

If she could get the doors closed she could trap the police there. Harwood pulled her phone out. No signal, but that wasn't a problem. She got the keypad up and tapped #003. She glanced over her shoulder to see Bashir and Ruqsana shepherding a trickle of people into the cell corridor. Gas was creeping in from the vents. Her eyes were starting to sting.

A voice answered. "You're breathing very hard."

Harwood pinched the phone between her ear and shoulder. "Police make me jumpy."

"Are you sure you're in the right line of work?"

"Let's put a pin in that. The Met and an army of bailiffs are storming the building. Color me unimpressed. I'm looking at a fuse box that controls the electronic doors. I want to flush them out. I take it you can access the schematics?"

"Trap and release."

"There's probably a fishing joke in there somewhere. Can you help?"

"Is that a genuine question?"

Harwood said nothing.

"Good. Please stay on the line, caller. OK, we have the schematics. Now listen carefully."

It was then the students shouted the police were coming inside. Harwood swore under her breath, balanced her phone on top of the fuse box, picked up the paperweight, and vaulted the counter. The police officer was carrying a flashlight and Harwood saw the scene in tableau, the officer falling through the door as it suddenly gave, landing in a pile at the feet of ten panicked people, who shoved the door once again, shutting out the backup. The officer was clambering to his feet, swinging a truncheon, as a teenager at the front picked up a chair and got ready to bring it smashing down.

"Freeze!" shouted Harwood. And it actually worked. The tableau wavered. Harwood shook the man who'd helped her. The badges on his jean jacket clattered. "Stand on that chair, pick up the phone on top of the box, and follow the instructions."

"Who are you?" he asked again. "Who's your contact down here?"

"Ruqsana Choudhury." Harwood scanned the badges on his

jacket, a poem of occupation. "If you do what the voice on the phone says, we can stop the police at the doors. I'm trying to keep everyone here safe and the building secure."

"How do I know it won't open the doors? You've just shown up and now the police are breaching."

Harwood let down the guard of her British accent. "My grandmother didn't trust the police in Algiers and my father didn't trust them in Belfast and I haven't trusted them since I stopped believing in the tooth fairy." She caught the badge on his collar against police brutality. "I'm not giving my body over to riled-up police in a dark basement."

He jerked into action. Harwood grabbed the chair from the hands of the teenager, shoved her way through the shoulders and legs of the crowd, and grabbed the officer by the lapels, hauling him to his feet. Then she pushed him against the wall and told him to stay quiet if he wanted to get through this, keeping her hand on his chest.

"Now we're talking," said a pale teenager with bulging blue eyes and a red nose that had badly healed over more than one break. "This will make 'em back off."

"What will?" said a woman whose hardened face said she did this professionally.

"A hostage."

"No one's talking about hostages," said Harwood, turning to the woman, "right?"

She nodded. "The aim is to occupy peacefully."

Someone else shouted, "Who said that was the aim?"

Too many factions, too many thumps at the door, too much fear and fury flowing from the police officer's chest through her hand and up her arm. She asked the woman for the name of the man now at the fuse box. It was Lee.

"Lee, how's it coming?"

"It's working!"

Harwood smiled at the police officer. "It's your lucky day." His chest was rising and falling faster and faster as the short pale kid eyed him with a lifetime's worth of hate. Harwood turned to the teenager. "What's your name?"

"Ruairi."

"Nice to meet you, Ruairi. I want you to gather everyone up and take them to the cells."

"Shit, why would I do that?"

Harwood took a calming breath, and watched him mirror it. "Because I need your help, Ruairi, please? The cell doors have been closed, the air is cleaner in there."

The police officer spat. "You fucking thugs."

Harwood blocked Ruairi with her shoulder, planting her feet—remembering a stray dog her father often tried to rescue from the streets when she was little, and how the dog would plant its whole center of gravity in one spot and become immovable, so that Harwood could coax and haul but the dog was stuck to the spot. The boy bounced backward as the police officer lunged forward, and Harwood swung with the paperweight.

The police officer slumped to the floor. Fuck.

Harwood knelt down, checked his pulse, and his breathing. Both fine. She gave Ruairi a breezy smile. "How about gathering those people for me?"

He was staring down at the officer. "My dad was a policeman."

"Was he a good one?"

"Any such thing?"

Harwood moved the officer into the recovery position. Thought, *I do my best.* "Come on, Ruairi. Lee, nice job."

The monitor showed the police realizing the doors that ascended were open, and evacuating the stairwell. No point kicking something that won't give.

"Here's your phone," said Lee. "How many people do I have to kill to get one like that?"

"At least two. Do you want to get out of here?"

"What do you mean, out?"

Bashir and Ruqsana had gathered about half the protesters in the corridor, a shaky column of around thirty people wearing gas masks or scarves. Around the same number again were setting up camp inside the cells, planning to continue the occupation for as long as possible. When Bashir saw Harwood at the rear of the column, he waved her forward. Ruqsana wanted to stay with the remaining activists. Harwood removed her from the group.

"I know you want to help these protesters, and help Zofia too. If you come with us now, you can do both. You'll go straight from here to the police station, with the benefit of not being under arrest yourself."

Ruqsana pulled her coat tighter around Hope.

"Think about Hope."

Ruqsana jigged Hope up and down, lips pursed so tightly they'd turned milky. She nodded.

"There's an entrance for Guantánamo returnees a level down," said Bashir. "It lets out into a security tunnel, repurposed from the Blitz." The building shook again. "Time to go."

Bashir led the column past a shower room where the tiles were dyed red-brown, and an empty armory. Gas chased them. Harwood held on to Ruqsana's arm with one hand, and felt the other gripped by someone—she turned and looked up at Lee. She squeezed his fist.

A short flight of stairs ended in a steel door. Harwood found the outline of a panel. She began to pry it off when Lee handed her a knife.

"Thanks," she said.

The panel popped off, revealing a keypad. Bashir raised the phone to his ear, repeating a series of numbers. Harwood punched them in. There was a clunk, and the door hissed open.

During the Second World War, bomb shelters had been constructed in parallel tunnels four hundred meters long with the idea of later integrating them into the Tube. Harwood felt the rumble of a train passing through the next tunnel. But not all of them had joined the network. Over time, the tunnels had been used as shelter for Caribbean migrants arriving on the *Empire Windrush*, overnight accommodation for crowds visiting the Festival of Britain, sewer routes, and archive storage, all part of London's underground city. This tunnel had been smoothed with concrete, a perfect gray whose occasional stains told stories of prisoners who'd been brought here and tried to struggle.

Harwood and Lee eased the door to behind them.

Bashir hung up the phone. "This way."

"How are we going to get out of here?" asked a young woman with a shaved head whose face had splotched purple in the gas.

Harwood asked her if she had a phone. She nodded. "Then I need you to shine your light for me. London runs on sewers and tunnels and electricity substations and countless other underground spaces, all of which have to breathe. Just like you do. That's it. You've probably never noticed the ventilation shafts all around you. That's how we'll get out of here. Point the light ahead, OK?"

The woman's hand steadied, the beam true.

The group jogged along a Tube platform with posters advertising back pills and nylons. A service hatch took them into another tunnel, then another. It was winter aboveground, but the second London did not know cold. Sweat sheeted Harwood's body. She kept hold of Ruqsana. Rats fled from the lights. Dust and grit choked Harwood's mouth and nose.

"It's this one," said Bashir at the front, lending his shoulder to a low wooden door, kept shut by a rusted chain. Lee and the woman with the shaved head helped him. The chain buckled.

Harwood shielded her eyes from the LED sunshine and breathed in the smell of drenched soil and mustard seeds, a combination her mind told her wasn't possible down here. When her vision returned, she realized they were in a deep-level air-raid shelter that had been transformed into a hydroponic farm. Lines of shelving filled the space, each one verdant with pea shoots or lettuce unaffected by changes in weather or seasons. Bashir, paused at the threshold, now zigzagged through the shelves to a newer door on the other side. He drew the lockpick from his watch and the door was open in thirty seconds, revealing a clean stairway, lit by a grid of sun. The ventilation shaft. The activists stood now dazed, breathing in the crops. Bashir told them to head up the stairs and let themselves out. He threaded through them, stopping Ruqsana with a hand on her arm. He steered her to a packaging production line.

Ruqsana bent over Hope.

"She OK?" asked Bashir.

"Fine." Ruqsana was laughing, near hysteria. "Her first protest was a roaring success."

Harwood sat down on the bench, guiding her to it. "Start them young. Why did Zofia think Robert Bull was bugging her phone?"

Ruqsana drew a hand over her face. Her palm came away gleaming. "Zofia would be listening to a podcast on the future of housing in New York or something, and the next day Robert Bull starts chatting to her randomly about the Greenwich Historical Preservation Society. He started to bring her coffee only on mornings when she hadn't slept well. She realized her phone was monitoring her sleep cycle, though she hadn't switched it on. Then he asked her to dinner. She told him she didn't socialize with colleagues."

"And he took it like a gentleman?"

Ruqsana was gently cleaning Hope's cheeks. "He said they wouldn't be colleagues long. It freaked her out, but then he laughed it off. Still, he wouldn't leave it alone, kept asking her out. Zofia even told him she was seeing someone, though they'd only had a couple of dates. And Robert Bull said he already knew all about it."

"Who was Zofia seeing?" asked Bashir.

"An American in Berlin," said Ruqsana. She shot a look at Bashir. "One of you. A government suit."

Bashir put his hands in his pockets. "Do you know the man's name?"

"I remember thinking his surname was sort of poetic. Felix— something."

The light on Bashir's phone swung up. He'd forgotten to turn it off. "Felix Leiter?"

Ruqsana shielded Hope's eyes. "Yes, that's it. You know him?"

"I know who makes his suits."

TWENTY-TWO

Icarus

Baikonur was a nightmare from a security perspective. The spaceport crawled over one hundred kilometers of steppe, laddered with dry streams and baked gullies and collapsed fences, over which Kazakh herders drove their cattle at will, only retreating across the shrubland when a rocket was due to fire. Since the Russians marched out, the decrepit warehouses and underground missile silos on the hinterland of the vast complex had become caches and hideouts for smugglers and looters. The local population had their pick of reasons to resent the spaceport, from mysterious illnesses to failing water. Fears of terrorism left the place jumping at ghosts. Perhaps it was time to start thinking of where to go—but then, were they not on their own land, given to them by their own God?

Joseph Dryden saw this question in the eyes of the cleaners, the canteen staff, the low-level maintenance crew, and saw the answering fear in the eyes of the newest private army guarding Baikonur, Paradise's own militia, formed of local men eager for a job. They had searched Paradise's party and the journalists upon entry, and Dryden had been forced to lose the stolen mobile phone before he was patted down. The base was a powder keg. But Sir Bertram seemed oblivious to it, the magician revealing to the world his latest trick. He dragged the press through howling wind to walk the new concrete runway that unfolded across the cracked earth. Support vehicles and trunks of cables and ground crew surrounded the repurposed 747 jet, which would launch a light rocket carrying Sir Bertram's latest array of low-orbital satellites.

Sir Bertram was explaining what made his satellites special. Instead of a satellite the size of a dumper truck costing four hundred million dollars, he was offering satellites the size of a human head costing as little as a million. Paradise's language was one of the many off-kilter things about him. Dryden had heard him agree with Hester, his publicist, to use a football to put the satellite into perspective—it was friendly, relatable. But now he was laughing as he told the press that a human head that cost a million would be the most overpriced computer in the world. Where most minds—this said as if he stood outside the rule—used just a fraction of their power, his satellites could line-scan the earth, taking photographs of landmasses that together formed a daily changing portrait of our world.

"Celestial, my quantum computer, can process these images in such detail, I can count the number of trees deforested in the Amazon, or pick out the blue tarpaulin pulled over mine shafts, or the cracks on a glacier foreshadowing imminent collapse." A journalist asked where he kept his quantum computer, an industry secret that earned a finger wag as Paradise plowed on. "This data, in conjunction with data from my ground sensors, will direct the movement of *Ark*, my yacht, and eventually my entire fleet, helping me direct the Cloud Nine seeding program. It will also empower me to alert local authorities to humanitarian disasters before they happen."

This last was delivered as an afterthought.

"Let's wager a bet," he called, gesturing at the 747. "I do not pretend to be a man of the people or a maverick of the business world. I do not claim I am committed to the welfare of others while dodging my tax bill. I do not own newspapers or fund political campaigns with the sole aim of driving disunity, dissent, and my profit margin. I do not pretend happiness doesn't come with a price tag, while strolling around barefoot on my private island."

Dryden wondered whom this stump speech was really aimed at. Yuri stood close by Paradise, scowling into the flashing cameras. Dryden had received his orders from Q on the way to Baikonur, including an abridged version of Yuri's CV. Isolate, interrogate, dispatch. He had no qualms with the last part. He just wished there was a fish tank around to drown him in.

"I will tell you what it is I *do*," said Paradise. "I put my money where my mouth is. I have developed a new mode of launching lighter rockets from the wings of a 747 jet, purposely designed for my smaller satellites, meaning they can be launched from anywhere in the world. Although I have bought this spaceport, and so do not need to invest in new launch technologies, I am switching to this new mode because it's better for the local environment. I am committed to making Baikonur work *for* its people, not off the backs of its people. My new launch method will make replacing faulty satellites fast, easy, and affordable. From this long-forgotten corner of the world, I release my flock of collared doves. I've been told it cannot be done. That a launch of this type has remained theory for a reason." A watery smile. "This jet has been rechristened *Icarus*. Our pilot today is Captain Katherine Drylaw."

On cue, the door to the 747 hissed open, and the pilot appeared, waving to the world's press. The cameras clacked and flashed. Sir Bertram rubbed his hands.

"Here's my hazard. I am willing to bet anyone here the amount I earn during one night, against the amount you earn during one night, that this launch is a success."

Captain Drylaw's wave skipped a pass.

"If you believe we'll see a ball of flame in the sky after liftoff, and you're right, I'll give you eighty-eight million dollars. If I'm right, and

Captain Drylaw survives making history, you sacrifice to me whatever slice of your salary pays for your beauty sleep. Any takers?"

Luke gave nothing away. The press jostled together like nervous pack animals, glancing around the expanse of the steppe, the distant stage being set up for a concert that would keep everyone entertained while they waited for touchdown. The blare and crackle of speakers was joined by a titter of strained laughter.

Sir Bertram cracked his knuckles. "If you'd been braver, I would have been obligated to give you my day's taking. I work through the night."

Elena Ilić raised her hand. "What is your day's taking, Sir Bertram?"

A shrug. "My personal worth grew by twenty-five billion yesterday." A mild smile. "It was a good day."

"That's supposing Captain Drylaw crashes. And dies. You'd give me twenty-five billion dollars?"

Sir Bertram put on his sunglasses with a laugh. "Captain Drylaw has the wings of an angel."

"How can you be so confident?" asked Elena, tilting forward against the wind.

Sir Bertram's gaze drifted over the plane. "I don't fail."

"You hold degrees in economics, international development, and politics, not engineering," pursued Elena. "You're not really an inventor, are you? You're a backer, an investor. These satellites and ground sensors could be selling intelligence data to governments and private firms, for instance, who can't afford to launch their own fleet of satellites, but would subscribe to your services. You could be spying on us all right now. How can you justify so much power in the hands of someone who was never elected?"

Luke shifted between the balls of his feet.

"Democracy is an illusion," said Paradise. "We live in a meritocracy. The public have to gamble that those of us with the power to save the world truly want to do so. Should they believe in such a childish dream? No. But it's the dream we have. Seeing the world from the perspective of my satellites has gifted me a vision of a whole planet united in its destiny, and its fate. The climate is collapsing. Is trusting me, and the many governments who have backed my technology, a risk? Does geo-engineering itself pose unknown dangers, even as it remedies existing dangers? Yes. Once I collect my data, I will possess the knowledge of the most effective sites to halt the melting of the sea ice. The first wound to salve. It might go wrong. It might make matters worse. Or it might just save the planet. The clock is ticking. Double-or-nothing time."

"But what gives you the right to gamble with the fate of the world?"

Sir Bertram's smile revealed a pointed canine. "Money." He clapped his hands. "Forgive my glibness. I'll tell you a story. My father was a businessman. He lived for money, because money represents power, and a man can never have enough power. That's what he taught me, anyway. My father specialized toward the end of his life in mining for neodymium, an essential rare earth metal used in electric cars, mobile phones, wind turbines—the future. But his mines spewed toxic and radioactive materials and were the site of multiple human rights abuses. After my father suffered a stroke, I made my start by changing the landscape of rare earth mining. I revolutionized the mines with my environmentally friendly extraction method based on salt-based systems. I brought pride and dignity to the workers, as I am here."

"What did your father think about that?" said Elena.

The wind turned and clouds scattered overhead like gulls driven over sand by pursuing dogs.

"We shared our last words at his deathbed. He said I'd never live up to him." Sir Bertram squared his shoulders. "And he was right. My father represents the worst of humanity. I pray to God I never live up to him."

"You've more than quadrupled his profit margin. There are rumors—"

Sir Bertram's publicist cupped her hands against the growing wind to shout: "Ladies and gentlemen, if you'll follow me, we must now return to the control room."

The armed guard pushed forward, and the press members swapped looks of bemusement and unreality as they were funneled onto the rusted minibus. Yuri wasn't following Ahmed and St. John. He was cutting through the crowd toward Elena Ilić. Dryden looked for Luke—he was already aboard the vehicle. Dryden drew his weapon, holding it at his side, and covered the cracked concrete runway double-time, blocking Yuri before he reached the journalist.

Dryden said over his shoulder to Elena: "Get on the bus. Keep your head down." He wasn't sure she'd heard him over the wind and the throb of the engines, but she hurried toward the line of journalists mounting the steps. He felt a prick on the back of his hand and re-acted by reflex, seizing Yuri's wrist and almost breaking it.

Yuri sneered. "Always the knight in shining armor, yes?"

"We're taking a walk."

The driver honked. Dryden saw Sir Bertram speaking to him quickly. The engines revved. Luke was standing in the gangway of the bus, watching Dryden with confusion on his face. And then the vehicle swung away, leaving Yuri and Dryden standing alone together in the desert.

TWENTY-THREE

Experiments in the Human Body

O04 seized Yuri in an armlock. They staggered across the launch area like two drunks stumbling from a lock-in. Joseph Dryden felt the ground shake beneath his feet as bitter chemicals hit the back of his throat. He was dizzy—fumes getting to him. His legs tremored. The 747 was preparing for takeoff. The roaring was terrible as the plane taxied down the runway. Dryden turned to watch. Yuri tried to elbow him in the ribs. Dryden kicked at the back of his knees, sending Yuri to the dirt, and then dragged him behind a corrugated warehouse. He slammed Yuri against the wall, raising his weapon.

"So funny," said Yuri. "You have orders to execute me. I have orders to execute you."

"With so much in common we should try dating." Dryden cocked the weapon. "Orders from who? Who knows I'm here?"

Yuri giggled. "Who doesn't? We were very unhappy when we discovered Bertie called you in. It is interfering with our plans."

The plane was climbing against the glare of blue sky rearing up behind the warehouse, leaving behind three white streaks like salt pouring from a shaker. Dryden seized Yuri's jacket and pounded him against the metal. The echo resounded in his skull. A trembling shock jolted up his arm. "What are you to Paradise?"

Yuri pulled a face. "A babysitter. No big fry. So why are you picking on me?"

"You're minding him for Rattenfänger?"

"What did you think, I am just hanging around in case he drops some scraps I can lick up? That's your job, Extra Special Secret Agent. Now I think I have enough of your questions and your bad attitude."

Dryden smiled. "That right?"

"Yes." Yuri opened his fist. A vial rocked back and forth in his palm. Dryden recognized the label. It was from the Island of Rebirth. "I have never experimented with anthrax. I am excited to try it out on you."

Dryden's smile faded. "You release that, you'll die too. Only, my bullet will kill you a lot faster than the anthrax. That is if I'm feeling merciful."

"You think I am so silly to expose myself too? No. You are going to drop your weapon, and we are going for a little drive together so we can talk while you still have a tongue."

"Why would I do that?"

"Because you are losing muscle control, of course. Right now a drug is targeting the neurotransmitters of your brain telling you to relax. So relax, *man*."

The prick on his hand. Dryden swallowed—or somebody did. Yuri had injected him with something. His throat seemed to belong to another body. He shook his head. His eyes were streaming. The gun suddenly weighed a ton.

"You see," said Yuri, "I enjoy my little experiments in the human body, but it is much more fun if the subject is compliant. You are feeling pliant now, aren't you, 004? Then we will go for a drive, and play a game of spin the anthrax. A game of kiss-and-tell, yes? Don't you have so much you want to tell me?"

The warehouse seemed to be falling down. Over its steep roof, the 747 reached cruising altitude. Captain Katherine Drylaw would be putting a hand on the lever and saying calmly: *Pulling now.* And someone in the control room would utter the magic word: *Release release release.* Dryden looked at his hand holding the gun. His fingers were releasing. The rocket dropped. It looked like a bomb falling from the plane. But then another incandescent line appeared from the rocket. Ignition. A ball of flames shone so brightly it mushroomed in Dryden's mind. The plane and the rocket were separating, their contrail lines forming a broken wishbone. The rocket was leaving the atmosphere. The plane soared in a triumphant arc, returning to earth. Mission success. His mission.

Dryden fired.

But his hand wasn't where it had been. The bullet was wide by an inch. Yuri froze like a cat caught in headlights. But no one was drawn by the sound. The air was on fire and everybody was cheering. Dryden heard their claps as he sagged at the knees and Yuri caught him.

A trampled fence. A blurred expanse. Hard earth reverberating through his knees. Yuri's weblike hands folding him into a passenger seat. Throat caked in dust. Engine coughing to life. Bumping over the dirt. Nobody around, no figures on the horizon. Miles streaked by, asking questions of him. How strong could the drug be? He was still awake.

Dryden studied the point of his elbow. Your body belongs to you. Always has. Always will. Even after the blast in Afghanistan. He just had to wake up. Come on, Q, wake me up. Dryden licked his lips. He had to concentrate on the words, just like after Afghanistan—but this isn't then. This is now. He is 004. "If a drug is targeting the neu-rotransmitters of my brain, all I have to do is override it."

Yuri glanced at him sidelong. "Take a poke around in there, yes? I'd be happy to jam a pencil through your eye and see what happens. Only I do not have a pencil."

"Be grateful for small favors, Ma always said. My implant works by stimulating my brain to pinpoint speech among noise."

"What implant?"

"So stimulate me, Ibrahim. And that's not a come-on."

"Who are you talking to?"

Dryden smiled. "Not you." Nothing was happening. He imagined Ibrahim and Aisha debating the risks.

Then Ibrahim's voice burred in his head: "This has never been tested."

"Do it now or lose a very expensive piece of equipment."

His whole body jerked, as if he were a puppet and someone had yanked him by the strings. Dryden slammed his elbow into Yuri's crotch. The UAZ-469 swerved, diving headfirst into a dry riverbed. The wheels spun, showering him in earth. Dryden hit his head on the dashboard.

When he came to, Yuri was hauling Dryden inside a hangar. An im-possibly giant structure with holes in the tin roof, raining light on the Soviet space shuttle rusting inside. It was propped on wooden blocks, a ghostly glory. The towering walls were lined with gang-planks. The concrete was stained and blistered. Yuri held the vial aloft like a medal. Dryden decided he didn't give a shit. He knocked Yuri with his shoulder and ran under one wing of the shuttle, breathing in decayed dreams and bird droppings. A shot ate the air. Yuri had Dryden's gun. There was a ladder propped up underneath the belly, climbing into an open hatch. There could be a radio or a weapon inside. He almost laughed at himself. His first instinct was still to call Lucky Luke for backup, after all these years.

"I see you . . ."

Deafening gunfire, an explosion of movement. Pigeons burst from the ceiling. The hangar itself seemed to sway. Dryden remembered a detail from the press briefing package. A Cosmodrome hangar had collapsed after an earthquake, killing eight people and destroying the last shuttle to make it into space under the hammer and sickle.

Dryden sprinted underneath the shuttle and grabbed the ladder. A bullet hit the metalwork. Climbing awkwardly, he gripped the ladder with the hand that worked best and fell into the body of the shuttle. He tipped the ladder over, hearing it clatter to the floor. He pulled the hatch to and locked it.

Dryden fought for breath. The inside of the shuttle had been raided long ago. He was lying on baize flooring, and had a vision of himself raked across the poker table with a stack of chips, Paradise or Yuri's win; Moneypenny or M or even Luke's loss—whoever it was he was fighting against, whoever it was he was fighting for.

The tube of the shuttle was lined in perishing mustard rubber. Silver panels and instruments clung on like limpets. What seemed like a lantern twisted on wires yanked from the tube. He picked up a spanner. A cabinet swung open. He flinched. One cosmonaut suit remained inside. A helmet glared from the top shelf. There was a sudden clang, and then the shuttle shook. Yuri was thumping the base. Dryden got up into a crouch and made it to the end of the shuttle, clambering through a tight door into the cockpit.

Dryden swore. Yuri was crouching on the nose of the shuttle.

Yuri tilted his head and grinned wildly. Then he raised the pistol. Dryden ducked. The glass cracked, but did not shatter.

There was a radio. Dryden crouched behind the left-hand pilot's seat, reaching blindly for the panels with both hands as another bullet thumped into the screen. He couldn't ask Aisha or Ibrahim to call

Luke: if he wanted backup, he needed to summon it himself. His hand kept missing the damn thing. How many more rounds did Yuri have?

Breathe. You know you were carrying a Colt 1911. You know it's single-action, semiautomatic, magazine-fed, and recoil-operated. These compound adjectives are your nightly prayers, your daily hymns. You know it holds seven rounds with one in the chamber. Play back the last minutes. He fired twice at the birds, once at the shuttle. Four more shots. Never mind that, you've found the switch.

Dryden offered a prayer to whatever God would still have him, and threw the radio into life. A hum answered.

He ducked as another bullet hit the screen. It shattered.

Dryden cycled through to the general distress band as glass rained on him. Yuri spidered into the cabin, his boot landing on Dryden's ribs. Dryden fought for purchase, for control of the gun. Yuri's bones snapped under his right fist. He liked the feeling.

The shuttle swayed, dropping off one of the blocks.

Dryden tried to grab onto something but his left arm had gone numb. He fell back, bashing the base of his chin on the metal edging of the cockpit hatch. The radio tumbled away.

When he blinked next, his vision throbbed red and purple. His mouth tasted of salt. His muscles creaked as if he hadn't used them for months. He sat dumped into the pilot's seat.

Ibrahim's voice: "Wake up, 004. *Now.*"

Dryden headbutted Yuri with all his strength. He hit glass. It didn't crack, only chased around Dryden's skull like a whisper around St. Paul's. But he could still hear. It was OK. The implant was OK. Yuri was dressed like a cosmonaut. Dryden had tried to headbutt his helmet. Yuri slapped him.

"What do you want from me?"

Yuri heaved a sigh, glossing the helmet. Perching on the control panels, he pointed the gun lazily at Dryden. His voice was muffled, but it still made the roots of Dryden's hair shiver. "I want to conduct an experiment on you, 004. I've never watched someone die from anthrax before. Not even my teacher, Colonel Mora, ever did that. Rattenfänger will be very impressed with me, I think."

Dryden swallowed. He focused on the gloved hand, the vial rolling to and fro in his palm.

"I even have a hazmat suit. You see, I'm not breaking any safety protocols."

"Anthrax takes days, weeks to kill a person. You're just going to sit here all that time?"

Yuri's tongue darted out of his mouth, rubbed at his lips. "Maybe I will have a picnic."

"You must want something, some information."

"Why must I?" He sounded petulant, a little boy denied a toy. "I just want to have some fun. Don't you want to have fun with me?"

Think. Think like your life depends on it, because it does. "Who told you I'm a Double O, Yuri?"

His shrug was mostly swallowed by the space suit. "Maybe Bond, James Bond spread his legs for me, huh?" He raised the vial. Shook it. "They say I should *terminate* you. This boy is pesky, they say, he knows too much. He'll ruin our fine day. They do not say *how* I should terminate you."

"What fine day? Why is Rattenfänger so interested in Paradise?"

"Rattenfänger *is* Paradise."

Dryden felt his blood slowing down as this picture came together.

Yuri continued: "Rattenfänger backed him. We gave him money to build his machines. We will use his power for our own ends."

"How? Terrorism?" he said. "Holding governments to ransom?"

"Such fine days as this. But he has got above his station. Lost his head. I wonder what will happen to yours."

Dryden watched the vial. "What's Paradise planning to do that Rattenfänger doesn't like?"

"A show of independence, maybe, impress his other investors, break away from his need of us. Or maybe he just likes to gamble. His behavior has become erratic. I was supposed to mind him, but he does not like our company anymore, so he hired you to get rid of us. Now I will show him the error of his ways. Bertie is no great ideas man. We only need his face for the posters. But we would like to have access to his ideas if he is going to be so uncooperative. I don't suppose you know where his ideas are hiding?"

"That's why you're supposed to be interrogating me. You think MI6 knows Zofia Nowak's whereabouts."

Another sulking shrug. "They think Zofia knows how to turn Bertram's big machines on and off. They want access to Celestial. I don't care so much."

"Why not just ask Luke?"

"Bertie cares for him. I have been told to keep Bertie agreeable if I can. But not you. Are you ready?" He opened his hand, and began to tilt his palm.

"Wait! That suit's been lying in the desert for decades! I can see at least a dozen holes in it! Do you want to die too?"

His hand wavered. The domed head wagged. "Perhaps you are right." He levered himself up. Squeezed between the chairs. The gun landed on Dryden's shoulder. "I will watch from outside. Goodnight, 004."

The vial fell. Had it broken? Yuri seemed to think so. The door closed.

TWENTY-FOUR

Revelation

Ibrahim's voice: "Get out of there as quickly as you can."

Aisha's voice: "Dryden? You've got to move."

Dryden laughed. Blood bubbled at his lips. No shit.

Another jolt through his body.

Dryden sprang to his feet, stepping over the vial, kicking the door, grabbing Yuri by the oxygen tube snaking from his helmet. It came loose, flapping and hissing. The gun went off, puncturing the hull. The shuttle sank another foot. Dryden grabbed Yuri's forearm, hurling him against the side, attempting to force him to drop the weapon. Another shot blazed across his cheek and ear, booming in his head. Dryden tore at Yuri's helmet. The thing came off. The door to the cockpit was swinging open and shut—was anthrax sighing into the air? Dryden grabbed the loose oxygen tube and strung it around Yuri's neck. Yuri's gloved hand jabbed at his eyes and mouth. Dryden wrapped the tube around Yuri's neck again and again, like stringing lights on a Christmas tree. Yuri was turning purple. His tongue appeared, a gorged rat. Dryden yanked. Yuri sagged to the floor. The gun spun away. Dryden picked it up. One bullet left.

The shot rang through the hangar, disturbing the pigeons that had just resettled.

Dryden left Yuri to rot in the space shuttle. He dropped onto the concrete. Blood blinded him, coursing down his neck, mixing with sweat under his shirt. His skull was pounding. Dryden sat on the floor, hanging his head between his knees.

Then the sliding doors creaked open. Luke entered, weapon ready. Paradise was at his shoulder.

Dryden wasn't sure whether to surrender or expect applause.

Luke lowered the weapon and hurried to his side. He knelt down. "I picked up the distress call. Shit, man—you've looked better. Where's Yuri?"

Dryden jerked his thumb at the shuttle.

Paradise picked his way around the mess to the shuttle, standing beneath the open hatch. He took a whiff, as if trying to drink in the smell of Yuri's death.

"Don't breathe too deep," said Dryden. "Possible anthrax exposure." He gripped Luke's hand. "You can't be here."

"All right," said Luke. He looked up at Paradise. "Sir, we have to leave, it's not safe for you."

Paradise swiveled on the spot. There was a long beat as he took in the sight of Luke with his arm around Dryden. A line deepened between his eyebrows. Then he nodded.

Fatigue rolled through Dryden's body, an incoming tide drawing him under. He was sprawled across the back seat of a UAZ-469. A strip of cloth masked his mouth in case of infection. Luke was driving. Paradise was studying him, twisted in his seat. Dryden wasn't sure if it was the muscle relaxer or the brain stimulations or the bullet that had nearly cracked his head open or any number of other injuries, physical and otherwise. Maybe it was the sensation of safety, the picture of Luke making entry with his weapon drawn, Luke backing him up like old times. But all he wanted to do was fall asleep. Paradise shook his knee.

"Thank you." Paradise's voice was precise, the words as precise as cut glass. "You performed your duty admirably."

Dryden glanced at the back of Luke's head. "What was that duty, Mr. Paradise?"

"Sir Bertram." A clap on the knee. "Don't worry, Joe. We're all friends here. Yuri represented an evil trying to steal from me. You've saved Cloud Nine. We'll get you medical attention immediately. Make sure none of those nasty spores got inside."

"You need to decontaminate the hangar. There are locals, people who might . . ." Another wave of fatigue rolled over him. The sun was high, a constant beat. Wind iced his joints.

"What a hero," said Paradise.

After the launch, when the journalist Elena Ilić got home to Sarajevo, it was in the blue haze between night and day; she dropped her bags on the living room floor, stripped off, and scrubbed every inch of her body. Then she fell asleep in her towel, collapsed horizontally across the bed. The familiar harmony of the muezzin's call to prayer and church bells told her she was waking up at home. Elena wrapped herself in a dressing gown, filled the copper *džezva*, and put it on the stove. Then she went to retrieve her phone and laptop from her bag. Her bag was gone. A chill riveted Elena to the spot. The water began to boil. She checked the hall, the cupboard, the bedroom. The coffee frothed to the top. She called her mother on the landline and asked if she'd used her key to come in and tidy; she cast cushions off the sofa; shoved the table aside. Knocked on her neighbor's door. The *džezva* overflowed, flooding the stove, dripping onto the tiles. She called the police. They told her she was imagining things. She called her editor.

He said, You win some, you lose some. These people are telling you they can walk in and out of your home when they wish. You lost this one. She asked him: But who are *they*? A cigarette-cough chuckle. Who they've always been. Be grateful you are alive.

"Are you there? Is anybody there?"

A damp cloth soothed his forehead.

"Luke?"

The beads of water threaded through Dryden's eyebrows and slipped over his eyelids. Dryden raised a hand. Fingers folded around his wrist, and returned his hand to the mattress.

"Luke isn't here," said Paradise. "And neither is anyone else."

Dryden opened his eyes. He was in the Cosmonaut Hotel. Bundled in the peach sheets. The stretch of floor where he and Luke had lain together was now occupied by Paradise, who'd drawn a chair up to the bed. Paradise wrung out the damp cloth onto the carpet, a darkening puddle. Dryden felt his face—butterfly tape crawled over his cheek and ear.

"I'm afraid your lungs are completely healthy," said Paradise. "Yuri wasn't much of a chemist."

"Afraid?" Dryden croaked.

Paradise beamed. "Luke is arranging our departure. Such a good boy. I never had a son, but if I had I would have wanted him to possess Luke's loyalty. My own father never cared for my loyalty. My father, my grandfather, my great-grandfather—these petty tycoons traded stakes in precious mines and slave labor as if possessing a pit in the ground mattered." Spit flecked his bottom lip. "My fathers had *very small* imaginations. They pushed the planet to the brink for banks and statues. They didn't know the meaning of the word 'profit.' My fortune will last *forever*, a cloud that will cocoon me while the seas boil. I don't mean to *live up to* my father. I mean to outdo him."

"With Rattenfänger's backing," said Dryden, trying to keep his voice steady.

Paradise caught his breath, wiped his brow. "Luke will be with me to enjoy the spoils. He's so much more than the army made of him. So much more than you made of him."

"He's a decorated soldier."

Paradise scratched behind his ear. "He was. After I discovered his connection to a Double O and realized his potential value for the future, I encouraged him to discard those medals, to wear a different insignia. Mine. They were only weighing him down, relics from a life that left him begging on the streets until I saved him. I suppose you still keep your medals in a drawer so you can polish them when you feel lonely and purposeless?"

"I have purpose." Dryden mirrored Paradise's hand, feeling his right ear. The implant was buried beneath it. It must still be working, despite the knocks. He was processing sounds fine. Just fine. His stomach tightened.

"You're a remote-controlled gadget that I wouldn't buy a child for Christmas." This was delivered lightly, almost pleasantly. "You've been hearing voices, haven't you, Joe?"

Dryden's fingers stilled at his ear.

"It's terrible, how the trauma of war leaves men such as you scarred mentally. Imagining you're a spy and there are friendly chirrups in your head telling you what to do. A pity really. You did me a great favor, removing Yuri from the equation. It was what I hoped you'd achieve and you did so with rather messy aplomb, but still—you got the job done. Bravo. I knew I could count on a Double O."

"How could you know who I am?"

"Celestial makes Q look like something from the back pages of an Argos catalogue. I encouraged Luke to bring you into the fold, though he was none the wiser. I hoped the famous Double O section could get Rattenfänger off my back. And you're all doing a fine, *fine* job. But I can't have you transmitting all our little chats home, Joe. No more secret conversations. Your parents should have taught you that it's rude to talk behind your host's back. An ingenious device, really. I have control of Celestial from here, and I was able to adjust your implant using the same remote surgery techniques your Q Branch employs. I've kept your hearing working. Don't want to upset Luke too much. But no more transmissions, no more gossiping."

"Luke would never go along with whatever mad scheme you've cooked up."

"Wouldn't he? *Behold, he cometh with clouds; and every eye shall see him, and they also which pierced him: and all kindreds of the earth shall wail because of him.* Perhaps Luke wants to be on the winning side for once. I have written upon him my name."

"*And he laid hold on the dragon, that old serpent, which is the Devil,*" said Dryden, "and beat the fuck out of him."

Paradise tutted. "I could trade Revelations with you all day, son, but I've a boxing match to attend, one last stop on my goodwill tour in full face of the press where Rattenfänger cannot reach me. And then I have a sea to burn."

"That's what you're planning?"

Paradise laid a mock hand over his mouth. "I've said too much."

"Have you told Luke who I am?"

Paradise sidestepped that. "I'm still deciding what to do with you. Perhaps send you to a better hospital. Luke would respect that. But I know Rattenfänger will only try and claim me now I've shrugged off their minder. They will not stop. And I do not want to lose Luke. Cannon fodder, food for powder—these are not celebrated terms, but they are transparent descriptions of how we've utilized men and women from our colonies in every war. You could provide me with that service now."

"Empire's over. I'm not fighting for you."

"Is it?" Paradise sighed. "I suppose you were never educated about the human zoos deep into the twentieth century—people from British, French, and Belgian colonies exhibited in model villages at world's fairs, children fed through bars, a man displayed in a cage in the Bronx with apes. Of course, it's considered abhorrent now. I consider it an honest expression of our complete disregard for the dignity of others. Human rights are a construct. It's all a game." A shrug. "Double O might mean the house wins in American roulette, but this is *my* house. And the house always wins."

"That man in the Bronx, his name was Ota Benga and he shot himself through the heart."

"So there is some knowledge other than your master's voice rattling around in that head of yours." Paradise stretched. A slice of light, punctured by the corpses of flies trapped in the window, speckled his legs and glinted from his watch face. "You let them experiment on you like you're a monkey."

Dryden sat up. Paradise flinched.

Dryden smiled. "If you're trying to rile me, you're going to have to come up with something more original than that. You're nothing new, *son.*"

Paradise swallowed, then gave a little laugh. "Then I take it you're not calculating how quickly you could snap my neck?"

"Want to bet?" said Dryden—and then moved faster than he ever had in his life, his hands finding Paradise's throat. The door banged open. Paradise's six-man security team fanned into the room, rifles raised. Poulain, the leader, was holding a phone. Its strobing screen drew Dryden's attention as Paradise flushed beet red in his grip.

"I did some experimenting myself," croaked Paradise. "I hacked the stream to Q using Celestial and gave you a little upgrade."

"One swipe," said Poulain, "your brain fries."

Dryden looked down at Paradise, contorted between the chair

and the bed, saliva frothing at his mouth. Then back at Poulain, whose thumb was hovering over the screen. What were the odds it was true? Was it even possible? He studied Paradise's eyes, which were veining red. Yes, this was the madman who'd use the device in his head to fry him. And he'd enjoy it, too.

Dryden let go. Paradise flopped to the carpet. He was laughing.

TWENTY-FIVE

In Search of an Honorable Man

Moneypenny drove with the top down, threading the frayed edge between a soft sky and the chalky folds and gashes of the Sussex Downs. The bite of frost kept her awake. It had been a long night. After returning from Mary Ann Russell's house, Moneypenny had paid a visit to Records, keeping one eye on 003 and 009's progress at Paddington Green. She placed a call to M, then to Felix Leiter, who was dodging her. It had been early morning by the time she reached Holly Lodge Estate, a block of mock-Tudor villas in northwest London made even more façade-like because Mrs. Keator lived there in the guise of a forgotten retiree among nuclear families whose jobs didn't involve any actual nuclear material. Mrs. Keator was waiting for her on the doorstep, and announced they'd take a turn around Highgate Cemetery, whose tree line was a smudge over the chimneypots.

Mrs. Keator breathed heavily through her nose, the only sound to break the hush, and Moneypenny knew better than to rush the master. So she stopped to pay homage to George Eliot and Claudia Jones and to enjoy the birds. When they passed Patrick Caulfield's grave—the letters D E A D descending cutouts in a stepped slab of stone—Mrs. Keator said there at least was someone with an admirable regard for reality. Moneypenny nodded, aware that the monument to Karl Marx waited up ahead with its exhortation that the philosophers have only interpreted the world in various ways: the point however is to change it. But Mrs. Keator was clutching a jam jar filled with water and sprigs of holly, and Moneypenny knew where they were heading. The headstone of Major Boothroyd, who had lived on the Archway Road in a block of flats that shared his vintage. Moneypenny had visited the Major just once for scotch in a narrow kitchen. The wilderness of the cemetery was clipped neatly around the grave. Mrs. Keator winced as she bent down, and Moneypenny helped her place the jar beneath the words "A Life in Service."

Moneypenny bowed her head.

"Out with it then."

A small smile. "You told me that Tanner acted like he had no idea we'd had prior contact with Yuri, or Michael Dobra, as he styled himself then. But Bill was the case officer when Mary Ann Russell and Bond debriefed about meeting Yuri. Russell asserts that Yuri asked Bond to join Rattenfänger in its infancy. That information is missing from the report."

Mrs. Keator shot Moneypenny a scouring look. "Pedestal unsteady, is it?"

Moneypenny returned the glare. "If Bond were a double agent, I'd be the first to put a bullet between his eyes. If we could find him. I want to know why Tanner's redacting files and withholding information that could have benefited my agent in the field. You've worked with him since the days when you both could sleep well." Moneypenny looked at the headstone. "So did the Major. What can you tell me?"

"Why not ask M?"

"You're already out on this limb with me."

Mrs. Keator sighed, hacked out a cough, then blew her nose noisily, shaking out the handkerchief—all motions, Moneypenny knew, to frustrate her interlocutor in the hopes they'd stop bothering her. Moneypenny waited. Eventually Mrs. Keator shook her head.

"Bill Tanner is an honorable man, without nearly so many chinks in his armor as your James Bond, who was running on fumes before he was captured—if he *was* captured, and didn't defect."

"I'm not arguing."

"Good. Keep it that way. And keep this for what it's worth, though I tell you it's not worth anything. Bill's been visiting the town of Lewes the second Saturday of every third month. Today, in fact. He doesn't know anyone there, and no one knows him. He's not filed any interests with security. He turns his phone off, bless him. Thinks that means I can't track him. Or perhaps he simply believes he's off-limits."

"How long has this been going on for?"

"First instance when his wife left him five years ago. Then nothing, then intermittent. Increased in recent months. I've looked into it—there's no significance to Lewes."

Moneypenny felt the hairs on the back of her neck stand up. She turned, seeing a family in the drab colors of recent mourning trooping down the lane. She knelt level with Mrs. Keator, damp earth seeping through her woolen slacks. "Bill's wife left him shortly before the first 009 was killed, didn't she?"

Mrs. Keator grunted, then lunged forward unsteadily to grasp Major Boothroyd's headstone. She patted the slab. "Bill Tanner is an honorable man. The Major himself trained him in what matters. Myself and the Major and Sir Miles Messervy—we were tempered by wars, hot and cold. Real wars, not wars on drugs or terror. We built the ramparts behind which this country remains safe. You are our inheritors. We chose you because we thought you competent. We didn't expect you to come snapping at our heels. You are well aware that you have my support, Ms. Moneypenny. But Bill was our first student. Our protégé, before you, or Bond, or the rest of these wet-behind-the-ears Double O's. He is an honorable man."

Now, Moneypenny dropped down into Lewes in search of an honorable man. She drove around the two-platform station with its clapboard sidings and car park. No sign of Tanner's bronze-beige 1984 BMW E23. The railway depot had been converted into a cinema-bar-café, and she took the narrow street at a purr, examining the people sharing small plates in the large windows. No Bill Tanner. Up the slight hill, past a shuttered pub, a record store with posters in the window calling for revolution and advertising Lewes's own currency. She examined the back of a hotel, a once grand spot on the stagecoach now expanded with a prefabricated annex that seemed soggy in the first drops of rain. No Bill Tanner on the balconies, balancing a chair on sagging asbestos tiles in order to relish the white cliffs. Moneypenny remembered Bill's wife painted landscapes.

She turned onto the high street, examining the tidy Queen Anne buildings, the cocktail and craft beer chain, the estate agent, a coffee shop painted in the slate gray that promised hipsters single origin beans. She couldn't see this as the kind of place Bill might move in retirement, or enact a love affair. She drew to a stop behind shoppers at the lights. The county Crown Court was on the right, a Georgian building in cool Portland stone with Doric columns flanked by three reliefs. Moneypenny read their stories from left to right. Wisdom. Justice. Mercy. The lights turned green, and the car ahead peeled off at the foot of the castle. No Bill Tanner ferreting antiquarian books or Baltic ceramics. Something else his wife would like.

Mrs. Keator hadn't been able to pinpoint Tanner's exact location—turning his phone off achieved that much. Moneypenny followed the high street until it was only houses—some real Tudor, some studded in flint, some cottages with bulging bow windows—and wondered where to turn next, the feeling that she'd soon rejoin a main road and merge with the countryside proving true. She paused at a crossroads, glancing down at the map on the screen where once her speedometer had pride of place. Her Majesty's Prison was on the left—a glance up at the foreboding wall only half-hidden by bare trees—and Lewes Victoria Hospital was to the right.

It was then Moneypenny saw Bill Tanner in the forecourt of a garage at the fork. He was climbing out of his car. He looked like he hadn't slept either. Moneypenny beeped her horn. When he saw her car, she thought the color in his cheeks drained a touch, but it could be the graying sky. Moneypenny pulled in.

"Hello, Bill. Car trouble?"

He wiped his forehead. "Scared the life out of me, Penny." He jerked a thumb in the direction of the garage. "Morris is an expert in vintage BMWs. We've been monkeying around with mine."

Moneypenny tapped the window frame of the Jaguar. "Don't trust Ibrahim and his toolbox?"

"That boy's got too many degrees for my liking. What are you doing out here?"

"Looking for you. Do you know this area well?"

"Not much, I'm afraid. Trouble at the office?"

A glance up at the clouds. "Time to put the roof up. Hop in, Bill. Let's go for a spin while Morris does his stuff."

Tanner moved to tug on his tie, but he wasn't wearing one. "You're starting to worry me, Penny."

Moneypenny said, "Better we talk off the books, friend to friend. We are friends, aren't we, Bill?"

He was still hanging on to his open door. "I've always thought so."

"Me too. So get in."

He glanced, almost imperceptibly, at the driver's seat of his own car. Then closed the door, hopped the low wall, and jogged around to Moneypenny's passenger seat as the rain broke.

———

The storm advanced over the Downs, a black line towing thunder. Moneypenny parked on top of the world. The wipers were a metronome to a silent symphony. Each swipe briefly opened a curtain on hundreds of neon-green miles electrified by lightning, and then closed again, dousing Moneypenny and Tanner in darkness.

"Mrs. Keator told me you acted like you had nothing to add to the scant file on Yuri. Now Mary Ann Russell says she and Bond reported it all to you. You were the runner in the field then. Except you're not in the field, you're Chief of Staff, and you haven't run an agent in decades. And it's *my* field."

"Try not to get too upset, old girl."

"Don't call me 'old girl' and I'll remain the picture of equanimity."

He laughed. He was drumming his fingers on the dashboard. The thunder landed a great paw on the roof.

"It's not like you to run off the books, Bill."

"How did you know I'd be out here?"

Moneypenny watched the windscreen wipers: the disclosure, the erasure. "What's out here?"

"I told you."

"Right, seeing a man about a car. Anything else?"

"Why don't you stick Q on me?"

"I intend to."

Bill jerked around. "On whose authority? Have you forgotten I'm your superior?"

"M's authority, mine—take your pick. Unless you want to fill me in now."

He tried to recover the look of shock in his eyes, tried to smooth himself down. "No need for high drama. I didn't remove anything from that file, and I don't recall James or Russell telling me anything much beyond contact had been made."

Moneypenny could smell Tanner's sweat. "And it didn't occur to you to let me know all of this when we looked at Paradise's circle before putting 004 in the field?"

"None of us are unimpeachable."

"Is that a confession?"

Tanner's hand drifted at his throat. "A point clumsily made. You and I both know the number of losses we've suffered recently only points to one thing. A leak. How am I to know who I can trust? You understand that, don't you? After all, you conveniently weren't there when this pass was made at James. Nothing to link to you. You were cleaning up in Vienna, but that wasn't your job. You should have accompanied James to Paris."

Moneypenny surprised herself and him by smiling. A clatter of hail drew her attention to the window. "We're all getting paranoid in our old age."

"Don't lose your equanimity, now."

She stroked her Nanna Ditzel watch and thought of Harwood's watch by Hermès. She said, "James never told me about the approach. I was his runner. He should've alerted me."

Tanner sighed. "Did anybody ever run James?"

Moneypenny's phone vibrated. She drew it from her jacket. Q Branch. She scanned her thumb and swiped Accept.

Tanner was watching her expression closely as she listened for more than a minute, but she betrayed nothing—no surprise or fear, no satisfaction, no fury.

Instead she said simply, "Understood," and hung up. Her gaze swept the land. "004 has gone dark."

TWENTY-SIX

An American in Berlin

Johanna Harwood was sitting outside the Hotel Adlon on the corner of Pariser Platz, in the center of what was once known as the City of Spies. Snow fell softly on the cloth canopy above. The pop-up champagne bar was doing good business, drawing people who'd come to see the Christmas tree as the great columns of the Brandenburg Gate turned gold with the last of sunset. She was using a hotel pen to write a postcard to her mother she knew she would never send, asking her mother if she remembered their trip to Berlin for a conference when Harwood was fifteen. They had one free afternoon together, and her mama brought her to this spot for one scoop of five-star ice cream. It was all they could afford but it felt like magic, becoming real magic when the waitress brought their tap water in flutes, and the one scoop of ice cream adorned with strawberries, two spoons, and a chocolate button stamped with edible gold leaf, reading: HOTEL ADLON. They'd been charged just three euros.

Harwood had spent today pretending to be a tourist. She'd asked for directions at the airport in enjoyably risible German, where she felt eyes on the back of her neck, turning to see a cab driver with a sign bearing a stranger's name. She meandered up Unter den Linden, catching the world rushing by in the windows of car showrooms and department stores, before moving into the window frame herself, settling into a booth in Café Einstein with a perfect view of tourists hunching over their phones to find themselves. Neither Rattenfänger nor Felix Leiter lingered under the trees nor angled their cameras her way. She idled in Ampelmann, a souvenir shop dedicated to the smart men of Berlin's traffic lights, where she bought the postcard of the green man with his hat tipped back and his arm and leg extended, striding forward. She stopped at a Christmas market, examining hand-painted baubles. The seller asked her if she was in Berlin for business or pleasure, and she told him she hoped both. Once she'd paid for a red star, she saw the seller send a text message, and his eyes followed her as she wolfed down a bratwurst, steam coiling from her mouth.

A waiter subtly stamped life into his cold feet next to her. "What can I get for you, please, madame?"

Harwood turned the postcard over. "One scoop of chocolate ice cream, *bitte*."

"It is too cold, madame, surely!"

"Just one scoop, please."

"But to drink, please, madame?"

"A glass of water, *danke*."

"But that is all you want, madame?"

"That's all."

A short and somewhat concerned bow, and the man retreated. Harwood's attention roamed over the banks and embassies crowding Pariser Platz, landing on the American flag. The US embassy was the last building to complete the remodeling of Pariser Platz from days when the sky was always the color of asphalt, and the Prussian wind, sharp as a knife, blew the rubble dust into one's eyes and mouth—Sir Emery's glory days as a Double O. Pariser Platz had fallen onto the Eastern side, Hotel Adlon reduced to three surviving bullet-marked stories and a restaurant done up in beige wallpaper and dusty potted cacti, where Sir Emery had arranged border crossings over thick-grained coffee. The honor of the last hand in the transformation of the center of Berlin had gone to the American government, which had bought a drafty palace on this plot in the thirties. Now, the pale and cautious embassy in monolithic white was separated from the public by a line of waist-high pillars, a buffer zone against car bombs.

Harwood glanced at her enamel Hermès watch by Anita Porchet; the red glow of the halogen heaters sparked against the geometric horses picked out in gold wire and fired in a kiln. Coming up on five p.m. She fixed her sights on the doors beneath the flag, and settled in to wait for Felix Leiter, the CIA's man in Berlin.

She was mildly disappointed. Bond had told her of Leiter's habit, one night in bed when the outside world seemed to no longer exist and Bond was looking both back and forward to what he called *a life after this*. He said Leiter seemed to know when Bond was going to appear, and would tail him, always wanting to get the jump. In New York, when Bond was undercover as a diamond smuggler, James had got that slight tingling in the scalp and an extra awareness of the people around him, enough to make him duck into a shop doorway on Sixth Avenue, only to find someone gripping his pistol arm from behind, and a voice laughing in his ear: "No good, James. The angels have got you." Felix had been front tailing. Another time, Bond checked into his hotel room to find Leiter arranging the flowers by his bed—"Part of the famous CIA 'Service with a Smile.'" So either Leiter had been undaunted by Moneypenny's request for information, and had not anticipated a Double O would be sent to Berlin to work him over when he denied her request, or it was a game he played only with Bond—a game Harwood had hoped to enter, just as she hoped Leiter would transfer his trust of Bond to her, because Bond had trusted her. Oh well. She'd have to try a front tail of her own.

The embassy staff were filing out now, pausing to admire the tree, or organize drinks after work. Harwood looked for Leiter's tall, lean frame, his mop of straw-colored hair streaked with gray. Nothing, though Moneypenny's intelligence had placed him firmly at Pariser Platz.

From the corner of her eye, Harwood saw the waiter approach with a tray in his left hand, though he'd been right-handed just minutes ago. She clicked the pen so the nib was exposed and curled her fingers around it as she would a knife.

"Now help me out here," a voice said, lugubrious and relaxed. "Who's tailing who?"

Harwood twisted and looked up into a hawklike face, the chin and cheekbones sharp, the mouth wry, the ash eyes buried in laughter lines. A trace of scars below the hairline above his right eye. A tan woolen coat hung loosely from his shoulders. His right hand was in his pocket, hiding the prosthetic. Felix Leiter set the tray down: tap water in two flutes, two spoons, a crystal bowl, one scoop of ice cream, strawberries, a chocolate button stamped in gold.

Harwood fingered the heavy ball bearings of her necklace, examining the tray. "You tell me, Mr. Leiter."

"Mind if I take a seat?" he said, his Texas accent surprisingly strong after years of postings abroad.

"I don't know who else is going to use the other spoon."

He pulled out the chair and sat down. She noticed the stiff fold of his left leg.

"Nice afternoon?" he asked.

"A little lonely, now you mention it."

A shrug. "You don't mind me saying, picking that red star from a whole bazaar of angels and Santa Clauses was plain cruel. Don't know how I resisted sending in the marines."

"Didn't you hear—the Cold War's over?"

"Must've missed the memo." He picked up the spoon and played it between his fingers like an expert card shark. "So you're the girl James couldn't stop praising, last time we spoke."

"Could be."

"Apparently you're the real deal."

Harwood picked the leaves from a strawberry. "Could be."

Leiter relaxed into his chair. "Boss sent you, huh?"

"Moneypenny found it hard to believe you'd refuse an old friend."

"Ouch. All right, real deal. What've you got for me?"

It couldn't be that easy. Harwood kept her thoughts from him, focusing on the bowl. "You could tell me something. Did James tell you about the ice cream, or is this the hotel's standard issue?"

"That's what you want to know?"

"That's it."

"Maybe I read the contents of your postcard."

Harwood looked from the card to the flower arrangement at the center of the table, calculating the odds of Leiter reading her handwriting back to front in the reflection of a vase in the dark without her noticing. "No good, Felix."

He laughed. "So maybe James was a lovesick pup and regaled me with tales of your sad youth. Or maybe the hotel staff have a thing for pretty ladies sitting alone."

Harwood pointed her spoon toward the embassy. "Don't suppose you're keeping Dr. Zofia Nowak or Robert Bull in there, are you? We seem to have a missing persons case on our hands."

Leiter made a show of squinting over his shoulder, as if he'd never seen the embassy before in his life. "In there? No."

"But you are stashing one or both of them somewhere?"

"I don't make a habit of stashing the women I date."

"Please, the chief Cousin in Berlin just *happens* to be dating a senior scientist working on privileged climate technology?"

"What, ain't I got the charm?"

"Did she?"

Another laugh. "Suppose we happened to get a whiff of something that downright stinks from Paradise Incorporated, and suppose when he opened up Factory Berlin, I was invited, and suppose that stank even more. Suppose I don't like being a mark. Suppose I saw a way of making the girl a mark without any harm done."

"No harm done? Depends what happened on these dates of yours."

"Hey, I'm no James Bond."

"No," said Harwood. "He wouldn't be sitting here with me eating ice cream when Zofia Nowak is in danger somewhere alone."

"More fool him." Leiter hunched. "Say, our boy eating ice cream anywhere these days, in your books?"

Harwood stroked her watch face. She said softly, "I haven't given up."

Leiter rallied, shaking himself straight. "Tell you what, real deal. How about you watch my tail and I watch yours back to my house. You can grill me some more and I can play dumb. I'm good at that."

Harwood pushed the bowl toward him. All that remained was the chocolate button. "Me too," she said.

"All right then," he said. "Let's go pretend to know nothing together."

TWENTY-SEVEN

The House by the Lake

They rode the S-Bahn southwest to the end of the line. At first it was standing room only, and they hung on to the rail, jostled together between bodies. Berlin was a circuit board of lights, sliding by the windows in strobes. At one point Harwood stumbled and felt Felix's right arm around her, and the smooth alloy of his hand at her waist. She met his eyes, startled by the frankness she found there. Then the golden cubes of city blocks were eaten by patches of darkness that swelled as the train shrugged off the noise and thrum of the capital, seeking out its edges. Leiter and Harwood sat opposite each other on threadbare seats, legs touching. His left knee was cold and hard. She looked through her own reflection to a makeshift and, she imagined, immovable community that straggled along the railway sidings: broken-down caravans, irregular allotments, tin huts, and among it all the dim and slow movement of people caught between history's currents, and perhaps content to be so.

When they stepped onto the platform, the air was crisp with pine. A hand-painted sign in black letter read *Berlin—Wannsee*. They followed a straggle of commuters into an octagonal hall painted in chipped mint green, passing beneath squat capital letters spelling AUSGANG in a futurist typeface washed up from the twenties. Outside, the loudest noise was the wind in the trees. A woman in her twenties with a backpacker air was locking up the station café; she waved and called hello to Felix in an Australian accent. He asked if she needed a lift home.

"I've got my bike, thanks, Felix." The woman wobbled away on a secondhand thing.

Harwood looked Felix up and down. "Service with a smile?"

"Nothing less, ma'am. You mind walking? I get pent up behind a desk."

She fell in with him, smelling the lake hidden by the regiment of trees. "How did you end up out here?"

"Let's say I miss a big sky."

Felix Leiter lived in a Gothic redbrick villa on the eastern shore of Wannsee lake, with the Grunewald forest pressing in to the north. Harwood eased from her boots and dropped her yellow canvas roll-top bag on a deep sofa—reading in the rental furnishings, the one rumpled chair, the game of solitaire on the coffee table, a more singular existence than she'd imagined—and passed to an arched window, hoping to sense the water. Nothingness stretched before her.

"Hell of a view in the morning," said Leiter, flicking through a stack of vinyl on the floor.

She shot him a smile. "That an invitation?"

A one-shouldered shrug as he dropped the needle of the record player. "Play your cards right." An old jazz number Harwood didn't recognize crackled through the speakers. "Let's see, what's for dinner . . ."

They shared an omelet at the kitchen counter, bent over the plate head-to-head, as if their two ice cream spoons had conjured a lifelong comradery. Leiter was open about his role in Berlin, trying to patch up the diplomatic hash left by his predecessor, who'd been summarily banished by Angela Merkel after being discovered tapping her phone. But Harwood was struck by the tightrope of his generosity—though he told her much, none of it was information she couldn't glean from her own intelligence reports. Afterward, he lit a fire, and opened up a cabinet to reveal a small cocktail bar. Harwood sat on the floor with her back against the coffee table. She stretched her legs out to the hearth, warming her cold toes. She made sure her dress did not ride over her knees. She watched the tension play over Leiter's shoulders as he poured himself a Haig on the rocks and then turned to her.

"What'll you have?"

"Would it break your heart," she said, "if I ordered a vodka martini, shaken not stirred?"

"Only a little," he said, and the smile reached his eyes. "Let's see. Three measures of Gordon's, one of vodka, half a measure of Kina Lillet. I forget anything?"

"Only the lemon twist."

Leiter clicked his fingers. "And a lemon twist. He really is the fussiest sumbitch I ever knew."

Harwood watched Leiter assemble the drink, seeing how he used his right hand, which gleamed white, to grip but not much else. He was avoiding her eyes. She said, "You knew Vesper, too."

He scratched his chin. "I was there when he met her and christened the drink," said Leiter. "I was there when she betrayed him over matters of the heart. He never knew when to fall in love. And when not to." He handed the glass to her, hitched his trousers, and joined her on the floor. "Let's skip the toast, I'll only promise you my soul."

Harwood sipped the martini, resisting the thousand memories that went with it to look Leiter squarely in the face. "Do you think I betrayed James, too?"

A short shrug. "James doesn't have many weaknesses. As the years went on, those weaknesses became fewer and fewer. But it's weakness that makes us human. Forces us to acknowledge our own mortality. I told him to quit. Told him this lousy job stinks. You know what it stinks of? Formaldehyde and lilies. And I thought he might quit, too.

But then you came along, and he knew weakness again, but it didn't make him cling to hearth and home. It only spurred him on."

Another sip. She thought back to James's fantasy of *a life after this*. She believed, in the early days, that he meant a life after retirement from active duty once he'd passed forty-five. Then she realized that his fantasy—which he'd make real in brief escapes—of a house on the beach with her wasn't a retirement plan. It was just a place for them to quit the world when it was sunny and he wanted to forget, a refuge for the next few years he expected to be alive. He couldn't imagine quitting for good. Only dying. 007 was a tragedy waiting to happen—if the tragedy hadn't happened already, long before she ever met him. Anybody attached to James Bond would end up mourning him, and she couldn't bear to be his last witness. She'd done that already in her life. She wanted someone who could dream of the future and mean it.

"And here's a coincidence," said Felix, drawing her back. "I wasn't the only operative trailing you today. I was shadowed by a couple of hale and hearty types with the look of eastern European mercs. So you tell me, Johanna Harwood, what's an old spy to think?"

"You tell me."

Leiter's jaw pulsed. "Jury's still out. If I thought *you* were the reason I'm down a friend . . ." He stared into the fire. "Well, let's just say I don't have any neighbors, and the lake is deep."

"If you're trying to scare me"—she set the glass down—"you're doing a terrific job."

"I don't imagine much scares you."

Harwood grabbed the poker, nudging a log deeper into the flames. "What was Zofia scared of?"

"You favor a blunt interrogation, huh?"

"I'm on the clock till midnight. Then we can try soft."

"Don't make promises you don't intend to keep, my mom always said."

"She must have been thrilled when you went into the deception racket."

"Was yours?"

Harwood leaned back, keeping hold of the poker. She raised it aloft a little. "I could fence with you all week, Felix Leiter, if the fate of the world didn't hang in the balance."

"You Double O's, always so dramatic. I got on fine with Zofia. Kind of girl anyone would get on fine with. Hyper-smart. Not strictly present in the here and now. But only 'cause her mind's doing bigger and better things. How can you resent her for that, when she's gunning for the angels and she wears her optimism on her sleeve where anyone can take a poke at it? An old spy like me gets a hankering for that kind of disposition. Comes over sort of protective. Guess that's why she confided in me about Robert Bull, private citizen of the United States of America and the Paradise Republic, security expert with a rap sheet for stalking and sexual assault in a former life, now expunged from the records. Curious company for Paradise."

"Did you see it coming?"

"Not soon enough. My order to put Bull under surveillance was going to come into effect the morning after Zofia stopped answering her phone. Let me tell you something, 003. It means something when the CIA can't find a person."

"Did you find Robert Bull?"

"The Berlin police arrested him at a hospital around the corner from her apartment. Nurses called it in. Blood on his clothes and under his fingernails, most of it not his. A damaged right orbital socket. Guess Zofia got in a punch or two."

Harwood wanted to ask whether or not Leiter had left Robert Bull in the custody of the police or disappeared him into a CIA black hole. But it would be too soon. He was dancing with her, and the rhythm was his. She raised her glass. "I'm dry."

"Can't have that."

One more drink, then two. His shoulders relaxed. When the fire began to struggle, he dropped a hefty block of wood into the embers, and the rush of red glowed over his face, shading a deep frown between his eyes. She wondered if he was not simply alone but lonely. Down a friend.

She asked, "How much does it mean, Felix, when the CIA can't find a person?"

Felix drummed the fingers of his left hand on the back of his right, a hard patter. "Believe me, I've put every informer from every circle of hell on the search for James. Nothing."

"How do you explain that?"

A short laugh. "I tell myself that James finally took my advice and is enjoying a permanent vacation on some tropical island beyond the scope of Langley or London or anywhere. It's either that or cry into my whisky, and I was taught by my daddy's belt never to do that. Matter of fact, James is the only person ever to see me bawl. Visited me in the hospital after . . ." He raised his right arm.

The chill that Harwood first felt when Bond described discovering the shape of a body on Leiter's hotel bed returned to her. The shape had been covered in a sheet. When Bond snatched the shroud from the face, there was no face. Just something wrapped round and round with dirty bandages, like a white wasps' nest. More bandages wrapped around the torso, blood seeping through. The lower half of the body was draped in a sack; the sack was mostly empty. Everything was soaked in blood. A piece of paper protruded from the gap in the bandages where the mouth should have been, like a thank-you card sticking out among a bunch of lilies. The card read: HE DISAGREED WITH SOMETHING THAT ATE HIM. As Bond recalled sitting on the edge of the bed waiting for the paramedics, watching over the body of his friend and wondering how much of it could be saved, there was a quietness rarely heard in his voice, as if he were back in the hotel room, enjoined in the wait for death.

She said gently: "Anyone would cry."

Felix gave her a brief smile. "Worse things happen at sea." Then he broke into laughter that blew through the room like a gale, sweeping Harwood up in it. But his gaze lost its focus, seeming to watch the scene from a great distance. "You want to know the meaning of terror, try the moment a great white bumps into your legs with all the weight of a tank, and you know it's just getting started. I thought I was gone for sure. Wrestling with sharks might make a good story for parties in Washington, but I'd rather have the sunken pirate treasure and a pretty girl to tell about. James gets all the luck." He inspected his drink. "He was there when I came to. Holding the hand I had left. That's a good parlor trick he's got. Just when you need a friend . . ."

"I haven't given up. Neither's Moneypenny."

"You haven't gotten married, either. James told me the fella's a genius."

Harwood found a hearty tone. "He likes to think he is."

"Still, not smart enough to watch his partner's back."

"It wasn't Sid's fault, whatever happened to James." Harwood's hand floated to the pocket of her dress, to her silenced phone, wondering how Sid was getting on with Ruqsana trying to trace Zofia's last movements on the other side of Berlin. They'd said goodbye at the edge of the Barbican, a lingering kiss in the snow, and then boarded separate planes. "James told Sid he was going to check a lead by himself and would be back soon."

"That's how you get eaten by sharks," said Leiter, knocking back his drink. "I was posted here because I lost my gun hand and I can't run a man down anymore. This is my reward. A house by the lake. A game of spies. Now you've come to play a hand, you and your boyfriend. You put him outta the way so you can bat your eyelashes at me. Why should I trust either of you? Bashir failed to follow basic protocol and let his partner follow a lead alone. He was the last person to see James alive. James told me he hoped to meet up with you, the famous real deal, after that mission for a last goodbye. Good money says one or both of you sold James down the river."

"Are you a gambling man, Felix?"

"Less and less."

"Say you get me access to Robert Bull, say I interrogate him, if I'm a double agent—or whatever it is you think I am—you can follow what I do with that information and then you'll have all the proof you need that I'm either a traitor, or an ally. If you stop me now, we lose any chance of finding Zofia and discovering whatever it is that Paradise has gotten himself into."

"Pretty confident of your interrogation skills."

"Did you think you'd end tonight by telling me you cried when you woke up in the hospital?"

He scratched his chin. "Can't say I did." Leiter's attention traveled to the poker, lying on the floor at her fingertips. "Can't say I haven't noticed you've kept yourself armed most of the evening, too."

A *tap-tap-tap* on the windows announced rain.

"You don't have any neighbors," said Harwood, "and the lake is deep. A woman takes her precautions. Besides, that list of people James trusts, the list of people *you* think might have lulled him into a false sense of security before his fall—that list includes you, Felix."

Flares spread across his cheeks. "You think I'd do him a lousy turn?"

"No." Harwood slid the poker away. "I'm trusting you. Why don't you give it a try?"

TWENTY-EIGHT

Running with Scissors

Mauerpark Flohmarkt. A Sunday morning in December.

Anya, a T-shirt designer, was watching her young daughter craft a perfect snowball. She shouted at her to clean her hands—that's dirty with the mess of people's boots—and then switched to English for the American tourists admiring her hammer and sickle print. Dropping the shimmering patty, her daughter stumbled between the metal legs of the table and careened toward the next stall, where two Turkish brothers with matching guts and balding heads sat side by side in green plastic chairs, ears brushing as thoughts slipped from one to the other, blankly observing the freaks and *Lebenskünstlers* bargaining for their Polaroids and Box Brownies. The brothers were immovable. Samuel and Erich, who ran a nearby café and took the free time afforded by Sunday closure laws to shop for retro china, knew the brothers were immovable and waited for the hipster ahead to give up haggling. They bought the Polaroid, loading a new revival film. Umbrellas popped like spring bulbs on a time-lapse video. Mrs. Linz tipped the contents of her attic on a long trestle table, tutting at hungover students squealing over her husband's junk—GDR memorabilia, typewriter ribbon, stamps, the genuine jewelry he'd never shown her . . .

Sid Bashir was distracted by this, something tugging at him, and so didn't see when Ruqsana Choudhury tapped her card on a seller's phone—forgetting, in the sting of bitter rain, his injunction to use cash only—and bought a Fisher-Price telephone for her daughter. Bashir bought a dozen Austrian stamps with the change from his pocket.

He'd persuaded Ruqsana to join him in Berlin in the hope that Dr. Zofia Nowak's tight-lipped friends would talk to another friend of Zofia's. Bashir had peeled off from Harwood because she said she could work her magic with Felix Leiter better alone. Bashir didn't want to analyze what that magic might involve—not from possessiveness, but because it was this adaptability of hers that made M suspicious, and each success seemed only to damn her further.

Ruqsana shook the toy so the goggle eyes cast a sidelong glance at Sid. "Remember these?"

"Hope won't even know what that is," he said, dinging the rotary dial.

Ruqsana lifted the telephone to his ear as the ring purred. "Your conscience is calling, it wants a refund."

"Tell it I'm busy saving the world for Western democracy and low petrol prices."

She nestled the toy into her bag, wondering how her mum was coping with Hope. "And you're doing a bang-up job. None of Zofia's other friends or colleagues know anything. And her neighbor looked at us like we were casing the joint."

Bashir peered at her over tortoiseshell glasses. He said, "That your spy talk?"

It was news to her that he wore glasses. He looked like Omar Sharif in one of those old films they used to watch. "I'd make a great spy," she said.

"Why's that?" He lingered by a stall where surgical tools were laid out on a black cloth. Picking up a dentist's mirror, he angled it this way and that. The sensor embedded in the screw of his glasses, which transmitted information to Q, had just sent an alert to his phone, which now buzzed three times in his pocket—there were electronic surveillance devices nearby.

"Well, as a for instance, I know you and that lawyer, Johanna Harwood, aren't just colleagues."

Bashir chose a pair of surgical scissors and dug a note from his wallet. "Jealous?"

"Mum will be. She maintains you and I are destined for each other."

"She's maintained that since we were six years old," he said, clacking the mirror and scissors together.

"She has staying power."

He laughed, leading her crosscurrent to the next row. She noticed he kept the scissors in his hands, pointing up, and recalled the way he used to walk so carefully with the little red safety scissors of their classroom, the blades pointed to the floor. She was always running.

Then Ruqsana bumped into a little girl at knee height, snot stringing between her fingers, a graze on her wrist. Ruqsana squatted down, saying hello, putting one arm around the girl's shoulders, as a woman appeared above her amidst a violent stream of Russian, and scooped the child up.

"How much for the hammer and sickle?" said Bashir.

Ruqsana tried to hide her blanch, realizing they'd found the T-shirt stall they were looking for, though Bashir's wandering had seemed aimless.

Anya, the designer, sought the protection of the table and glared at him, not really because of anything Bashir had said or done, but because her heart was still hammering at losing sight of her daughter. "Twenty."

"Nice designs."

"*Ja, ja.* You want it?"

"Do you have a women's fit?"

"Unisex."

"Let me guess," said Ruqsana. "Johanna Harwood appreciates irony?"

Bashir grinned. "Not really. Do you have a business card?"

Anya stuffed the T-shirt in a paper bag, and thrust a card his way.

"D'you think you could draw us a map on here?"

"You don't have Google?" said Anya.

"Out of data," said Bashir.

"What you want?"

Bashir hunched over the stall, as if to watch her draw on the card. "You were taking English language classes with Zofia Nowak. Don't look up. Zofia hasn't been attending classes because she's in trouble. Your tutor said the two of you had got friendly, but there's no trace of your friendship online. We think that made you safe, to her. No one knows you exist."

Anya hissed: "What is this?"

"We need to know where she is. Her life is in danger."

The little girl was crying again. Ruqsana pulled the Fisher-Price telephone from her bag and shook it so all the bells and dials trilled at once. The girl's squeals turned to giggles. Ruqsana murmured, "My name's Ruqsana Choudhury. Did Zofia ever mention me?"

Slowly: "How do I know you are who you say?"

Ruqsana slid her phone from her pocket, keeping it low, and opened up the photo of her and Zofia.

"Please," said Bashir, "the longer we stand here the more danger you're in."

"Then leave!"

"Zofia needs our help."

Anya blew out her cheeks, then stabbed her pen twice on the card, leaving no mark, until the ink spurted out and she wrote one word. "There. Now go. Get away from me."

"*Danke*," said Bashir, dropping the card into the bag. He put his arm around Ruqsana. "Let's find some lunch."

Bashir steered them down the alley of stalls, aiming for the eastern side of the park, which was blank with snow, but still busy: a reggae drumming circle; a performance troupe with more piercings than he'd ever seen on a set of people; locals and tourists snaking between them. He wanted to use the crowds to get across the park and then disappear, but the flea market was too congested, they weren't moving at all. He glanced down at the dentist's mirror, clutched in his left hand. The scissors were in his right, and he tightened his grip on them when the mirror caught sight of two military-aged males, white, shaved heads, civvy clothes with combat boots, both with their eyes locked on the back of his head.

"What's wrong?" said Ruqsana.

"Do you remember the way back to the station from here?"

"What?"

"The station—you remember the way?"

"Yes."

"I want you to follow me to the fragment of the Berlin Wall at the top of the hill. You've never seen it before. You're fascinated. We're going to walk to the far end. You're going to stand on the eastern side while I'm on the west. I tell you to, you're going to run for the station. Find a police officer, ask to be taken to the American embassy. Once you're there, speak only to Felix Leiter. OK?"

Ruqsana felt a bewildering calm come upon her, as if the whole world had narrowed to the foot on either side of her, to Sid's reassuring voice, to the way his knuckles shone redly with the grip on the scissors, to the thump of her heart in her ears. Her throat was very dry. She hadn't noticed that before. OK, Sid, she said, except it didn't make it out of her mouth. OK, show me your fragment. That's interesting, Sid, why was Mauerpark known as "the death strip" during the Cold War? Because this stretch of ground ran between two parallel concrete walls that together made up the Berlin Wall. Now it's a three-hundred-meter-long graffiti wall. His eyes were trailing the Wall at head height, as if he had X-ray vision, and could see ghosts haunting him on the other side, or atoms mirroring his movements across the universe—metaphors and similes jumbled up in Ruqsana's mind, as she remembered a quiz in primary school in which they were instructed to spot the difference between the two: the sun *is* a penny, and the sun is *like* a penny. Ruqsana couldn't work it out, she was only just learning English then, and Sid gave her the answers. Now Sid gave her history, moving her fingertips to brush the neon paint. Yes, look at that, I'm touching history. You better go on the west side, Sid, you're the dirty capitalist, I'm the dreamer. What's that, Sid? Run? OK, Sid, I'll run.

She set off, the bag with the Fisher-Price telephone bashing against her thigh, *ring-ring-ring*. She took one look over her shoulder as she sprinted in a curving arc down the hillside, one look that afforded a glimpse of the western side, where what she saw was computed in flashes: Sid and a man who reminded her of a club bouncer hugging in the shadow of the Wall; Sid's arm moving in short, swift jabs; and each jab produced a bloom of blood, as if Sid were piercing a balloon filled with red paint, a project Ruqsana and Sid worked on for a science class, she couldn't remember the science behind it, something about the amount of time it took for the paint to slump out and the balloon to deflate, which the man was doing, sagging over Sid's frantic arm—all that in a microsecond, but there was no time to process it now, because another man with the same look of a club bouncer was bursting from the market and charging her way.

Ruqsana saw the open expanse of park before her, beyond the drummers and the artists. The man was catching up. She didn't want to cross that great blank with him behind her, to leave the crowd of people and head toward the desolate Sunday emptiness of the streets around the station. So she zigzagged, a feint that the man fell for, stumbling in the snow, as she sprinted back toward the market, your best sprint now, Ruqsana, a relay race with Sid, records to keep at sports day—and yes, she'd made it, into the comforting thicket of oblivious people.

Samuel and Erich, the café owners, steadied Ruqsana as she bowled into them, the flash of Erich taking a Polaroid swallowing them all. They asked if she was OK, bending to pick up her bag. Ruqsana realized she was crying and hid her face in her hands. Erich put his arms around her, a confused laugh as he said—Not to worry, there there . . .

It was Samuel who realized that the paroxysm of Ruqsana's shoulders was too extreme for tears. He pulled Erich away, saying—She is having a seizure!

Anya heard this cut through the crowd. She swung her daughter onto the lap of one of the Turkish brothers, and elbowed her way past these idiots holding her up. She was a few feet from the Indian woman—the rude man had called her Ruqsana—when every nerve she had screamed at her: *stop*. A man who reeked of secret police was stooping over Ruqsana, telling the surging onlookers she was epileptic and they must find her bag. Anya scoured the ground. There was the silly telephone lying in the snow, giving a merry ding every time someone kicked it. But the rude, insistent Indian man had put Anya's card in his own shopping bag. Anya glanced back at the secret policeman and saw a needle peeking from his fist. He'd injected Ruqsana with something.

Anya darted down one lane, then the next, seizing Mrs. Linz: Did you see an Indian man . . . The hoarder's widow gave a heavy shrug. Anya swore, staring east, then west, until she heard a scream from the selfie trap—her name for what was left of the Berlin Wall. Anya started up the hill, slipping and struggling, until she saw a glint of plastic in the gray snow. The Indian man had thrown the bag toward an overflowing bin, not cleared since yesterday. Anya snatched at it: the stupid T-shirt, the card with the incriminating word. Around the bin, the usual mountain of beer bottles, left out by idealists for homeless people, who would collect them and earn some money from the recycling plant. Anya ripped the card up into twenty pieces, and posted each one into a different bottle.

When Anya finally straightened, a stream of people were flooding from the Wall toward her. She called out to them: "What do you see?"

She was told there was a fight, one man stabbed another, then they were both shoved into a van!

Anya twisted around, searching for sight of Ruqsana, but she was gone too, and so was the secret policeman.

Where Ruqsana had stood, there was now only Samuel, looking around for the Polaroid picture he'd dropped, and Erich, holding the Fisher-Price telephone aloft in puzzlement, as if expecting someone to answer its call.

TWENTY-NINE

Barbican Redux

Wannsee lake was a sheet of marbled paper, gold running into green, stirring softly as an invisible hand urged the inks first this way toward the grand villas opposite, from which smoke curled languidly, and then that, to the distant shoreline marked by puffs of trees. The mist cleared through the forest and the sky controlled its blushes, fading pink to blue. Harwood walked the edge back to the main road, messaging the information she'd gleaned from Leiter to Moneypenny. She clicked her neck, sore after a night on the sofa. Felix Leiter really was no James Bond. Traffic was light, but still she watched the progress of a rental BMW in the windows of parked cars. The station café was open for commuters. The Australian backpacker was arranging pastries on a glass shelf at the cabinet. Harwood asked the barista what Leiter normally ordered.

"Filter coffee. Make that two?"

"Espresso for me. And a doughnut." She imagined Leiter's grimace when she returned with the sixth food group of American policemen. "Beautiful place."

"Isn't it?" said the woman, slapping the reluctant coffee machine.

Harwood moved aside for a man in overalls who was reaching for the napkins. His reflection slipped over the tin box, and she realized it was the ear and beard she'd glimpsed in the rental BMW—weren't overalls and a BMW a strange combination? The thought combined with a smell that stiffened Harwood's spine, some particular combination of drink and sweat and petrol that took her back to the interrogation cell and told her: Rattenfänger.

He took two napkins, said *danke*, and plodded to a table in the back. Harwood watched his reflection recede, and then slipped two fingers into the box, pincering the napkin she'd seen blossom from his meaty fingers. He'd folded it around a Polaroid wrinkled and smudged with fingerprints. The photograph showed Ruqsana Choudhury in a crowd, and behind her a man gripping the infinitesimal glint of a needle. The Rattenfänger operative now watching her over his coffee had scribbled instructions in the space meant for captions, along with three words in French: ALLER JUSQU'AU BOUT. Three words that could translate to any number of idioms—*go through with it, stretch a point, stay the course*—but really translated to a warning, and so much cliché. This isn't a game, and you're in too deep now to turn back. So don't try it. If you're having second thoughts, it will be her funeral, and most likely Sid's too, because there was no way Sid just let Ruqsana be taken. Harwood balled the Polaroid into her fist. The blood cells in her face seemed to be contracting. She was burning red, struggling to breathe.

Had it truly been only a few days since Rattenfänger came to the Barbican, or was it a lifetime? After she'd completed the tests at Shrublands, Harwood had returned home tender, prodded one too many times. When she got the call from Moneypenny that Ruqsana Choudhury had reached out to Bashir and they would soon make contact, she took the box of Turkish lokum she'd picked up at the Istanbul airport and crossed out the name with a sharpie, writing the Greek *loukoumi* over it. That would make Mrs. Kafatos, her father's old friend in Defoe House, cackle. While Mrs. Kafatos rummaged for two plates to divide the sweets, Harwood swapped around the postcards that showed their backs to the stairwell. She moved one to the center that read *I come bearing gifts.* It was the signal agreed with Rattenfänger. Then she retreated to her flat, drew a bath, and lay staring blindly at the white tiles. She felt just as numb as she buzzed Bashir up, pulled on a dressing gown, watching herself in the mirror, this strange automaton that had taken over her body since she'd given Rattenfänger the three words they wanted to hear on top of that mountain in Syria. *I'll do it.*

And beneath that, so many more words. I'll do it, if you stop hurting me; I'll do it if you let me limp out of here breathing; I'll do it if you reverse time and give me back Sid Bashir as my fiancé; I'll do it if you reverse time and give me back James Bond as my—whatever it was between us; I'll do it if you reverse time and return me to childhood simplicities, to good versus evil, to love I could trust and a home with a fixed compass point, though these last binaries were things she'd never had, they'd been missing from day one, and it was only in her disintegration that she believed Rattenfänger could salve all her wounds. Bond would have shaken his head over these wishes. Never job backward. What-might-have-been is a waste of time. Follow your fate and be satisfied with it, be glad not to be a secondhand car salesman, or crippled by an injury in the field—or dead. Your strength lies in myth. Myths are built on heroic deeds and heroic people. Be glad to be the boy who stands on the burning deck.

But she hadn't stood on the burning deck as the ship sank. She'd uttered the three magic words every agent dreads or longs for in interrogation, depending on which side you stood—*I'll do it*—and when she opened her door to Sid in the Barbican, she was no more than a puppet on a string. Except, when Sid brushed his hair back and offered her a goofy grin, an electric bolt went through her, animation that lasted until they fell asleep, animation that meant she could put the reasons why out of her mind, and simply pull pleasure from him and give in return because she wanted him, and wanted them.

Then she woke. Sid's shortwave radio was playing Chinese propaganda broadcast from America about the good quality of life in Hong Kong. And a red laser was washing over the ceiling. It wasn't a stray light from construction cranes. It was the signal she'd been waiting for since saying those three words.

The sweetest vulnerability Sid possessed—and also the saddest—was that he wouldn't wake up if she kissed him softly first on the shoulder, which she did next, and he did not stir as she slipped from bed and walked naked into the living room. There, she switched on the darkroom safety light, which pulsed red before fizzling out. She'd learned that the signals of betrayal were so numberless, it seemed a miracle no one counted them. Though she didn't put much faith in this lasting—Sid never let any number go by him. She padded into the kitchen, and opened the highest cupboard, pulling out her go bag. She dressed in black.

Her father had been the one to rig the emergency escape door so that it always stood unlocked, though the Letraset pane remained unbroken, and seemingly unused. An escape route that left no wake. Harwood did not arm herself. She knew better than that. She pushed at the door with the flat of her hand and it swung open noiselessly.

Harwood avoided the lift in case Sid heard the slide of the doors over the radio, wails that reminded her of a toy her mama had brought back from some trip. It was called a groan tube and was designed to encourage Harwood to speak—she'd watched her parents mutely for as long as she could. They made enough noise between them. Family legend said that her first word was a complex sentence with at least three subordinate clauses. First you had nothing to say to the world—Mama would comment—and now you insist on talking it around. But she'd never forgotten how to listen. She listened well enough to know what her mother meant. *You can't talk this world round.* Well, here I am, Mama. Just watch me.

It was twenty-eight floors down. She took the stairs one at a time.

Let Rattenfänger wait. They were the ones who'd left her aching. She took the Podium exit, striding into the embrace of the mist. They'd told her to meet them on top of the conservatory. The walkways were a map of invisible breaches, puddles immediately soaking through her quiet plimsolls as she followed the puzzle of flyovers and stairs. The wet echo of her steps jumbled with her pulse. She felt certain someone was behind her. When she looked over her shoulder, the mist gazed blankly back. She thought she heard a noise, a sharp crack or clang. But the Barbican was built for secrets, the concrete so thick there had once been a fire in a tower apartment and nobody knew about it.

A traitor always feels watched. M said that once. A training session, reviewing an old case—how 006, an early comrade of Bond's, had gone bad, while others thought him good. Binaries again. James had sat in silence at the back of the training room, watching. He'd been the one most convinced of 006's goodness. Just as he was convinced of hers.

She made the jump onto the conservatory roof holding her breath. The drone of bees rose to meet her. Be sweet to the world, and it will be sweet to you. She moved closer to the hive. The growl grew louder. She hovered a hand near the latch.

"What took you so long?"

"I'll do anything for a room with a view," she said.

"As we've discovered."

The Rattenfänger operative emerged from the mist. She could only half-make out his features, but she knew the languid timbre of his voice from those days when it was her only company in the darkness.

It was Mora. Her aim had been true. She'd missed the vital organs.

Harwood gripped the latch of the hive, but did not release it. You can be ready with a weapon or ready with a first aid kit. She'd long ago opted for the weapon.

"What is this gift you have for us?"

"A lead on Dr. Nowak. She made contact with Ruqsana Choudhury before she disappeared, a lawyer volunteering to defend climate justice activists. Now Choudhury wants to talk."

"That's the pretty ribbon. What is in the box?"

"I was terribly bored as a child at school," said Harwood. "Desperate to grow up. My grandmama said to me, if you learn one thing from childhood, let it be patience."

"What an edifying lesson. And was your patience rewarded?" She could feel the heat of his body shimmering through the rain. "Are you happy now you are all grown up, sweet Johanna, whose expert aim kept me alive so tenderly?"

She breathed shallowly. "Happiness is for other people."

"How do *you* live, then?"

"Patiently."

"How very mediocre. I spared your life and released you back into your patient goldfish bowl because of your access. I want Dr. Nowak. She was going to blow the whistle on Paradise's backing. Robert Bull was ordered by Paradise to shut up that whistle. He was ordered by Rattenfänger to bring me that whistle. He failed both paymasters. Sir Bertram has locked us out of Celestial, his quantum computer—he is only alive because we hope he can be encouraged back to the fold and give us access once more. But if he does not, she will."

"Do you know why Sir Bertie's broken away from you? What he's planning?"

The purple lights of the conservatory lit up his leer. "We are not such good friends as that, sweet Johanna. You will gain access to Bull. We believe he is being held by the CIA. Find him and get in the room with him alone—I am not interested in how. He was tasked with silencing Dr. Nowak when it became clear she had discovered we are Paradise's backers. Instead he played his little games and lost her. We do not tolerate failure. Show him that."

"Double O agents don't kill prisoners."

A shrug. "You are not a Double O agent anymore. Count yourself lucky. The rest are dead, or soon will be."

"All of them?"

He wagged a finger at her. "You must get over this obsession, Johanna, wasting your most fertile years pining for James Bond. You have swallowed his myth like a child swallows medicine. All of your country's strength lies in myth—the myth of Empire, the myth of Churchill, the myth of Scotland Yard and Sherlock Holmes. The myth of James Bond. Myths are built on heroic deeds and heroic people, perhaps. Or perhaps they were only ever fantasy."

Harwood felt as if she were streaming between moments: now listening to Mora enjoy the sound of his own voice, then listening to Bond employ almost the exact same words. At some point between those two moments, the two men had exchanged ideas. Her pulse picked up.

Mora continued: "This man, he is a fantasy. The cars, the women, the gadgets, the endurance, the courage, the one man to hold the line and never waver." Mora's finger landed at the midpoint of her collarbone. A jab at her brachial plexus. She clutched her chest, blind spots appearing at the edge of her vision. "Time to move on. You are the new hero of the Secret Service. And aren't you doing M proud?"

Harwood eased back, bumping into a hive. The awful drone swelled around her. She massaged her throat. "I'll call you as soon as I know what Choudhury knows. We're negotiating making contact at Paddington Green, the former police station, where a protest has turned into an occupation. You want to impress me with the depth of your penetration into the UK intelligence and justice systems, keep the police away from the building." Something he'd failed to do, the Met for whatever reason disregarding the law of whomsoever else Mora had his claws into. Which meant the leak that had sold Bond down the river was not all-powerful.

His voice dropped to the rumble of a train announcing its arrival in the shiver of the tracks. "I haven't *impressed* you already?"

A crawl passed over her scalp. "I'm sorry if you think you left an impression," she said. "It's only, I've known more memorable men."

Mora laughed. "And that, little girl, is why we've taken certain measures tonight to remind you of your duty to us. You won't find 009 waiting for you in bed."

Harwood pursed her lips. "We need him. Choudhury will only trust him. They've been friends since childhood."

"You're the actress. I'm sure you'll find a solution. Meanwhile, Mr. Bashir is going to be our guest for a time. If *you* impress *me*, you'll find him returned to you in mostly one piece. I wonder what nightmares I can give him this time."

A scraping sound undercut the growing patter of rain. Harwood's whole body relaxed. She smiled. "You forgot something," she said, "about Double O's. We don't believe in nightmares."

"Why's that?"

"We don't sleep."

She turned and dropped off the side of the building as Bashir made his presence known.

Now, Harwood's chest was airless. When the Australian barista faced her at the counter of the station café, she felt as though she'd lost something. She wanted to check her pockets, to pat the air in search of some nicety, some easy cue, but she'd lost her mark, and stood senselessly on the tile floor, under the gaze of the operative in the corner, without any mask at all. Rattenfänger had taken it from her.

THIRTY

Murder in Macau!

Macau had once been, in M's language, a tiny Portuguese possession only forty miles from Hong Kong, the last stronghold of feudal luxury in the British Empire. Hong Kong had offered the old Double O the finest golf course in the East, Shantung silk suits tailored in twenty-four hours, and a morning massage with a view through French windows of a big orchid tree covered in deep-pink blossoms, touched off by a confiding butterfly that would alight on a man's wrist while he wolfed down scrambled eggs and bacon.

By contrast, Macau—a ferry ride over the Deep Bay, paved with a hundreds-strong fleet of junks and sampans—was announced by rotting godowns with sun-faded lettering and crumbling façades of once grandiose villas. Macau was then chiefly famous for the largest "house of ill fame" in the world. At nine stories, Hotel Central had counted as a skyscraper. The higher up you went, the more beautiful the hostesses, the higher the stakes, the better the music. On the ground floor, a local laborer might talk to a girl from the neighborhood while gambling for pennies by lowering his bet on a fishing rod through a hole in the floor to the basement tables. Those with longer pockets progressed upward until they reached the earthly paradise on the sixth floor: the croupiers all women, reigning with an unimpeachable air of authority over the décor of a once-expensive French café now on its way downhill. A British spy might try his hand at fan-tan and hi-lo and read the palm of a hostess who called herself Garbo. Above the sixth floor were the bedrooms, but you would live up to your reputation as the perfect English gentleman and decline the offer, showering Garbo in a minor snowstorm of twenty-dollar notes and protestations of undying love before leaving on a wave of virtue and euphoria—this last delivered with a wink—all in the name of charming actionable intelligence from some aggrieved gangster about the workings of floors eight and nine.

If Joseph Dryden got out of this mess, he'd report back to M that the Venetian hotel in Macau had thirty-nine stories, making it three times the size of the biggest casino in Vegas. In fact, everything here was bigger than Vegas. Macau offered the only legal gambling in China, and after Portugal's exit in 1999, American business was ushered in. Macau's casino revenue was now five times that of the Vegas strip. The hotel even had an indoor canal system with gondola rides beneath a painted sky. If you ever escaped the hotel, you'd probably miss the dilapidated ferro-concrete housing of the Street of Happiness, where cooks and cleaners lived on one meal a day, overshadowed by the City of Dreams, a new identity raised from mud flats using enough sand to rebuild the pyramids. That is if you made it out alive. To Dryden, that was feeling less and less likely. He wouldn't want to bet on it, walking in lockstep with Luke past the gondola pilots belting out arias.

He wanted to turn his hearing implant down, but couldn't afford to dull his senses, even if it was no longer transmitting back to London. That was just what the City of Dreams wanted. It wanted him to believe he was walking through a piazza on a beautiful sunny day with a gorgeous man on his arm. It wanted him to believe it was day when it was night. It wanted him to believe he could afford to gamble everything, when he knew he could afford to lose nothing at all. He'd already lost too much. Dryden wasn't sure what Paradise had told Luke about his identity, or his implant. But somewhere between Star City and the City of Dreams, Luke had stopped meeting his gaze, becoming askew, the off-kilter energy of an addict who's just used and believes he can keep it a secret.

Sir Bertram was in high spirits, exchanging rapid bets with St. John and Ahmed. Dryden dug his hand into his pocket. They were here—ostensibly—to speak with the Macau government about the new Hong Kong–Zhuhai–Macau Bridge, the world's longest sea-crossing bridge, which connected Hong Kong to Macau. Eighteen workers had died during its construction. But that wasn't Paradise's concern. He was here to raise the impact of the bridge on the critically rare Chinese white dolphin, whose numbers were plummeting. Dryden didn't need Paradise's publicist to tell him, in a place of the world's biggest buildings and tallest bridges, this was the world's most transparent lie. Sir Bertram was here for the same reason actors and royalty and politicians were here. The Venetian was hosting the Murder in Macau!—exclamation mark guaranteed, murder hopefully less so. King versus Chao. The heavyweight championship was on the line. So was Macau's reputation. They'd lined up a night of fights featuring Olympic winners and foreign nobodies, hoping to persuade the Chinese television-watching public that boxing was the new national sport. It was the mother of all gambles. It could save boxing, dogged in the States by accusations of corruption and falling ticket sales. It could make Macau, once and for all.

And Paradise was betting against. As security and ingratiating executives steered them through the din of the crowd pressing into Cotai Arena, the Venetian's own Madison Square Garden, Dryden could hear Paradise's shrill laugh at St. John's plaintive whine: "What do you know, Bertie?" What Bertie knew—and Dryden would love to beat out of him exactly *how* he knew—was that Chao was going down in the third, and he was telling the bookies to take note. The

Venetian staff led them through the barriers to the changing rooms, a network of halls with all the usual backstage props: trolleys of shampoos and toilet roll parked in corners, raised voices in other languages behind cupboard doors, where cleaners would most likely be sitting on upturned buckets placing their own bets. Dryden wanted to give them a knock and tell them to put it all on King in the third. God had seen something.

The hallway between the two boxers' changing rooms was flooded with bouncers and hangers-on and people who didn't need to be there. Sweat and polish spiced the air. Dryden drummed his fingers on his empty holster. Poulain, the head merc, had locked up the weapons on the plane, and Luke had said nothing.

Sir Bertram's braying voice left Dryden stiff as he was now urged in front of King, his longtime hero. He grew stiffer still as Lucky Luke ran his mouth, telling King he and Dryden were boxing champions in the army. King's warm smile pierced Dryden's heart. Wrong place, wrong time, City of Dreams.

Chao bowed to Paradise, unfailingly polite as he told Paradise he owed his rise to the great country of China, thank you very much. Luke forced a handshake on him with a goofy, ignorant grin, which Dryden didn't recognize and despised. He watched Luke's palm slide away. Nothing seemed to have changed hands. Could Chao be planning to take a dive? And was King in on it? Or could Paradise arrange their fates without them even knowing?

Dryden leaned into Luke, buffeted by the men behind. "You got a phone on you, man? I'll take a picture with you and the champ."

Luke only laughed. "You know better than that. No phones around Sir Bertram."

"Right." Dryden turned to a member of staff, hoping that either Luke didn't know the full extent of his presence here, or did know and was conflicted enough to play blind. "You got a phone I can borrow? For a picture?"

"Certainly, sir—"

But Luke cut him off with a raised arm. Dryden glanced over the heads of the crowd. Some of them were holding phones in tight grips. Nothing lay unattended. There was no pay phone on the wall. After all this time when talking to himself meant talking to Q, he'd forgotten what it was like to be cut off, to be truly alone.

Standing with Luke's arm around him, Dryden almost sagged into his old fighting buddy, almost said to him—Help me, I'm alone for the first time in my life. Because even when his brain got scrambled after Afghanistan, there was Luke to pull him out. But when Dryden searched Luke's expression now, he could find nothing there but fixed blankness, hard and unforgiving.

He had to find a way to communicate with Moneypenny. He'd turned up no method on the private flight from Kazakhstan—where Luke had taken the passports and Dryden's own wallet for "safe-keeping" without an extra word—or dinner on the *Ark*, Sir Bertram's yacht equipped with the cloud-seeding device, now harbored in Hong Kong. Dryden searched the hall again, settling on a man with sweat on his brow balancing two clipboards and two phones. The clatter of photographers filled the room. Dryden murmured, "Excuse me," and edged out of the way.

Luke's hand landed on his shoulder. "Time for Murder in Macau!"

They were ushered into Cotai Arena, where dazzling lights and the roar of fifteen thousand people made Dryden's jugular pound. He was following Luke's climb toward the best seats in the house. Dryden fought the yanking feeling of abandonment, of shipwreck. He tapped his watch again. No signal. The lines that ran from him to Q had been well and truly cut and somehow Aisha and Ibrahim knew nothing about it. No alarms were sounding—it must be that they wouldn't sound until the hearing implant broke completely, leaving Dryden deaf in his right ear, with his left unable to access his language center, beset by din and confusion.

Sir Bertram was crowing to a retired basketball player: "Down in three!"

Luke bounced on up the stairs, in the grip of some new mania. "Come on!"

"Aren't we watching from the Royal Box?" asked Dryden.

Luke grabbed him around the shoulders. "Nah, mate!" His eyes were gleaming. Just like they had when Luke took substances he shouldn't in Afghanistan, after they'd lost men, or done things they shouldn't, not because they were against orders, but because the orders made no sense, and they should have known better. "The real fight ain't here! We're leaving!"

Dryden ground his teeth. "So where is the real fight, Lucky Luke?"

"Hotel Central!"

"That's a ruin these days."

Luke raised his fists, jabbing the air with a one-two. "Let's see if we can't knock it down!"

THIRTY-ONE

The Real Fight

Hotel Central

The holes remained in the ceiling of the basement at Hotel Central, but it had been years since anyone lowered their bets on a fishing rod from the ground floor. The building had been bought by developers with the aim of a grand reopening for the anniversary of Macau's return to China, but its famous teal tower remained clad in scaffolding, stuck in a long argument no one expected to be resolved. In the meantime, its basement had become home to Macau's thriving underground mixed martial arts scene. Tonight's knockout tournament was designed to rival the championship bout itself, and every bare-knuckle boxer and Muay Thai legend was here. There were no rules, save one: no weapons in the ring. For, as Dryden had reminded Luke, your fists are lethal weapons.

Cotai Arena

The crowd were warmed up by matches between young Chinese stars and Mexican hopefuls, the latter bloodied and beaten in a steady stream of hometown success.

Hotel Central

In the basement, the first bouts meant blood. Paradise sat with St. John and Ahmed and other men he knew from nights like this on tattered velvet chairs and sofas scrounged from the top floor. The screams of the crowd were a blare in Dryden's head on the ground floor, where he was trying to talk Luke down amidst the detritus of the former bar. There were no hostesses now, only humorless men with no teeth who were handing out numbers. Luke was pulling gloves from a duffel bag. He was jumping from foot to foot.

"Look, man, you don't have to do this!" Dryden shouted over the howls. "If this is what you meant, about Paradise asking you to do something—"

"It's already done!" called Luke. He was stripping down to his trousers, toeing off his boots.

Dryden grabbed his arm. "Luke, what have you done?"

Luke tugged on boxing shorts. "Chao, he's going down in three!"

Dryden pressed in. "How do you know that?"

"Sir Bertram, he doesn't just like to gamble! He likes to control the odds!"

Dryden hauled Luke closer. "*What have you done?*"

"Nothing, man! I just slipped Chao a picture, that's all. A picture of his son."

"You've put a kid in danger?"

Luke's eyes were bigger than poker chips. "He'll be fine! You gotta chill out, mate. Where's your famous cool?"

"Where is he? Where's Chao's son?"

"Why? You can't report it, anyway."

Despite the smoke and heat of the excitement around him, Dryden went cold, right through the middle of him.

Luke landed a not-so-gentle punch on his arm. "Not got nothing to say, 004?"

Dryden balled his hands into fists.

"Sir Bertram told me on the flight what you're really here for."

"I was sent here to protect him from himself. Two of his top team are in the wind and he's been dropping big money on the dark web. Now I see it's on illegal fights, and I'm here to protect *you* from yourself. The Luke I know would never endanger a minor. You were that minor, once."

Luke sniffed. "That what you were doing at the Cosmonaut Hotel? Covering my back, right, Joe?"

"I didn't mean . . ." Dryden was jogged by another fighter.

Luke shook his head. "That's the truth, ain't it, Joe? You never *mean* it. None of it. You're just out for yourself."

Dryden clamped his hand around the back of Luke's neck, trying to hold him in place. "First Paradise had you kidnap a child, now he's going to make money off watching you bleed for him in the ring. This isn't you, Luke."

"How would you know?"

Dryden breathed in Luke's sweat. "I won't let you fight alone."

Luke shoved him. "Then get in the fucking ring and gimme something to aim at."

Cotai Arena

Finally, the bell rang on the main event. King advanced from his corner smiling, despite the pressures of retaining his championship. He was still smiling after landing a flurry on Chao, culminating in a punch that ballooned Chao's left eye. Chao, a southpaw famed for his fearlessness, responded with a forward-moving attack that unleashed a torrent of body blows, pulling fans from their seats. But when the bell rang, King shook his head and said smilingly to Chao: "Nope."

Hotel Central

Finally, Luke's number was called and he burst onto the chalked floor with a bloodthirsty grin on his face. His opponent was a head taller and several buses wider, a bare-knuckle fighter who laughed at Luke's gloves. Luke wiped the laugh from his face with a hook that Dryden—pushing through the crowd to watch from Luke's corner—knew well. It landed in the big man's ribs, shaking his foundations just as the hotel shook around them in the stamp of feet on the floor. Luke danced away from his opponent's giant rib, dancing and weaving now, ducking in to land a jab, taunting the man, before ending it with a quick combination that no one but Dryden saw coming. The bare-knuckle boxer hit the floor, unmoving. KO. Dryden looked over to Paradise. He was red with pleasure.

Cotai Arena

Second round, King landed six blows to Chao's face but couldn't send him to the mat. Chao remained unmoved until the last seconds, when he got King against the ropes and pounded him as if seeking revenge. The referee had to pull him off.

Hotel Central

Luke's next opponent was a jujitsu fighter whose skin was almost entirely black with tattoos that told the story of jails across Asia. Luke was at a disadvantage, limiting himself to the techniques of boxing, and soon the fighter's elbows and knees drew blood. Dryden put one foot on the ropes.

Paradise was screaming for Luke to kill the bastard.

Dryden bit his lip. He wanted to tear Paradise's head off. Poulain lurked in the corner, and waved the phone at him now with its strobing device, ready to fry Dryden's brains. A thud brought Dryden's attention back to the ring. The jujitsu fighter was on the floor. Second knockout for Luke. Dryden didn't remember him getting two KOs in successive matches, ever.

Cotai Arena

The bell rang to open the third round. King emerged more cautiously, nursing a cracked rib. Chao was hesitating, just out of reach. He didn't press the advantage, instead hovering passively within the limits of King's reach. The crowd began to boo.

Hotel Central

Zhang Yi, who oversaw gaming for the Triads in Macau and was supposed to be watching King versus Chao, had never before been witnessed in the basement of Hotel Central on fight night. He preferred to take his slice of its profit at a distance. So when the bookie's men moved away from the doors to let him in, the drunken crowd took hardly any notice at first. The final round of sixteen had seen three losers dragged out and dumped in the alley, for a taxi or an ambulance, or neither. Lucky Luke was back in the ring for the semifinal, now the solid favorite. His opponent was a former Olympic judo competitor, thrown out for steroid abuse, whose veins still popped. Luke bounced in his corner, ignoring Dryden's shouts. Paradise's voice cut through the throng: "Odds on my boy kills the Olympian!"

Cotai Arena

King jabbed, waiting for Chao to respond. Chao's guard was up, but only feebly. King looked to his corner, his eyes asking what was going on. The crowd howled.

Hotel Central

Zhang Yi sidestepped Ahmed. He laid a dry hand on Paradise's shoulder. Dryden read his lips, the precise enunciation: "Are you enjoying Macau, Sir Bertram?"

"You're blocking my view," said Paradise, accepting bets now that Luke would kill his opponent.

Dryden tugged at Luke's ankle. Nothing.

So get in the God damn ring.

Dryden circled the ring, ducked under the ropes, and advanced toward the Olympian, who turned baffled eyes on him. "Sorry," said Dryden, and then delivered a feint followed by a flickering punch that he knew would knock the man out, and it did.

Hotel Central erupted. Bookies and bouncers surged. Dryden shrugged, turning to face Luke. He rolled his sleeves up. "You wanna kill someone, Luke? Here I am."

Cotai Arena

The arena had dropped to a confused hush. Chao was hardly bothering to defend himself, looking around wildly. The seconds were counting down. King was shouting at him to fight. Then he threw up his arms in frustration, and backed off. The bell rang. The commentators nearest were shouting into their microphones: "It would seem the champ doesn't want this one lightly, and Chao—widely considered a favorite tonight after King's recent shaky performances—is now screaming at the King camp to fight on. We were told to expect Murder in Macau—well, ladies and gentlemen, we can only give you mayhem in Macau . . ."

Hotel Central

Zhang Yi raised a hand. The basement hushed, the fighters and the gamblers finally recognizing him. He put his thumb up, a stiff gesture, but one which meant the same here as it had to gladiators. You get to live. Dryden had beaten the Olympian.

Which meant, if the tournament continued, he would fight Luke. Dryden focused on the Triad boss's voice—his implant still allowed him to amplify it above the noise of the room. If only Q could hear what he was hearing.

Zhang Yi swept St. John aside with a peremptory gesture, taking his seat. He pressed his shoulder to Sir Bertram's. "I received an interesting communiqué this evening, Sir Bertram, from a man named Mora."

Paradise paled. The bell rang. Dryden stood still, watching Luke advance one nervous step, then another. His gloves hung at his sides. Dryden looked back at Zhang Yi's lips, the voice swelling.

"A colonel with Rattenfänger, a group with which we occasionally collaborate. Mora tells me you had been paying off large debts at fights such as this in other territories for some time. Until recently, when you started to win. He tells me you do this by rigging matches. He tells me you have developed a taste for such odds."

Dryden was pacing now, matching Luke's arc across the floor. He swayed left to right, watching the conversation over Luke's shoulder.

"He tells me you are even the kind of man to rig the King–Chao match, though what method you might use for such a feat he did not know. He merely asked me to detain you for him. I can't say I understand the conflict between you, nor do I care. I left the Venetian as Chao's feet turned to concrete. As if he were trying to throw the match. King refused his offer. We look absurd. Now I see how well your fighter does here. Are you a magician, Sir Bertram?"

Cotai Arena

The audience in the Cotai Arena were screaming bloody murder.

Hotel Central

The stinking men in the basement of Hotel Central were baying for the same.

Zhang Yi snapped his fingers. The suited Triad gunman next to him raised his gun to Sir Bertram's temple.

"You enjoy watching your employees shed blood for you?" said Zhang Yi. He crossed one leg over the other. "My father once owned this hotel. He was the first gaming tycoon in Macau. He brought baccarat to the island. He respected profit. My father grew a business empire. He built hospitals, Sir Bertram. I fear you are not a very good businessman."

Sir Bertram's face gleamed. He was tipping forward in his chair, blinking at the floor.

Zhang Yi scratched his temple. Then he drew a silver cigarette case from his jacket, tapped one out, and searched his pockets for matches. When the cigarette was lit, he waved it in the air. "You have had fun with my toys. Now let us play with yours." He raised his voice. "To the death, if you please. I don't really care whose. Yours, his"—the smoke trailed as he gestured to Sir Bertram—"it's merely a matter of sequence, by this point."

Dryden scanned the room. Triad at every door, loosely holding machine guns. The crowd caught in uncertainty, hardly breathing. Ahmed squealing. St. John studiously silent. And Sir Bertram's feet folded inward, as if he were trying to fold into himself.

Dryden raised his guard and faced Luke. He breathed: "What happens to the kid? If Chao doesn't go down?"

Luke's feet were slowing. "I told them—I didn't mean it. I thought Chao would throw the fight."

"Told them what?"

Luke stopped moving.

A gunshot split the room. St. John's brains hit the wall. Paradise screamed. The gunman forced the weapon into his cheek, shouting at them to fight.

Luke flushed, swore, then threw a half-hearted punch. Dryden's eyes burned. He swayed backward. The gloves were dipped in chloroform. That's how Luke achieved so many KO's. He shook his head. Luke fumbled, grabbing the Velcro of the gloves between his teeth, about to pull them off. The spray of bullets almost brought the ceiling down. Dryden hunched under the rain of plaster and dust. Luke froze.

Zhang Yi said, "I am happy to kill any man I do not feel performs." He turned to Paradise. "Shall I start with your blue-eyed pet?"

Dryden swore and then closed in on Luke with a stream of jabs and then a hook. Luke stumbled, almost hit the deck, shock and panic on his face.

Dryden got him on the ropes, pounding at his ribs as he shouted, "Where's the kid?"

Luke tried to shield his face. "Chungking Mansions! Orchid Tree Guest House! They're supposed to call me first!" Then he ducked and Dryden's swipe went overhead. He landed a punch in Dryden's stomach, forcing him back.

Dryden regained his footing, dancing out of the way of the poisoned gloves. He knocked Luke to the chalk with a left hook. Luke got to his feet. Dryden's second left hook was to the head. Luke dragged himself back up to the ropes, lurching across the ring on uncertain legs. Dryden caught him in a sweat-soaked hug, panting into his ear, "To the right side of the head, above my injury. Paradise cut off the transmission but there ain't no cavalry charging in so base must think I'm fine. Gotta break the whole damn thing."

"Fuck that, man," whispered Luke.

Dryden let Luke slip away and then came at him with the most punishing combination he could, letting every ounce of fury and disappointment—with Luke, with himself, with the Service—pour through his arms until he saw the light switch in Luke's eyes. Dryden got his feet side-on so that his right temple faced Luke and let his guard drop, holding his breath and closing his eyes.

The punch landed above his right ear.

THIRTY-TWO

The Bridge

Dryden is lifted from the ground. A fertilizer bomb worth twenty-five dollars has taken out his million-dollar armored personnel carrier. First, the primary blast. Ignition sparks a chemical reaction. In the same second, gases expand in a spherical shield faster than the speed of sound. The shock wave captures any object it encounters in a balloon of static pressure. It arrives as a blast thump at the very center of Dryden's chest that seems to pull out his insides. Then the pressure falls, forging a vacuum, shattering any organ or bone that contains air. A surge of supersonic wind chases out the vacuum, picking up objects from the ground and pulling them apart. That's the secondary blast. Dryden's ankle breaks, his lung perforates, his head is crushed against the roof of the vehicle before he is smacked back down, fracturing the base of his skull and slicing the nerve beneath his right ear. He is sprayed by bone fragments—the man next to him is gone.

The next thing Dryden is aware of is Luke—who was riding in the vehicle behind—crouching over him and shouting: "Are you good? Are you good?" Except the words are swallowed by absolute silence cut with ringing so terrible it makes Dryden want to retch as the black box of the vehicle seems to spin with blood. He scrambles for his weapon, seizes the rifle, and taps Luke on the shoulder: I'm good. The personnel carriers are pinned down. They fight their way out, though Dryden doesn't know if it's Christmas or Tuesday—he does know how to kill. He's always known that.

It takes a day or so for Dryden to realize the ringing is only getting worse, and that it demands all of his reserves to process even the simplest of speech, often absorbed in a wall of sound. It takes a few more days for him to report that he can't hear anything in his right ear at all, and then only at Luke's urging. He is medevacked to Birmingham and then Headley Court, the military center for traumatic brain injuries. He can't hear Luke say goodbye.

Dryden is usually the first man through the door after a breach. He's felt the thump of a blast countless times, but that day, that bomb, is different, for reasons the doctors cannot explain. *Perhaps it was just your time*, one says philosophically. Doctors won't be able to tell him if the shock wave entered his brain through his eyes, nose, ears, mouth, or whether it traveled through his vasculature into his neck and brain. In the First World War, they thought the shock traveled to the brain through spinal fluid after an explosion. They called the aftereffects shell shock. Then the higher-ups decided those men suffering headaches, paranoia, hallucinations, anxiety, hearing loss, speech loss—they were just cowards. Something wrong in the head. Dryden suffers all those things now.

Dryden is told that his right ear is sensorineural deaf. His intact left ear will now struggle to distinguish speech from noise because of auditory processing disorder, a result of his mild traumatic brain injury. They tell him the right ear is a problem with the hardware, the left ear a problem with the software. Promising data is published on traumatic brain injuries, once believed to be a myth, now understood as the signature injury of the Iraq and Afghanistan wars among Western troops.

At first, he commits to multidisciplinary treatment from doctors, psychologists, occupational therapists, physiotherapists. They help restore his balance. They offer strategies for recovery. They want him to meditate and practice yoga, but breathing deeply moves his body back to the moment he'd hype himself up for action. He can't sleep. His mind is making up sounds. Tinnitus drives him to punch a hole in the bedhead. Migraines mean he lives in darkness.

Sometimes, he can hear speech just fine—a mist lifting. Other times, people's words bleed together with surrounding sound; even in a one-to-one conversation their sentences scramble, their meanings turn inside out. The owner of the corner shop tries to chat, and Dryden feels so ashamed by his confusion he runs out, forgetting to pay. He's then so ashamed by this he doesn't go back, paralyzed in his flat. His days are filled with occurrences like this. He can't sort noise from noise, and the nearby train line and beep of cars and drills of construction are one awful blare.

Anxiety grips him. Shadows lengthen. Army buddies urge him to get a PTSD diagnosis, get some support, but he finds the conversations too difficult. He can't bear the idea there's something wrong in the head, not when he's kept himself so contained since he was sixteen, never spilled outside his borders onto anyone else. He feels suicidal at times, but then Luke returns from his tour. Dryden can breathe again. He can relax his shoulders. *Same old cool*, Luke says. But then Luke isn't there, he is called back up. Dryden is alone.

Until Moneypenny visits him at the local pub, explaining patiently that she has access to cutting-edge brain-computer interfaces that can combat APD. She tells him she needs a man with his skills and experience. A man with his courage. He is bound to Q. He is bound to a new purpose. He sleeps at night. He never misses a shot. He does miss Luke.

004 hit the floor of the Hotel Central basement. The room collapsed into a static haze. Luke towered over him shouting, but Dryden couldn't pick out his voice. He could see his lips moving, though. Luke was shouting: "Are you good? Are you good?"

Dryden closed his eyes.

Aisha hung her damp woolen coat on the hook behind the laboratory door and then removed her knee-high boots. She and Ibrahim had a no-dirty-shoes-on-the-reinforced-glass policy, so she kept a spare pair of pumps in her bottom drawer. Picking up the kettle to see if any water remained, Aisha felt the heavy slosh and set it to boil before scooping out her shoes so as not to waste time. *Time and motion studies*, that was her father's mantra. Aisha's dad worked for twenty years as the head caterer at the Oval cricket ground, and swore the time and motion studies of a kitchen were more intricate than quantum mechanics. Aisha glanced at Q. No change. There never was, but still Aisha checked on Q with the same instinct that saw her greet house plants.

She and Ibrahim had been taking alternate shifts so that one of them was always awake with Q since Mary Ann Russell's report. It wasn't that Aisha and Ibrahim didn't trust Q's secondary caretakers. It was simply that they trusted themselves more, and that was a valuable thing. The hush in the Regent's Park building told them trust was in short supply. So Aisha was startled when Ibrahim marched back into the lab. She was supposed to take the night shift.

"What's wrong?"

"Maybe nothing," said Ibrahim. He was standing in holey, mismatched socks. "Diagnostics pinged earlier, then settled down. I've run systems checks and it seems good, but I don't know—Q doesn't seem right."

"I thought Q *doesn't emote?*"

He bit his lip. He had the gray look he'd get when he forgot to eat.

Aisha chucked an energy bar from her bag at him. "What kind of ping?"

Ibrahim caught it, but dropped the snack onto his desk. He swiveled his screen to face her. "004 stopped transmitting in Baikonur. That's what it looked like, for a moment. Then his vital statistics and his location came back. Macau. I called in, but 004 told me to go dark."

Aisha's feet suddenly felt too big for the pumps. She kicked them off, flexing her stockinged toes on the cool surface. "Do we have confirmation that the signal is originating from 004 himself?"

"He gave me the right code. It's not possible to hack the stream. Right?"

Aisha pulled up Dryden's location and readout. Macau. Brain waves and heart rate normal. "Q can't be fooled," she said. "Not by any computer in this realm of time and space. Except one perhaps. The computer designed by Dr. Nowak."

"The systems checks are clean," said Ibrahim. "They've just come back and it's spotless. I'm being paranoid. He went dark."

The tea was over-brewed. Dark clouds drifted on the surface of the liquid. "Macau. The big fight. That was Paradise's next press stop. Turn it on."

Ibrahim brought up the live feed. Chao was staggering around the ring, his guard dropped. They were in the seventh. King was dancing, jabbing, calling for Chao to try and hit him. The boos of the crowd almost drowned out the commentators.

Aisha tapped the keyboard, asking Q to find Sir Bertram, Luke Luck, or Joseph Dryden in the Cotai Arena. Q scanned the faces and body masses. Nothing. They weren't there.

Ibrahim peered over her shoulder at the other monitor. "004's hearing aid is functioning. He should be able to hear everything around him, and call in if he wants. He heard me—he answered me. The equipment is functioning."

Aisha raised an eyebrow. "Unless it was an AI-generated voice, a soundalike."

Ibrahim picked up the energy bar again, dropped it again. "He had the right code."

"Q generates the codes. If Q were breached, or if someone here leaked—"

The crowd in Cotai Arena exploded. King was refusing to come out of his corner. The referee was shouting that refusal to fight meant forfeiting the fight. King gestured at Chao—*Tell him that.* Aisha watched Dryden's readouts. No reaction.

"Come on, Joe," she said. "Give us something."

The monitors screeched. No readout. No brain patterns. No stimuli.

Ibrahim placed a hand on the glass separating them from Q. A sweaty mirror appeared beneath his fingers. "Either 004's hearing aid just broke," he said, "or 004 just died."

"He broke it. He's talking to us. He's asking for help."

"How do you know that? We can't know that."

"Don't you see?" said Aisha, pointing at the screen where King was still shaking his head. "There aren't only two options, functioning or not functioning, winning or losing. King is using a third, for whatever reason: he turned the fight off. Dryden's equipment isn't sending the diagnostics reports it should—it's not even sending the audio it should. So he turned the whole thing off, knowing it would trip the fail-safe alarm."

It wasn't Lucky Luke who tried to drag him out of the ring. It was a man who smelled of night jasmine and tobacco. Night jasmine? Did he mean that? Certainty wriggled from his grip. Dryden shallowed his breathing, telling himself that didn't matter, just like the awful rushing vacuum around him didn't matter. What mattered was the metallic smell of the man's machine gun, and the thud of the weapon slinging against Dryden's arm.

Dryden opened his eyes. He had the Triad man on his back before the man could register what was happening. Dryden tore the machine gun free, picked out the man holding the gun to Paradise's head, aimed, fired. The Triad went down without pulling the trigger. Dryden sprayed the ceiling. The pops were so distant, it was like bubble gum bursting. The ceiling buckled, collapsing on Ahmed. Luke was overcoming another member of the Triad. Dryden felt him at his shoulder. Luke was saying something to him, but Dryden couldn't hear him. Luke's voice was gone.

Luke seized him by the lapels, then signed: "Shell game."

Dryden swallowed, nodded. Yes, he could do that. He took out the two men by the exit with clean shots as the fighters and the gamblers streamed around him. Luke had Paradise. Dryden covered their exit. They spilled into a humid night. Dryden looked around, struck immediately by the smell of duck soaked in honey and wrapped in plastic, and human sweat disguised with cheap deodorant against nylon shirts. He needed two identical vehicles. The taxi rank. A fleet of black Toyota Crowns. Dryden pointed Luke at them, and then defended the rear, pacing backward across the busy street—traffic swerved around him—the Triad piling onto the pavement. Dryden took aim. One. Two. Three. Luke tapped him on the shoulder—exfil. He'd found two cabs both advertising the King–Chao bout. The two drivers were ranting, mouths gaping like mimes, waving their arms. Luke was bundling Paradise into the passenger seat of the rear vehicle.

Dryden grabbed him by the elbow, signing: "Over the bridge. I'll get the boy."

Luke hesitated, then turned as if Paradise was calling him. Luke signed: "Meet you there."

Dryden jumped into the taxi. The engine was already running, fare racking up. He shifted into gear and swung the Toyota into the road. People scattered before him. Their screams were a muted whine. Dryden's instinct was to ask Q to map a clear route to the Hong Kong–Zhuhai–Macau Bridge, but he was alone. He glanced in the rearview mirror, saw Luke's vehicle lurching after him. Not alone, in any sense—Zhang Yi's men were in three pursuit vehicles.

Ibrahim raised his head from his hands as the alert sounded. He almost pressed his nose to the screen.

"Q's picking up reports of gunfire at Hotel Central, and two taxi drivers have got on the radio to report vehicles stolen at the scene."

"Are the vehicles LoJacked?"

Ibrahim gave a drawn-out yes as he found the identification.

Aisha called up the satellite. "I've got them—two taxis in convoy moving onto the bridge connecting Macau to Hong Kong, and three more in what looks like pursuit."

"You need a permit for that bridge, hang on . . ." Ibrahim skim-read, then snapped his fingers. "Taxis have permits. The bridge is thirty-four miles long, eighteen point six of which is sea crossing. It dives into a tunnel for four miles between two artificially constructed islands to allow ships to pass overhead. The bridge connects two former colonies through mainland Chinese territory, so driving starts on the left-hand side, then goes through a checkpoint and merges to the right-hand side, then another checkpoint and drivers return to the left. The Macau checkpoint is wired but unmanned. The Hong Kong side is under repair."

Aisha watched the two taxis speed across the deserted bridge toward the first checkpoint. "Whoever's in pursuit might have enough sway to stop them at customs." She lifted her head to Q's chamber. "Unless we could raise the barrier."

———

The bridge snaked into the night ahead and behind, seemingly connected to nothing. Below, the Pearl River Delta yawned blackly, lit only by the shimmer of shipping. Dryden opened the windows to admit a blast of air, despite the grit of pollution that waxed his face. The car was at least fifteen years old, maybe more, but it pushed eighty just fine. He was coming up on the first check. Dryden hoped the taxi driver's license plate would open the barriers automatically—that was if Zhang Yi hadn't called ahead.

Then again, he'd never seen a barrier he couldn't break.

Dryden slowed down, lifting a hand to Luke, hoping he caught it: "Ready to switch."

There was just one guard in the customs box on this side at the barrier, watching a screen. The guard got up and stood in the doorway. Dryden could see him shout to his opposite number. They were armed.

And then the barrier lifted.

Dryden couldn't hear his own laugh but didn't care in that moment. He raced through, Luke close on his tail. The lanes jinked to merge onto the right-hand side. Dryden slowed down, letting Luke pull up almost level. He stretched over and forced the passenger door open. Sir Bertram was huddled in the back. Dryden checked the rearview mirror—the pursuit vehicles were almost at the checks. They had to swap without being seen. But Paradise was clinging onto the door, too scared to jump. Dryden kept the car steady. They were running out of time. The road signs were changing from traditional characters on a blue background to simplified on green. The pursuit vehicles made it through, merging onto the right with them just as Paradise dared the scramble from Luke's car to Dryden's, landing on the passenger seat with a bump.

Dryden shouted at him to close the door. Paradise hesitated, studying Dryden's face for a fraction of a second, and then closed it. Could he tell that Dryden's head was ringing louder than a fire alarm?

Paradise was saying something now, but Dryden couldn't understand it—it was as if he were talking through water. Paradise laughed. Dryden could see the spittle at his mouth from the corner of his eye.

Dryden clicked his neck. He'd hoped to keep Paradise to himself, get him into an interrogation room while the Triads pursued Luke instead—a cold hope, but he was feeling pretty damn cold right now. The pursuit vehicles must have seen them make the switch—they knew he had possession of Paradise. If he wanted to save the boy and keep Paradise from the clutches of the Triads, the best bet was to go for the kid solo and trust Luke to support him, trust that Luke wanted out. If he wanted to save the boy. Another cold thought. Was he even capable of saving the boy like this? And could he trust Luke?

Dryden thought of the expression on Luke's face as he called, "Are you good? Are you good?"

Well, are you good, Luke?

You only ever truly trusted one person in your life, Joe Dryden, and it was him.

He glanced at Paradise, who was now gripping the seat, fear in his eyes as Dryden pushed ninety. The Triads believed Dryden had possession of Paradise, and would keep believing it if they could switch back without being seen. Luke could keep Paradise safe while Dryden saved Chao's son. But they had to gain more distance before the next checkpoint.

"It's vehicle-to-vehicle interdiction!" said Aisha, wiping sweat from her upper lip. "Dryden's trying to get far enough ahead but he's being outmatched by the pursuit vehicles' engines. They need more time to perform the exchange."

"How do we give them more distance?" said Ibrahim.

"What's the make of the pursuit vehicles?"

"You're going to hack their electronics from here?"

Aisha tossed her hair over her shoulder. "I'm not going to. Q's going to."

"There are fail-safe systems, you'll only have control for a few seconds."

"That's all Dryden needs."

The pursuit cars were slowing, a sudden drain as if their engines were winding down. The road dipped into the tunnel, crossing beneath a concrete island. White light filled his vision—LEDs bouncing off tiled walls. Dryden swerved into the next lane, his body rattling with the car as he maintained the line with Luke. The groan of the engine vibrated up his legs. The door of the back seat was lolling open. Dryden clamped one hand on Paradise's arm, letting him feel the bite of his grip, and then shoved. Luke peeled away. The whole thing had taken seconds.

Dryden checked the rearview. The pursuit cars were only just dipping into the tunnel. He was clear. The tunnel whipped by in streaks. Dryden gunned it. The blows from the fight with Luke were beginning to make themselves known to him. Ribs burning. Blood crusting his right eye. The wind squeezed his skull, a terrible hollow. But the next barriers were already open. Giant cranes swayed in and out of his vision. Girders sprang from concrete like wild antennae. The last stretch of the bridge was not secured. Let's hope that doesn't apply to the concrete. Hong Kong arched ahead, a blinding array of lights climbing into cloud. A two-lane choice: the port, or the city center. Luke peeled off for the port. Dryden said a prayer, and peeled off for the city. The pursuit vehicles followed. His prayers were answered. Ask for trouble, son, and you'll get it.

THIRTY-THREE

Chungking Mansions

The stink of Hong Kong harbor drifted first into the confusion of moldering vegetables and incense and fish on ice, then the *dai pai dong*, where seemingly thousands of Hong Kongers shared dishes of drunken chicken and egg custard. Dryden threaded the taxi between glowing skyscrapers, trying to block out the blurred holler of people crowding too close carrying birdcages, birds that flapped and panicked at Dryden's window, the bicycles, the umbrellas, the children. He kept half an eye on the rearview mirror—no pursuit. Yet. Bumping the taxi onto a curb, he switched off the engine. Then prized apart the lockbox that had been shunting about the well. It popped open. Dryden stuffed the change and notes into his pocket. Flipped down the mirror. He spat on his sleeve and did what he could about the blood on his face. His white shirt was now crimson. Dryden pulled it off. His T-shirt had fared a little better. It would have to do for now. He wrapped the shirt around the Triad machine gun and tucked it under his arm, climbing out of the Toyota.

Dryden joined a flood of people coursing across the broad road. The gold lettering of CHUNGKING MANSIONS was hard to pick out among the neon, a modest entrance to the complex where Chao's son was being held, masking the two-story mall that served as the foundation for fifteen more floors spread over five separate buildings. Most of the people crossing with him were ethnic Cantonese by the look of them, but as Dryden slipped toward the doors he was met by a quick flick of interest from a group of Middle Eastern men wearing ivory thobes. They lost interest just as quickly, moving aside.

Chungking Mansions was a hub for traders, migrants, asylum-seekers, travelers, small-time entrepreneurs, restaurants, bedsits. Its reputation for crime had been somewhat mollified by the growing presence of CCTV cameras inside, all feeding to a monitor room where guards watched for anomalous behavior. The security existed in a space between the law of Hong Kong and the law of Chungking Mansions. If the police asked for footage, they weren't going to say no; but they also weren't going to hassle peaceful migrants in this complex known by some as a ghetto, as a gold mine, as the Little United Nations. The whole world was here trying to thrive. Dryden watched the watchers, skipping up the stairs. The ceiling was mirrored, and a glance revealed an upside-down harried version of himself.

He loosened his arms and shoulders. Clocked businesses left and right—Hui's Brothers Foreign Remittance Company Limited, Quick Quick Laundry, Indian gods and goddesses, the Côte d'Ivoire flag hanging over a shop marketing renewable energy products to African wholesalers. Outside, minorities were nearly invisible. In Chungking Mansions, Dryden blended in, or would have were it not for his current state. He pushed aside hanging prayer mats to reach a menswear shop selling not classic knockoffs but, as the sign gamely said, *expansions of the classics*. Dryden bought a brown Sandown trilby and a herringbone overcoat. He pointed at the changing room and the old man waved him on. Dryden balled up his bloodied shirt and stuffed it beneath the bench. Slinging the machine gun strap over his shoulder, he tucked the weapon under his arm and shrugged into the coat. He put the hat on and rejoined the concourse, keeping his face to the floor.

Next: a phone. Chungking Mansions was the true City of Dreams.

The shop opposite, bedecked with the Ugandan flag, delivered him fourteen-day phones returned by European customers within two weeks of purchase. Dryden chose an ancient Nokia with no Internet connection. The trader began to protest, pointing to new iPhones, before looking sharply beyond Dryden's shoulder. Dryden followed his gaze, and then turned back just as quickly. Nine Triad men in sharp suits and mean moods congested the passageway.

Dryden urged money into the man's palm. He was about to pull away when the trader's dry fingers tangled with his. He looked up into the soft jowls, the white eyebrows, the gentle eyes. The man said something—Dryden recognized the shape of the word "help."

He nodded.

A smile of silver fillings. The man gave a gentle tug and Dryden slipped behind the counter, then through the back curtain, receiving the parting pat on his shoulder with a two-fingered salute. Dryden made for the door opposite, pausing to check a map of the complex. The Orchid Tree Guest House was on the thirteenth floor. He took the stairs two at a time, dialing as he ran.

Aisha's phone chimed in the plexiglass depository box to which they all surrendered their devices upon entry to Regent's Park. Bob Simmons was watching the big fight in his office, but was pulled away from the pandemonium by the brief glow. He would have logged it in the back of his mind as something to tell Aisha about later had the call not cut off after three rings, and then started again. He remembered that from his days in the army. Simmons unlocked the box. Unknown number. He got to his feet, and answered.

There was no one there, only heavy breathing and a bouncing echo. Then a voice cut through the noise: "004."

Simmons straightened. "Copy, 004, hold on." Simmons picked up his own secure line and called up to Moneypenny. Her secretary,

Phoebe, said she was down in Q Branch—she would transfer the call. Moneypenny answered.

"Ma'am, 004 is calling on Dr. Asante's mobile. If I bring it down in the lift I'm afraid he'll cut off."

Moneypenny said, "Put him on speaker next to the receiver, Bob." Simmons arranged them both on his desk and switched off the fight. Moneypenny's voice expanded into his office. "004, this is Moneypenny."

Dryden said again, "004 reporting. Say—I can't—"

Dr. Suleiman's voice took over. "We know about your hearing. We know you might not fully understand us. That's OK. Tell us what you need."

There was nothing, just the sound of breathing.

Then: "Orchid Tree Guest House. Chao's son. Q compromised."

"Copy," said Moneypenny. "We're going to text you the information. Keep the line open if you can. Stay with us, 004."

The six men paid by Luke Luck to kidnap Chao's son from his piano lesson that afternoon had been arguing for the past hour about what to do with the boy crying in the bathtub. They had called the number Luke gave them and there was no answer. One said it would be better just to leave the boy here, someone else would find him, he couldn't identify them after all. Just wash their hands of the situation. The others said they should kill him anyway—leave no danger that they could be traced by the police or the Triad. They were desperate men—they had to be to take on an assignment like this. It had seemed like easy money. No way Chao would let his son die. But the squeaky boxer had botched the job. Would they see any money now? The leader was losing his nerve. He screamed at the others to shut up and pulled the pistol from his coat. He'd been doing this repeatedly, and at first the others thought nothing of it. But then he wrenched open the door to the bathroom and told the boy he was sorry—he didn't have a choice.

Dryden was still running when the Nokia buzzed. The texts came like staccato gunfire.

We've been hacked. Trying to identify. Watch your six.

He didn't need to be told that.

The texts continued, telling him that satellite imaging showed six men enter the complex before the fight. One of them carrying a minor. The Chungking Mansions security footage was film, not digital, no outside access. But the phones that had been in the Triad pursuit vehicles had now split into two groups. The Triad obviously believed he had Paradise and were intent on finding him. One set had ridden the elevator to the top and were sweeping their way down floor by floor. The other was sweeping the corridors on the way up. They'd soon meet in the middle, where a room picked up by CCTV camera on the skyscraper opposite showed six adult males. No longer any sign of the child.

Dryden's heart skipped a beat. He checked the machine gun. It was the FN Minimi, a squad automatic weapon with an open bolt, designed for carrying by platoon or squad support soldiers. The rear sight was adjustable for wind and elevation, and this one had an adjuster for night vision. The magazine was half-spent. Or half-full. He smiled to himself, coming to a stop at the door to floor thirteen by a fuse box.

Another text. *You are at the northwest corner. Triad approaching from southeast counterclockwise. Turn right, then left. Door immediate left. Go now.*

Dryden slipped the phone into his jacket pocket, and then crowbarred the fuse box with the end of the gun. He threw each switch. Knocking off his hat, he flicked the gun sights to night vision and stepped into the corridor with the weapon raised. He trod the faded red carpet softly, counting seconds, head down.

When he reached the door, the night vision made the orchid tree painted there glow. Dryden took one cooling breath and kicked the door in.

Night vision showed him six Asian military-aged males, all armed. He took out two, clocking the seconds, and then dived as his phone buzzed. A volley of shots from the hallway outside, the Triad opening fire. Feathers and plaster and wood exploded all around him. Dryden scrambled beneath the bed. The kidnappers were blasting the Triad, the Triad blasting the kidnappers. The bathroom door was open. There was a boy crouching on the tiles, hands over his head. A man had a gun to his head. He was saying something, though he hadn't seen Dryden—he was shouting into the room. Dryden got himself into a firing position beneath the bed. He recognized the word "hostage."

Not for much longer.

Dryden whistled softly.

The boy glanced up, saw him, froze.

Dryden moved his head to the right.

The boy cringed to the right as Dryden fired.

It was a clean headshot. The kidnapper's gun did not go off.

The room was still. Dryden squeezed out from under the bed. There were bodies everywhere. No survivors, Triad or kidnappers. The acrid aroma of gunpowder and blood got inside his nostrils, a queasy familiarity because it was so comfortable. Dryden stepped over the body of the leader and reached out a hand to the boy.

The boy grabbed hold of him. Dryden smiled, lifting him into his arms. He pressed himself against the wall of the room, taking a split-second look into the main hallway. People were running for the stairs and the lift. No sign of the Triad.

He raised the phone to his ear. "Hearing intermittent. Going for Paradise on the *Ark*. Luke's on side. Send back up."

The Nokia buzzed. Dryden read the text: *Paradise hacked Q. Proceed with extreme prejudice.*

Dryden briefly wondered if Moneypenny or Aisha or whoever was at the keys had meant to text extreme caution. Then he took a last look at the smoking room. Probably not.

He hung up and stepped into the hall, bouncing the boy in his arms. Eight years old at the most, face streamed with snot. Dryden gave him a wide smile. There was a tap on his shoulder. Dryden turned around. Lucky Luke clapped him on the arm, peering into the room over a cheap pair of sunglasses that mostly hid his bruised eyes.

He signed: "Trust you to start World War Three."

Dryden took a small step back. Signed: "Just cleaning up after you. Where's Paradise?"

Luke signed: "We need your help. It's Rattenfänger."

Dryden nodded. He was about to say he'd just get the boy to safety when he saw Paradise's security team approaching in the lens of Luke's glasses—two of the contingent attached to the yacht.

The boy fell from Dryden's arms as electricity coursed through him from a fifty-three-million-volt stun gun.

THIRTY-FOUR

An Untidy Scandal in the Spy War

Felix told Harwood the story of the Great Tunnel as the lift descended beneath Berlin.

"Sometime in '55, you Brits were studying the town map for Greater Berlin when a bright communications man spotted that the main trunk of cables from East Berlin to Leipzig ran right under a bulge in the American sector. These cables carried traffic from the East German army, even an official Russian teleprinter line. All very hot stuff if you're a bright communications man in 1955 Germany, I think you'll agree.

"So you Brits persuade us Yanks to dig a tunnel under the field from a nearby American radar station. Known as Harvey's Hole, after the CIA's then–man in Berlin, who'd been chucked out of the FBI by Hoover himself for drinking on duty. A lot to unpack there, but who has the time? For months, hundreds of people deciphered all the juicy gossip whispered down those cables twenty-four hours a day. It was a God damn coup. Except it wasn't. There was a mole in the British secret service. Can you imagine? George Blake. He'd been taking the minutes when Harvey's Hole was dreamt up. The Soviets let it go on for months to protect Blake's cover. Until one day, an Eastern telephone repair gang picked up a fault in the line caused by rainwater, and got to digging in the field.

"The Brits and the Yanks cleared out, but didn't have enough time to dismantle the farm's worth of machinery lighting the tunnel up. So along come some Russians with tommy guns and pop their heads down, and what do they find? All the gadgets are labeled GPO, property of the United Kingdom General Post Office. What followed was a brouhaha, an untidy scandal in the spy war, and no one likes those. So we put up a sign in the tunnel that said rather stiffly, BEWARE: YOU ARE NOW ENTERING THE AMERICAN SECTOR, and we beat a humiliating retreat. But real estate is real estate, and the Agency isn't going to let a perfectly good listening post under the capital of new Europe go unused, now is it? Even in the wake of our most recent untidy scandal. My predecessor intercepted Angela Merkel's texts down here. I just use it to disappear folks I don't like. Including Robert Bull."

The lift doors opened, and Felix made a wide arc with his arm. "After you, real deal."

Harwood stepped into the kill box—a cell of bulletproof glass with a grille ceiling for gas and the unblinking eye of a camera dead ahead. She imagined there was some device in here for reading her heart rate, too, and breathed steadily as Felix brushed past her and raised his right hand to a black panel. What had been the opaque plastic of his prosthetic, lacking even the five tones a mortician artist would add to bring life to an open casket, now glowed green in the bath of the screen. It read the prosthetic as if it were a barcode.

"Neat trick," said Harwood.

"Thanks," said Felix, as a panel of glass slid away. "Cost me an arm and a leg."

Harwood raised an eyebrow.

"Only I can make that joke. Come on, you've got a date."

"So what else can you do with it?" she asked, following him into a low hall that flashed blue and white. Sensor sweeps for weapons.

"Wouldn't you like to know?"

The tunnel could have been any corridor on any army base in the world, but still Harwood felt the pressure of the city stamping above her and the walls curving in, the pressure of closed doors left and right seeming to peer at her, to ask—What exactly are you going to do now, 003, with Sid Bashir in the hands of Rattenfänger, and your mission to complete? How about an untidy scandal in the spy war?

Felix Leiter had persuaded the Berlin police to let him take this headache off their hands after they picked up Robert Bull in hospital following Zofia's disappearance. When Bull woke up, it was to a sweltering cell with no furniture and no windows and no real air. There was sand on the floor. He shouted at the guards who brought his food to tell him where he was. He seemed to think Egypt was most likely, because he demanded to talk to Reed Jacobs, an Agency recruiter posing as a good-time guy at the embassy in Cairo.

When Leiter looked into the nature of the link between Bull and Jacobs, he found the two had met at a glad-hand party put on by the European Bank for Reconstruction and Development at the Nile Ritz-Carlton, where Sir Bertram was wooing some Internet infrastructure folks with satellite talk. This was a pattern of Robert Bull's working life, making nice with security types wherever Sir Bertram did business, whether they were pure as the driven snow or all shades of gray.

When his guards neither confirmed nor denied he was in Egypt, Robert Bull searched their blank faces for clues. He next pleaded with them to repeat his name to Lucas Wells, the CFO of a limited liability company who, among other things, contracted Filipino workers for six dollars a month to clean out interrogation cells on a US naval base in Diego Garcia, a militarized island in British Indian Ocean

Territory. Put Egypt and Diego Garcia together, and it would seem Robert Bull was comfortable with the flight plans of Extraordinary Rendition, and believed he was being detained in some out-of-the-way desert where he would be tortured by the CIA.

He was half-right, Felix told Harwood now, inspecting her face as she watched Robert Bull sweat on the other side of the one-way mirror. "He saw sand and thought CIA. That means Sir Bertram is up to something the CIA would be interested in, wouldn't you say?"

"Unless he thinks Zofia Nowak's two dates with Mr. Leiter of the US embassy really meant a lot to you."

"They did," said Leiter, throwing a switch. The cell went dark. Robert Bull screamed. He clearly didn't like what happened here in the dark. It lasted for a full minute. "But he's more scared of something outside his imaginary desert than he is of me. You say you can get him to squeak about what happened to Zofia and where she might be now. Time to work your magic, real deal."

Harwood paused at the door to the cell. She was carrying a folding chair, and checked the ease of the hinges, focusing on the mechanism. At the heart of every agent is a hurricane room. You were never imprisoned in this cell. No man ever tied you to a chair here. No man rasped your skin with needles. No man laughed while things happened that you will not name. Your hurricane room is empty of anything that might hurt you. You are safe in your hurricane room. You can turn gently in circles, enjoying the freedom of no histories and no obligations, while 003 does her job. Mora wanted Zofia's location, and Bull dead.

At the click of the door, Robert Bull attempted to spring from the floor, but he was yanked back by shackles.

"It's OK," said Harwood. She raised her voice. "Switch the lights on, for heaven's sake." The room washed white. "Aren't the restraints a bit much . . ." She set a bottle of water on the floor between them, casting a noon shadow. "I'm Ms. Goodmaiden. I've heard any joke you can come up with so don't bother. I'm a UN observer and I'm here to vouch that your human rights aren't being contravened. I can see I'm a little late." As she finished saying this she unfolded the chair and set it down so that her back was to the mirror, all the while watching Bull unfurl like a fern dazed by sudden spring. Then he tore the lid off the bottle and poured most of the water down his shirt because his hand was shaking. She added, "I suppose you know they're planning to hold you responsible?"

His relief switched bitterly. He spluttered: "Responsible for what? You bitch, I've been suffocating in this fucking hole for months."

"Not that long, Mr. Bull. I'm afraid they've played some tricks on you."

"I'm head of security for Bertram Paradise! I don't belong here!"

"If not you, who does belong here? Sir Bertram?"

Bull opened his mouth wide enough to spit the answer at her, and then stopped. His eyes were suddenly fearful. They swept to the mirror. He said, quietly now: "I don't belong here. I shouldn't be here."

Harwood sighed. She crossed her legs. Dusted sand from her boot. "Have they given you regular meals and water?"

"No."

"They say different."

Bull exploded to his feet, but made it no further. "Whose side are you on?"

"Would you say you're experiencing weight loss or dehydration? Or any deterioration in your mental health?" Harwood closed her eyes as Bull screamed himself hoarse and empty of obscenities. His spit landed on her cheek. She wiped it away. "Are you quite done?" She played her next gamble coolly: "It says here you raped Dr. Zofia Nowak."

He twisted, stumbling on the chains. "That's a lie!"

"Because she stopped you?"

Bull wavered. "What kind of observer are you?"

Harwood leaned forward. Lowered her voice. Imagined Felix Leiter's narrowing eyes behind the mirror. "I'm the observer Rattenfänger sends when its employees fuck up, Mr. Bull."

Bull clutched his stomach as if she'd winded him.

Felix whistled and relaxed into the corner of the listening booth, crossing his arms. If this was an interrogation gamble, it was a damn bold one. If it was something else . . . Felix dug his phone from his jacket and swiped to Control. The crackle that always reminded him of old-fashioned walkie-talkies answered. He said: "Keep an eye on the locks on interrogation room one. That door opens on my word only."

Harwood watched fresh sweat map from Bull's armpits. She continued softly: "You were given a very simple task, Mr. Bull. Eliminate Zofia Nowak. We didn't tell you to harass her. We didn't tell you to assault her. We told you to shut her up. Now you're here, and she's free. Do you see the problem?"

"They told me to make it look real! Most murdered girls, it's the boyfriend that did it. I thought if it seemed like she'd been harassed by a boyfriend, it would be open-and-shut. I had it all planned. But she fought back, she got away . . ."

"The police found a great deal of blood in her apartment."

"They told me to make it look real . . ." The words drifted from him, as if he were leaving his body.

"Quite the imagination you have."

"Get me out of here, and I'll give you Paradise. He's run out of patience being your whipping boy. Gone into business for himself. Cooking up a way to send you his final regards. Zofia told me everything. *Get me out of here.*"

Harwood remained still. "If Zofia worked it out, what do I need you for?"

"I know the details!"

"Are you a scientist, Mr. Bull? I didn't realize. The only thing you have going for you right now is that Dr. Nowak's value has gone up in the world. Rattenfänger no longer want her dead. They'd like her ideas instead. Sir Bertram has become too much of a liability. Do you know where she is?"

"I know where she'd hide! Her grandmother!"

"Zofia Nowak has no living relatives."

"She found her birth family," said Bull hungrily. "She's adopted! I can find her grandmother!"

"That won't be necessary," said Harwood, standing up. "What were you going to do with her body, once you'd raped and killed her?"

"Fuck's sake, what does it matter now? I did my best!"

Harwood raised her eyebrows. She gripped the top rung of the chair. "I'm afraid you've outlived your usefulness, Mr. Bull."

He lunged forward. The chain snapped him back. "No! Paradise will pay you double whatever Rattenfänger are paying you for my release!"

"Why would he do that, when you just sold his chief science officer to me for nothing?"

Harwood's phone vibrated. She pulled it from her pocket. Signal from Moneypenny. The code took a moment to untangle itself in Harwood's mind. 004 was MIA. Paradise's yacht had disappeared from all satellites. And the sensor in Bashir's glasses said 009's heart was failing.

She released a breath she didn't know she was holding. "They told me to make it look real, too, Mr. Bull."

Behind the mirror, Felix was striding to the door, but it was too late. He glanced over his shoulder as Harwood slammed the chair into Bull's larynx so hard she broke his neck.

THIRTY-FIVE

Too Good to Be True

A re you with us, Mr. Bashir? Play up, play up and play the game."
He is eleven years old and he's off school for a term. He broke his leg skateboarding. It's the worst pain he's ever experienced. He can't go on the history trip to Normandy. Friends go to Snappy Snaps and print copies of group shots for him, from which he's absent. School sends work home, and he lets it pile up on the little desk squeezed under the window until the light bleaches the cover of his science textbook, paling the cross section of the human head so that it has no skin and becomes a skull. He refuses games of chess with his dad. His mum worries about him. She brings home a portable radio from lost and found at the hospital. It is green, a world receiver. She lies in bed with him, teaching him about medium waves and short-waves, about modulations and frequencies. He turns the dial and an unknown language bursts through the crackle. It is magic. He is afraid to breathe, aware for the first time of the world talking around him, afraid he might swallow it whole. The radio becomes his teacher. He listens to American preachers and Romanian news and French pop songs. At night there is less radiation from the sun, and he thrills when he reaches Japan. He listens to Bollywood music with his mum,

who gives him a lecture on film history, rummaging in cupboards for tapes he's never shown interest in before. He gets out of bed.

But the radio is too loud. It is talking over their film night. There is a voice, crooning from the blare, asking him if he won't play up, play up and play the game. It is the voice of his nightmares.

Bashir opened his eyes. He flinched. Mora was smiling down at him. A proud, ghastly smile. The tattoo of the death's-head hawk moth peered over the collar, smiling at him too. Bashir shook his head. He was losing it. He was seeing ghosts.

Mora tapped him on the forehead. "Welcome back to the land of the living, Mr. Bashir. You will have to forgive my men. They took offense at your scissor trick." Another tap. "Stay with me, son. Tell me what you see. How many fingers?"

Bashir jerked upright, and was pinched by handcuffs. He was tied to a chair. He was naked. He was cold. Surgical lamps breathed down his neck. A police radio was chattering. His feet were in a bucket of water. There were wires in the bucket, and water all around. He followed the wire to a battery, which was on a rusted trolley, along with a pair of scissors, a set of Austrian stamps, and dental tools. His finds from the market.

Bashir fought the panic that gripped him by the throat and filled his mouth with the taste of copper. He was in an operating theater, a pit circled by seating that climbed to the ceiling miles above, cracked and choked with living ivy. Moss glimmered on the walls. Rain and wind whistled through weeds piercing the windows. A masked man lounged in the nosebleeds in front of a door, cradling an MK. Another masked man waited by the trolley, disconsolately stroking the battery switch, ready to throw it again. A third sat slumped in a chair, pale as ash, shirtless. Bashir's stabbing victim. Bandages wound around his waist, an IV threading blood into his arm.

And Mora, very much not dead, talking as he took Bashir's pulse. Bashir blinked. It was surely a miracle he'd survived Harwood's shot.

"We are in an abandoned military hospital complex, Mr. Bashir, in the Taunus Mountains. Patients with tuberculosis recovered here far from civilization. Or didn't. You said goodbye to your mother in the hospital where she worked at nights as a psychiatric nurse, I understand. Breast cancer, wasn't it? You developed a hatred for hospitals after that. Yet you fell for Dr. Harwood. I am afraid Freud would find you most predictable. You have been bullishly uncooperative, my men inform me. Most gallant with the whereabouts of Zofia Nowak. But I must insist you give me her location now. I hope to keep Bertram Paradise alive as the useful public face of Cloud Nine, but he is proving most unreliable. Zofia's brains will have to do. I'd suggest singing your song now. After all, you might not survive another shock. And then what would happen to Ruqsana? The injection we gave her is lethal, I'm afraid. She desperately needs an antidote."

Mora stood back. Bashir reared upward, taking the chair with him. Mora slapped him with a great open hand, sending him to the floor. His glasses shattered. The arm of the chair cracked, just a little. Bashir lay still, panting. In the reflection of the puddle, the iron bed where Ruqsana lay inert at the center of the pit was flipped upside down, shuddering, and he could believe it wasn't real—believe instead that he was fourteen years old, lying top-to-tail with Ruqsana on his bed, demonstrating the radio, falling in love as she translated a Spanish cooking program. She was going to do languages at Oxford. She had it all planned out. He just wanted to find some way to edge his hand into hers.

But that was then. Now she was unconscious and unresponsive, her face clammy and the pulse in her neck pounding, because of him.

A tut, and Mora grabbed him by the hair and hauled him and the chair upright. "I am surprised at you. I thought you would have more concern for your childhood friend. She will die without treatment for the poison we gave her. And yet you will not play with us. How do you live with yourself, Mr. Bashir, adhering to such utilitarian philosophies? What do you tell yourself at night, when you wake from nightmares?" Mora wiped his hands. "Perhaps you wake from nightmares of me."

Bashir grated his tongue along his teeth. "I've got bigger demons."

Mora chuckled. "That's more like it." He strolled over to the bed. Ruqsana had been dropped there without ceremony. Her arm hung over the side. Mora held her hand, crossed her arm over her chest.

"Don't touch her!"

"Too late to be the knight-errant now, my boy. We'll be burying her soon."

"I don't know where Zofia Nowak is, I don't know anything about Bertram Paradise, I'm here on holiday with Ruqsana."

"You departed from the apartment of Johanna Harwood for a romantic getaway in Berlin with another lady? Perhaps there is more James Bond in you than I imagined," said Mora, now crossing Ruqsana's other arm over her chest, as if arranging her for burial.

"What do you know about James Bond?"

Mora laughed. "Reverse interrogation, I applaud you. He trained you well. Tell me, did you develop these good looks as a teenager, or later? I imagine an awkward youth, unable to control your gazelle-like limbs, all elbows and thumbs, just hoping Ruqsana will notice you. Then, overnight, an Adonis appears. Was it then you became so callous, so cold, when you realized how easily she would give it up?"

"Fuck you."

"How original. Perhaps your blood turned cold when your mother died. I wonder how little Hope will manage, when *her* mother dies." A look at his watch. "I would give Ruqsana another fifteen minutes."

"OK, OK—give her the antidote and I'll tell you."

Mora chuckled, bowing down to the bucket. He flicked water at Bashir's groin, laughed when he cringed.

"We're just here on holiday!"

"Why the sudden interest in stamps?" Mora picked up the packet, holding the tiny alpine scenes to the light. "The Russian T-shirt designer, she wrote something down for you. Zofia's location. Did she write in the margins?" He turned the stamps over. "Perhaps I should be looking for invisible ink. I know how you Double O's love your tricks."

Every muscle in Bashir's body tensed as Mora strolled toward him. He tapped the stamps against a cut on Bashir's forehead. "How about it, son? Do you come bearing gifts?"

Bashir snapped his teeth at Mora's fingers. Mora reared back, laughing. Then he dug two fingers into Bashir's throat, dragging him closer. The radio flared again, inviting him to swim in its waves. The room was growing darker. He was learning about numbers stations, shortwave bursts of code used to communicate clandestinely across extremely long distances in territories where it would be impossible for an agent to use open communication. Bond is teaching him, an old dog with old tricks—who says this? M, laughing as Bond retorts that he's only as anachronistic as his teacher. First, an interval signal: a song, or a poem read by a voice like a newscaster. Then, a series of numbers in the same voice.

Lines from the verse assigned to Bashir lulled him now:

> *Go where you will: I have no more to say:*
> *You have had what I could give; take it and go.*
> *I will not argue who 'twas struck the blow;*
> *The thing is broken, throw the bits away . . .*

Now, the numbers. But the numbers wouldn't come. Instead, there was Mora, asking if he came bearing gifts. Why had Bashir chosen the Austrian stamps as his decoy, from the whole world on offer? What had been asking for his attention? The postcard facing into the Barbican stairwell, the surveillance Harwood claimed were posted by Moneypenny . . .

Still, some hope: "You've been watching me?"

Mora clicked his tongue. "Not you, son."

Bashir's stomach dropped.

The whine of hinges as the guard lounging above rose and his theater chair sprang shut. The doors opened. The guard said something
in Arabic. Johanna Harwood stood framed in the doorway, surveying
the scene. The guard moved aside, relaxing his grip on the gun. Harwood passed him and took the stairs down. Bashir looked for binds at
her hands, but she was free. He shook himself, searching for the gun
she would have trained on Mora, a second shot, fatal this time. But
her holster was empty.

"Johanna?"

Harwood reached the foot of the stairs. She cast her eyes over the
bucket, his legs, but did not look any further. She turned to Mora. "I
have Zofia's location. Robert Bull is dead."

"Johanna, what are you doing?"

Harwood's gaze flicked between the wounded soldier and Ruqsana.
She said, "I see you've been having your own fun."

It wasn't clear to whom this was directed, but Mora laughed, and
blocked her path to Bashir. At first it seemed like he meant to embrace her, but then Bashir realized he was patting her down, sweeping beneath the club of her hair, underneath her arms, squatting down
to run his fingers over the seam of her jeans, creep beneath her shirt.
Harwood let him, her attention on Ruqsana.

"Poison?" she said.

Mora rose and planted a kiss on her forehead. "Your expertise
is needed for my lieutenant. Multiple lacerations. Luckily his armor
caught most of it. But our man Bashir here is persistent. Stan, tell the
lady how much it hurts on a scale of one to ten."

The wounded soldier looked like he was going to curse Mora,
then bit his lip. His legs shook.

Mora said, "Time to play the ministering angel."

"Let me look at Choudhury first," said Harwood. "I've got what you wanted."

"That's not how this works."

Harwood turned to the soldier standing over the trolley. "How many volts is that?"

Mora put his hand on Harwood's shoulder. "Do you want a demonstration?"

Still, she would not meet Bashir's eyes. "I know how batteries work."

"Bitch," said someone—him. Bashir. He said it again: "You bitch. I trusted you. I believed in you."

She met his eyes then. She was pale, but he could detect no feeling. He was trembling. Trembling with enough rage to break the chair into a thousand pieces.

Harwood said, "If something seems too good to be true, Sid, it usually is. You can't tell me this is a surprise." Then she shook her torso as if passing through a chill, and asked Mora, "Do you have a first aid kit or am I to use a rusting needle on Stan?"

"You spoil him," said Mora, before pointing to a leather duffel bag open on the floor.

Harwood retrieved the field kit and then knelt between Stan's legs, telling him softly that she was going to take a look. Bashir could see over her shoulder as she peeled the bandages back and a shock of red spilled over her hands. She called for clean water, snapping when no one moved. The soldier by the door jerked to attention and went to follow her orders, leaving his post. One less guard at the door.

Think, Sid. Wake up. She's right. You saw this betrayal coming, even if you didn't want to look it in the eye. So get out of your hurricane room and wake up. He was zip-tied to the chair, but one arm had cracked. If he gave it a good wrench, he'd get his left hand free.

"How did you find Bull?" said Mora, now arranging Ruqsana's hair in a fan on the bed. "Suitably shocked and awed by the CIA?"

"Holding it together," said Harwood, not looking around, "until I got there."

"Then you put the fear of God in him?"

Now she turned, gave him a smirk. "The fear of you in him."

He applauded. "Careful, Johanna, you'll get me hot and bothered. And he gave you the location just like that?"

She returned to her work. "More or less. He said that Sir Bertram has run out of patience with Rattenfänger dictating how he use his technology. You want to, what, use it to hold the world to ransom?"

"I appreciate your imagination. And he told you that, just so?" He clicked his fingers.

"I told you the human touch would be more effective than some quantum computer calculating Nowak's location."

"In order to set a quantum computer on the problem, we'd have to employ Sir Bertram's—a small problem when he is no longer answering our phone calls. The prodigal son who does not return."

Harwood shrugged. "You could always use Q."

Bashir stiffened. Mora's hands stilled on Ruqsana's hair.

"I suppose we could have ordered you to run the numbers through Q, yes."

Harwood told Stan to stay still, and then said: "You know too much about me not to have a man on the inside already. You turned me because you knew Moneypenny was getting suspicious, not releasing information to your original source."

Mora reclined in the second row, propping his colossal legs up on the back of the chair in front of him. He pulled his sleeve back, lifting his watch up for Bashir. "I received some of my training from your government, during a brief peacetime. I also enjoyed a sojourn in one of your interrogation cells, during a longer wartime. Johanna is right—I made a friend there. Interrogation goes both ways, as 003 has just demonstrated. A clever girl. She earned my respect in Syria.

I know what you are taught to endure. She did well. You, too, have met my expectations physically. But emotionally, mentally—I did not expect you to let your calf love, your childhood crush, this crusading single mother, die in order to keep one little secret. I don't know whether I am impressed or appalled. Maybe I'll flip a coin. And now to no avail. You see, Mr. Bashir, your Johanna Harwood is actually *my* Johanna Harwood. She was brave like you, for a time, until time grew too long and her knight in shining armor failed to appear."

Bashir spat. "I don't believe you."

"More gallantry."

"I don't believe you turned her then. Syria was for show, wasn't it? You knew we suspected her, so you wanted to prove her loyalty. She passed the lie detectors because she hadn't turned under your torture. She turned long ago." Bashir snapped at Harwood: "It was you, wasn't it? It was you who betrayed Bond. Betrayed me. You're the scalpel. You . . ."

"Mind your manners," said Mora.

The soldier by the trolley flipped the switch. Bashir was dislocated, out of the room, out of his body, out of time, waltzing with Harwood on the balcony after proposing, head-banging to grime on his living room rug with Ruqsana, copying Bollywood moves with his mother, thrashing in the chair, its left arm breaking. The thing is broken, throw the bits away . . .

The pain ebbed away like the ticker-tape static between radio stations. Harwood was speaking calmly, but not to him, to Stan.

"Hold still," she said, "and stop squirming. A man makes his own luck. A woman makes her own choices. And I might choose to sew my signature into you."

Bashir straightened. His bones were jelly.

When he had told Harwood of Bond's last words, she'd grown very quiet, and he'd wondered then if she was regretting choosing him over Bond. Now, it came to him with the sensation of a blow that she might have been reviewing another choice. A choice not to betray—but to appear to betray in service to a higher ideal, and so, possibly, lose everything without even the consolation of love. Could it be true?

"What's the poison?" said Harwood, as above her Stan swore.

"Tricyclic antidepressant," said Mora. "Nothing fancy, I'm afraid."

"Seizures?"

"That would account for her broken ribs," said Mora, ambling to the hospital bed, where he poked Ruqsana in the side. She jerked but made no sound. Mora winked at Bashir. Bashir snarled.

Harwood said, "She'll need benzodiazepines and activated charcoal."

"You missed your calling," said Mora.

"Tell that to Stan," said Harwood, and ducked as Stan went to grab her hair. "Stay cool, Stan, or I'll sew you up inside out."

The soldier flipped the switch again. Bashir could hear his mother's heart monitor. He could hear his dad crying, awful moans—face pressed to the wall of the hospital room, bashing his head there, the first and only time Bashir saw his father cry. Bashir reached for his mother's hand. Now his father was laughing. No, it wasn't his father, it was Mora, crying with laughter, and Harwood was telling them wearily to cut it out, that she could lead them straight to Zofia Nowak.

"A little late to care about 009's welfare now," said Mora.

"Nowak is nearby. She's living under an assumed name in Frankfurt. I can take you to her."

Bashir sagged in the chair. That was where Harwood's father had taken her the night he thought they were being targeted, the night he attacked the homeless man. Sweat crept over his face. But Zofia Nowak wasn't in Frankfurt. She was still in Berlin. That's what the T-shirt designer had written down on her business card. He spat blood onto the floor.

"I think we'll keep dear Sid here," said Mora, "just in case you have a change of heart."

Harwood stood up. She was rolling the sewing needle over her flat palm. The reflection bounced off her watch, glinting in the green light of the choked windows. "I'm not so easily changed."

Sometimes, the thing that was too good to be true turned out to be even better than you knew.

Johanna was wearing rubber-soled boots. He'd never seen them before.

The sniper fire was his mother's heart rate, it was the pip of the BBC World Service, it was the Greenwich Time Signal telling him he was still alive.

Felix Leiter reloaded. He lay prone on the roof of the sanatorium opposite. A thatch of stars made a jagged silhouette of the forested mountainside. He adjusted his scope and fired again through the wild window, an explosion of vines and leaves puffing green in his vision. This time the bullet hit the soldier by the battery, who pitched forward, throwing the switch as he went. Well, nobody was perfect.

Leiter swiveled the gun to the surgical lamps. Pop, pop, pop. He adjusted again, in time to see 003 kick the bucket at Bashir's feet so that the electric wires flopped onto the floor, and the puddles flared blue. Bashir pulled his feet up just in time. The soldier she'd been patching up did a jig. Good thing Harwood had borrowed his fishing boots from the boot of his car after assessing the situation. Leiter finished the soldier with a bullet to center mass.

Harwood had disappeared. He searched for Mora, sweeping the theater. The giant was gone. He swung the scope to the front of the building, and saw two cars starting up: a matte gray Alpine A110S, which he hadn't seen hidden in the tree line, and a black Mercedes G-Class. Their engines gave a combined roar, and both vehicles jumped forward. He returned to the window, checking for surviving Rattenfänger. Harwood had one hell of a cool head, watching them fry 009. He hoped to God that cool head was on his side, and this wasn't a not-so-merry dance she was leading him on.

A second roar drew his attention back to the pack of Mercedes parked slalomed across the hospital forecourt. Four more cars were starting up now. The rats had escaped. Leiter put his next bullet in the front wheel of one, and his second in the back wheel of another. He cursed when the third bullet caught a ricochet and the vehicle broke the compound.

Still, two out of four ain't bad for an old killer like me.

He wished Harwood luck and packed up his rifle, barking orders into the mic at his lapel for a medic to prepare benzodiazepines, activated charcoal—and a defibrillator. Bashir was rigid in the chair.

THIRTY-SIX

Allegiances

Johanna Harwood kicked free of Felix's boots, pulled open the door to her Alpine, and dropped into the bucket seat, its low-slung cradle a familiar comfort that registered at the back of her mind as a return to safety, a return to herself. But she wasn't safe yet. And neither, perhaps, was Sid, depending on how quickly Felix could medevac him out of that ghoulish hospital to a real one. At the press of a button the engine surged to life, thunder in her chest. Harwood swallowed her fear for Sid, punching the red button on the steering wheel that demurely read SPORT, and raced out of the compound for Frankfurt, feeling the bump of old paving stones in her bones.

Shifting down a gear using the paddles, temporarily overriding the automatic gearbox, she slammed her foot on the accelerator, and muttered a prayer of thanks to Moneypenny for getting the car here as she surged onto the mountain road. The torque forced her back into the Dinamica eco-suede in a sudden push that took her back to childhood in Paris, when her mother had driven a classic yellow Alpine A110, a car she'd found as a wreck and restored to beauty, proving to possess a surgeon's hands. If the street was empty, her mother would wink at her and floor it. It thrilled Harwood as a child. It thrilled her now, whipping by the snow-topped trees and confidently taking the corner of the mountain pass, her headlights revealing, on her right, a great wall of trees, some needle-thin, some thick clusters, and above them steeply pointed roofs and a translucent moon; the ground copper with fallen leaves and snaking with arrows that disappeared into the gloom, a curved promise; and on her left, a steep drop into blackness illuminated by the distant flash of train signals.

Harwood jabbed the touch screen to life. The map of the Taunus Mountains glowed to life, a low range thick with forest, broken up by a straggle of villages and thermal spas running south to Frankfurt. The highland was bounded by three rivers: the Rhine to the west, Main to the south, and Lahn to the north. A forty-five minute drive. Harwood squinted as headlights flared to life in the mirror. It occurred to her that forty-five was the statutory age of retirement for Double O's, but she'd never been to a retirement party. It was a polite way of saying your life expectancy was forty-five, at best. She glanced at the mirror. Two cars pursuing, Mora most likely in one of them. They either thought she was telling the truth, and were now trying to beat her to Frankfurt with the intention of finding Zofia, or they thought she was lying, and wanted her dead. Or something in between. Whatever their motivation, she didn't care—only wanted to pull them off course, and leave the real run to Zofia free.

They were driving the new Mercedes G63. The off-road vehicle was almost two and a half times heavier than the Alpine, and had none of its grace, seemingly designed with a ruler and set square—all harsh lines and ninety-degree angles. The roof of the Alpine would only reach the door handles of the Mercedes. Where Harwood's Alpine A110 was a modern facsimile of her mother's even tinier car, the Mercedes G63 was a new take on the 1970s Mercedes G Wagon, a civilian version of the 4x4 made for the German army. The weight of the G63 demanded significant torque from the twin turbo engine. The vehicle could spring from nought to sixty in 4.4 seconds—something they were demonstrating nicely now. The Alpine could do nought to sixty in 4.2 seconds, but it would be the weight that mattered—constructed mainly from aluminum, the Alpine offered speed, responsiveness, and agility. With double wishbone suspension and a mid-engine, it was a nimble thing, taking corners better than any other car she'd driven. Harwood told herself this now as the Mercedes gained ground behind her. Forty-five minutes, forty-five years, what did it matter? This is the race of your life. So floor it.

The halo of the D button on the flying bridge between the seats turned from white to blue as she stabbed to engage the manual gearshift. Harwood switched to track and urged the car to sprint, the worn tarmac beneath the wheels a thrum through her muscles. Another corner coming. She took it well and jumped forward, gaining valuable seconds. The two Mercedes were falling behind. The mountainside dropped away before her into a gully ceilinged with mist, caught by the occasional sodium flare of lampposts and cats' eyes. Harwood glanced at the speedometer. The Alpine usually had a maximum speed of 161 miles per hour, limited by its coding. Q had taken the limits off, and she wondered how much speed she could gather as she hurtled ever downward, now controlling another bend, imagining herself a piece of paper drifting smoothly across the surface of a table. A snarl as the Mercedes bumped back into the rearview mirror.

Harwood realized she hadn't heard the sound of her own breathing for endless minutes. She gripped the steering wheel at the nine and three positions, ballooned her stomach, imagined her ribs expanding outward, her chest filling—and breathed out slow and steady. Her hand was shaking at the three—had been shaking since she finished stitching up Stan and no longer had something to do to keep her mind from Sid's pain. She shook it out, gripped again. Shifted, tapped the accelerator as a clear stretch emerged ahead. Her hand was no longer shaking. Fast and steady.

All you have to do is make it to Frankfurt. All you have to do is forget the image of Sid jerking in the chair, naked and bleeding, as the volts devoured him. All you have to do is forget the look of pure hatred in his eyes. All you have to do is forget the limp body of Ruqsana Choudhury. All you have to do is forget your medical training, and everything you know about trauma to the human body. Think, instead, about the piece of paper gliding over the table toward you. Moneypenny is offering you an assignment. It's an offer, not an order, because it's dangerous in more ways than one. Lose your life, lose your sanity, lose your soul, take your pick.

"You are in a unique position," Moneypenny had said, "a position I want to exploit in order to flush out Rattenfänger. Q's assessment is that the only way Rattenfänger could have so successfully targeted our agents is through recruiting a mole on the inside of MI6. Q also identifies Rattenfänger as the most likely organization to have captured or killed James."

Harwood had sat up straighter in the chair. As a practiced snake charmer herself, she recognized the tactics of manipulation—calling him James, not Bond or by his number, served to underscore the particular intimacy both Harwood and Moneypenny had shared with James, though whether it was the same intimacy Harwood didn't know. The most successful method for blunting a tool of influence was to recognize it. She recognized it in that moment, but didn't want to blunt it. Sensed an opportunity coming to finally *do* something, to stanch the bleeding, and was ready to accept it, no manipulation needed.

"If Rattenfänger have access to our information, they'll know you and James were close for a period. They'll buy it if you go off book to look for him in Syria. I'll begin dropping breadcrumbs now. You'll have to withstand interrogation long enough to make the break seem real. They may offer you something to bring it about. If it's an end to the pain, say yes, but not too soon. If it's James's location, even better, but don't press it. If it's money, privileges, say no. They'll be aware of your profile as a doctor. It will be clear to them that you're not in this game for the rewards. You want to help people. You're an idealist. Let them use that, if they find an angle. An end to the bloodshed, perhaps. One man's life in the big picture still meaning something to you. That sort of thing."

Harwood had smiled, repeating lightly, "Yes—that sort of thing."

Moneypenny managed to snag a waiter. It was a dying summer evening, and they were in the Keeper's Garden at the Royal Academy, a courtyard walled in by the many sides of the gallery. Giant tree ferns bowed overhead, fronds damp from recent rain reaching out to stroke Harwood's hair. The RA was open late tonight to members, and Harwood had found Moneypenny half-hidden in this gully of shadow. No natural light reached them, and no one else had chosen to risk the clouds. They were alone, apart from the waiter, to whom Moneypenny rattled off her order now: Hendrick's gin, lime juice, syrup, rose liqueur, and Cocchi Americano, shaken and strained into a frosted highball glass over crushed ice, and finished with a sprig of mint and a long strip of cucumber, whatever they had to hand. Harwood had seen this drink appear at Moneypenny's table with white rose petals in the past, and wondered if the bartender would attempt to win a smile and a tip from Moneypenny with the same tonight. She didn't look in a giving mood.

"Gin and tonic, take your pick on both," Harwood told the waiter, winning an appreciative glance for not adding a second bespoke request, and even as she did so wondering why it was so important to her to be able to win allegiances, big or small, lasting or fleeting. He vanished, as only good waiters could. She reclined, offering her attention to the ferns. "How old do you think they are?"

"Two hundred and fifty years," said Moneypenny. "The RA imported them from Australia under a special license—when the rainforest gets cut back there, the ferns are usually burned."

Harwood hooked her finger into the delicate curve of the frond. It was like a pinkie swear. "How did they survive the journey?"

Good question, Harwood thought now, as a bullet thudded into the rear window, which Q Branch had fortunately replaced with ballistic glass. She glanced at the wing mirror and saw Mora leaning out of the passenger window of the lead vehicle. The road was getting bumpier, and his second shot—aiming at the tires—missed just as Harwood swung, smelling the rubber burn as she lurched down the hill, the brakes working overtime. The front discs of the G63 glowed red as their brakes smoked too. The road was curling down toward the train track, which cut through the mountain pass. There was a level crossing. The map, with a few adjustments from Q, was live, not just for traffic, but for all vehicles. It showed her a freight train barreling toward the foothills.

Harwood stepped on it, watching the speedometer climb to beyond the usual maximum limit. But she didn't need numbers. She could feel it in her blood, just as she had felt a racing in her blood at the table with Moneypenny. The drinks had arrived. The aroma of British summer chased by the bittersweet Cocchi Americano—wasn't there always something bittersweet about British summer, and about Moneypenny, too, whose cool and direct eyes made one wonder where she could have gained her laughter lines.

"You'll agree to take orders from Rattenfänger," said Moneypenny, "and you'll be true to your word. You must convince them you can be relied on, if not trusted. Make it look real, 003. Make them trust you—as only you can. You won't surface until you've identified the mole in MI6. Only I will know you're a triple. We must control the flow of information if we're to discover where we're leaking. It will mean lying to M, lying to the other Double O's, lying to Sid. Convincing them to give you their trust when they ought to most suspect you. You can do that, can't you?"

Harwood recognized this as the phrasing of a hostage negotiator trying to prompt a *yes*, as saying *no* would suggest you couldn't manage, weren't up to the task, would mean uttering words of failure: *No, I can't do that*. The most effective way to blunt a weapon of manipulation is to recognize it. Again she recognized it. Again she did nothing to blunt its impact.

She said, just as lightly as before: "Yes—I can do that."

Rattenfänger had wanted her to locate Zofia Nowak. Mora wanted Nowak's ideas so they could access Celestial and cut Paradise loose. Mora also hoped Zofia could tell them what Paradise was planning. In the meantime, he had his protégé Yuri keeping Paradise under surveillance, still not quite convinced Paradise had the temerity to be a loose cannon.

Harwood had done as Moneypenny ordered. She'd lied to Sid, lied to Felix, lied to herself about the trauma a body could endure. But she still hadn't secured the identity of the mole. It was only when she peered through Felix's sniper scope and watched Sid's heartbeat peter away that she acknowledged to herself that her oath as a doctor, her oath as a human being, meant there was only so much she could endure. She told Felix to follow up the lead on Zofia's biological grandmother by himself: to trust no one. She was going to throw in the towel, end her run as a triple without getting the identity of the mole, Moneypenny and the whole lot of them be damned. She just wanted to get Mora away from Sid and Ruqsana.

And yet—and yet—while Sid thrashed in his bonds, and Ruqsana's minutes ebbed, she found herself winning allegiances, big or small, lasting or fleeting. Mora had given her the answer perhaps without realizing, at least without caring. The mole, the leak in MI6, had once interrogated him. All Moneypenny need now do was run Mora's file through Q, and wait for the name. Harwood released the nine o'clock position on the steering wheel, finding the crown of her watch on her right wrist. The watch was a gift from Moneypenny, the simplest of gadgets: it emitted Morse code directly to Moneypenny's watch.

A flash in the rearview mirror stole Harwood's attention. Mora was craning from the window again, her lights reflected on his MK. Another spray made the glass creak, and jolted Harwood in her seat. Her thumb stuttered over the crown of the watch. Damn it. A corner was coming up in which she would face Mora across the hypotenuse formed by the mountain's angles—between them a fifteen-hundred-foot drop. Harwood slipped her Glock 17 from the holster Velcroed to the driver's door and snapped off the safety. She took the corner and slid to a momentary halt. The drop yawned before her. Across the gap, Mora was still reaching out of the window. Harwood leaned across the passenger seat, steadied the gun on the frame of the Alpine, and fired twice.

The headshot missed by the width of a flinch. The second bullet struck home in the rear wheel. The car spun, tunneling not over the precipice but into the forest. The second vehicle took over, checking momentarily, and then lurching forward. Harwood dropped the gun onto the seat and accelerated so fast she smelled burning rubber just as the road jinked and the car reached for thin air. She shifted down, refusing to lose momentum, and controlled the curve.

The second car was coming on, but Mora was out of the race— for now. For sure he'd have a spare tire in the back. She wondered how quick the driver's pit stop time was—she knew Mora had only so much patience. He'd demonstrated that in Syria, repeatedly. *You'll have to withstand interrogation long enough to make the break seem real.* It had seemed abstract, even make-believe, under the giant tree ferns in a cavern of slick shadows on a warm summer evening. Mora had made it concrete. Harwood checked the map. Registered the position of the oncoming train. What Sid would call a fun mathematical co-nundrum.

Harwood stamped on the accelerator, gripping the wheel with her right hand and finding the crown of the watch again with her left. She tapped out three sentences in Morse code. *MI6 interrogated Mora. He turned interrogator. Find name.* Moneypenny's Nanna Ditzel watch would be letting off what would sound like a very strange alarm. She breathed out through her nose. Mission success. Time to go home, 003.

Harwood bumped down onto the road running parallel with the train. The level crossing was red. The freight was bearing down on them. Harwood could feel its pressure through the open window. She eased the brakes, watching the pursuit vehicle in the rearview mirror plunge toward her, the driver wanting to take advantage of her stop. Harwood revved the engine. The freight was shrieking. Mist parted from its long spine. The Mercedes screeched to a halt behind her, realizing what she was thinking—the doors opened, two men with MKs jumped out, shouting at her to switch off the engine and get out of the vehicle. Harwood smiled and floored it just like her mother, surging over the tracks as the train filled her vision, breathing in its dust and grit and power, and making it to the other side.

Laughing, she thumped the wheel with a closed fist and gave the Alpine no relief, the torque now accelerating through her as she slammed onto the opposite road and thundered south. The move had given her seconds, perhaps minutes, as the Rattenfänger climbed back into the car, waited for the train to pass, and made it over the tracks. In the Alpine a few minutes was all she needed. She was gaining on Frankfurt. They'd be watching her on satellite, would see that once she'd shaken them she wasted no time in gunning hell-bent for the city, and perhaps conclude she'd been telling the truth about Zofia's location. She hoped so. She must pull them away from Felix and the real location. Fatigue was sapping at her edges. The precipice jumped and jolted in the mirror. The last thing she'd eaten was a croissant that morning, hours, years, before smelling Sid's fear, before calculating Ruqsana's odds, before breaking Robert Bull's neck.

A foghorn made her sit up straight. A long-haul truck was turning the corner ahead, and the driver had pulled his horn at the sight of her—more likely the blur of her. Harwood hugged the mountain wall, rocking in the wave of the truck. The truck driver, startled, had lost control, and the rear end was now careening toward her. She scraped the Alpine against the rock, already mourning the matte finish. The exit offered by the gap between the truck's rear end and the wall was narrowing. Harwood relied on the brakes and they repaid her, swallowing the car's speed with the suddenness of a vacuum. The truck pulled off. Harwood slumped briefly against the wheel, laughed again, and pressed the throttle. Minutes gained, minutes lost.

She was on a thin stretch of road when the headlights reappeared, walled on one side by mountain. The deadly drop waited ahead. The second pursuit vehicle, back in pursuit. Harwood felt again the sensation of the Keeper's Garden: the towering walls, the closed-in courtyard, the sense of no way out, a darkness closing in, which she didn't resist but welcomed, as if she'd been waiting for it her whole life. The Mercedes was closing in.

The Alpine A110S had been modeled after the iconic Alpine A110 Berlinette, the car of her mother. There were five silver switches beneath the display screen, just as there had been in her mother's car. The fifth switch on the right had been intended to control a soft top, until the engineers decided it would compromise the rigidity of the car's structure, losing valuable microseconds. But the switch stayed. You might update an icon; you might even drive an icon into the twenty-first century—but you can't upgrade it. Icons are forever.

So what was the Q Branch to do, with a switch that did nothing?

Harwood slowed down a touch, letting the Mercedes get within a meter. Then she threw the switch. Let there be light. The night blazed a blinding white behind her as if pulled to the center of the sun.

The taillights were equipped with an incapacitating strobe light that used a range finder to measure the distance to a target's eyes, so that it could adjust the light level and control the amount of damage inflicted. First the taillights emitted an ultrabright pulse that would blind the target.

Harwood dare not look in her rearview mirror, but she heard the Mercedes swerve.

Next the taillights emitted light pulses that changed color, dousing the mountain pass now in the flashes of a siren, now in the flashes of a circus writhing in the mist, each pulse longer or shorter than the last without any pattern. It overwhelmed the human brain, bringing on vertigo and nausea. Critics of the incapacitating strobe light said that the target could simply close their eyes and push through the nausea. But you mustn't close your eyes when you're driving. The vertigo brought on by the changing pulses was nothing compared to the vertigo of driving over a cliff edge.

003 threw the switch off and turned to watch the Mercedes sail over the edge. She clicked her tongue, shifted gears, and sped on to Frankfurt.

THIRTY-SEVEN

An Old-Fashioned Shoot-Out

Frankfurt Südbahnhof was so small compared to Frankfurt Main that it would be easy, expecting something much bigger, to ask for directions to the station and discover you were already in it. The station opened onto Diesterwegplatz, where tram tracks cut crescents across the cobbles. Plane trees harbored few leaves. A café, a chemist, and a post office all lined up neatly like in a picture book. No one waited on the benches for a night bus. Nobody was borrowing a city bicycle from the gaggle beneath the twin teardrop lampposts. The rasp of the Alpine's engine chased birds from the trees, stretching membraned shadows under the branches. When the engine fell silent, Harwood was left with the clicks and tings of the overheated car contracting in the cold, and the ragged pound of her own exhilaration, which turned to a sharp tang as the exhilaration flipped inside out. She heaved a breath, and pressed her forehead to the wheel for a moment. The snow hit the windscreen in a patter. She'd parked in a fan of cars, most of them crystalline with ice.

She could have chosen anywhere in Frankfurt to make her last stand, if that's what it was going to be—but in truth, she'd been here just the once in her life, and the night had ended at the café. The owners—who lived above, she imagined—had opened their doors, though it was past midnight then too. A woman in a bright nightgown gave her a hot chocolate to stop her howling under a policeman's apprehensive gaze. Now, the announcement of a sleeper train drifted over the wind. She didn't catch the destination. Harwood imagined posting the car keys through the letter box of the café and boarding the train. She'd find an empty berth and just close her eyes. Wake up in a place that she did not know, and did not know her.

Or not. The discontent of an engine pushed too hard screeched toward her. It had been a three-minute grace. So that's how long it took Mora's man to change a tire. Harwood grabbed her own boots from the back seat as the Mercedes burst to life in her rearview mirror, taking the road into the Platz at a sharp angle, churning snow. She reloaded her weapon, restarted the engine, and slipped out of the car through the passenger door, keeping it from clicking shut. Harwood hunkered in the snow behind the mid-engine. Q Branch had suggested cladding the car in armor, but that would have compromised the Alpine's speed. The door of a car gives little to no protection against active shooters. The only part of a car that provides cover against steel-core penetrator rounds is the engine block. She wormed onto her stomach now, shuffling into the prone sniper position. She was pinned between the Alpine and a VW Golf that had been parked for so long its wheels were sunk in snow.

The slam of a door—just one. She'd seen two figures in the car on the road. Either Mora had ditched his tire changer, or the other way around. The snow-covered cobbles gave an inch worth of space beneath the low carriage of the car, and in the dark it wasn't enough to get a shot off from the ground. The Rattenfänger operative was most likely hovering behind his engine, reading the terrain. She wondered if he'd seen the movement of the door, or was he now trying to pick out her silhouette in the driver's seat?

A crunch in the snow. Then another. Harwood saw his shadow swell in the amber puddle of the lamppost.

"You are there, 003?"

A soft voice, not Mora's. Harwood prayed that didn't mean he'd somehow got hold of Zofia's real location.

Another crunch.

"You will take me to the scientist now. No hard feelings. We are professionals doing a job."

Harwood smiled. Snow seeped into her clothes, and she was grateful to it for shocking her awake.

Another crunch.

"Just tell me the location and we can forget everything."

He was approaching the boot of the car. His shadow was elongated by the gun in his hand. It would be a test of skill and speed. Stand up and shoot faster than he could, then get back behind the engine in case they both missed and he went for the second shot, following her motion. An old-fashioned shoot-out. The kind of thing they practiced in training all the time.

The kind of thing Rattenfänger would practice in training all the time too.

"Come out now, and we will find the scientist together." The thick, almost polystyrene sound of boots sinking into snow, as the operative took up his stance.

Harwood measured the gap between herself and the fifth silver switch. In the time it took her to dive for it, the mercenary could have a shot off. The bulletproof glass ought to withstand gunfire. Ought to. Harwood glanced behind her at the Golf. It looked like it had been parked here days ago, perhaps left by someone who'd taken the train somewhere for the weekend. It was a nice car, a new model and well cared for. Let's hope they keep their alarm in good working order.

She extended one leg, finding the rear wheel of the Golf, and kicked with all her strength. A small bounce, and then a wail.

The shadow flinched. Harwood rose, fired once. She was ducking as a bullet thumped into the boot of the car—the shooter had imagined she was taking cover behind a front engine, tried to find the angle, and failed.

A hush, and then the windows looking down on her turned yellow as the inhabitants switched on their lights.

Harwood's nostrils flared, breathing in the gun smoke, the snow, the panic, remembering window shutters opening like great blinks that night after her father left the man lying on the cobbles and the police arrived.

Sirens spooled through the air.

Harwood stood up, walking into the clear, gun raised. Harwood remained for just a moment, threatening the street, the building, the sky, the peace, threatening nobody at all. She returned to the side of the Rattenfänger operative. She'd found center mass. Four fatalities in a night. Five, if Choudhury didn't make it. Six, if Sid's heart gave out.

The doors of the station were clanging shut. The screech of tires approaching. Harwood then crossed to the Mercedes. There was a radio on the passenger seat. Harwood scooped it up, and returned to the Alpine for a systems check. The shot had been a through-and-through, and missed the Alpine's vital organs.

Harwood made it out just minutes before the police established a cordon. Degrees of grace.

THIRTY-EIGHT

Zofia Nowak

Zofia Nowak's biological grandmother lived in a nursing home—or an assisted living community, as the brochures stacked on the reception desk promised, Leiter translating from German. He flicked one with his fingernail, before giving the woman behind the desk a bright, I-mean-no-harm look. A long time since he was in the field, and the mission was an old folks' home. He tried not to take it personally.

"You say you are a friend of Zofia, Mrs. Schulz's granddaughter?"

"Yes, ma'am."

A doubtful glance back at the monitor. "You are not on the approved visitors list."

"Can't have every Tom, Dick, and Harry walking in off the street to try and swindle the old broads out of their pension funds, right?"

The receptionist was likely a college student trying to make a little extra money, and stuck on the front desk because she was young, white, and buxom, as his ma would have said, in contrast to the porter steering the burdened trolley around the corner toward the security doors, a black woman whose shoulders were wilting. The receptionist perked up briefly at Leiter's portrait of a con artist, before deflating. Nothing so exciting as swindles around here, it would seem. Just give me half a minute, honey.

"Don't suppose you'd give Zofia a ring for me, in that case, tell her I'm here?"

"We do not disturb our residents before breakfast." The dawn chorus was only just beginning. "You do not have Zofia's number yourself?"

"You know Zofia," hazarded Leiter with a reckless grin, "hates technology."

"Oh, that is true, Mrs. Schulz is always telling me how her laptop is broken and I have to arrange for IT support because Zofia who has three degrees cannot even fix it."

Some resentment there. Maybe not a college student. Felix noted the bags under her eyes. Maybe working nights to support a young family, someone who could use a bit of extra dough, but still had her professional pride, not letting him in just like that. Leiter looked beyond the desk, where the security doors stopped passage into the main nest of the building. All the windows were wired, too. God, don't let me end up in a place like this.

Would you prefer the alternative?

"You ever noticed any strange behavior from Zofia?"

"It is unusual, highly unusual, for a resident to have a relative move in here. And Mrs. Schulz says she didn't even know she *had* a granddaughter."

"Uh-huh." The porter was running for a touchdown. Leiter bent an elbow on the counter, and fished a badge from his jacket. It wasn't a German police badge, but also wasn't quite not a German police badge. Gifts of the trade. "You got good instincts. I'm here on a fraud case. I'd like to do this quietly. There'll be a reward for Miss Nowak's capture."

Wide eyes. A nod. "Room 103." Leiter winked, then hurried after the porter, helping her navigate the trolley over a fold in the carpet before the doors closed. In his experience, it was always easier to persuade your way across a threshold when it was opening anyway. He wondered what 003 would make of that. She was a skilled interrogator, he'd give Harwood that, wryly admitting to himself that she'd been interrogating him the whole time they were together, and if he hadn't given the farm away, he'd certainly conceded some of the cattle fields. Maybe a couple of barns. The porter gave him a grateful nod.

The building was arranged in a horseshoe around a frosty lawn. Leiter tracked to the right, counting doors down from fifty, listening to the pipes waking up. It had stung his own professional pride that the CIA—and himself particularly—hadn't picked up that Zofia was adopted. He was mildly mollified when his search through official records came up blank, as did Q. So either Robert Bull had been lying to Harwood, or Zofia was adopted in some less official capacity. He'd agreed to a watertight seal with Harwood on Bull's tip. Bashir had the place, gifting Leiter one word before losing consciousness, the word Mora had tried to pry from his tongue: Pankow. Harwood had the person, a grandmother. An effective team. Somehow, Robert Bull had worked out Zofia was adopted. Robert Bull was a stalker. What did a stalker see that others didn't? Everything.

Leiter had followed the movement data on Robert Bull's phone, matching it to the movement on Zofia's phone, which had been uploaded to the cloud. At some point, she stopped taking it with her; presumably once she realized Bull was snooping. But he still had Bull's shadow footsteps, and he followed them to Café Chagall, a smoky Russian place lit by candles and loud with conversation at three a.m., the walls half-paneled and half-plastered in music posters and flyers. It didn't seem Bull's style; it did seem Zofia's. Bull's phone told Leiter that the creep had lingered in the passage to the ladies' room, where one poster advised women experiencing harassment or violence on a date to ask the bar staff: "Is Luisa here?" The staff would then call the woman a cab, or call the police, whatever seemed necessary.

It was a small place, and Felix felt Bull wouldn't have gone unnoticed long. He had asked the tattooed woman at the bar if she remembered Zofia, explaining he was following up on a harassment case, his

less than official badge once again in hand. She stared at him from beneath metallic blue eyelids—a look that said even if she *did* know he'd
just neutralized multiple targets with a sniper rifle, she still wouldn't
give a damn. Then she told him Zofia sometimes came in with Anya,
the T-shirt designer Bashir had spoken with—who'd since split
town, wisely. Leiter asked the barwoman if she remembered Zofia
reporting trouble with a guy, using the Luisa code word. The woman
gave a heavy shrug, exchanged rapid debate with the needle-thin
woman keeping the cocktail production line going by herself, and
then nodded. Did they have any security cameras? Just one, and who
knew if it worked. But if it would help stop the slime, OK. He seemed
a real nasty piece of work. Felix had nodded. You're not wrong.

The footage had revealed what Leiter had hoped for. That Zofia,
feeling surveilled in her own home, had hoped a public space would
gift the privacy she needed for an act of desperation—seeking refuge
in the arms of strangers. Leiter had fired up the computer himself and
zoomed in on the letter Zofia had written at a table by the window,
before catching Bull in the mirror and hurrying away. Leiter guessed
Bull had caught just enough of the letter in the mirror to decipher its
first sentence.

The letter touched Leiter. *I know this will sound strange, but I think
you might be my grandmother. I'm an orphan. My parents died when I
was young. I recently discovered, through a genetic test, that I am not 100%
Jewish as I thought. My DNA is linked to your son, who I see died many
years ago, as is the DNA of many other people in the same area. If your son
was a sperm donor, as I imagine, I know he would have been promised
anonymity long before DNA testing was viable, and you may never have
known about his generous act. I am writing because I am alone in this
world. I cannot in good conscience bring children into it, knowing what I
do about its future. But I am lonely.*

What struck Leiter most was the way Zofia paused, lifting her
head like a deer hearing the crack of human footfall, before committing

herself to the last lines: *I have less and less faith in my work. It is being put to uses I never intended. I hope you will forgive this intrusion. I have run out of places to turn.*

Leiter thought about how isolated she'd become, most likely bullied by Paradise, the world's savior—who would believe her? Harassed by Bull, a creeping awareness of his presence in every inch of her life. Watching the clock count down on the planet's chances. She simply didn't want to be alone. Leiter wished he'd turned off the good ol' boy charm and listened to her as a man, not an agent.

Now, he drew up in front of Zofia's "grandmother's" room. Snap out of it, Leiter. You're nobody's port in a storm, just the smiling face of the CIA.

He knocked softly. A loud creak of bed or sofa springs sounded from inside. Leiter waited. A clipboard hung next to the door. It read in the rushed hand of a nurse: BERTHE SCHULZ, ☺ MUSIC, PUZZLES ☹ FAMILY, SPORTS. Things to mention and not to mention. The word "family" had recently been rubbed out, but someone had used the wrong kind of pen for the whiteboard so it couldn't disappear fully. Leiter liked the idea of an old dame to whom small talk about sports made you persona non grata. After all, time is short and getting shorter. Shuffling feet made their way to the door. Beneath the dos and don'ts was a note written in a small but inescapable hand. "Distressed by losing bladder control." Leiter winced a little, hoping for Mrs. Schulz's sake that she couldn't read this PSA.

The door opened. Mrs. Schulz was five foot nothing in her slippers and faded housedress. She smelled of rose petal water. Her eyes gleamed like beads, assessing him just as quickly as he'd assessed her. Leiter wished he had a hat to remove.

He switched to German. "Ma'am, I'm here to talk with Zofia."

The doorknob rattled in her hand. "Are you with the police?"

"Yes, ma'am."

"I wish to see your identification."

They should hire you for reception, Felix thought as she frowned at his ID.

"You are not with the federal authorities."

No bullshit about Friday's game, now. "I'm with the American embassy, ma'am. Zofia's in a lot of danger. My name's Felix Leiter. She may have mentioned me. I'd like to help her out, if I can."

"You are American?"

"For my sins."

"Zofia did not say you were American. Your name sounds German."

"Once upon a time." Felix lifted his gaze over her head. There were framed silver records on the wall. On the table what looked like a two-thousand-piece puzzle shaping up to be Van Gogh's *Starry Night* lay incomplete. A pot of coffee with one mug waited on a console by the French windows. "Zofia's not here, is she?"

Mrs. Schulz closed the door by an inch. She said in biting English: "Did you smooth-talk your way in here, Herr Leiter?"

He mirrored her switch with a simple "Yes, ma'am."

"Did you talk smooth to my granddaughter?"

"Sure tried."

"She thought well of you. She even considered asking for your help."

"Wish she had, ma'am. I thought a lot of her."

"She did not think a lot of your employer."

Leiter gave his best who-me smile. "Smart girl. If she'd been a little smarter I'd have had her in a safe house."

Mrs. Schulz stepped aside. Leiter eased the door shut behind him. "Were you surprised when Zofia got in touch with you?" The connecting doors were open, revealing a divan bed with sheets that shone like plastic, and a camping cot.

"I suppose you, too, are going to tell me she is a con artist."

Leiter saw that her ankles were swollen. "Mind if we sit?"

She poured him a cup of black coffee and they sat admiring the bed of hellebores.

"The director of this institute," she said primly, reverting to German, "was highly suspicious too, but I am in sound mind, and there are no rules against taking in one's own granddaughter. I certainly pay enough."

"Only, I can't find any evidence of Zofia's DNA test."

"She erased it. She is good with computer technology."

He smiled. "That she is."

"My son did donate to such causes when he was a medical student."

"He was in the sciences too?"

"He would have been proud of Zofia. We watched that man's launch on the news. His big speech about his computer and his yacht. Those are *my* granddaughter's inventions."

"She has a lot to offer the world. I'd like to make sure she gets to do just that."

Mrs. Schulz brushed her dress, though it was spotless. "How should I know you are Felix Leiter, not this man Robert Bull." She pointed a shaking finger to his leg. "Zofia told me you are an amputee."

Felix twitched his trouser leg up. "Hard to fake that one. She tell you what Bull did?"

Her face hardened. "Yes."

"He's dead now."

"Good."

He sipped his coffee. "I thought so."

"Then Zofia does not need to be scared anymore."

"Almost. But if someone else finds her before me, she's going to need a friend. I'm a friend, Mrs. Schulz."

"I cannot help you. After we watched the news program, she said she must act. Must tell the truth about that man. She phoned someone. Then she left."

Leiter kept his voice languid. "Did she take her phone with her?"

"She smashed it and spread the remains on the flowers."

Felix clapped his hand on his thigh. "Well, as my ma would say to keep from cursing—hellebores, hellebores, hellebores. What time did she place the call?"

"When that man's rocket left the atmosphere."

"Did you get a sense of who it was she was talking to?"

She tipped her hand this way and that. "Not a friend. Zofia sounded not so relaxed as that. Perhaps a journalist. She said she would take a plane, I remember that because she is very against planes. She was to arrive at this place at seven twenty a.m."

"And she left immediately after that?"

"Yes."

Leiter drained his coffee. "You've been a big help, Mrs. Schulz." He stood up. "Mind if I go snooping in your flowers?"

"You have already snooped everywhere else."

He laughed. "Occupational hazard." He was stepping into the frosty soil when Mrs. Schulz called after him. "You will help her, Herr Leiter?"

"Yes, ma'am."

"She has my son's eyes."

He wavered. "Yes, ma'am."

Leiter left the scene with his jacket pocket ruined by damp fragments of a burner phone. He'd get it to the lab, see if they could whistle him up a miracle. But before that, he'd call the only friend he could trust in this situation. He'd ask Moneypenny to consult that magic eight ball they called Q, and run departure times, radius of travel, arrivals, and cross-check with the locations of any known associates in the case, especially journalists. A bit of Pinkerton snooping. Leiter doffed his no-hat to the receptionist and cleared the grounds, pulling out the phone that wasn't in pieces. The sun stroked his face. He sighed, remembering Zofia's confession: *I have less and less faith in my work.* He was glad, in a corner of his heart, to have faith in his work today.

THIRTY-NINE

Lake Bled

The magic eight ball spit out a name and a place. The name: journalist Elena Ilić, flagged already by 004, known for her critical reporting on Sir Bertram, someone Zofia might trust. The place: Lake Bled, Slovenia.

Elena camped there as a child, summers spent pleading for ice cream at the castle restaurant on the hill above the lake; rowing across the brilliant surface to the island at the center, where they'd ring the church bell and make a wish; and sometimes simply floating in her swimming costume, turning in a gentle circle in the wake of boats, battlements bobbing in the periphery of her vision, then thick forest, dry road, sun glittering inside the beads of water on her face. It was the place that made her feel safest on earth, so she told Zofia Nowak to meet her on Bled Island. But Elena's family had never visited in winter, and the trees surrounding Lake Bled were spectral strangers. This defamiliarization left her uneasy. As a child, the future had seemed certain. Now she waited on the shore of the island and watched the lakeside through binoculars, where a *pletna* oarsman waited for Zofia in the traditional boat.

Harwood and Leiter were on the road from Šobec Campground.

Harwood had driven through the night, meeting Felix at Trieste Airport, but Zofia wasn't there. Q told them about the campsite, the place where most of Elena's childhood photos were tagged. The administrators, shocked to be woken by the sort-of-police, had no record of anyone matching Elena or Zofia pitching in the site. Harwood and Leiter stalked among the slumbering tents to the white water river, where Harwood splashed her face, pressing a glacial hand to the back of her neck, thinking of Bashir waiting for word in the hospital. The radio was in her pocket, but it had fallen silent. Mora had realized he was compromised. Aren't we all, thought Harwood now as she whipped around the edge of Lake Bled. Leiter was watching the thermal satellite on the display screen. "We've got movement on the island, and one person at the boats."

Harwood looked across to the island, and had to shield her eyes against the silver glare of binoculars. "Your nine o'clock, Felix. I'd bet that's Elena, worrying about Zofia."

Leiter reached for a rubber-insulated scope Velcroed behind the seat. Elena was practically standing in the water. Zofia must be late. "That's her, watching through binoculars. The man in the boat looks to be waiting to row Zofia to safety."

"Let's hope so."

The screen pulsed. A taxi was dropping someone off at the shore of the lake. Leiter raised the scope again. He watched Zofia Nowak get out and look around with her shoulders hunched. She was clutching a rucksack to her chest. He resisted the surge of hope. She wasn't safe yet. Zofia saw the oarsman, who raised his arm in the boat. She swung the rucksack onto her back, carefully negotiating the icy path to the jetty.

Straight road appeared ahead. Harwood told Felix to hold on to something and the Alpine sprinted with a cavernous echo. It was hard to tell at this speed, but it struck her that, while Zofia looked up, startled, the oarsman did not provide the double take warranted by the appearance of a sports car on an empty road at dawn. She scanned the hilltops. "Does the thermal show any sign of a sniper?"

Leiter did not ask why, only moved the map on the Alpine's screen with his fingertip. "Castle roof, we've got a faint signature at the restaurant. Bit early for setting up."

"How faint?"

The boat wobbled under Zofia, triggering the map to find the disturbance. "Damn it," said Leiter, watching the oarsman manage the boat with confident strokes into the body of the lake.

The sudden stop of the Alpine at the foot of the castle churned up grit and stones. Harwood climbed out and ran down to the jetty. Her gun waited in the shoulder holster beneath her coat and she almost drew it then and there, but something about the way the oarsman now lowered his head to Zofia's to share a whispered conference made her pause. Zofia stiffened. She gripped the side of the boat, then stilled. The boat seesawed gently in the water.

The radio in Harwood's pocket spat to life. "Hold very still now, Johanna." It was Mora. Harwood's flesh pimpled. "Or I will shoot Dr. Nowak. Open your coat."

Harwood heard the crunch of snow as Leiter halted on the path behind her. She raised her hands, then slowly did as Mora said.

"Throw that weapon into the lake."

Harwood bit her lip to keep from swearing. The gun made only a small splash.

"Tell Agent Leiter to discard his weapon, also into the lake. He has one good throwing arm left, I understand."

Harwood looked over her shoulder at Felix. He was six feet from the car. He flushed red, then chucked his sidearm in a wide arc.

"Take the radio from your pocket. Then remove your coat. And your sweater. Your socks and shoes, too, I think."

This time Harwood did swear, then peeled off her layers, tossing them onto the silvered grass. When she pulled her socks off, ice clamped her bare feet. She was left in her jeans and T-shirt. It felt like a sudden fever. She opened the line on the radio, trying to keep her teeth from chattering as she said, "You went to a lot of trouble to get to her. You wouldn't shoot her."

"Trouble? I only listened to the birds. So good at picking up breadcrumbs. But I would like to keep this civilized, so stop dancing on your tiptoes like a puppet, sweet Johanna, or I'll shoot Dr. Nowak in the stomach."

Harwood lowered the soles of her feet into the snow. She breathed. "Go ahead and shoot. I'm a surgeon. I'll take my odds."

"Like you saved Sid? I am told he died from sudden heart failure forty minutes ago."

Harwood almost dropped the radio. She swiveled to Felix. He shook his head.

"I told you not to move."

A bullet slammed into the Alpine's front left tire. She froze, half-turned from the lake now. The shot had come from the battlements. The sniper who had declined to shoot her in Frankfurt. She could hear the creak and slap of the oars as Mora made his way to the far side of the lake. The cold spreading up her legs was white hot. Light was dancing over Leiter's face. Not the red beam of a sniper in the battlements. The reflection from Elena Ilić's binoculars. Harwood saw Felix smile and relief expanded in her chest, a wave against the pain, the same relief she'd felt on missions with Bond when fun would show in his eyes just as it all went wrong. Leiter's arms were spread, too, but he pointed Elena with one finger to the castle.

For the briefest of seconds, the reflection from Elena's binoculars followed his gesture and found a metal surface in the battlements, forging a momentary star that blinded the sniper—who fired. Harwood and Leiter had already both dived, Leiter behind the car, Harwood into a rowboat, hunkering beneath its rim as the whole fleet clunked together.

Leiter popped the rear boot. It was small, but with space enough for his sniper case. How quickly can you assemble a sniper rifle with only one hand? That had been a game once, in training. The answer—damn quick.

Mora's voice snapped through the cold air: "I *will* shoot her."

Harwood reached for the oars, trying to keep her head down. A round missed her by a hair's breadth, rollicking the water. She said into the radio, "I've called, Mora. You can either show me your hand or leave the table."

"Or raise."

The next bullet pierced the boat. Water rushed in. She had to jump into another one. She couldn't see whether Leiter had assembled the rifle he'd slung in the back. She wished they'd had it prepared, despite the border they'd crossed. Measures of grace. Measures of faith. She scrambled for it. The noise of Felix firing round after round into the battlements was pure music. But it wasn't just the gun. Harwood struck out into the lake as the monastery bell clamored. She smiled. Elena Ilić, doing whatever she could, even if all she could do was make some noise. Like a good journalist should.

"Have you got the shooter?" called Harwood.

"He's a squirrelly son of a bitch!" called Leiter.

Harwood was gaining on Mora and Zofia, even as her arms seized in the bitter wind and ice floes knocked on the hull. Mora was rowing with two hands. That meant he'd trusted the sniper to keep the gun moving between Zofia and the agents. He would be armed. But he'd have to stop rowing to pull his weapon.

A shot fired and the bell stopped, its peal a dying echo. Harwood lost the rhythm of the oars for a moment.

So the order had been to take care of the journalist, too. Or else the sniper was simply irritated by the bell.

Leiter moved his scope over the island. Elena lay in a still and bloody heap at the base of the bell. A clean headshot from the sniper on the roof of the castle. Leiter breathed through his nostrils and retrained his sights on the tower. The sniper had found a nest that offered no angle, using an old archer's window. Leiter put two rounds through the slit, shots that would have earned him a merit badge, but it was no good; the shooter must be lying crooked. Leiter had always been a good shot with any armament you cared to name. When he lost his shooting hand, they told him the days of heroics were over. He begged to differ.

Leiter scanned the courtyard restaurant. Outdoor burners stood like sentries over each table, all blanketed in snow, probably not used much this deep into December. He hoped they kept the propane stocked. Leiter loosed three bullets, one after the other, into the heaters. *Boom, boom, boom.* He smiled. He'd always wanted to lay siege to a castle.

Harwood instinctively ducked. A fireball erupted from the battlements. She saw Mora check just as she had, and then redouble his strokes, but Zofia—perhaps realizing there was no longer a gun directly at her head, perhaps simply no longer caring—was now struggling. Harwood could see the bead of Felix's sniper rifle dance over the fighting forms.

Harwood shouted, "Zofia, get down!" The wind stole her words. But it didn't matter. She was almost there.

Then the red bead of Leiter's gun disappeared. Harwood looked over her shoulder. The last shot hadn't been from his rifle. The sniper had survived the blast. Leiter lay motionless by the rear wheels of the Alpine. The white grass beneath him was rusting.

Harwood felt the disturbance of the bullet as she threw herself flat beneath the bench seats of the rowboat. Something very cold touched her, and for a moment she thought it was actually something hot, that it was her own blood. But it wasn't. It was ice water. The bullet had pierced the boat. She was sinking. Mora was disappearing from reach. Harwood controlled her breathing to avoid hyperventilation, filled her lungs with air, and dropped over the side into Lake Bled as another shot shattered the boat.

Shock grabbed her by the throat. Harwood forced her arms to drive deeper. Another bullet stirred the murk. She knew it was working because she was losing light. She couldn't feel her body, only the cold around it. She had been trained to hold her breath for up to four minutes under water. Harwood twisted, treading water slowly, closing her eyes. Her feet were blocks dragging her down. Lake grasses hugged her neck, wrapped around her like limbs. Her T-shirt ballooned, delivering a punch to her ribs, her chest. Her jeans dragged at her. In training, a buddy waited by the side of the pool with their eyes on the clock. Harwood tried to count the seconds herself now. How far would Mora get in four minutes? Would Felix survive four minutes of blood loss? And did the sniper—who seemed to know her combat training in the Frankfurt shoot-out—know just how long she could hold her breath? Would they wait for the fifth minute? She was reaching it now. Her scalp was freezing over, her lungs were burning, her mind was screaming. *Swim up.* Harwood waited. A delicious ease spread through her limbs. That's it. Relax. And breathe.

Harwood jolted in the water. Don't breathe. You'll drown.

Minute six.

Harwood broke the surface, gasping, dizzy, sick. She was rocked and pushed by the swell. She couldn't move her arms. Weeds clung to her face.

No bullet came.

The fragments of the boat drifted nearby. Harwood's teeth were the fall of hammers. It seemed to take hours to get her arms to move, to get to the shell, to cling on, to float.

Lake Bled was empty. Mora was gone. He must have had a car waiting on the opposite shore. How fast was his head start? She could swim to the western shore, repair her tire, pursue. Minutes of grace.

She turned around, finding Felix Leiter prone on the eastern shore. Minutes of faith.

Harwood set off swimming, more slowly than she ever had before, all of those minutes bleeding away. When she reached the shore, it took three attempts to pull her body out. She crawled across the jetty. Made it to her feet on the bank. She was shaking violently. She couldn't think.

"Harwood?" Felix's eyes were open. He was scanning the sky. "Mora, he's got Zofia . . ."

Harwood scrambled up the bank, crying out as her feet seemed to break in two. She hauled the front boot open. Wrapped herself in a thermal blanket. Grabbed the first aid kit, then dropped it. Retrieved the box from beneath the car, opening it with shaking hands as she rushed around to the rear. Felix was the color of ash. He watched her with a removed curiosity.

Harwood sloshed pure alcohol over her palms. It burned. "You're going to be OK. Stay with me. You're going to be OK." *I'm a surgeon. I'll take my odds.* Had she meant it?

"Zofia," said Felix. His gaze darted between clouds. His breath puffed into wisps. "You've gotta get Zofia. Go. Now. This is fine. I'm fine with it."

Harwood looked up at the open road and then said, "I'm not fine with it."

She knelt by his body, opening his coat, then his shirt. Blood spilled over her arms. He was wearing a bulletproof vest. She wanted to kiss him. But the massive round had half-penetrated, lodging in his chest. The sniper had been going for the heart.

Harwood's hands were trembling. She took a shot of the alcohol, shook herself fiercely, and laid out her tools.

FORTY

Trouble in Paradise

The *Ark* was the largest yacht of its kind. Measuring almost 143 meters long with a gross tonnage of 12,600, she was powered by a hybrid diesel-electric propulsion system aided by three masts that represented the tallest and most highly loaded freestanding composite structure in the world. The steel superstructure and curved windows gave the ship the look of a mirrored whale cutting through the ocean. The yacht was also equipped with a communications net that detected and dampened microwaves. But that wasn't why it had disappeared from the face of the earth. Our sense of omniscience is only as strong as our surveillance, and Sir Bertram's new low-orbital satellite array had a capability never mentioned in the specifications. He had hijacked every existing satellite that would detect the *Ark*'s route. He'd erased himself. And he'd erased Joseph Dryden.

It was no use Dryden telling himself he'd been in worse hells than this. He was stripped. No armor, no backup, no brother-in-arms, his hearing shot through, his self shot through. Dryden gripped his knees in the far corner of the gilded cage. The chain of the white tiger kept the animal inches from reaching him, if that. The tiger was snarling, a low growl that filled Dryden's chest like the vibrations of the primary blast. The tiger had been fed as little as Dryden in the last six days.

When exhaustion tugged Dryden under, the white tiger lunged, the chain and the cage shaking like an earthquake, and Dryden would jerk awake and press himself against the bars, the tiger's breath on his face. Eventually, the tiger would settle into the corner, its eyes meeting Dryden's, asking questions of him to which he had no answer. The cage was bolted into the floor of the main saloon, which stretched all the way from the foredeck to the aft, the forward area open to the elements. The *Ark of Paradise* was sailing into the Sea of Okhotsk. Dryden thought that if the tiger didn't kill him, the cold would. He was only kept alive by the tiger's insistence.

The open deck bristled with gigantic spines. The yacht reminded Dryden of a lionfish, its spiked towers ready to spray not poison but a mist of particles that would paint the clouds white, cooling the sea. At least, that's what the world had been told. When Dryden had turned to find Lucky Luke in the corridor of Chungking Mansions, relief and the sting of betrayal had overlapped each other. He'd believed Luke was there to ask for his help, but Luke was only there to deliver him to Paradise. He woke up on the yacht, the tiger sniffing at his mist of fear. Sir Bertram was sitting on a white velvet armchair, legs crossed, one foot tapping the bars. Luke stood at his shoulder, paler than the sky. Paradise was talking, talking, talking, syllables sliding and crashing into each other, mouth twisted into something halfway between a sneer and a smile. When Dryden didn't reply, Paradise kicked the cage and the tiger lunged. Luke jumped forward, signing rapidly.

Luke's words did not match Paradise's expression as the lunatic spoke on and on. He signed to Dryden, his hands shaking, that he was sorry. Paradise had ordered the security team on the yacht to locate and kill Dryden before departing Hong Kong. Luke persuaded Paradise to keep him alive, persuaded him that a Double O could arrange amnesty with MI6, arrange refuge from Rattenfänger. He hadn't known what was going to happen.

Dryden had arranged his bruised and bloodied hands: "I could have taken them. I could have arranged amnesty for you."

Sir Bertram kicked the cage again. The tiger prowled, the fall of its feet the fall of ammunition.

Luke signed: "He wants to hear you speak."

Dryden settled his gaze on Paradise. So the man wanted to find out if the language center of Dryden's brain would scramble his words, if he could even find the nerve to give voice to them. So the man wanted to laugh at him. If you could call him a man. Dryden kept staring until he had the satisfaction of a bead of sweat appearing in Paradise's eyebrows, despite the knife-edge wind. Dryden swallowed spit, cleared his throat. He didn't know if the words would come out right—he didn't care if Paradise laughed at him—he moved his gaze to Luke.

"Life's about choices, man, the ones you make in the hard times. I was born poor and black and gay. I know about hard times. I served my country and lost my hearing and nearly my mind. I got back up. I know you saw hard times. I know you suffered. I know I wasn't there for you when you'd been there for me, and I'm sorry for that. But you never got back up, man, you got down in the dirt with this false god instead, and that's all on you. Our choices define us, not our words. So don't give me your guilt. Do something. Shoot him in the head."

Sir Bertram jolted. Luke's eyes were wide. His hand drifted to the gun in the shoulder holster. Behind, the security team raised their rifles. Poulain brandished the phone, the device that would fry Dryden from the inside out. Paradise swallowed, his Adam's apple sliding down his throat as if making it through rubble. Then he laughed. Luke's hand froze.

Sir Bertram stretched to rub Dryden's head. "Don't be too disappointed," he said—Dryden followed Luke's hands—"it's only a little heartbreak, and you've got bigger things to concern yourself with. I had hoped the impressive 004 would be able to free me of Rattenfänger. The gangsters want to use Cloud Nine as a ransom device. But it transpires, and here's a twist in the tiger's tail"—another kick at the tiger, another lunge—"you were actually helping Rattenfänger. Every word you broadcast to Q was leaked to Rattenfänger."

Dryden croaked, "How do you know that?"

"I'd switched you off, but still Mora knew exactly where to find me in Macau. Dear boy, you came here on good faith, but I'm afraid that faith was misplaced from the start. I'm no savior, and MI6 never wanted to save me. Someone at the top wanted to hand me over. They'd have me be a victim, of one stripe or another"—another kick, a sudden swipe that shredded Dryden's shirt and skinned his shoulder as Paradise laughed—"but I have never been and will never be a victim. I am accelerating the climate crisis for profit. The spray is designed to darken the clouds. I am going to melt the Sea of Okhotsk, cut off the oxygen to the Pacific, and drive the collapse of glaciers. It will open new trade routes. I have mapped them with Celestial. My friends are paying me for the new trade routes I will open up."

Dryden removed the hand he'd pressed to his shoulder, inspected his blood. He signed with slick fingers: "He doesn't care about the people it will affect. What about you, Luke?"

Luke repeated the question to Paradise. Listened queasily. Signed: "He says collapse is inevitable, these companies are content to make money from it while they're alive. The rest is collateral. He says human beings are just units of profit or loss. He says—he says you'll have a front-row seat."

Salt and ice ate at Dryden's face. He considered Paradise and said slowly, measuring his words: "You're not the first white industrialist to put a man who looks like me in a cage, and I'm sure you won't be the last. But before we reach the Sea of Okhotsk, I'm going to feed you to this tiger."

Paradise chuckled.

That was five days ago. Dryden had endured Paradise eating dinner with his security team on deck, consuming champagne and lobsters and steak tartare and smoked salmon and caviar and cocaine and coffee and ice cream, Paradise seeming to gorge like a Nero denied. The spiral staircase that opened onto the deck was lit up with projection of live footage from the underwater observation pod molded into the keel. Images of cracking glaciers hovered at the corner of Dryden's vision, filtering into his dreams, until one night he flinched awake to find Luke crouching by the bars. There were tears in his eyes. His sidearm was missing. He was picking the lock.

Luke was whispering, and Dryden tried to puzzle the words together: "Paradise is finally asleep. I didn't know he'd do this to you. I thought he was a good man. I thought Rattenfänger were trying to steal his technology. He gave me my life back, gave me my sense of being a man back. I had orders to follow again, but I knew they were wrong. I shouldn't have gone along with the fights, Chao's son—when I found out you were using me, I lost it, lost myself. But I'm here now. I've brought you some food and a knife." He fed a parcel through the bars. "I'm going to get the device off Poulain, then slit the throat of anyone who resists me."

Dryden remembered Moneypenny asking him as he left her office: "Who could resist you, Joe?" He whispered the same to Luke now, not convinced he wasn't in a dream. Luke laughed, pressed something sweet to his lips—and then electricity coursed through Luke and into Dryden. Before Dryden lost consciousness, he saw Poulain stick Luke again with the Taser. When he woke, the livestream from the camera in the hull showed light struggling through chinks in the ice. They were getting closer to the heart of the sea. There was no food, no knife, no Luke. The tiger was whispering a promise to kill.

Luke did not reappear on deck. Dryden didn't know if he was still alive. But he knew the ship was just a day and a half away from the release site. Now, Dryden tapped the ground softly with the only thing he had in his pocket, a coin that had lingered since he'd stolen the contents of the taxi driver's strongbox. The tiger opened one baleful eye and regarded him. Dryden almost laughed. He wanted to ask— You got any bright ideas? Because I'm all out. The tiger swiped the air, raising its head, and then fell heavily back down, blue eyes settling on the clouds. The chain shivered. Dryden inched forward. The manacle was showing strain. He looked at the joints of the cage.

FORTY-ONE

Dagger Complex

Bashir didn't stir on the hospital pillow. He didn't want Johanna to know he was awake. She was sleeping in an overstuffed chair by the window. The wear of the last few days showed in gray stamps on her face. She had been treated for hypothermia after she brought Felix Leiter in to the Dagger Complex, and now drifted between Leiter's room, Bashir's, and Ruqsana's. Leiter was recovering. Ruqsana was not, the coma consuming seconds, minutes, days. Her mother was told that she'd experienced an unknown allergic reaction. Bashir knew he ought to call Mrs. Choudhury, but every time he picked up the heavy phone by the bed, he lost his nerve and surrendered it to the cradle. He knew he'd only do all the wrong things: ask Mrs. Choudhury for sympathy when he ought to give it; ask her—who'd known him since he was a boy, when she was running the nursery at the Barton Hill community center—how he'd got here. How he'd gone so wrong as to take the coincidence of friendship and let it darken Ruqsana's skies so terribly.

Bashir's parents met over iftar at Barton Hill. Bashir's father was Sudanese, his mother Pakistani. Bashir's mother had arranged the Islamic Cultural Fayre in Bristol every year. He remembered cringing by her side after September 11th under a banner that read: DON'T PANIC I'M ISLAMIC. Remembered the football tournaments she organized, swapping nations among his teammates like trading Pokémon cards: Somali kids, Pakistani, Indian, Bangladeshi, Kosovan, Indonesian, English. His mother wrote constant applications for council funding, requesting volunteer linesmen, a flip chart for a scoreboard, even public sector presence. His mates would ask if his mum was round the bend, inviting not just the police to the Fayre, but the army, fire brigade, and Crown Prosecution Service, who all touted their wares from stalls decorated in red, white, and blue. They wanted Muslim probation officers, Muslim firefighters, Muslim friends who would keep ears and eyes open. (That last suggested only between the lines.) His father, tall and skinny as a goalpost—something Bashir had inherited—watched all this from the sidelines, hovering near his Bristol Blue taxi, wanting to run away from the stiff smiles of the police and their like, but pinned there by his wife's inexhaustible efforts. And amidst it all, Bashir: desperate to stay inside, to play chess, and get away from the good intentions of his mother and the reluctant faith of his father. But he never had. So here he was. A spy who brought the only friend he looked forward to hanging out with at the Fayre into danger, and left her there, not even for his ideals, simply for his philosophy. One life. Many lives.

He knew what Mrs. Choudhury would tell him. What were you thinking, Aazar Siddig Bashir? Your mother taught you that to save one life is to save all of humanity, and instead of honoring her memory you sacrifice my daughter to your cold calculations.

And for what? They'd lost Dr. Zofia Nowak. They'd lost 004 to Paradise, disappeared from every satellite image and shipping report. They'd lost Paradise, or perhaps to him. They'd lost to Rattenfänger.

"That doesn't look like a nice place to be," said Harwood. She was awake, the blanket folded neatly on the back of the chair.

"Where?" said Bashir.

"Inside your head. Ruqsana has a very good chance of recovery, Sid."

He cleared his throat. Studied the morning shadows on the floor. "I never should have involved her in any of this. I should have listened to myself."

"I didn't know you had doubts."

Sid laid a hand over the bruise on his chest. "At the beginning of all this. When I was mounting the rescue op in Syria to recover you, I was doing it because M thought that you'd have likely turned—it had been so many days. Or that you were a double already. He thought we could use you. I could use you. It wasn't a rescue mission."

She linked her hands between her knees. Her expression gave away nothing.

"I wanted to want to save you because I love you. I wanted to want to save you because whoever saves one life saves all of humanity. That's my mother's philosophy, my parents' faith. I wanted it to be the whole reason, my whole commitment. But it wasn't. It was a fraction of a calculation. M told me to get close to you again, reignite our relationship, and watch for betrayal. I did it, even though I knew it was unethical." A bitter laugh. "And I didn't even do a good job of it."

Harwood crossed to the bed and sat by his feet, correcting the fall of the blanket. "We were both playing a long game. You know that. You lie to me. I lie to you. Maybe we should've got married after all."

That made him smile. "So what's the truth?"

"The truth." She looked off, beyond the wall of the room, beyond the US Army base, into the past perhaps, or the future, somewhere that truth could be easily described. "The truth is I love you, Sid. Always did, always will. The truth is I had a job to do, and so did you. Always did, always will."

"Except we failed."

"I've given everything for this mission, and I'm not prepared to admit failure. Moneypenny is running down who in MI6 interrogated Mora, and in the meantime Tanner is in a precautionary sweat box—apparently he'd been making mystery visits to an unknown contact, and keeping certain things back about Paradise's circle. We're closer than ever to finding the mole. Aisha and Ibrahim are trying to shut down Paradise's satellites to reveal his ship. And M is working on convincing the government to launch an ASAT against Paradise's satellites if Q can't shut them down. 004 will be doing everything he can to bring Paradise into the light. Ground teams have swept Baikonur for the location of Paradise's own quantum computer to see if we can turn the satellites off at the source. If we find that, we can shut down his satellites from his own control station. Everybody's doing their jobs, Sid."

"Except us."

"You tell me, then, with that astounding mind of yours. What's our job?"

"Save Dr. Nowak from Rattenfänger. It doesn't matter if we save Paradise or stop Paradise—whatever's the flavor of the day. If Rattenfänger gains her knowledge—gains *her*—all of this will have been in vain."

The door bounced open, knocking against a wheelchair. Felix Leiter maneuvered himself across the rubber floor. He winked at Harwood.

"You shouldn't be up yet," said Harwood.

"I'm good as new, doc. Here's a souvenir for you." A shell casing glinted in his palm. "Sniper got sloppy once. Might be all we need. Seven-point-six-two-millimeter round. I'll send it to Moneypenny with a bow, see what your lab can figure."

"Any idea on the identity of the shooter?" said Harwood. "A sniper that good belongs to a fairly elite club. You've probably met before."

"You flatter me. I got one theory, but it's just a hunch. James ever tell you about Trigger?"

Harwood nodded. The sniper posing as a cellist Bond had let escape in a shooting match in Berlin after spending three days constructing a fantasy around her beautiful pale blond profile. Harwood had been as unimpressed as M was back in the day. But she'd quieted down when Bond reminded her she was new at this game—wait until the murder really hits you, and you'd do anything to have Tanner sack you from the Double O Section so you can settle down and make a snug nest of papers as an ordinary staffer. Then scaring the living daylights out of your opposite number and maybe taking her left hand instead of killing her won't seem so foolish.

Harwood had reminded James of that snug nest of papers when she told him it was over between them. She asked if he truly believed he'd make it there, if he truly *wanted* to make it there. James had asked her the same in return. "We're the same model," he'd said.

She had disagreed then. She wondered now.

Harwood cleared her throat. "I thought James injured Trigger enough to put her out of the game?"

Leiter tossed the shell case, plucking it from the air. "You don't see me hanging up my gun. Trigger had an impressive profile as a shooter, and her signature still crops up every now and again. One theory is the Russians chucked her for failing against Bond and she went freelance. Her work has crossed my desk a couple of times."

"You see her signature here?" asked Harwood.

"Something in the movement . . ."

"The sniper shot Elena. That wasn't necessary. Does that fit Trigger's MO?"

"Hard to say. She's ruthless."

"So much for James's long-range, one-sided romance."

"Don't sell yourself short," said Leiter. "James likes 'em ruthless." Then his raptor's gaze settled on Bashir. "Sorry, kid. Hear you're the brains of the outfit. The million-dollar question. Where does Rattenfänger disappear people? Johanna, Mora never gave you a sense of where they might be stashing prisoners? You must've talked about James."

"I tried," said Harwood. "No give."

"Wherever he's got Dr. Nowak, it's someplace without technology, right?" said Leiter. "Otherwise Q would have found her instantly. Same with James."

Bashir touched his foot to Harwood's knee. "When you agreed to be captured by Rattenfänger, did Moneypenny know where they'd take you?"

"No. But she knew what to follow." She raised her arm. "She had my location in my watch. Mrs. Keator developed a homing device and Morse code emitter that wasn't detected by Rattenfänger. Trust the classics."

"But Q eventually picked up satellite footage of you entering the compound," said Bashir. "That's how we found you."

"That's what Moneypenny told you. She had to wait until my breaking would seem convincing to Rattenfänger. She always knew where I was."

Leiter whistled. "You are the real deal."

"Did Moneypenny doctor the footage?" asked Bashir.

"Not by herself," said Harwood. "Mrs. Keator was a co-conspirator."

"Did they direct Q *not* to watch the compound?"

"No, directing our satellites away from Syria would have raised suspicion," said Harwood. Her eyes narrowed. "But still, Q didn't pick up on me entering the compound."

"How's that possible?" said Leiter.

"It's not," said Bashir. "Are you sure you were in the compound for the duration of your capture?"

Harwood tapped her watch. "One way to find out."

FORTY-TWO

Double or Nothing

The *Ark* had gone as far as it could. The Sea of Okhotsk, the northwestern arm of the Pacific, was bounded by the Russian-controlled Kamchatka Peninsula to the east, the Kuril Islands to the southeast, and Sakhalin Island and the eastern coast of Siberia to the west and north; the Japanese island of Hokkaidō tapered its southern limits. This deep into winter, navigation was limited to those who lived on the water as fishermen, and even for them it was often impassable. The high quantity of freshwater flow from the Amur lowered the salinity and raised the freezing point, forming giant ice floes that creaked over the surface. The sea ice had been melting since the 1950s as oceans warmed, and was projected to shrink by about forty percent by 2050. The Sea of Okhotsk supported one of the most diverse and abundant marine ecosystems in the world, responsible for pumping oxygen into the heart of the Pacific. If the Sea of Okhotsk melted, it would trigger a cascade failure, killing marine life and melting ice caps throughout the ocean.

Joseph Dryden breathed on his fingertips. He couldn't move his hands. The tiger snorted in response, a brief puff of warmth that Dryden wanted to drown in. In the last day, Dryden had been shuffling closer to the tiger, inch by inch, prompting it to lunge at him. It had broadsided his coat, stripes of the fabric wound in its claws. The links in the tiger's chain were yawning. The cage, shaken by the tiger's thrashes and frozen by the winds, rang like glass.

Sir Bertram strode onto the foredeck. He was flanked by the six security guards and six additional crewmen, all armed. Paradise squared his shoulders before the spines that would release the deadly particles into the marine cloud layer. He was carrying a laptop, the first time Dryden had seen him handle technology.

"Time for a new world!" Then he laughed, pointing overhead. A Steller's sea eagle broke up the white sky.

Dryden dragged the coin from his pocket. It was the heaviest thing he'd ever lifted. He wet his lips. Called—croaked—"Sure it's not an albatross?"

Paradise gave him a glance, then seemed to decide to ignore him. "Initialize the start-up sequence."

The crewmen moved to the spines, each taking a winch at the base. Paradise was focused on the laptop.

Dryden leaned his head against the bars. "Want to make a bet?"

Paradise's gloved fingers stilled. He was twenty paces from Dryden. He took three steps closer. "You have nothing to offer."

"Heads," said Dryden softly, forcing his words into order, "you turn off the machine. Tails, I give you Nowak."

Paradise took a step closer. "Speak up, boy."

Dryden clenched his jaw. "Heads. You turn off machine. Tails. I give you Nowak."

"You don't know where she is. Anyway, why would I care?"

Dryden shrugged. "Afraid of the odds?"

Paradise scoffed, then checked his watch. The crewmen were busy at work, calling numbers and words Dryden couldn't pick out.

Then Paradise said something—Dryden read his lips—"I'll take that bet."

Dryden tossed the coin, catching it on the back of his ashen hand.

Tails.

The tiger growled.

Paradise took another step. "Poor luck, Joseph."

Dryden rubbed the coin. It winked. "Double or nothing."

"You have nothing else to offer."

Dryden picked out the word "offer." He got to one knee. The tiger stirred. "Luke. Where's Luke?"

A ripple of discontent crossed Paradise's content expression. "Below. He is behaving like a petulant child. *I've* gifted him opportunity, *I've* gifted him purpose, *I've* gifted him stability, *I've* gifted him family. And now he sulks because there's one toy I deny him. *You*, a deaf brute of absolutely no value or use."

"Double or nothing. I'll forgive him."

Paradise's eyes narrowed. "I won't let you out of that cage."

Dryden shrugged.

The crew were cheering. There was a tremor through the deck. Something had started.

"Don't you want Luke to see this?"

Paradise narrowed his eyes. He nodded.

Dryden tossed. The coin clattered on the base of the cage. The tiger lumbered to its feet. Dryden stood up, retrieving the coin. He was within an inch of the tiger's range. He showed the coin. Tails.

"You just don't have luck on your side," said Paradise.

The crew were applauding. One of them brought Paradise a bottle of champagne. Dryden couldn't work out what they were saying. But then a jet of spray launched into the sky, making him duck. It was starting.

Paradise lifted his watch. "Or time. It will be irreversible within thirty minutes. After that, the damage will be done. No one can stop me now. Even if your precious MI6 were to spur Russia or Japan to act, and even if they could find me, it would not matter. The world will think it was a terrible accident. One only I can correct. You, I'm afraid, will not survive the tragedy. Tiger meat is only so much dead weight. I've won." He seized the champagne by the neck. Then snapped at the crewman: "Fetch Luke."

The crewman hurried away.

Paradise's words were oozing into each other. Dryden edged into the weakest corner of the cage. He was within the reach of the tiger. He thought he could feel the breath of the animal on the back of his legs, if he could feel anything. The flickering projection of water on the staircase seemed to be clouding, but perhaps that was his fading eyes. He reached through the bars, holding up the coin.

Paradise took a step closer. He sneered. "Double or nothing?"

Dryden tossed the coin. It glittered through the air. Paradise bent closer, saying something Dryden didn't catch because he was throwing himself to the floor as the tiger lunged for his back and the animal's bulk brushed the top of his head. The chain snapped. The wall of the cage smacked to the deck. The tiger landed on Paradise's chest.

Dryden saw red. The tiger tore Paradise apart, gouging and scraping and wrenching. He could see Paradise was screaming but the sound bled away with the rest of him. Everything inside him, whatever he amounted to, was smeared across the deck. The tiger snapped Paradise's limbs like wet kindling. Steam rose from its shoulder blades, its paw prints a crimson signature.

The crew and the guards stood frozen for a moment, and then opened fire. Dryden hugged the deck. The tiger seemed to weave past the shots, hissing and clawing the air, and then leaped on Poulain. Poulain dropped his rifle, which clattered across the deck. Dryden reached for it.

Dryden stood over Paradise. The man was a soggy mess. His eyes were wild white blanks in shreds of scarlet. Dryden considered Paradise's last double or nothing. He considered his sum, his parts, his worth. Then he said, "Nothing," and shot him in the head.

The tiger slid into the main saloon. A security officer and an armed crewman dead. Five guards remaining, all carrying, plus five crew. Dryden dropped to one knee. His fingers were bleeding, split apart. His trigger finger was calcified. He'd used his last reserve. He couldn't move. He braced himself for the end.

Then Lucky Luke came out firing.

FORTY-THREE

A Hillside in Syria

Harwood and Bashir walked deeper into the caves in lockstep, weapons ready. The ground was slick, stealing and stretching their reflections, which were doubled in the needles of stalactites groping for them overhead. The cave stretched into the hillside, a deep network of tunnels shielded from thermal or ground sensor penetration because of high levels of lead. They had no permission to operate inside Syria, no cover stories, no false identities, no legends, and no backup. Solve an international incident without starting another international incident. Harwood lifted her collar against the cold. The light from the entrance faded, eclipsed, gone. Her breath twisted in the remaining glow of the flashlight attached to her Glock. She glanced at Bashir. He nodded to her. Time to finish this.

The movement of Harwood's watch had revealed she'd been in the compound for her full time in captivity—at least, beneath it. The tunnels had been used by warring factions and freedom fighters for decades. Moneypenny found geological surveys in the British Library dating back to the nineteenth century and fed scans to Q, which predicted the most likely entry point roughly ten klicks to the south.

Aisha was incensed, demanding to know why Q wouldn't have picked up Harwood's body mass index and gait, even if she was hooded—they'd searched this satellite footage already, as Harwood had been captured in Syria. She spooled the satellite captures back through time, finding the day in question, and had the answer, though it wasn't one she liked. There were Mora and his troops dragging Harwood into the cave entrance. But it didn't look like Harwood. The body was completely different. The prisoner wasn't even wearing a hood. The face was different too. The obvious answer was that this was simply a different prisoner being taken into the compound via the back door. But facial recognition rang a bell. This person was a primary school teacher who was alive and well in Scotland. She had gone through a body scanner at Edinburgh Airport the day before the footage was taken.

Dr. Nowak's quantum computer represented an artificial intelligence capable of learning someone's face and body and mapping them on top of someone else in a live satellite feed. But you'd have to control the satellite first. Moneypenny had thrown her drink at the wall. Rattenfänger had backed Paradise, and in return he'd built a code into his computer for them, using his array of satellites to erase prisoners from the world's eyes. A new form of rendition. Zofia's own designs had been used to make her disappear. And Harwood. And, Moneypenny would bet all the money in her pocket against all the money in Paradise's pocket, James Bond too. Aisha managed to peel back the layers and find the original image beneath. Harwood's limp figure. She'd found Zofia Nowak next, exactly as Bashir had predicted. Ibrahim suggested they use Bashir's brain instead of Q and got a shoe thrown at him.

The satellite feed told them Dr. Nowak was inside with Mora and a company of Rattenfänger men. Harwood probed her muscles for memory of these sloping rock surfaces, these icy needles, these scattering rocks beneath her feet. But she must have been unconscious, carried by Mora into the tunnels to the subterranean cell. She'd been pumped full of chemicals for days—could recall only slices pulsing with light and noise, Mora's fingers probing her nerves, Mora's mouth over hers, Mora's laugh—but she must have been carried to the cell above ground when Rattenfänger knew Bashir was approaching. When the mole told them a rescue op was underway.

And Mora let Bashir set the place on fire, let him play the hero, because they were planning to wind Harwood up and set her running in the field. Rattenfänger would have had not only a mole in the office, the hand holding the spear, but also a mole in the field, the tip of the spear.

But Moneypenny had seen them coming, turning Harwood to a triple. Now Mora would be doing what he did to her to Dr. Nowak, forcing her to give them access to Celestial—another mind to crack open like a jack-in-the-box and twist what springs out. Harwood squared her shoulders.

Harwood and Bashir had studied the schematics on the plane before parachuting into the Mediterranean Sea and making land incursion. They had decided on a backdoor assault through the least passable tunnel, entering separately, banking on the element of surprise. The tunnel was narrowing. According to the plans, it would branch ahead. The left branch was a fair-size passage and led to a chamber cut by a river. The right would shrink to a meter square for a passage of one hundred meters, and then split before feeding into the same chamber. Their gambit was to take the least accessible, and least likely to be guarded.

"Did you ever find out Mora's real name?" said Bashir, breath shivering between them.

"No," said Harwood. "Why?"

"Mora—it stems from the Kikimora, right? I looked up the folktale. It's Russian. Mora's linked to several terrorist actions in Russian cities. Do you think he chose a Russian name because he's their nightmare?"

"You're wondering if he has a particular grudge against Russia?"

"Moneypenny can't find the British agent who interrogated him. Maybe it wasn't one of us, exactly. Maybe it was a Russian ally. When we had those."

"Colonel Nikitin?"

"Worth asking if he's had any nightmares lately."

Harwood smiled at Bashir. Then she said softly, "Did you have nightmares? After your encounter with Mora?"

He ducked under the sloping ceiling. "Did you?"

"You know I did."

Bashir paused at the entrance of the shrinking tunnel. "I read a couple of folktales that included methods of repulsion, ways to keep the Kikimora from your home. You can recite a prayer or poem before you fall asleep. Or leave a broom upside down behind the door."

"My money's on the broom."

Bashir chuckled. "Me too. Though I've had this poem going round and round in my head. It was assigned to me, when James taught me clandestine communication.

"Go where you will: I have no more to say:
You have had what I could give; take it and go.
I will not argue who 'twas struck the blow;
The thing is broken, throw the bits away . . ."

Harwood touched Bashir's arm. "You're not broken, Sid."

"Mora said different." Bashir's voice was constrained. "He said I was broken out of the package. Maybe I am. Look what happened to Ruqsana. To you and me."

Harwood gripped Bashir's arm. "Mora's a homicidal maniac. Let's not take his life advice." That shook a laugh from him. "Whoever saves one life saves all of humanity. We were both raised believing that. Zofia needs us now."

Bashir faced the narrow entrance of the tunnel. Then he offered Harwood his closed left fist, and his gun hand. "Pick to see who goes first?"

She tapped his left hand.

Bashir opened an empty palm. "White goes first."

"Which one of us is playing white today?"

"Me." Then he kissed her softly.

Harwood felt his touch linger as he disappeared into blackness. She dimmed her light, wriggled her shoulders into the gap, and followed. Rock scraped her shoulder blades and she tossed her coat behind her, going on hands and knees. Cold water leached through her clothes. She inched underneath a bulge in the rock above, wincing as it gashed her scalp and neck. She felt the hot beads of blood. She shouldered on, hearing Bashir grunt ahead of her. Something scurried over her legs.

"Almost there," whispered Bashir.

The chamber they were aiming at was the largest in the hillside. It was a good bet prisoners would be kept there. Before reaching it, the tunnel would branch west and east, dropping into the chamber at opposite sides. Harwood would take one, Bashir the other.

As they packed their parachutes, Bashir had told Harwood that strategically, surprise is considered a force multiplier, a tactic that increases the effectiveness of one's forces in war while reducing casualties, facilitating the destruction of a significant quota of the enemy's forces at a lower cost to the attacker by throwing the inherently stronger defense off psychologically, reducing his readiness and resistance. The outnumbered side is able to take the initiative by concentrating her best forces at a place and time of her choosing. Surprise temporarily suspends the dialectical makeup of warfare by neutralizing an active opponent from the battlefield, meaning the probability of an event can be calculated, or even determined, with a higher degree of certainty. Surprise transforms war from a strategic interaction into one of logistics and probabilities. It ends the duel before it begins. Surprise removes the need for war.

Harwood had asked him why, in that case, he was lacking the irritating look of victory that stole over him in chess. Bashir had not met her gaze as he told her that surprise came with a high-risk price tag. It is impossible to guarantee that the surprise will come off, or when it will wear off, and any failure will doom the mission. Unless surprise produces complete victory, the capacity for surprise to transform war is fleeting, and soon lost. Launch a commando raid of twelve men against a high-value base behind enemy lines and achieve surprise—that small force could end a war. Fail to achieve surprise, and that small force is immediately wiped off the board as if they'd joined the frontline regiment and walked into gunfire.

What they had to hope was that Mora simply did not believe the Double O's were capable of finding Rattenfänger's subterranean base, especially without advance warning from his mole—and Moneypenny had Tanner isolated with no way to warn Mora, if Tanner was in fact the mole. This surprise attack would seem impossible to Mora, especially with Bashir hospitalized; both Moneypenny and Felix Leiter had broadcast on as many channels as possible that Bashir was still in hospital, as he probably should be, but try telling him that. If a surprise attack seemed highly unlikely to Mora because of the diminished numbers and intelligence vulnerabilities of the Double O's, it would be less risky for the Double O's, because Mora would be less prepared. The greater the risk, the smaller the risk actually becomes.

Checking Bashir's parachute, Harwood had asked him: "So what's our risk here?"

Bashir had finally met her eyes. "That Tanner isn't the leak."

Now, they reached the branch. Harwood tapped Bashir's shoulder—good to proceed. Bashir set the timer running on his Casio watch and crawled east. Harwood took the western tunnel. The ceiling was climbing, thank God. The burning between her shoulder blades raged down her spine as she stretched. There was light at the end of the tunnel. Could mean a reason to hope. Could mean you're dying. Toss you for it.

Harwood curled herself like a fossil into the earth, listening for sounds. The tumble of water. A mechanical whirring, like a fan. And a scream. It caught Harwood in the gut. She checked her weapon, drew the stale air in deeply through her nostrils, and edged closer to the cusp of the entrance.

A crescent vision of water spilling from a grille at the north of the chamber, and the slick trail of a river curving northeast. Harwood had to check that she was seeing what her brain told her she was seeing. The river was spilling over glass. The floor of the chamber was glass. Beneath it, the nerve endings of a quantum computer bathed in golden light. Paradise's quantum computer sat inside the heart of Rattenfänger—but they must not know how to operate it, must be locked out, and that was why Zofia Nowak was bound in the middle of the floor. She was crying. Her left arm flopped from the socket. There were two steel tables set up in front of her. One offered a laptop. The other, a tray of injection needles and pharmaceutical liquids. A masked Rattenfänger soldier held a gun to her head. Four more guarded the main entrance, which was next to the waterfall grille at the northwest. Another stood at the table of poisons, his hand hovering over the needles as Zofia begged him to stop. Bile crawled up Harwood's throat. That made six soldiers. And Mora, who was stooping over the waterfall, drinking from a cupped hand. Then he splashed his face, and turned to face Zofia with raised eyebrows and a look of impatient disappointment.

"Well, Dr. Nowak? I promised you five minutes' relief. That's five minutes."

Zofia flinched.

Harwood felt sweat on her brow. She remembered this—a carousel of relief and pain, except the moments of relief never seemed to last as long as he'd promised, and grew ever further apart. Not this time. She had a clear shot. And, finally, she was going to take it.

Harwood fired. The bullet lodged in the air at the entrance to the chamber. No—not the air. She ought to be able to smell the water, smell Zofia's panic, smell the chemical stink of it all. But she couldn't. Bulletproof glass casing blocked off the tunnel.

They saw you coming.

Harwood twisted—over her shoulder, a laser grid closed off the retreat.

At the same time, Bashir appeared at the eastern entrance and opened fire. His tunnel was open. The first shot took the head off the guard holding the weapon at Zofia's head. And the second would have hit Mora's center mass, if he weren't standing behind a shield of bulletproof glass. A slow smile spread over his face as the remaining guards trained their weapons on Bashir. Bashir was outnumbered six to one, with absolutely no surprise on his side.

FORTY-FOUR

Crossing Saturn

Bob Simmons knocked softly at Moneypenny's door. Moneypenny called for him to enter without looking away from her screens. The audio from HAVOC on the plane skirting Syrian airspace spooled into her office. It was a comfort to hear Felix Leiter's drawl, though she knew he was breaking every doctor's order.

"What is it, Bob?"

No answer.

Moneypenny glanced up. Bob looked stricken. "What's happened? Sun blinked?"

Bob Simmons sidled in, accompanied by two other security officers—Precious Mosaku and Don Nicholson—who were both armed. They moved aside for Mrs. Keator, who was shaking, her usually pale cheeks spotted red. She could see Phoebe standing with her hands vaguely raised by the coat rack, watched by another officer, Jay Russo.

"Mrs. Keator?"

"A transmission is leaving this building from your station."

"I've got an open line to Felix Leiter."

"That's not it." Mrs. Keator looked like she was having trouble breathing. "You're transmitting your screen activity. Including 009 and 003's plan of approach."

Moneypenny laid a hand on her keyboard. "That's not possible."

Mrs. Keator beckoned Aisha Asante inside. "Go ahead."

Aisha paused at the threshold, biting her lower lip. Then said, "Sorry, Ms. Moneypenny."

Moneypenny's stomach flipped as Aisha took apart her machine, trailing its wires like fishing lines. "I can't possibly be transmitting."

The device was smaller than a fingernail. Aisha held it up to the lamplight. "This is it."

"I've never seen that before in my life," said Moneypenny.

"You were going to frame Bill Tanner," said Mrs. Keator, "and you had me help you."

Moneypenny slammed her fist on the desk. "We don't have time for this."

"You're going to sit here under Bob Simmons and Mosaku's watch until M arrives. Be glad it's them, not me."

"You can't release Tanner," said Moneypenny. "You have to listen to me."

Mrs. Keator shook her head. "I'll let M decide what to do with the two of you. He put the Double O's under your care. He trusted you. I trusted you. Bill trusted you, too."

Moneypenny came out from behind her desk. Mosaku and Nicholson both raised their weapons by an instinctive inch, and then froze. Bob Simmons got himself between them all, his arm raised.

"All right, everyone," he said equably, "let's keep the peace."

Moneypenny glanced back to her phone. She could hear Leiter say they had failed to cross Saturn. Each stage of the mission had a code name. Successful landing had been Mercury. Penetration of the tunnels, radioed in by Harwood, Jupiter. No contact was expected beneath ground because of the depth and makeup of the soil. Harwood and Bashir had given an estimate of how long they thought it would take for them to neutralize Mora and make contact. And that time had passed.

FORTY-FIVE

Countdown

Luke's first shot hit the merc closest to Dryden, a pink mist appearing where the man's head had been before his body hit the deck. It pushed Dryden into action. Luke was alternating between firing at the guards and firing at the spines, taking cover behind the wall of the saloon. But the cloud-seeding spray was still releasing toward the clouds. Dryden ran for Luke, sliding on water and blood, righting himself, until the two were back-to-back in the saloon.

More armed crewmen appeared on deck from the spiral staircase that peeled through the ship. The stairs were lit up with the live projection from the underwater observation pod, and the men merged with flickering algae and seaweed, faces studded by frostfish. A bullet brushed the projector and its footage knocked and splayed across the walls. Luke sprayed the foredeck. Dryden got off one shot in three toward the stairs, his trigger finger threatening to snap from frostbite. The crewmen broke into the saloon, three fanning to the left and taking cover behind a table laid with champagne and salmon, and three to the right, taking cover behind a white velvet sofa—all chased by the giant shadow of a whale whose projection reared over the glass walls.

"Engine room! We have to cut the power!"

Dryden was aware of Luke shouting behind him, but couldn't pick out the words.

Luke's left hand appeared in Dryden's peripheral vision, signing rapidly: "Engine room, cut power."

So all they had to do was get to the lower decks. Dryden fired left—hitting a champagne bottle in a fountain of spray—and right. He crouched as the guards returned fire, Luke now twisting to use Dryden's shoulder as a steadier. Dryden did the same, firing past Luke to the deck. He grabbed Luke and sent him sliding across the floor as a security officer came out from behind the cover of the spines and fired. Then Luke seized Dryden by the chin and turned his face so he saw the tiger leaping over the white velvet sofa.

Dryden nodded. They raced to the stairs, falling into writhing seaweed made of light as they crashed down, past the guest quarters—Dryden saw two cleaners cowering behind the bed, who raised their hands at the sight of him—then past the main bedroom, where he glimpsed Paradise's white velvet chairs, a white chaise longue, a bed in white satin, and all of them spattered red, Luke's guards lying dead on the white rug, and down again. Gunfire chased them, Luke and Dryden exchanging places, covering and running, covering and running. The minutes were ticking down—how long until it was irreversible? Dryden thumbed blood and ice from his watch: nine minutes and counting. He joined Luke in barricading the door at the base of the stairs with everything they could find—chairs, a dish cupboard—to the tremendous crash of glass.

The underwater observation pod lay ahead. The three curved elliptical windows revealed a looming rock encased in cracking ice and erupting in bubbles. *And I saw as it were a sea of glass mingled with fire.* The light from the camera flashed in his eyes, and Dryden imagined the projector filling the deck with his ravaged face. The observation pod included a sofa and a glass table, on which waited another bottle of Dom Pérignon '46 in a chilled bucket. Dryden had the small bite of satisfaction that Paradise would not be alive to watch from these padded seats as the sea ice melted. Then a muffled *whoomph* told him the shooters had made it through the barricade. Dryden checked his ammunition. Empty.

He tapped Luke's arm. Luke shook his head. Dryden picked up the champagne, good for a club if nothing else, and followed Luke down the last wind of staircase to the door of the engine room. Luke shot the lock, and then stood back for Dryden to kick it in. The metal jumped up his legs and reverberated through his chest as the door popped its frame and bounced back. Dryden tapped Luke on the shoulder and left him defending the door. Luke dragged the steel sheet back into position. How many minutes, seconds, could he hold the line?

The engine room was both diesel and electric, so vast Dryden couldn't see the far end. It was a cathedral to machinery. The warmth scorched his numbed bones. Think, he had to think. He just had to shut off all the ship's power, and the spines would deactivate. But he couldn't speak to Q and ask how, he didn't have a tactical operations center at his back, he just had himself. You want to stop the electrics. That's what it runs on. And the sun ain't blinking. No electric magnetic pulse from heaven. No signs from God. No twists of fate, no lucky hand. Dryden glanced at Luke, who was waiting for the breach with sweat on his brow and his mouth set in a firm line. He shook himself. You want to break something that was engineered to within an inch of its life to withstand any pressure the sea or air or fire could throw at it. So break the safeties. Break everything.

The door budged. Luke pushed it back.

Five minutes until the cloud-seeding spray took permanent effect.

Dryden seized Luke's shoulder. He signed: "I'm going to overload the engine."

Luke looked between him and the door. He signed: "It was my job to keep you safe. I'm your 2ic."

Dryden signed: "Not anymore."

Luke touched the side of his face, almost brushing his ear. He signed: "I'm sorry."

Dryden caught his hand and kissed his palm. Running down the galleys, he counted off valves and pipes he didn't understand until he reached a steel-paneled wall with his name on it: WARNING—DANGER. The gauges showed needles on the diesel tanks hovering exactly in their safety lines. Dryden hauled at each lever, pushing each gauge into the red.

The door bent.

Four minutes.

A seam of metal on the tanks popped. Buckled. Hissed. The reek of gas.

Dryden wrenched a lever off and struck it against the metal until a spark snaked in wavering air. A lick of flame erupted into the engine room. The clanging tinnitus in his head turned to wailing. Sparks showered down on him. The circuits were overloading. The needles on the valves were banging their heads against the red lines. He slid for cover behind a row of pumps. Sprinklers turned on, dousing him, but the sparks continued. A bang punched him in the chest.

One minute. Pray it was enough.

Dryden poked his head into the galley. Luke was emptying his clip. The door crashed in and guards clambered through it. Luke was down. Two immediately moved to the safety controls. Two others fanned out in search of Dryden. And the last aimed his rifle at Luke's head. Dryden whistled, drawing his attention as fire licked at his back.

FORTY-SIX

Hurricane Room

The guards forced Bashir to his knees, shouting at him to get his hands behind his head and his face on the floor, shouts to surrender his weapon, a rifle butt to the cheek—Harwood watched it all with paralysis stretching through her limbs, under Mora's beneficent smile. He winked at her. Zofia's look of relief and euphoria was crumpling into despair.

Mora waved a hand. "Take him apart."

Bashir's body jerked and thrashed under the guard's boots.

Mora sauntered over to Harwood and tapped a knuckle on the glass as if taunting a goldfish. "So good of you to join us, sweet Johanna, I've missed your cold heart. Don't let me down now—those aren't tears I see in your eyes, are they? If you had just done as you were told, little girl, then your lover would be tucked up in your bed right now. Maybe even both of them. Tell me, did James and Sid ever enjoy you that way? Or each other? I'd love to know—"

A crack of bone interrupted him. The guards had all recoiled, a human reflex perhaps at what had just happened. Bashir's ankle flopped. Mora grinned at Harwood through the glass, his head perfectly framed by its circle.

Harwood raised her gun and fired between his eyes. The bullet lodged in the material.

Mora clicked his tongue. "Touchy." He swung away, ruffling Zofia's hair. Zofia shrieked.

Harwood kicked the glass—nothing. Of course, nothing. She inspected the rock around the casing. She doubted a bullet could crack it or the new iron bolts. She fired another bullet in the exact position of the last—a crack veined through the surface, but it did not give. Mora clicked his fingers and another guard grabbed Zofia by the neck and stuck his gun in her face. Harwood cursed under her breath. Inched around. She chucked a loose stone at the lasers—it crisped and shattered before falling to the ground. Harwood patted her pockets, and then her watch. She yanked it from her wrist, turning it inside out to reveal the gold-plating underside of the face. She just needed Sid to distract them. Mora might do it for her. He was enjoying the sound of his own voice once again.

"That looks like a nasty break, son. You should really have a doctor look at it." Mora laughed, touching the tip of his boot to the lurid gash. "Do you call it probability or fate, Sid, that circumstances would lead you both back here, and once again Johanna would be imprisoned, and you would face me alone, this time the lives of not one but two lovely ladies hanging in the balance? I suppose you tossed for which tunnel you would take. Let's call that my good luck. I had hoped it would end this way. Last time, Johanna broke free a little earlier than she was supposed to. A willful girl. I never got to finish my kiss goodnight."

"Wait." Bashir heard his own voice as if from miles away. "What happened to fair play?"

"I thought you skipped civics," said Mora.

Bashir got to one elbow, then another, then gripped the wall behind him and pulled, feeling all of the blood drain from his face and his stomach rise into his throat.

Mora watched with eyebrows raised, and then clapped slowly. "Would you like a medal?"

"A rematch."

"You want to fight me for the women? How very patriarchal."

"Whoever saves one life saves all of humanity."

Mora sneered. "Quaint."

The waterfall thundered around them. Bashir blinked the sting of sweat from his eyes. The chamber was round, with the waterfall crashing from above into a sheer drop below, its spray kept from the quantum computer by a long chute of glass. The computer hung, suspended, beneath where Dr. Nowak sat tied to a chair. His efforts had been futile. But if he could just buy Johanna some time, he knew she'd think of something.

"Scared?" said Bashir.

Mora laughed. He floated back. A distance of twelve feet between them, and Mora between Bashir and Dr. Nowak. He beckoned with one finger.

Bashir had to stay out of his deadly reach, avoid Mora's lethal jabs and pokes, and avoid putting all of his weight on his broken ankle— every time he did he felt as though he was going to faint. Bashir raised his fists, limping in a half-circle as Mora prowled from side to side. Mora swiped. Bashir veered, trying to get in a blow as Mora retreated, but the giant moved in a blur. Mora came again. This time Bashir was too slow, and Mora's index finger jammed into his solar plexus. He lashed out with his good leg, catching a blow to Mora's hip, but his other leg buckled and Bashir was off-balance when Mora came for his throat, his arms, his chest.

It was happening again, he was being dismantled, and he'd only managed to land one hit. Mora had him in a bind—there was no best play left to him, no blockade, no Boden's Mate. Mora pincered Bashir's torso between his knees and Bashir's neck between his fingers, contorting and breaking him. His mouth came for Bashir's, the moth's wings groping and flapping from Mora's steaming neck, and Bashir was paralyzed, could not move, could not breathe. A demon was squatting on his chest and he was crying out for help but no one would come and the demon's mouth was swallowing his last breath.

He is in his hurricane room. Only the room has changed. It is not white or empty anymore. It is a room in the community center where his parents met. He spent hours in this room as a boy. The walls are faded salmon, a color he will later associate with rooms set aside for waiting in hospitals, but he does not know that pain yet. The window is stained glass, a project his mother organized, and his father watched from the side, pride pouring from him. Bashir is elated, his mother has arranged all this, and hangs by the artist's elbow all day, wanting to be in the thick of it. He's not learned reserve yet, either. The stained glass window shows a moon in the top left corner, silver rays rippling a midnight sky. In the top right corner, a sun burns, gold shimmering in summer noon. The moon and the sun pour onto the famous multi-colored Victorian terraces that peer down on Bristol from the hillside. On the hill itself, the children have designed emblems of what matters to them in the city. The artist let Bashir include something that didn't belong to the city, but belonged to him. A chess piece. A knight. Bashir touches its rippling solder outline, and then turns to embrace the rest of the room. The usual boxes of craft supplies are missing. But the rug is still there. Bashir sits down. He remembers this fabric with a sigh. The red-and-orange border, the blue-and-green inlays, the deep-purple curves, and the tree at the center, alive with fruit and birds. Bashir strokes the branches. He breathes. He learned to play chess lying on this rug with his father. And when he reaches out, a set carved in sandstone is waiting for him. Your move—a voice tells him. Johanna's voice.

Mora's mouth remained over his, sniffing at his last breath. Bashir bit down on Mora's tongue, raised his throbbing hands to Mora's neck, and twisted. It was like trying to wring the body of a boa constrictor. He spat out the tip of Mora's tongue and all the blood that came with it and kept twisting. His vision was spotting—he could just see Mora's eye, Mora's cheek, turning purple. Shouts, screams. He couldn't make Mora's neck break. But it didn't matter. Mora wasn't breathing.

"I'll shoot Nowak! I'll shoot her!"

In the tunnel, Johanna Harwood edged the back of her watch into the path of the laser. The beam bounced. She adjusted the angle, the metal already melting, a bounce burning her arm—and then it lined up, the light searing the damage she'd already caused to the bulletproof glass, which shattered. Harwood dropped to the floor and fired, killing first the guard standing over Zofia, then the two hauling Mora's body off Bashir. Two by the door got shots off—one missed, one hit—Harwood took out the shooter on the left in the first numb moment of the bullet finding her shoulder. She was empty, no time to reload.

Harwood strode to Zofia's side and tipped up the medical table, hurling the vials and needles along with the table itself at the guard, who ducked. He was still in a crouch as Harwood followed the path of destruction, stabbing him in the neck with the first needle she could find. He grabbed her arm for a long moment, light-blue eyes fixed on her, and then convulsed, smacking the ground. Harwood yanked the needle out and hurled it, catching the final shooter in the thorax. He collapsed as his finger squeezed the trigger, a wild arc. Dust and rock rained down.

Harwood turned to Bashir. "Are you OK?"

"I'll live."

Harwood grinned. "Check he won't."

Bashir nodded, pulling himself up to Mora's massive form. He checked his pulse, hating the slime of his neck beneath his fingers. No movement. He checked his wrist—the same. Then put his palm in front of Mora's ruin of a mouth—only the still heat of death.

Bashir dragged himself across the rock to the waterfall, drinking in the shocking cold, spitting out the taste of blood.

Harwood found secateurs among Mora's tools and cut Zofia's binds, quickly holding her before she collapsed, squatting at Zofia's feet. She held the scientist, feeling Zofia's tears in her hair, trickling through her scalp.

"I'm going to put your arm back into place. I'm a doctor. Count to three with me, OK? One, two, three." A snap, a shriek. Zofia panted into Harwood's neck. "We're with the British government. You're safe. He can't hurt you again. You protected your work." Harwood straightened Zofia. "Can you show me where it hurts?" Zofia's hands moved slowly. Harwood followed their path, keeping up a kind chatter as she checked the marks of Mora's torture. "You're going to be just fine. We'll take care of you. Rattenfänger wanted you to give them access to the computer. I know you were trying to blow the whistle on Paradise. I know what Robert Bull did. He's dead now. But Paradise has disappeared. We can't find him because Paradise is using his satellites to shield his ship. I need you to access the computer and shut those satellites down so we can bring Paradise to justice, OK?"

Zofia stiffened, tried to pull away.

"Hey, hey—look at me." Harwood found Zofia's green eyes and smiled into them. "I'm not with Mora, I'm not with Rattenfänger. Don't look at Mora. Just look at us. We're on your side."

Zofia swallowed. When her voice emerged it was reedy, strangled. "How can I trust you? How do I know you won't take me into your custody?"

Harwood bounced on her heels, still squatting before Zofia, her hands opened peacefully. "When we take you out of here, Felix Leiter is going to be waiting for you. He's going to make sure you get your life back."

"Mora said he was dead."

"He underestimates my surgical powers. We don't have time to debate this, Dr. Nowak. You've got to make a choice. We've come a long way to find you. All we want to do now is bring Paradise to justice and secure your safety. Please, believe me."

Zofia rubbed her wrists, then the marks on her arm. Her gaze stayed steady on Harwood's face. She nodded.

Harwood smiled. "Thank you." She drew the table with the computer console closer. "Can you do it from here?"

Zofia moved her hair from her face with a shaking hand. She nodded. Harwood stood at Zofia's shoulder, watching her type. A satellite map took up the screen. Bashir was sitting at the edge of the waterfall, his attention shifting between Zofia and Mora's body.

"Either Tanner wasn't the leak," he said, "or he wasn't acting alone."

"I know," said Harwood softly. She laid an encouraging hand on Zofia's shoulder when the doctor looked up. "Don't worry. Carry on. Do you want a drink of water?"

"I've got it," said Zofia. She didn't seem to have heard the question. "I'm disabling the satellites. The ship is in the Sea of Okhotsk. I can see a plume of smoke."

"Can you zoom in at all?"

"I can process the image . . ."

"Let me look at your ankle," said Harwood, lifting her face to Bashir.

A sharp breath drew Harwood's attention. Mora was moving. There was a rifle on the ground. Harwood hugged herself around Zofia. A shot exploded into the chamber. For a long and infinitesimal second, Harwood waited for her body to report its damage. But the throbbing in her shoulder and the scorch to her arm and the hundred small cuts did not bloom or shrink. She moved an inch, asking Zofia if she was OK—she nodded—and then another shot answered. They were both OK because Bashir had returned fire—returned fire as he put himself in the path of the bullet.

FORTY-SEVEN

Fire in the Engine Room

Joseph Dryden knelt over Luke, the rifle of the dead guard now in his arms. Luke was unconscious. He fired into the smoke of the engine room. Noise swamped him. Gunshots appeared from the flame. Dryden grabbed Luke and hauled him to the corner. The ship shuddered and moaned. Dryden imagined his situation report—outnumbered and overwhelmed by opposing forces, 2ic injured, Alpha suffering frostbite and burns and God knew what else. Dryden did not lower his sights. He was still squeezing the trigger when the gun stopped responding. I'm out of ammunition, and there's a fire in the engine room. So get out of the engine room.

Dryden cast the weapon aside and lifted Luke in a fireman's hold, yelling out as he did so, his muscles tearing. He clambered over the ruin of the door and into the hall, heat pressing behind him. He knew the remaining officers would be having the same thought—abandon ship. He just had to get to the tender garage first, the vast chamber below containing a small submarine, a limo tender, and a sports tender. Dryden moved into the hall, and almost retreated immediately. Water was flooding up the stairs. A bullet whistled by. Up, the only choice was up. Dryden took the stairs two at a time, careening into the walls, just keeping hold of Luke—until the ship lurched and Luke fell and Dryden smacked his knee on the stairs. Another bullet thumped the wall above his head. He tried to stand. His knee tore.

Luke woke with a grunt. "My turn," he said, hauling at Dryden, lugging him up the stairs one by one, then at the bend lifting Dryden over his shoulder, making the last flight.

But Paradise's men were closing in behind. Luke set Dryden down in the saloon, almost slipping, the floor awash. The live camera projection from the observation deck was glitching—strobes of sea grass and the shadow of sharks ate them. Both men heard a ripping and tearing—they looked up through the glass ceiling to see the masts collapsing, a terrible demolition. Luke grabbed Dryden's hand. Dryden looked round—Luke was staring at the opening of the foredeck, at the busted cage and Paradise's corpse—the tiger was pacing the deck, growling at the sky. Then the remaining three officers reached the top of the stairs.

The flickering footage of a sea crab closing its pincers was shadowed by rappel lines and the fan of a rotor blade. Dryden looked up. Helicopters hovered overhead. Commandos were dropping on deck. Six, twelve, eighteen of them landing on the foredeck, barking commands. Dryden couldn't pick out their words, but raised his hands anyway. Luke did the same. Dryden waited for a last-ditch bullet, but Paradise's soldiers were surrendering. Two of the commandos were carrying a net, which they hurled over the tiger. One drew a plastic-looking gun, shooting a dart into the creature's flank. Then the commandos formed a diamond, protecting their own Alpha, who landed on deck with a thud, a few years perhaps since he'd been in the field. But the man removed his harness with economy. He had a big, square figure and moved powerfully through the ruin, stepping over glass and bodies, with only a lingering gaze for the tiger. His dark eyes glittered. He offered Dryden his hand, flashing a gold-toothed sunburst of a smile.

"Tiger Tanaka. Pleasure to meet you, 004."

Dryden blinked. He lowered his arms. When he took Tanaka's hand, his whole weight almost went, and only the steel grip kept him upright.

"M is anxious to speak with you."

Dryden shook his head. He couldn't keep his eyes open enough to read the man's lips, and the words meant nothing at all. Luke got between the two men with just his shoulder, a slight guard as he said something. Tiger Tanaka nodded slowly. He spoke to Luke. Luke nodded, said something else.

Then he turned to Dryden and signed: "This is Tiger Tanaka of the Japanese Secret Service. He says your boss wants to talk to you. Medical's on standby. Early days, but they reckon we turned the device off in time. No lasting damage. I've explained I was Paradise's second-in-command. He's going to take me and the survivors into custody."

Dryden grabbed Luke's hands, silencing his fingers. "Wait," he said. "That's not . . ."

Tiger Tanaka stood back. He ordered his soldiers to secure the prisoners and leave the Cloud Nine to burn or sink, whichever happened faster. He didn't want it: Tiger Tanaka did not need a crystal ball to tell him the sea ice was shrinking and that their days were running short. Speak of next year and the devil laughs. He put little to no faith in shiny toys. He watched Joseph Dryden. Tiger Tanaka put his faith in other things.

Luke shook his head. Dryden felt tears on his cheeks—they were his own. He wiped his face on Luke's shoulder. Luke's arms came around him.

FORTY-EIGHT

Oaths

I can fix this, Sid, I can fix this—stay with me. You're not broken, do you hear me? You're not broken." Harwood was slicing open Bashir's shirt and pulling the bulletproof vest off him, the good-for-nothing bulletproof vest, whose plates had shifted when Bashir had been kicked on the ground, a tiny and fundamental flaw that now meant Aazar Siddig Bashir was bleeding out from a shot to the upper chest despite her efforts to stanch the flow. "You're going to be fine. Ruqsana's going to be fine, and you're going to see her again, and you and me, Sid, you and me, we're going to . . ."

Bashir laughed, a gurgle. "What're we going to do, Johanna?"

"See this?" She pulled the engagement ring from her neck, and slipped it on her finger. "See, Sid? I do. I do. I already wrote my vows—you're the best man I've ever known, that's what . . ."

He smiled—it was a wan shadow crossing his face.

Harwood caught at the fleeting tails of her training, applying pressure that made him cry out, shouting at Zofia to find her a med kit, anything, anything at all.

Bashir's hand caught hers. "Too late. I do, too."

Harwood pressed her forehead to his. "It's not too late. I can fix this."

"Johanna . . ." Bashir's lips moved over her skin. "You're not the mole, are you?"

Harwood flinched, sitting back by an inch. Tears spilled over. "You don't think that, do you, Sid?"

He studied her through narrowing eyes. "No. M's going to walk us down the aisle."

Harwood buried her face in his neck, aware of the convulsions of her own body, then suddenly realizing that she did not want to panic him in his last moments—the guilt of this making her cry all the harder, and then draw it in, a short and sharp breath. She shook her hair back and gave him her best smile. "You did it, Sid. You saved Dr. Nowak. You saved one life that could save all of humanity."

He shook his head, a small movement, but one that seemed to stretch into the years he wouldn't occupy. "I saved you, Johanna. I know where I want to marry you."

"Where, Sid? I'll arrange it now. We'll do it now."

"The community center. My hurricane room. There's this window . . ."

Harwood waited. A film spread gradually over his eyes, chasing out the final spark. Harwood felt her heart dislodge, a physical crack. She was holding a dead man's hand.

A chuckle sounded behind her. Harwood turned. Mora was laughing. He lay sprawled on his back, one mammoth hand clamping his thigh, where Bashir's bullet had clipped him. Blood spooled from his mouth. Harwood felt time slow in her veins. She got to her feet. Dr. Nowak stood six paces back, out of breath, a medical kit dangling from one hand and horror stamped on her face. Harwood studied the litter on the floor. She picked up one of the needles, reading the label. She squatted down at Mora's side.

"I suppose that elixir won't send me to a sleep of sweet dreams?" His voice was cloudy, an unsteady red fountain.

"The right amount would. It would keep you unconscious until

Leiter and Moneypenny get the authority to send a retrieval team in here, for you and all this equipment. That's what the right amount would do. But it's been a long time since med school."

"You swore an oath, Dr. Harwood, to do no harm."

"I took another oath."

Mora grunted. "You bend with the breeze. That's what I like about you."

Harwood recalled Dr. Kowalczyk saying the same: *Your word is worth so little?* Recalled the pin of her stare as she asked: *Why did you kill the bastard, instead of capturing him for interrogation?* Back then, the truth was that she made a shot which looked like a killing blow but wasn't, at Moneypenny's orders, despite everything the monster had done to her. This mutability, her capacity to bend with the breeze, had meant Sid asked her with his last breaths if she was a traitor. Now, the truth would be that she delivered a fatal shot because the monster had taken her lover and she had a license to kill.

Mora grunted, squeezing his leg.

"Kill him." Harwood heard Dr. Nowak come closer as she said again: "Kill him. He doesn't deserve to live. The world would be better without him."

Between blinks, Harwood imagined the window Bashir might have described, if he'd been granted a few more words, imagined him waiting for her, imagined M's hand on her elbow as she reached the aisle. Then she straightened.

"I don't live in that world. He has valuable intel. Pass me the med kit."

Mora sighed, resting his head back on the stone. "That's my girl."

Harwood sneered. "When you wake up, it will be to a cell darker than this one and the old friend who interrogated you for company. Your real mole." She took the kit and swabbed Mora's neck before easing in the tip of the needle.

Mora's eyes eased shut. His voice was deep with contentment as he said, "I look forward to seeing him again . . ."

Harwood paused in unpacking the gauze and needle. She looked from Mora's face, the laughter lines, the deep crevice that turned down at his lips, a smirk tucked permanently in the lower right-hand corner; he lost nothing of his self in sleep. Then she looked to Bashir, whose inquisitive gaze, now dulled, was turned to the roof of the chamber; there was no pinch of worry between his eyebrows, and his lips parted slightly as if ready to ask a question, to ask the world what he could give.

Harwood got to work.

FORTY-NINE

Repercussions

The light burned red as M closed the door behind him. He paused there, resting his head on the soundproof padding. Standing behind her desk, Moneypenny imagined the gauntlet he'd run, the questions on the faces of the other Double O's, Q Branch, Bob Simmons. Her grip on the files she was stuffing into her bag was unsteady. She relinquished the bag, and it thudded onto her desktop.

"Sir, I would have driven over to Vauxhall."

M gave a one-shouldered shrug. "Don't grieve and drive, I always say. Mind if I raid your liquor cabinet? We can drink and sit, instead."

M was stiff-backed as he poured them both a whisky. Then he twitched up his trousers and sat down on the black leather sofa, which had been softened by countless late-night counsels. Moneypenny joined him, taking the glass. It felt too heavy. Everything felt too heavy.

"To 009," said M.

"Sid Bashir."

They both drank.

Moneypenny wiped a thumb across her lower lip. "I posted two guards outside Bill Tanner's office. One was removed to guard me. I suppose we can call that a budgeting problem."

"I'll raise it with the minister next time we golf."

"I should have put Tanner in a holding cell. I just—he gave me the tour on my first day here. He was already seasoned then. I couldn't imagine it. Unlike Mrs. Keator and you, who it would seem had no trouble imagining me as a traitor."

"Don't undersell yourself," said M. "You imagined it just fine, Penny. That's why you cleared the office you stuffed him in of pointed objects and nailed the window shut."

"It didn't help," said Moneypenny, opening her left hand. The wiring from the light fitting had cut across her palm as she tried to hold Bill up with one shoulder and free the cord from his neck.

She had been moments too late. If only Aisha had realized a few minutes sooner that the log indicating that Moneypenny checked the transmitter out of Q Branch had been falsified, or if Harwood's report that Mora used the pronoun "him" to describe the figure Mora turned during his own interrogation had been analyzed sooner, or if Q had spat out Tanner's name as that interrogator sooner, or if, or if . . .

M took Moneypenny's unmarked hand and quickly squeezed, then released her and sat back with a sigh. His face was stone. "Bill Tanner and I were pups behind the Iron Curtain together under Sir Miles Messervy. We used to haunt a *palais de danse* in Berlin rigged up with telephones and pneumatic tube postal service connecting hundreds of tables so that strangers could make dates or pass anonymous compliments. Bill once set me up with a girl who turned out to be an East German agent, quite the shock over pillow talk . . ." M shook his head. "Always good for a laugh, Bill. He'd keep you smiling when the going got tough. More than once he snatched my balls from the fire, James's too—the whole God damn Service." For a moment his face cracked, then he sniffed and cleared his throat. "Bloody silly thing to do, hanging himself. Could have got him out of a tight spot, if he'd just told me about his son."

Moneypenny pulled the crumpled note from her pocket, but did not open it. Tanner had an illegitimate son he'd never disclosed to the Service or his wife, who had left him five years ago, after she discovered the truth. The son was in Lewes Prison. When Moneypenny ran a background check on the prisoners, Q missed the son because there was another man's name on the birth certificate. But Tanner's wife confirmed it. On the phone with Moneypenny, she asked what all this was about, and fell completely silent as Moneypenny explained, the phone almost slipping from her hand, which was slick with sweat, her own and Tanner's.

They couldn't explain how Rattenfänger had discovered the son's identity, but they had, and used it to blackmail Bill. He said no at first. Then his son suffered an "overdose" of spice and almost died on the floor of the prison laundry. After that, Tanner said yes. The former 009 had been the first victim. And Tanner kept saying yes. The new 009 was his last victim. Moneypenny wondered what Sid would have to say about the statistical likelihood of that, the sublime nature of coincidence.

Tanner had signed the note with one word—"Sorry." Moneypenny looked over the entrails of her computer. Tanner had installed the bug just before he was put into isolation, a last-ditch attempt to keep his end of the bargain and save his son's life.

Moneypenny rested her drink on her knee. She looked at the black window—beyond it, the doll's house squares of yellow lights, ordinary lives in London playing out. "Mrs. Keator told me Bill Tanner was an honorable man."

"He was," said M stiffly.

"Tell that to Sid." Moneypenny's voice rose. "Tell that to the six Double O agents for whom we hung memorial stars in the past two years." She stood up. "Tell that to James Bond."

M ducked his head, took a drink. He scratched his stubble. Then he considered her with a mild gaze. "You wanted the job, Penny. This is the job. You can't tell me you didn't see this coming. You put 003 in as a triple agent without my knowledge."

"And you put 009 on her without my knowledge. These are my Double O's. It's my field and my right to run it as I see fit. You should have told me what you were doing. Instead, you put an unknown element in my field, endangering my operation. You stuck to the old boys' club, and now one of your old boys is dead and so is my agent."

M pounced to his feet. Moneypenny did not retreat. "That's quite enough. We were both mole-hunting, and neither of us trusted each other because we're not wide-eyed naïfs, so stop acting like it now. Sid died in the line of duty to his country. That was his job. Be grateful there was no worse collateral damage. You lost the journalist, but the lawyer you used will make a full recovery. Chao's son is back home. So is Dr. Nowak, and let's hope her gratitude will mean we can benefit from her capabilities. 004 is recovering in hospital. 003 came through. We won more than we lost. What I lost was a friend. So don't lecture me."

Moneypenny noticed his hand was shaking. She took his drink, placed it on the desk amidst the cables and papers. She heaved a sigh, catching sight of a report from this morning that Phoebe had buried under all the others as low-grade important. It was from the Communications Department. They wanted her to know that the sun had blinked.

She topped up M's glass and her own, returning his drink to him.

Moneypenny raised her whisky. "To service."

M touched his glass to hers, a dull clunk. "Service."

FIFTY

Hole

Johanna Harwood remained fixed as around her a joint task force negotiated by the US filled the chamber. They had opened up the access to the quantum computer and carried out its gold armaments like ants conveying treasure to their queen. Harwood sat at the edge of the waterfall, the spray hitting her back the only thing telling her this was real. Medics lifted Bashir's body into a bag and carried him away, as if he were just another component. Mora did not stir when they rolled him onto a stretcher and pulled a hood over his head, the first stage in his own rendition for interrogation. Dr. Nowak was told that Felix Leiter was waiting for her on the surface, and he wanted to know if that was really her grandmother. Harwood didn't catch the answer. She was having trouble focusing.

A medic looked at her shoulder, a sluggish slump of blood, and told her she needed to have a surgeon look at it as soon as possible. Harwood nodded, but did not get up, just kept pressure on the wound. She studied the chamber, the dimensions, the angles, the seconds— could she have made it into the chamber sooner? Would that have saved Bashir's bulletproof vest? She stared down at the glass floor, and the remains of the computer below. Her reflection was dusty. The chair where Zofia had been bound was whisked away. She had the feeling of being the last one on set, the production over, the players and their parts abandoned, the props and costumes cast aside. What had this place meant, after all? A hole for disappearing people.

Harwood sat up. There was an opening in the chamber to the left of the main door, leading to a dim tunnel. It was closed off by steel bars. Harwood asked a forensics officer if she could borrow his bolt cutters. He seemed about to argue, but then gave her the heavy thing, turning back to his business. Harwood got to her feet. She limped to the bars. They were chained shut, nothing fancy. Harwood's shoulder seared as she bit down with the tool, and then the chain clanked to her feet.

The darkness stank of stagnant water. She remembered that dampness on her skin. Had she been kept down here? Harwood moved down the tunnel, trailing the bolt cutters. There were cells left and right, recesses in the rock, no greaseproof paper fluttering from the walls here, no bench, no toilet. The doors bolted into the caves were meant for cages. Each cell had a metal bowl, meant for dogs. The first one showed signs of recent occupation—a stain on the sandy floor, the bowl half-filled, water matted with hair and grime. Zofia Nowak's cell? Harwood moved on, the gears of her mind catching up now. A place where people disappeared. She had disappeared here, forced into a fog of disembodiment. Had he been here at the same time? Had he listened to her screams? Had Harwood heard his own in return?

He could still be here now.

Harwood held her breath. She daren't call his name, daren't tempt it. She passed empty cells—perhaps she'd been held in this one, curled into a corner marked with the scratchings of prisoners trying to hold on to time, or this one, where the bowl had been crumpled, perhaps in an attempt to beat open the lock—Harwood reached the end of the tunnel. The door of the final cell hung open. The sandy ground showed signs of a man being dragged out by guards. Harwood stood at the threshold, her heart hammering.

The cell was empty. But a hand had gripped a stub of stone and carved three numbers into the rock face, so deep it would have left the fingers bloody. 007.

Acknowledgments

Thank you to Corinne Turner for making my dreams come true. I am so grateful for your faith, encouragement, and friendship. Thank you to Simon Ward for your support and passion. Thank you to Phoebe Taylor for your generosity and insight. Thank you to Ros Taylor for your kindness. Thank you to the best agent there is, Sue Armstrong. Thank you to Jonny Geller, Viola Hayden, Kathryn Cheshire, David Highfill, and the whole team at HarperCollins UK and US.

Many people were generous with their time and expertise during the writing of this book. Thank you to the friends and family who read versions and discussed ideas. Thank you to the Royal Centre for Defence Medicine. Thank you to Seb Brechon at Alpine and Andrew Franklin at Thruxton. Thank you to Fedor Bryant-Dantés for sharing your stories. Thank you to Will Daniel-Braham, aka Big Billy, who remembered the code. To Simon Latimer, whose mind could power a quantum computer. To Tom Godano, my action adviser. To Antony Herrmann, who knows the coolest things. To Dr. Lucy Brooks, my medical adviser. To Jess Gaitán Johannesson and Adam Ley-Lange, who advised on science and whisky and kept the secret. To my father, Craig Sherwood, who has been everywhere.

Thank you to Billy Brooks, who took me to see Bond in the cinema for the first time. Thank you to my sister, Rosie Sherwood, for walking and talking. Thank you to my mother, Ellie Baker, for always being there. Thank you to my husband, Nick Herrmann, for living the creation with me—and listening to the Bond themes on repeat for three years.

Thank you to the Fleming family for the honor of a lifetime.

Ian Fleming

Ian Lancaster Fleming was born in London on May 28, 1908, and was educated at Eton College before spending a formative period studying languages in Europe. His first job was with Reuters news agency, followed by a brief spell as a stockbroker. On the outbreak of the Second World War he was appointed assistant to the Director of Naval Intelligence, Admiral Godfrey, where he played a key part in British and Allied espionage operations.

After the war he joined Kemsley Newspapers as foreign manager of the *Sunday Times*, running a network of correspondents who were intimately involved in the Cold War. His first novel, *Casino Royale*, was first published in 1953 and introduced James Bond, Special Agent 007, to the world. The first print run sold out within a month. Following this initial success, he published a Bond title every year until his death. His own travels, interests, and wartime experience gave authority to everything he wrote. Raymond Chandler hailed him as "the most forceful and driving writer of thrillers in England." The fifth title, *From Russia with Love*, was particularly well received, and sales soared when President Kennedy named it as one of his favorite books. The Bond novels have sold more than sixty million copies and inspired a hugely successful film franchise, which began in 1962 with the release of *Dr. No*, starring Sean Connery as 007.

The Bond books were written in Jamaica, a country Fleming fell in love with during the war and where he built a house, "Goldeneye." He married Ann Rothermere in 1952. His story about a magical car, written in 1961 for their only child, Caspar, went on to become the well-loved novel and film *Chitty Chitty Bang Bang*.

Fleming died of heart failure on August 12, 1964.

www.ianfleming.com

THE JAMES BOND BOOKS

Casino Royale

Live and Let Die

Moonraker

Diamonds Are Forever

From Russia, with Love

Dr. No

Goldfinger

For Your Eyes Only

Thunderball

The Spy Who Loved Me

On Her Majesty's Secret Service

You Only Live Twice

The Man with the Golden Gun

Octopussy and The Living Daylights

NONFICTION

The Diamond Smugglers

Thrilling Cities

CHILDREN'S

Chitty Chitty Bang Bang